Where is the Number?

by

Nicholas Temple-Smith

First Published in 2019
by GWL Publishing
an imprint of Great War Literature Publishing LLP

Produced in United Kingdom

ISBN 978-1-910603-68-0 Paperback Edition

GWL Publishing
Forum House
Sterling Road
Chichester PO19 7DN

www.gwlpublishing.co.uk

Nicholas Temple-Smith was born in north London and educated at Westminster School. He spent several years working in Canada for a non-governmental non-profit corporation which organised work camps in low income rural communities, particularly Indian reserves and Inuit villages. This allowed him to travel extensively across that vast country, spending time in every province and territory. Returning to England, he took up a career in sales, eventually running his own company. As often as circumstances permitted, he travelled, especially to South East Asia. He also discovered an interest in (some might say obsession with) jazz and hot dance music of the 1920s and 1930s, and he amassed a collection of over one thousand 78rpm records, and a few hundred LPs and CDs. In addition, he served for ten years as a special constable in the Metropolitan Police.

He moved to Florida in 2001, where he now lives with his wife. He gained a degree from Santa Fe College in Gainesville and, as he has been since early childhood, is a voracious reader of books – real books, made of paper. In spite of his travels, he considers himself one hundred percent a Londoner.

Dedication

To my parents, with love.

Here was a royal fellowship of death!
Where is the number of our English dead?

Shakespeare: *Henry V* Act IV, Scene 8

The Middlesex Regiment was real, but the battalion described in this narrative, the 35th, is entirely fictional.

35th (Service) Battalion, The Middlesex Regiment
(The St. Marylebone Rifles)

Partial List

C.O.	Lieut-Col. M. C. K. Wintergrass
2 i/c	Major B. D. Fullerton
Adjutant	Capt. G. de V. Case
R.S.M.	Sgt Major T. F. Callow
A-Coy. Commander	Major W. A. Henderson
2 i/c	Capt. R. S. W. Huntingdon-Roberts
C.S.M.	Sgt Major R. Bull
1 Platoon	Second Lieut. Charles Snow
2 Platoon	Second Lieut. Arnold Snow
	Sgt. Fred Quill
	Lance Corporal Edwin Marvell
	Pvt. Bert Giddington
	Pvt. Harry Travis
	Pvt. Roland Selway
	Pvt. Wilfred Leuchars
	Pvt. Hubert Snibley
	Pvt. Colin Tunniford
	Pvt. Jimmy Hope
	Lance Corporal Matthew Clay
	Pvt. Joseph Marren
	Pvt. Eddie Ross
	Pvt. Johnny Winslow
	Pvt. Alec Millcross
	Pvt. Les Mosterby
	Pvt. Vic Rangle
	Pvt. Percy Glass
	Corporal Seamus O'Malley

Prologue

Two young men, happy and smiling, walked arm in arm along London's Piccadilly on a Friday afternoon, bathed in the glorious golden sunshine that sometimes comes at the end of a sublime summer. Around them, the capital seemed bright, benevolent, all that they could wish for. Today the very buildings, trees, and parks were their friends. They smiled at the people they passed, raised their hats to strangers, and felt content with life in general, especially with what it had just brought them. They were on their way home to tell their mother they had been granted commissions in a new army regiment; they were going to go to war.

On that same day, as the Kaiser's grey army continued its march westwards through Belgium and northern France, in an attempt to capture Paris, life continued as usual for thousands of men hundreds of miles from the front line, as the catastrophe of war steadily engulfed Europe.

In north London, a man awoke from a drunken sleep, which was not unusual for him and, as he made tea for himself, he decided to go to a dance that evening. In Marylebone railway station, four men from north Oxfordshire, in town to attend a funeral, decided that since they were in London – where most of them had never been before – they might as well see something of the place and take a later train back to Banbury. An office manager from Ealing went home from work early with a headache, something he had never done in his working life; so when he let himself into his little house he had an unpleasant surprise. A young man from a very good family sat in a hotel room in Bloomsbury, reading for the tenth or eleventh time, his father's telegram ordering him back home to Scotland at once. In Surrey, a retired sergeant of the regular army once again ignored the sudden pains that slashed across his chest without warning, leaving him short of breath, trying to convince himself that he must have eaten something that had disagreed with him. In Kent, three young men impatiently waited for their day's work at the bank to end, so they could hop into the motor car that one of them was lucky enough to own, to pop up to town for the evening. A lovesick young man sat in a deck chair in Regent's Park, listening to a military band playing a selection from Gilbert and Sullivan, and tried to imagine the joy his girlfriend would feel when he told her he had actually found someone willing to publish his book of poetry.

Across the Channel, men in khaki, blue, and grey fought and died – the first several thousands. Millions more would follow.

Part One

Joining

Chapter I

The Two Young Men

Charles and Arnold Snow were twins: well born, well educated, well nurtured. Life had been good to them and they had very few complaints. Despite being twins, they had been born in different years. Charles was born at ten minutes to midnight on the last day of December 1894. To everyone's surprise, his mother's labour had not ended and, half an hour later, Arnold had arrived. This gap in their ages – which had placed Arnold's birth in 1895 – gave Charles the excuse to refer to his twin as 'my younger brother' or even, to Arnold's great irritation, which was why Charles so often did it, as simply 'the boy'. They were fraternal, not identical twins and no one ever had any difficulty in telling them apart. Charles was a good two inches taller than Arnold and was possessed of fair hair, in a marked contrast to his brother's unruly dark thatch. Both of them would have seemed equally at home in a library, laboratory, or on a rugby pitch. Their father, a kindly man of whom they had fond but few memories, had died when they were still very young, while their mother, after two years of profound grief, had fallen in love with and married a widower several years her senior, who loved her as much as she loved him.

He was Colonel Hugh Hardy, a professional soldier since leaving Rugby at the age of seventeen, who had been badly wounded in the South African War. In fact, he had lost an eye, which unfitted him for active service and he had spent the remainder of his career behind a desk at the War Office. It was of little consequence that his superiors told him that the work he did was as valuable to the nation as leading a regiment into battle; he knew which of the two alternatives he preferred. He was, above all, a soldier, so he did what he was told. He was very proud of the two stepsons he had accepted as his own when he had married their mother. They had only been ten years old then; now they were young men who had finished at Westminster School, had spent a year with relatives in Canada, and were both about to enter Oxford University. Charles had decided to read Law, while Arnold had opted for Classics, though as yet he had no idea what he wanted to do when he graduated.

None of that mattered when the tangle of alliances in Europe, which had been forged over previous decades, drew one country after another into war. Austria declared war on Serbia. She had been wanting to do this for ages, and the assassination of the heir to the Austro-Hungarian throne in Sarajevo by a Serbian nationalist gave the Austrians the excuse they needed. Serbia's ally, the enormous Russian Empire, then declared war on Austria. Germany, Austria's ally, declared war on Russia, and France, bound by treaty to Russia, declared war on Germany and Austria. Germany had defeated France in the 1870 war, and had for years readied a plan, in case they needed to do it again. This plan involved invading France through neutral Belgium. Belgium's independence was guaranteed by Great Britain, so when the field-grey soldiers of the Kaiser crossed the border into Belgium, Britain gave Germany an ultimatum. This was ignored, and Britain and her Empire declared war on Germany and her allies. What had seemed like a little local assassination had become a world war. The house of cards had collapsed.

All of the countries involved had large standing conscript armies, numbering several millions, except Great Britain, which had a small, professional force. More men, men in their thousands, would be needed for this conflict. The Secretary of State for War, Lord Kitchener, who had been appointed upon the outbreak of hostilities, realised that Britain – her small regular force of some two hundred and fifty thousand men not withstanding – had almost no army. Had he asked Parliament for conscription, he probably would have got it, but instead he called upon the public for one hundred thousand volunteers. His expectations were exceeded many times over. It appeared this was a popular war. The country was almost unanimous that it was about time Germany was put in her place, and there was no shortage of men willing to volunteer for service for the duration of this war – which everyone confidently expected to be little more than a few months. So that was why Charles and Arnold Snow had knocked on the door of their stepfather's study one evening and asked for his help and advice.

As a former serving soldier, Colonel Hardy was delighted that these two young men, in whom he took such pride, wanted to join the Army, but he was enough of a realist to acknowledge that they would be delaying promising careers elsewhere. With that in mind and out of a sense of obligation to his wife, their mother, he asked them if they were sure.

"Yes we are, sir." Charles was most emphatic. "We've thought about it a great deal and we believe it's our duty."

"There's been no shortage of recruits, you know," said the colonel. "There's no need for everyone to go."

"Yes, sir, we know. But we wouldn't feel right staying safe at home while other chaps were out there taking all the risks."

"And," Arnold added, "this might be our only chance; of seeing what war is like, I mean. Once Germany has been defeated, there may not be another war again for some fifty years or more."

"And that's just it, sir," said Charles. "The war's already two months old and everyone seems to think it won't last much longer than Christmas. We'd really hate to miss it."

The colonel smiled. He knew just what they meant. It was the same feeling that kept him seething with frustration behind his desk, when all he wanted was to be back in action. He remembered the colonial wars, in which he'd fought, as an exciting adventure; a by-and-large safe activity. Regarding his own injury, he thought of himself as one of the unlucky few. The odds in favour of survival were substantial. He nodded indulgently at the two men standing before him.

"If you're set on it, I'll see what I can do. There are new regiments being formed all the time. The 'New Army', they call it. You'd have a better chance there than getting commissioned into a regular regiment, or even a territorial one. You're both in good health and you both did well in the Corps Cadets Force at school. There shouldn't be a problem. Leave it with me."

As the twins began to thank him, another thought occurred to him.

"Best not mention this to your mother just yet. Women can be very funny about these things, you know. Let sleeping dogs lie for the time being, I think."

Charles and Arnold agreed, thanked him again and left the room, pleased that they had taken this step and impatient for things to start moving.

The colonel waited about two weeks to receive an answer to his enquiries. It was good news and he looked forward to passing it on to his stepsons. That evening, when he got home, he told the butler to ask the two young men to join him in his study.

"Good news for you both," he said, once they had entered the room and closed the door. "All being well, you'll both be commissioned into one of the New Army regiments, the 35th Middlesex. Their unofficial name, which is probably what everyone will end up calling them, is the St Marylebone Rifles. Rather like all those Pals regiments they've been raising up north."

"The Middlesex Regiment," exclaimed Arnold. "The 'Die Hards'."

"That's right," agreed their stepfather. "It's a good regiment, with an honourable history. I expect you'll both do very well with them."

"Thank you, sir," said Charles, who was the more practical of the two brothers. "What do we have to do now?"

"You'll need to go and see someone at the War Office next week. I'll give you the details. You'll have to pass the interview and that's when it will become official, but between you and me I don't think there'll be any problem. You're just the sort of young men the army is looking for."

"We're ever so grateful, sir," said Charles, and the colonel made a self-deprecating gesture.

"Never mind all that rot. I'm glad to have been of help. Besides, I just did the easy part. You two have the difficult bit."

"You mean winning the war, sir?"

"No. I mean you have to tell your mother."

They did so that evening, at dinner. It was a quiet, family evening, almost cosy; just the four of them around the table, candles burning as opposed to the electric light, and two of the household's four servants in attendance. The men spent the first few minutes of the meal talking about nothing in particular, mainly fishing and the career of some bright young man or other with whom the twins had been at school. No one mentioned the war and their mother wondered why her sons were avoiding the one subject that they liked to discuss above all else. Then, between the mulligatawny and the lamb chops, the colonel announced that the two boys had something to say, which they duly did.

Their mother took it as well as could be expected for someone who had just been presented with what was almost a fait accompli. She was a sensible, educated woman and she knew that this was an argument she would probably lose, so she gave in gracefully, after only a token protest.

"It's only until the war is over, Mother," was Charles's attempt to console her. In fact it was no consolation at all.

"That's right, my dear," chimed in the colonel. "And it can't last very much longer; a few months at the most."

"But how can anyone be sure of that?" she asked.

"A matter of obvious fact. Look at the huge armies that each country is putting in the field. Hundreds of thousands of troops, millions of guns, and artillery pieces and horses. That's to say nothing of the respective navies. No country can afford that for long. The war simply can't last more than a few months, or all the countries involved would bankrupt themselves. No, I don't see this going on much longer than the end of next spring at the latest." He beamed at his stepsons. "And these two will have to go through training, and that takes time. They'll probably get in on the fighting at the tail end of the war, just in time to see a little action before it's all over. Probably not much more danger for them than a hard-fought game of rugby. No need to worry."

Of course, she did worry. She was desperately afraid, even as this conversation took place.

"In the end it won't really make any difference what I say, will it? You're going to go anyway, aren't you?"

Not one of the three men could think of anything to say. They didn't want to contradict her, because they knew she was absolutely right.

"Go on, then," she said after an awkward silence. "I know you'll both pass your interviews. You'll probably make very good officers. I'm sure I shall be very proud of both of you."

Her two sons beamed with pleasure and the colonel thumped the table. He said, "Jolly good show," and told the butler to go down to the cellar and fetch a bottle of champagne. When their glasses had been filled, he said, "What shall we drink to? The war?"

"No," said his wife. "I'd rather drink to a swift victory and the safe return of my two sons."

So that was the toast they drank.

On the Friday of the following week, Charles and Arnold attended their interviews at the War Office. They were astounded to be ushered into a waiting room full of young men, all apparently there for the same purpose. They began to wonder, for the first time, if the number of applicants might not exceed the number of vacancies. In a hushed conversation, Arnold told Charles that if he didn't achieve a commission, he'd go straight round to the nearest recruiting office and join up as a private soldier. Charles wasn't sure what he'd do – the possibility of not succeeding simply had not occurred to him.

Eventually they were seen; Charles first, then Arnold and they both passed their interviews. They were told that officially they would have to wait for written notification, but unofficially their applications would be successful.

It was a wonderful afternoon, so they decided to walk home, from Whitehall to Berkeley Square. They were so happy with the turn of events that they linked arms. Life was good.

Chapter II

The Thief

Frank Claybourne woke slowly, aching and uncomfortable. Last night, or early this morning to be exact, he had fallen asleep fully clothed, after doing one of the few things he did really well – he had drunk far too much. That was where most of his money went: booze and gambling. When he tried to justify his hand-to-mouth existence, he reasoned that there was little point in saving his money, so he might as well just spend it and have a good time. In his line of work there was always more money to be found. Life was meant to be enjoyed after all and, perhaps, he really had managed to convince himself that the way he lived his life actually did constitute enjoying it.

He heaved himself off the rumpled and rather malodorous bed which took up almost half the room and sat on the edge, stroking the stubble on his chin, while trying to ignore the foul taste in his mouth. He had seemingly taken off his jacket and tie before collapsing in a drunken sleep, but had left his shirt and trousers on, which now looked crumpled. His shoes had stayed on too. They were tight and uncomfortable, having been on his feet for about eighteen hours, so the first thing he did was to ease them off, letting each one thump to the floor. He flexed his toes, allowing them a moment to enjoy their release from the constriction of his old brogues, and then he set about heating a kettle on the gas ring in the corner, which was the sum total of his cooking facilities. He inspected the dubious remains of a brown loaf that sat on a chipped plate upon the counter. It was a couple of days old and looked as stale as its age would suggest, but it was all he had in the place, so he ate it with neither pleasure nor enthusiasm. It was just something to fill the stomach, he told himself; he'd eat properly that evening.

Then he saw the envelope on the floor by the door of the room. He hadn't noticed it when he had come home; well, he hadn't really been in a condition to notice very much of anything. He knew what it was before he even picked it up. Inside, as expected, was a note from the landlord, far less polite than the one he had received the previous week, telling him that he was now four weeks in arrears with the rent and that, unless he could clear the outstanding amount and pay in advance for next week's rent, he, the landlord, would take steps to ensure that he, Frank Claybourne, was forced to quit the premises as soon as possible.

Frank Claybourne wasn't surprised. He had received many notes like this in the past. It was all part of his way of life and he had no intention whatsoever of paying the outstanding rent. He had spent the last few years living in a series of rooms throughout London. All he needed was a place to sleep and leave his few belongings, all of which fitted nicely into a medium sized suitcase. His plan was always to stay in one place as long as he could, but if he couldn't pay the rent he simply stuck it out until the last moment, before disappearing into the night. He never put down roots or made friends. This room was in Bayswater, but he had also lived in similar rooming houses in Camden Town, St Pancras, Bow, Lewisham and more; so many he had lost count. He'd calculated that he could usually live rent-free for three or four weeks in each place, while being dunned for the outstanding money, and then vanish. He knew no one would ever go to the trouble of trying to find him; not for that sort of cash.

So he had, at his best guess, two or three days left in this room, which he would leave with no regret at all. The plan would be to work tonight and, if tonight wasn't successful, tomorrow night too and then move to somewhere new the day after, having packed his few belongings and walked out. He was confident he'd have the money for a couple of weeks' rent at a new place, and probably quite a bit left over, because he knew he was good at what he did.

His chosen trade was to steal from women. It was a very lucrative line of work for him. He didn't have the ability, or the patience, to work through long, involved confidence tricks on them, to get entangled, or even marry them for their money. Instead, he chose a more direct method. He liked to meet women in public places – dances and concerts being the best of all – and to pick them up. He was admittedly good looking and, when he was sober, he was a witty and interesting conversationalist. He also was a very good judge of women, otherwise he would have been in prison long before now. He could tell, when picking out a dancing partner, which woman was likely, especially after a lot to drink, to allow him to come home with her. That was not the way nice women behaved, but there were many who were pleasant enough, but not so 'nice', who did act that way and Frank Claybourne stole from them. They almost always had some item worth lifting, or even a bit of cash lying about, but what he liked to take best of all was jewellery. Small enough to slip into a pocket, he could always fence it for something approaching a reasonable price. What was more, women advertised the fact that they owned jewellery by displaying it round their necks, on their fingers, attached to their ear lobes, or pinned to their costumes. Over the years, he had developed an eye for such things, so that, while he was by no means an expert, or even an authority, he could, nine times out of ten, spot cheap imitations. Using common sense helped. If a young woman whose demeanour indicated that she worked behind the counter of a draper's shop, or in a stuffy office, was wearing big dangly earrings, they would obviously be imitations. She simply couldn't own real jewellery that expensive. A discreet little gold ring, perhaps with a diamond or ruby, possibly a family heirloom? Now, that was more likely to be real. Claybourne's method – which was nearly always successful, let it be said – was to give them lots to drink and then to go home with them. To their homes, of course. When his prey was asleep, either after sex or simply having passed out from too much drink, he would steal what he could. Sometimes they slept with their rings still on, but usually they took their jewels off, and he always made sure to note where they put them. He also made away with watches, cash, anything that he found when going through handbags and purses that would be remotely of value, but he hardly ever took anything that he couldn't fit into a pocket. Then he would slip away. He had developed a knack of moving very quietly, and he seldom disturbed the sleep of his victims. They always lived alone; he made sure of that by allowing the subject casually to arise during conversation and, if they lived with anyone else, he wouldn't pursue them any further, so he was never disturbed by anybody while making a quiet exit in the dark. Additionally, his victims seldom reported him. How could they? To do so would be to admit that they were the type of woman to invite a man to their home, unchaperoned, on first or second acquaintance. A lot of it may have gone on behind closed doors, but in 1914 no one wanted to admit to it. So, most of them suffered the loss of their possessions and lived with the humiliating knowledge that they had been duped, rather than admit to anyone what had actually happened. A few did go to the police, but they had very little information to give. Claybourne, of course, never used his real name and there was nothing distinctive about him: he was medium sized, with dark hair, brown eyes, and a London accent. How many tens of thousands of men were there in the capital who looked just like that? The police noted the information, realised that there was a petty thief at work picking on women living alone, but since he had never been violent and there were so many more things to worry about, they left it there. Unless they could actually catch him in the act, which was unlikely, their efforts at fighting crime would have to be directed elsewhere.

Tonight's work, Claybourne decided – for that was how he regarded his criminal activities – would be at a little dance hall he knew in Clerkenwell. He had been there before, a couple of months back, but he hadn't actually been successful, so it was worth another try. He had a hard and reasonably fast rule that he never went back to a location where he had managed to connect with a victim. There was always the risk that if he did, he'd be recognised by someone from whom he had already stolen, and the last thing he wanted, of course, was to have the alarm raised and his collar felt by the local constabulary. That was why he had decided that, after he had worked a few more locations in London, he'd move to the provinces and try his luck in Birmingham, Manchester, or just about anywhere in the country you could think of that had a female population large enough to enable him to live anonymously.

It looked like a lovely afternoon, so he decided to go for a walk to clear his head, before coming back to the rooming house, where he would wash in the communal bathroom and change in to his working clothes – shirt, suit and tie, all kept immaculately clean, unlike the rest of his clothes and the room in which he lived. Then off to the dance, pausing probably to eat something along the way.

At a small and reasonably respectable restaurant near Marble Arch, a washed and scrubbed Frank Claybourne was seen that evening, eating a plate of cottage pie, washed down with a couple of beers, before taking a bus to Clerkenwell, where he made his way with a self-assured step to the dance hall. It wasn't the most sophisticated of places, catering as it did to the middle and lower middle classes, but it attracted enough paying customers to keep in profit and for many people, most in their twenties or early thirties, it was somewhere they went regularly for their entertainment.

Claybourne paid his shilling, which was the price of admission, before making his way into the hall, to the dance floor. *No hurry*, he told himself; *just take a little while to survey the room. It's early yet, so plenty of time, old chap, plenty of time*. He bought himself a ginger beer. He liked to get his victims drunk, but he himself always stayed sober while working. It was only between jobs that he drank himself into insensibility.

There was a fairly large dance floor and about twenty couples were already up and dancing. At one end of the floor was a raised dais, fringed with potted palms, without which, it seemed to him, no place of popular entertainment was complete. On this dais was a reasonably competent band; six men dressed in formal evening attire. Claybourne recognised the tunes they were playing, popular songs of the time that everyone knew, and most people could dance to – *He'd Have to Get Under, Where Shall We Go Tonight?, Everybody's Doing It*, and *A Popular Girl* – and several ragtime numbers as well. Some people, mainly the older generation, didn't approve of ragtime. They said it was 'depraved and degenerate' and that it would 'ruin the morals of the young'. No doubt that provided extra enjoyment for those younger people who liked it, buying ragtime records to play at home and dancing to it with great enthusiasm in public. Claybourne thoroughly approved. He didn't really believe for one moment that ragtime music would deprave anyone, but just on the off chance that it did? Well, a general loosening of morals by one and all made his job that much easier.

People were arriving all the time and Claybourne kept his eyes open for a likely prospect. It was no use, of course, setting his sights on a woman who arrived with a male companion. No, it was far better to concentrate on those women who arrived in groups. It was very rare for a woman to come unaccompanied. They almost always travelled in packs and came to dances such as this in groups of two, three, or more. It seemed that in each group there was usually one woman who was more popular with unaccompanied men than her companions. He had learnt to forget her and to go for the ones who didn't get asked to dance quite so often. Find one of those and, once he had made sure she didn't wear a wedding ring, the thing to do was to isolate her from the herd, dance with her often, make conversation in which she was able to say as much as he did, and then lower her resistance by buying her as much drink as she would accept. It wouldn't take long to assess whether she was the sort who had something worth nicking and if she did, well he would insist, of course, on seeing her home. London was full of ruffians nowadays, he would never forgive himself if anything happened to her. Sometimes they wanted to go home in the company of the women they had arrived with – so it was to Claybourne's advantage that he pick someone whose friends would be constantly occupied by other young men.

After a couple of ginger beers and a dance or two with likely prospects whom he rejected as unworthy of his criminal attentions, Claybourne saw a group of five young women arrive together. One, louder than the rest, was clearly the dominant member of their group. He mentally rejected her – the others would miss her too soon if she tried to leave with him and too many other men would be attracted to her. Two of the women sat together, as though uneasy at being out in public, and the remaining two chatted to each other and their loud friend, seemingly thoroughly at home in a dance hall. So, Claybourne thought, these two were worth some scrutiny. Walking round the dance floor, rather than across it, so as to attract less attention from any nosy spectators, he approached the two women. One was about five feet, with mouse brown hair and a wide smile. The other was a little taller, with hair that had obviously been coloured and her make-up was a shade more obvious.

Claybourne stopped by the two women he thought of as 'Possibility One' and 'Possibility Two'. He put on his best smile, which experience told him women went for. No point in wasting time with a lot of small talk; women came here to dance.

"Would you like to dance?" he asked Possibility One, the short mousy-haired girl.

She and Possibility Two looked at each other for a moment and then burst into a fit of giggles, the kind that young women in groups seemed so prone to and that Claybourne found so irritating. Then Possibility One turned back to him and smiled.

"Alright," she said. "I'm not that good at it though."

"Never mind," replied Claybourne, smiling just a little wider and holding out his arm to her. "I won't tell anyone if you won't."

This won him another giggle, before Possibility One took his arm and they went out onto the floor. The band was playing a waltz, nothing at all energetic, so they could make a bit of conversation as they danced.

"My name's Luke," lied Claybourne. He always picked biblical names when he was working. Within reason, of course – he never claimed to be called Judas, for example.

"I'm Edna." She was reasonably well spoken, though not at all top drawer. Claybourne could tell.

"You're not a bad dancer at all, Edna. You've probably had a lot of practice."

"Thank you. I do like to go dancing now and again."

"Always here?"

"No, usually closer to where I live," she answered.

"Where's that then?"

"Streatham."

That was on the other side of the Thames.

"You're a long way from home, Edna."

"Yes, but my mum and dad don't mind if I stay out once in a while, though they do insist that I stick with my friends, and they always wait up for me till I get home."

"Very wise of them," said Claybourne, as he struck her off his list of possibilities. The waltz ended and he escorted Edna back to her friends. Then he turned his attention to Possibility Two, who eagerly accepted his invitation to dance. Indeed, she seemed as though she had been expecting it.

It was another waltz. She was a better dancer than Edna and Claybourne was a very good dancer himself. Again, he took the opportunity to speak to his partner, whose name, he discovered, was Amy. She had a self-confidence that Edna didn't and he found himself enjoying the dance.

"You're here with your friends?" he asked, though the answer was obvious.

"Yes. Well, I don't know you'd say we were actually friends, not all of us, but we work in the same office, so we thought we'd go out together for an evening. Seeing as it's Friday and pay day."

"What work do you do then?"

"I'm a typewriter."

Was a typewriter the machine, or the person who used it? Claybourne smiled. He had heard the word used in both ways. Still, he knew what she meant and it seemed to him that a typewriter would earn more than a shop assistant, or a factory girl.

"Oh yes? All of you?"

"No, just me and Sylvia," she said, indicating the woman whom Claybourne had decided was the leader of the little group, who was now dancing with a young man in uniform. "The others are junior to us, working in the records department."

"Where at?"

"McLaughlin & Maggs – that's a shipping company. In Leadenhall Street, I'll have you know."

Leadenhall Street was where most of the top shipping companies had their offices. A good sign.

"I'm impressed," said Claybourne, and he was. This was the sort of woman he had been hoping to come across.

"What do you do?" his companion asked.

"I'm in sales. I travel the country selling machine parts. It's hard work but it can be rewarding."

"Why haven't you joined up, then?"

"I tried to, but they wouldn't let me." The ready-made lies rolled very smoothly off his tongue. "Because my company does a lot of very important work for the Army, they need me in my present position. Actually, I'm not really supposed to tell anyone that, so please don't mention it to any of your friends."

"Oh, I won't," she exclaimed and he could tell by her expression how she was thrilled to have been told even this little scrap of important information about the war effort. She'd enjoy that, would hint to her friends that she knew something very important, but of course she wasn't allowed to tell them. What's more, the air of secrecy he had just given himself made him that bit more attractive to her.

"But tell me, Amy," he said, "how is it that a lovely girl like you has to go to a dance with your chums from work? I'd have thought you'd have a young man of your own. I'm not complaining, of course, otherwise I'd not be able to dance with you myself, but it does seem strange."

"I do have a young man," she replied, sounding almost defensive. "But he's away."

"Oh?"

"Yes. He joined up as soon as war was declared and now he's off in a training camp in Yorkshire, or Lancashire, or somewhere a thousand miles away. So he couldn't come out with me tonight, you see. But I'm sure that even though he's in the army he'd want me to enjoy myself. Stands to reason."

"I'm sure you're right."

"Besides, we're engaged."

"Really?" said Claybourne, wondering if this fiancé would be an obstacle.

"Yes, the night before he went away he asked me to marry him. Gave me this." She held up the third finger of her left hand to show Claybourne an engagement ring – gold, with a very small diamond in it. Nothing vastly expensive, but Claybourne was sure he could get a reasonable price for it.

"Very nice."

"Yes. Mind you, I was a bit surprised when he popped the question, seeing as we hadn't known each other all that long. But I mean, he was off to the war and he seemed like a nice man, so I accepted. It was the right thing to do, wasn't it? It would have hurt him otherwise, don't you think?"

"I'm sure it would have. You seem like a very nice person to me, Amy. He's a lucky man."

She blushed a bit beneath the make-up.

"Thank you."

The waltz ended and, after they had applauded the band, he walked her back to her seat at the edge of the dance floor, but as they got there, the band struck up a tango.

"Can you tango?" he asked. Something told him that she could.

"Yes. Can you?"

"I certainly can. Let's show everyone how to do it."

A grin of devilment lit up her face and Claybourne knew he was making progress.

"Yes, let's!"

They did the tango very well indeed. Not everyone could do that dance and a lot of couples had left the floor after the waltz, so they had plenty of spectators. That was not especially to Claybourne's advantage, but at the same time it did much to proclaim his right of possession over this woman for the evening and it seemed only natural that, after the tango, she should stay with him for several more dances – waltzes, foxtrots, and a two-step. She was a good dancer, almost as good as he was. They had connected and Claybourne was feeling good about the evening. Between dances, he took her to the bar and bought her as many drinks as she wanted, which turned out to be quite a few. She started with a sherry, but confessed to him that she really enjoyed beer, so that was what he bought her; real beer for her, ginger beer for himself. She was enjoying herself and, in the heady atmosphere, it wasn't too long before the drink began to affect her. With her tongue and her judgment thus loosened, Claybourne found out that she lived with her sister. Originally, when they had first arrived in London, they had stayed at a hostel for single young women, but they hadn't liked the long list of rules they had been expected to observe, so they had found a nice little flat together, just off the Edgware Road. What was more, her sister was away looking after a sick aunt in Taunton. Amy liked dancing, ragtime music, and modern novels. She was not going to be a typewriter for the rest of her life, but she would get married when her soldier fiancé came back from the war and have lots of children, after she and her husband had managed to enjoy as much of life as they could while they were still young. Her family in Somerset wanted her to return to the village where she had been brought up, but she couldn't bear the idea of that. After two years in London she was now a city girl, and that she would stay.

"I don't blame you," said Claybourne when she told him this. "I feel just the same way. London's in my blood too."

She didn't reply, but simply smiled at him and let him hold her a little bit closer.

It was time to move to the next phase, Claybourne decided.

"I rather think your friends disapprove of you dancing with me so much," he said.

True, her friends, or at least the quiet ones who hadn't danced with anyone all evening, were looking in their direction with neutral expressions, but a neutral expression could usually be taken to indicate anything you wanted it to. After he had put the suggestion in her head, Amy imagined that her friends were glowering their censure at them.

"Who cares?" said Amy. "Besides, they're not friends, I told you. Just girls from the same office. I don't care what they think anyway."

"I expect you'll probably hear all about it from them when you all go home."

"They don't live anywhere near me. We arrived together because we came from work, but we won't be leaving together."

"You're not going home on your own, surely?" He managed to sound surprised.

"Why not?"

"For one thing, there are all sorts of people about. For another, it's a very long way."

"I'll be fine," She insisted, "I'll take the Underground Railway and I'll be back home in two shakes. I've done it before."

"I dare say, but that was probably before the war, wasn't it?"

"What's the war got to do with it?"

"Well, since the war began, London has been full of men who've come to town to enlist. You can't be too careful, you know," he said, without being at all specific what it was that Amy couldn't be too careful about.

"I've never thought of it like that," Amy said.

"Then it's a good thing I was here to warn you, isn't it?"

"I suppose so."

"Never mind supposing. It's true. Now, let's have another couple of dances, then I'll get some more beer in. And do you know what I'm going to do after?"

"No, what?" she asked, with a smile.

"When the time comes, I am going to escort you home, see you back safely."

"Go on! I can't ask you to do that," she protested, her expression betraying that she wanted him to do exactly that.

"You aren't asking, I'm telling," he countered. "I'd never forgive myself if anything happened to you."

"You're a real gent, aren't you?"

"I am that. Now drink up – we've more dancing to do yet."

He kept her with him for the rest of the evening. After a while, her friends decided to leave, or at least the three who hadn't danced much, if at all, and hadn't allowed themselves to be claimed for the evening by any of the young men present. Amy waved them off, telling them she was going to stay for a while longer because she was enjoying herself and that she'd make her way home later. She'd see them all at work on Monday morning. Claybourne bought her a few more drinks and then decided it was time to leave. She wasn't exactly drunk, but she was getting loud and a bit unsteady. He didn't want her to have too much, or else he'd never get her home.

When the time came, he walked with her to the Underground station, where they rode together to Baker Street and from there they walked the mile or so to her flat. It was in a dark little building in Penfold Street, but her flat itself was clean and neat. It consisted of a small living room, a tiny kitchen, scarcely more than a large cupboard really, and a bathroom. There was also a closed door, which Claybourne guessed must have been the bedroom that Amy normally shared with her absent sister. Amy hadn't hesitated to ask Claybourne in, "For a cup of tea, to fortify you before your journey home." Claybourne, of course, hadn't hesitated to accept.

"You're a lovely girl, Amy," he said after she had brought in the tea and they were sitting practically knee to knee in the little sitting room, with a fire starting to blaze in the tiny grate. "It's been a wonderful evening. I can't remember the last time I enjoyed myself so much."

"Go on!" She waved his compliment away, obviously delighted by it and hoping to hear more.

"No, that's God's honest truth. I had a lovely time at the dance hall. I hope you enjoyed it a bit too."

"Of course I did, silly. If you go there a lot, I hope we can do it again another Friday evening."

"Unfortunately, I don't think that'll be possible for a long time," he said, watching her face fall, "I have to travel a lot for my work, you see, and the things I do for the government. Can't go into detail, of course, but I do know that I'll be out of London for a long while. In fact, I leave tomorrow."

"Shame," she said, and she meant it.

"Yes, it is a shame," he agreed, putting down his cup to lean forward. He took her hand in his. "And that's why I can't resist the temptation to take the chance to do this." He kissed her on the cheek.

"Hey, you shouldn't do that," she cried, making no attempt to resist.

"I know I shouldn't, but the thought of leaving you this evening without knowing what it was like to kiss you was too much. We'll probably never see each other again."

"Don't say that, it's too sad."

"But it's probably true. And this has been one of the best evenings of my entire life," he lied.

"Go on with you."

"No, I mean it. As soon as we started to dance, it was as though I'd known you for ages."

She was taken in by this, so much so that she looked him in the eye for a moment and then she kissed him, full on the lips.

"I know, Luke," she said, as she drew apart from him for a moment, "I felt the same way."

He put his arms round her and was very pleased to feel her leaning into him. He kissed her again. This was the point where things would either go his way or he'd be thrown out of the place. He had to tread carefully. A little testing of the water would not go amiss.

"I don't want to stop kissing you," he said, "but I feel funny about it while you've got that ring on."

"What ring?" she asked. Either she was much drunker than he realised or her attachment to her fiancé was very tenuous indeed. It took her a moment or two to realise what he was talking about. Then she held up the finger bearing the ring in question. "Oh, you mean this? Well, if it distracts you that much, I'll just take it off." So she did. "It's not like I'm being disrespectful to my Billy," she told him earnestly, and he made sure to make a great show of agreeing with her. "But he is a long way off and there's nothing wrong with you and me having just a little kiss and a cuddle, is there? Seeing as you were good enough to see me home."

She put the ring on the little table by the armchair.

"Nothing wrong with it at all," replied Claybourne, who was very pleased with the way things were developing. He had already noted two or three small items worth taking.

One matter was pressing and he couldn't avoid dealing with it, so he asked her to excuse him while he went to the bathroom. As he stood there peeing, he decided that the ring, her brooch, a small carriage clock, and a china ornament he'd seen on the mantelpiece – which may have been valuable, or may have been worthless, but was small enough to take away – were all fair game. There might even be more. Right now, his job was to get her to her bedroom, have his way with her, and then make away with the loot while she was sleeping it all off.

However, when he got back to the living room a few moments later, he found that she had passed out in the armchair, her hands dangling at her side and her head thrown back, mouth agape.

"Amy? Are you awake?" whispered Claybourne, fervently hoping that she wasn't.

There was no response.

"Darling, can you hear me?" he murmured hoarsely and he was rewarded with a snore.

This was an unexpected bonus. He could get on with things straight away and make a quiet exit while she was still spark out. He didn't mind not having her, because he never really enjoyed sex while he was working. It slowed things up too much.

First he went to the bedroom. Two small dressing tables were in there, no doubt one for each sister. He searched through the drawers of each and was delighted to find a small wooden box with jewellery in it. It all went into his pocket. He could sort the good stuff from the rubbish later. In another drawer, under a pile of lace hankies, he found a gold-coloured locket, containing a tiny lock of hair. Then he headed back to the living room. Amy was still asleep, breathing noisily. He pocketed her ring and opened her handbag. The purse inside yielded three pounds in notes – he didn't bother with the coins. She still had her brooch on and he didn't want to risk disturbing her by unfastening it so, with regret, he left it. Finally, he came to the carriage clock and the small ornament. The clock was too big to go in his pocket, just, but the ornament he dropped in, where it knocked against the ring with a soft clink.

Soft the clink may have been, but as often happens to people fast asleep, that minute sound achieved what louder noises had not managed.

Claybourne was about to leave the room, which would have left him but three or four paces to the front door of the flat and to a successful end to this evening's business, but he never made it.

"Oi, what do you think you're doing?"

Amy had woken and it had taken her only a second or so to realise exactly what Claybourne was up to.

"Nothing, darling," was the best response he could give, but he was standing there, with her clock in his hand, about to leave the room. He didn't think she'd be convinced, and he was right.

"You devil." She was out of the chair now, absolutely livid. "You were going to nick that stuff, weren't you?"

"You were asleep, darling. I couldn't wake you and I wanted something to remember you by. I didn't think you'd mind."

"Wouldn't mind? I wouldn't mind that you were stealing a valuable clock from me?"

Claybourne wished she would keep her voice down. He might be able to talk his way out of this, but it wouldn't be easy if she alerted her neighbours with her yelling.

"I didn't realise it was valuable. I'm sorry, I'll put it back at once."

Meanwhile, her eyes had gone to the small table, beside the chair from which she had just leapt.

"Where's my ring? You've pinched my engagement ring, you coward. And where's the china fawn off the mantle? You've swiped that too, haven't you?"

He had, of course, but he couldn't very well say so. In fact he wasn't given any time to answer, because she lost what little of her temper she still had and came at him, hands out and claws extended. She managed to make contact with one hand and made a nasty scratch in Claybourne's left temple, before he had the presence of mind to try and push her away.

It was very unfortunate that the way he attempted to fend her off was by trying to bash her in the face, because he forgot that he was holding her carriage clock in his right hand and, instead of delivering a slap, or even a punch, he managed to strike her on the forehead with the corner of the clock. It stopped her short, and he heard the noise that is made when metal connects with flesh and bone. She clapped a hand to her forehead and blood seeped between her fingers. On her face was an expression of shock rather than pain. She seemed very startled that events had taken this turn, but she made no sound. Claybourne watched in fascinated horror as she took a step away from him and then keeled over backwards.

It was even more unfortunate that she fell backwards from that very spot, because it meant that, as she fell, the back of her head struck the corner of the mantelpiece. That made an even louder noise than the clock, and she crumpled to the floor.

"Oh Christ," muttered Claybourne. He stood transfixed for several seconds before he could bring himself to bend down to her, but he knew, really, what he would find. She was lying there, completely motionless, with her eyes half open. He listened for the sound of her breathing, but there was none. He felt for a heartbeat, but there wasn't one.

Don't panic, he told himself, though his every instinct was telling him to do exactly that. *Think. Can I tell the police? It was an accident, after all. But it won't look like much of an accident because she has a bloody great wound in her forehead where I hit her with the clock, as well as the hole in the back of her head, where she bashed herself on the corner of the mantelpiece. So I can hardly say she fell backwards accidentally. But it* was *an accident. It was only an accident because she fell badly, after I hit her. She died because I hit her when she caught me stealing from her. Killing someone while committing theft, that's murder according to the law, no matter how accidental it was. If they catch me, they'll hang me. Right, so I can't report it,* he decided. *I'll just leave. But what if they catch me? Calm down, for heaven's sake, and concentrate. Now, did anyone see me arriving here with her? No, I don't think so. What about at the dance hall? Her friends saw me, but they don't know anything about me. I gave Amy a false name and I told her I was a travelling salesman. And as far as I can remember she didn't have the chance to tell anyone anything about me. I kept her with me all evening. Did anyone notice us together on the Underground or in the street? I don't know. We didn't do much to attract attention. But just a moment, there was that tango, wasn't there? The two of us making an exhibition of ourselves in front of all those people. I just couldn't resist showing off, could I? Shit. I'd forgotten that. What I have to do, and that right speedily, is to make myself scarce. Get out of London and stay out. Wait till this all blows over, then wait a bit longer. Don't come back until next year perhaps. I can't take any chances,* he told himself.

He debated leaving his loot behind, but decided there would be little point in wasting it. In fact, after a few moments' hesitation, he unfastened her brooch and took that too. She would be discovered sooner or later and it was obviously a murder, not an accident. Breathing heavily and sweating, but otherwise keeping control of himself, he looked round the room to make sure he wasn't leaving anything behind to identify himself. He had come with nothing except his hat, which he now put on. A final glance at her, cursing his bad luck at what had happened, and he opened the door of the flat. It was late, the corridor outside was dark and no one saw him leave.

He made his way to his room in Bayswater on foot. When at last he reached it, he locked his door behind him and collapsed on his bed. Then panic took hold of him and he lay there shaking and weeping – weeping out of self pity, not for the life he had taken.

The next day, when he woke from a restless sleep that had been anything but refreshing, he made his way to one of the many pawnshops he had patronised over the previous year or two. He made a point of never using the same establishment too often and only did business with those who advanced him money for whatever he took to them, without making too many enquiries.

So, that morning he walked along the Marylebone Road, to an establishment he had not visited for some months. There were two or three other customers there before him, desperate to raise something for what little valuables they had. Claybourne hung back, pretending to examine a selection of musical instruments, telescopes, and sundry other items for sale, which were on display down one side of the room. He didn't feel comfortable standing in a queue. The less people who saw him, the better.

A lugubrious woman with a dirty face was turned away from the counter after trying, unsuccessfully, to convince the pawnbroker that a pile of what were obviously rags, were in fact silk. She walked out of the shop swearing loudly, and Claybourne found himself to be the only customer there. The pawnbroker stood on the other side of the counter, behind a metal grille. He was there to provide a service, if he chose, for customers who were in urgent need of cash. They came to him, so there was no need for him to offer a cheerful welcome.

"Yes?" was his only greeting to Claybourne.

By way of reply, Claybourne put the diamond ring, the brooch, the locket, the carriage clock, and the jewellery he had found in Amy's bedroom, on the counter and pushed them through a little hatch in the grille. He had not brought the little china ornament because it had broken in his pocket during his scuffle with Amy.

"Hmm," grunted the pawnbroker, and he put a jeweller's glass in his right eye, then picked up the ring. He scrutinised it for a few moments. "Diamond's real enough. Not very big though. More like a chip than a stone. Gold's real too. Only nine carats, though. Got a hallmark. You've been here before, haven't you?"

"I don't remember," Claybourne said, taken by surprise.

"Strikes me that I remember you. Came in a few months back, with a signet ring and a gold pendant."

"I don't think it was me. I've never been here before."

"I reckon you have. I'm good with faces. Not very good with names, but I usually remember faces." He chuckled. "No matter. Let's have a look at what else you've brought me."

He looked at each of the items in turn. He nodded a few times, looking at all of Claybourne's offerings on the counter, sighed once, then lifted his head to look Claybourne straight in the eye.

"You got provenance?"

"What?" Of course, Claybourne knew exactly what he meant and the question was not unexpected, but he wanted to delay, even by a few moments, admitting that he had no such thing.

"Proof of ownership. Do you have anything to show that all this belongs to you? A receipt, bill of sale, something like that?"

"No. I won this lot in a card game. Not the sort of place where you hand out receipts. But it's mine alright."

Claybourne had been through this bit of verbal fencing many times when dealing with pawnbrokers and, while it didn't stop them doing business, it never worked to his advantage.

"Difficult," said the broker. "It makes things so much easier if you have some sort of paperwork."

Claybourne stayed silent, waiting to see what sort of figure would be mentioned

"That's a nice ring and the clock's in good condition too. The other items are pleasing enough in their own way, but without provenance, I won't be able to advance you as much as I'd like to."

The very idea of a pawnbroker regretting that he couldn't offer more was, thought Claybourne, so ridiculous that it was almost funny. He kept quiet and waited for the verdict.

"So, taking all that into account, I can only offer you eleven pounds."

"Eleven quid? The ring's got to be worth more than that on its own!"

The pawnbroker was used to customers who argued, but it didn't matter to him one bit. He held all the cards.

"Eleven pounds. It's more than I advanced you for that signet ring, as I recall. Take it or leave it. Up to you."

So Claybourne took it. He gave a false name, signed a chit and received eleven one pound notes. With the cash he had stolen from Amy's purse, that made fourteen pounds. This was normally enough to keep him quite well for a week or two, assuming he didn't throw it away gambling or drinking, which he frequently did.

Normally, he would collect his belongings from his room and unofficially vacate the premises, finding new lodgings in another part of town, where he could live for a few weeks, or months, while doing a job once or twice a fortnight. Now, however, he had to reconsider. As much as he hated to admit it to himself, he had committed a murder and the police would be looking for him, so it was really imperative for him to follow through with his plan get out of London. He'd have to venture into the unknown territory of the provinces. The police would undoubtedly question Amy's friends, who would of course tell them that the last time they had seen their colleague alive she had been leaving a dance hall, with a man who had picked her up. So it might be advisable to stay away from dance halls, tea dances, and all his usual hunting grounds for the time being. Another kind of work was what he needed, for a few months at least.

He got the idea when he was passing a café, just south of Crawford Street. Three soldiers came out, looking very confident, in a martial sort of way, in their new uniforms. As they walked past him, they were talking about paying over the odds for food that wasn't much better than the grub at the barracks. Claybourne told himself not to be ridiculous; that it wasn't his sort of thing at all. Although, it was the perfect way to drop out of sight for a while. But he could get killed, for God's sake. *Not likely though,* he thought, *with the war bound to be over in a few months, or so everyone says.* He could get killed hanging around London waiting for the peelers to nick him. He'd never even considered it, really; he'd always thought it was a mug's game. A mug's game it may have been, but right now it could be a godsend, just what he needed. Maybe they wouldn't take him, he thought, but why ever wouldn't they? They were looking for one hundred thousand men, and he was the right age and in good condition. *Go ahead and try it,* he told himself, *and if it doesn't work, then think of something else.* But he couldn't just dither.

The nearest recruiting station was less than half a mile away and Claybourne walked straight there, before he could change his mind. There was a queue of about two dozen young men, and a few not so young. Some were in working clothes, others neat and tidy in suits. The one thing they all had in common was a buoyant enthusiasm and, in spite of himself, Claybourne allowed this mood to take him over too. He didn't want to tell anyone he was only joining so he would have somewhere to hide, obviously, so he played the patriotic recruit in order to fit in. It was a pleasant morning and he was starting to enjoy himself.

The queue moved reasonably fast and soon he found himself at the front of the line, facing an elderly man in a sergeant's uniform, who was sitting behind a table, over which was draped a Union Jack. The sergeant seemed as cheerful as the men he was dealing with.

"Name?" he asked, pen poised over a buff-coloured form.

Claybourne had naturally intended to give a false name, but he automatically started to answer with his real name, and had already uttered one syllable before he could stop himself.

"Christian names?" said the sergeant before Claybourne could correct himself.

"Matthew Mark," replied Claybourne. Using the saints and apostles as a source of aliases was a hard habit to break, it seemed.

"Date and place of birth?"

Claybourne gave a date of birth that deducted exactly one year from his true age and said he had been born in London, which was true.

"Right, take that through there," said the sergeant, handing him the form and pointing to a door.

Through the door was where three army doctors were examining recruits. They listened to Claybourne's chest, looked into his ears, tested his eyesight, told him to drop his pants and cough, and asked him a number of questions about his medical history. He passed, of course, because he was in good health and shortly after, he was back in the first room, with a dozen or so other men who had been accepted. So that was how Matthew Mark Clay, aged twenty-four, signed the necessary forms and swore the oath that made him a soldier for the duration of the war, in the 35th battalion of the Middlesex Regiment. The recruiting sergeant beamed upon them all and, if he had any doubts about their suitability, or how they would fare in the army, he kept them to himself.

The rest was an anti-climax. Clay – Claybourne that was – had more or less imagined that he and his new comrades would be taken to a barracks where they would immediately begin the business of becoming soldiers. In fact they were all told to leave an address where they could be contacted. In about a week or so, they would receive notification of when and where to report for training. Reminding them that they were in the army now and that, if they didn't show up for training, they would be found and arrested by the police and sentenced to a long stretch in prison for being absent without leave, the sergeant ushered them all out into the street, where the queue of recruits had got longer, before he admitted another dozen or so into the building.

Clay had given his address as Poste Restante, at the Trafalgar Square post office. He certainly couldn't use his current address and he had no idea where he would be staying until orders came. In fact, after he had rescued his suitcase of possessions from the rooming house in Bayswater and had sat for an hour over a cup of tea, a couple of fried eggs, and some toast in a café in Baker Street, contemplating his options, he decided that the best and most economic course of action was a hostel. As a result, Clay spent his last days out of uniform with the Salvation Army, where he remained sober and law abiding. He checked the post office in Trafalgar Square every day for mail and ten days later, he was rewarded. Two days after that, he bade farewell to the staff at the hostel and made his way to a drill hall in Hammersmith. He was told to bring no more than one suitcase, and since one suitcase was enough to hold everything he owned in the world, he had no trouble obeying that order. As he walked from the bus stop to the hall, he heard the sound of dance music, a lively two-step, coming from somewhere nearby.

"I'll be back," he said to himself. "In a few months when this little lot is over, I'll be back."

Chapter III

The Men of Banbury

Joseph Marren had never seen anything like London. He knew it was big, of course. After all, it was the nation's capital, the centre of the empire, where the king lived, and where parliament sat, but he had never imagined that a town could be so vast. He had arrived the day before, with three of his friends from Banbury, in Oxfordshire. After they had reached Marylebone Station in northwest London, they had taken a short walk, before boarding another train that went underground and had ridden that for what had seemed like ages. Then they had taken a bus, then changed to another bus, and at the end of their journey they had still been in London. It was incredible. He had been so breath-taken, so absorbed by what was going on around him, that he had been unable to concentrate on what he had come to London to do in the first place, which was to attend the funeral of one of his friends. Poor old Wally Timms had left his father's farm and had come to London to try his hand at making his fortune, but he hadn't been there more than a month or two when tuberculosis got hold of his lungs, and he'd died soon after.

Now, Joseph sat with his three chums in the station cafeteria at Marylebone, sipping tea and killing time until their train left for home, in just over an hour. No one had much to say, really. They were all of them enjoying the experience of being in London, but none of them thought it was quite right to talk about it, especially considering what they had come to town for. Not very respectful to poor old Wally. Joseph looked round him, not for the first time, taking in the size of Marylebone Station. All those locomotives, waiting at all those platforms. Steam, smoke, noise, crowds of people everywhere. He had never been in such a huge building in his life. He sipped his tea again.

"Big, ain't it?" he remarked.

"What is?" asked his friend Harry Travis.

"Marylebone Station. It's much bigger than our own station at Banbury."

"Well, it would be. Stands to reason. This is one of the mainline stations in London. Trains come from a great many places in England to this terminus. It has to be big."

"Did you say 'one of'?" enquired Bert Giddington.

"That's right," replied Harry, who was the only one of the four who had ever been to London before. That had only been for twenty-four hours a few years ago, on trade union business, but he felt that it entitled him to speak with authority on the capital. "There are lots of railway termini in London. One for each of the railway companies. Besides this one, there's Victoria, Paddington, Kings Cross, Euston, Charing Cross, and several others."

"London Bridge too," chimed in Sam Barker. At over fifty, he was the oldest of them and he had read a bit about London in his time.

"Aye, London Bridge too," Harry conceded, with just a touch of irritation. He was showing off how much he knew about London and he didn't want anyone else sticking his oar in.

"And they're all as big as this?" To Joseph that seemed beyond belief.

"Oh yes." Harry quickly reinstated himself as the knowledgeable one of the group. "Most of them, anyway. Some of them are even bigger."

"Get on with you!"

"It's true. This is London, you know, not Banbury. Of course things like stations are big here."

"I don't see," said Joseph slowly and deliberately, as though he were thinking all this out very carefully, "how any railway station could be bigger than this. I'd have thought that this was the biggest station in the world. There can't be enough trains in all England, not for that many stations, if they're all this big. It just doesn't seem possible."

"Well, you're wrong," Harry snapped. He didn't like being disbelieved, especially when he knew he was correct.

"I think he's right you know," Sam said to Joseph.

"I still don't believe it," said Joseph, and he was telling the truth there.

"Well, let's prove it, if you don't believe me," snapped Harry.

"How?"

"We'll go take a look, that's how."

"We can't do that," cried Joseph, taken aback by the suggestion. He may have been curious, but he was not very adventurous. "We've got a train to catch."

"Yes we can. There are lots more trains back to Banbury today. We'll just find out when the last one goes, so we can make sure we're back here in time to catch it, then we can go exploring."

Joseph was the type who, once he had made plans, he didn't like to have them disturbed. When the four of them planned this trip a couple of days ago, they had agreed that they would catch an early afternoon train back to Oxfordshire. "I'm not that fussed, you know, if other stations are as big as this one. I was just making conversation."

"Well, never mind stations then. But we're in London. Why not take the chance to look around? You never know when you'll be back here, if ever."

"Sounds good to me," chipped in Bert Giddington, and Sam nodded in agreement.

"It don't seem right, that's all," said Joseph. "We came to London for a funeral."

"Yes, and we've been to a funeral, ain't we?" remarked Harry. "So why don't we take advantage of the fact as we're 'ere and see some of London – Buckingham Palace and such like?"

"I'm game," said Bert.

"Me too," added Sam.

"Good!" Harry was triumphant. "That's settled. Of course," he said, looking at Joseph, "you can always stay here if you want. No skin off our noses if you don't want to come. But why chuck away this chance? Let's have a laugh before we go home. It's what Wally would have wanted us to do, I shouldn't wonder."

So Joseph allowed himself to be persuaded, and the four men from Oxfordshire, having gulped down whatever tea was left in their cups and made sure that there were several more trains that day which called at Banbury, headed out for the rest of London; or at least for however much of it they thought they could see in the next few hours.

Once the decision had been made, Joseph became increasingly enthusiastic about the venture. "I'd like to see Big Ben," he told the others. "I've always wanted to, ever since I was a nipper and my Auntie Violet gave me a box of chocolates for Christmas and on it there was this picture of Big Ben. The hands were at ten past two, they were, and it looked so majestic and dignified and I thought how wonderful it would be to see it, and to hear it strike the hour. Do you suppose we could do that?"

His companions didn't see why not and the others by turn suggested Trafalgar Square, the Bank of England, the Crystal Palace and – for some reason, known only to Bert Giddington, who suggested it – Bow Street Magistrates Court. "Yes, why not, we'll see as much as we can," they said to each other. "What interesting accounts of our trip we'll be able to pass on to our friends and relatives when we get home." It made the prospect of work the following Monday somehow less daunting. Joseph, Sam and Bert were farm workers, Harry worked as a road mender, and none of them particularly enjoyed what they did. Friend's funeral or no, this trip to London was probably one of the high points, if not *the* high point, of their year.

They left Marylebone Station unsure of which direction to go in, but their impression of London was that there would be something worth seeing at every turn. They were a cheerful group, feeling the exhilaration of setting off on a minor adventure. Joseph Marren at twenty-two was the youngest of them, and looked even younger. Bert Giddington was two years his senior but at times, quite often really, he felt even older; marriage tends to mature a man. Harry Travis was twenty-eight but looked older, and he knew it. There were more than a few streaks of grey in his hair and wrinkles upon his face. While Joseph and Bert were tall and slim, Harry was shorter and stockier, but there was a dependable solidity to him which extended to his personality that signalled he would be a good man to have on your side.

As it happened, they were going in the right direction and the first place they came across was Madame Tussauds. They paid their entrance money and spent an enjoyable hour looking at the waxworks, especially the Hall of Kings and the Chamber of Horrors. They stared back at Dr. Crippen and gasped at the Tortures of the Hook, and Harry explained to his chums that yes, that really was the actual guillotine blade that had cut off the heads of so many French aristocrats.

After the waxworks, they found they had lost their bearings a bit and ended up walking back the way they had come. A few minutes later, they found themselves in Baker Street. Bert and Sam were both book readers, so they recognised the street name at once.

"This must be where he lives," said Bert. "There can't be two Baker Streets in the same city."

"Where who lives?" Joseph wanted to know.

"Sherlock Holmes."

"Don't be daft," said Harry.

"No," said Sam. "The lad's got it right. Number two hundred and twenty-one it is."

"Two hundred and twenty-one *B*, Sam," Bert corrected him.

"Yes, you're right enough. I forgot the B. I suppose it must be somewhere hereabouts."

"Do you reckon he's at home?" asked Bert.

"He could be, if he's not out working on a case," said Sam. "Maybe we'll get to meet him."

"Well, I don't know as we can just barge in; without an appointment, I mean."

"Maybe if he knew we'd come all the way from Oxfordshire, he'd give us a few moments of his time. Just so we can say hello, like. And perhaps Dr Watson might be there too."

"Yes, that's true, he might be."

Joseph had only vaguely heard of Sherlock Holmes, so he was taking no part in this discussion, but Harry was listening to this little exchange with disbelief.

"Are you two soft in the head or something?" he burst out.

"What do you mean?" asked Bert.

"There's no such person as Sherlock Holmes. He's just a made-up character from a load of detective stories. He doesn't really exist."

"Doesn't really exist?" Bert was outraged. "I've never heard of such rubbish in all my life! Of course he exists. Those stories are all true. Do you think I don't know the difference between made up tales and true stories?"

"Yes, I do actually, after listening to the pair of you carrying on like that."

"Steady on," said Sam quietly. "I've read those stories too, you know, and I reckon they could only be real life accounts. They didn't seem like fiction to me."

"You see?" cried out Bert triumphantly.

"Fine. Have it your own way. Let's call on the famous Mr. Holmes and see for ourselves."

They walked up Baker Street, looking at the door numbers as they went. They found number two hundred and twenty-one, but much to their surprise – the surprise of two of them, that is – it was immediately followed by number two hundred and twenty-three. Harry was all for calling off this wild goose chase, but Bert and Sam wanted to make sure before giving up. So, Bert knocked on the door of number two hundred and twenty-one, a two storey building that appeared to consist of several offices.

An elderly gentleman in a pin stripe suit, wearing gold rimmed pince-nez, opened the door to them.

"May I help you?" he enquired.

"Yes please," said Bert, with Sam standing behind him. Several paces back were Harry, looking disbelieving, so as to show that this foolishness was nothing to do with him, and Joseph, who was watching the proceedings with a detached equanimity. "We were wondering if Mr. Sherlock Holmes was at home."

For the briefest of moments, a look of exasperation crossed the old man's face, as though this was a question he had frequently been asked by strangers knocking at this door. Maybe it was. For some reason he looked straight at Harry, who shook his head slightly and shrugged, and the two of them shared a moment of disbelief at the expense of Bert and Sam.

"I regret, sir," said the man, with the greatest of courtesy, "that Mr. Holmes is not here, and we do not anticipate his return for quite some time, if at all."

"How long do you mean?" asked Bert.

"Probably at least not until after the cessation of hostilities, I should imagine."

"Fine. Thank you very much," said Harry, taking charge. "We're sorry to have troubled you. We'll be on our way now."

As the old fellow closed the door, Harry ushered his friends away and they walked back the way they had come.

"Told you he was real, didn't I?" said Bert in triumph.

"Where's your proof then?" said Harry.

"Weren't you listening? That man told us he lived there but he wasn't in," said Bert.

"He was just trying to spare your feelings, that's all."

"Rubbish! You just don't want to admit you're wrong."

"You still think he lives there? There isn't a two hundred and twenty-one B in Baker Street. We all looked for it and couldn't find it."

"You know what I think?" Bert asked Harry.

"No, please tell us. What do you think?"

"I think Sherlock Holmes is doing war work. The man said he wouldn't be back till after the war at the earliest."

"That still doesn't explain why there is no two hundred and twenty-one B, does it?"

"Course it does. You see, I reckon he's probably on some very important case, tracking down German spies or something, and if the spies cotton on to the fact that he's after them, they might try to break into his flat to see if they can find any notes, or something that will tell them how much he has found out."

"So?" said Harry.

"So he's taken the number off his door, so no one can find where he lives."

"Taken the number off what door?"

"Well, I don't know, do I? If he's taken the number off the door, how do I know what door it is? It stands to reason, doesn't it?"

With Bert and Harry arguing like this, the four of them made their way south along Baker Street, until they reached Oxford Street, at which point they all agreed it was high time they had some refreshment, so they stepped into the nearest pub.

Harry got in four pints of bitter and they sat round a table, sipping in silence for a while, enjoying their day out again. Any thoughts of disrespect to their late friend Wally were dispelled. This was an enjoyable lads' outing. A little while later, after Harry and Sam had both lit pipes and Bert had rolled his own cigarette – not very expertly, as shown when he'd applied a match flame to it, which caused at least a third of it to flare up and turn to ash before he had even had a chance to inhale – Harry put the question to them as to where they wanted to go next. The problem here was that none of them, not even Harry, who was the natural leader of the group, knew exactly where they were, and that meant that they didn't know how far away anywhere was. Joseph, who was a useful cricket player, suggested Lords, but he was overruled because, of course, in October the cricket season was over and if they did get all the way to Lords – although they had no idea exactly where it was anyway – there would be nothing to see.

Sam rather fancied that he had heard of this street, Oxford Street, before. Maybe there was something important there? Harry said he thought he'd heard of Oxford Street as well, and he was sure it was probably the most important thoroughfare in London. Well, one of them at any rate. Now that he came to think about it, it had looked very busy as they'd walked along it.

"Excuse me," Bert called to a man, reading his newspaper at a table next to theirs, "This is Oxford Street, ain't it?"

The gentleman looked up from his paper for a moment at conceded that yes, this was certainly Oxford Street.

"What's in Oxford Street then?" Bert asked.

"What's in it? Shops and offices, mate, that's what. You've got Selfridges along the way a bit. That's the biggest one, but there are many more. You from out of town?"

"Yes, we're here from Banbury," answered Bert.

"Never heard of it. Where's that?"

"It's in Oxfordshire," Bert told him..

The man shrugged. That was somewhere outside London and therefore not a place he cared to waste time thinking about.

"We're just here for the day," Bert went on.

"Well, there's a lot to see in Oxford Street that you probably don't have in Banbury, wherever that is. It's a long street, with Oxford Circus at one end and Hyde Park at the other." Then he returned his attention to his newspaper and his pint.

"Did he say there's a circus here?" asked Joseph, "I like circuses. I saw one when I was a nipper."

The man with the newspaper looked up.

"It's not that sort of circus," he said, "It's just the name of a crossroads."

"Not a proper circus, with clowns and the like?"

"No."

"So we don't have to waste time going there," said Harry. "I think we should have a look at this park. See what's there."

"What was that Selfridge thing he was talking about?" asked Bert.

"That," answered Harry, "is a very big shop. A department store, it's called. Might be worth putting our heads round the door."

"Why? We've got shops in Banbury. Don't need to come all the way to London to see what a shop looks like. Let's go to the park. Should be some girls there worth looking at."

So they left the pub, found out from a passer-by which direction to walk to get to Hyde Park and hadn't gone more than a few hundred yards before they found themselves outside Selfridges. Now, this was not the sort of shop they had in Banbury – this was the biggest shop they had ever seen by a long chalk. It had an entrance that looked as though it belonged on the front of a palace, and it was several storeys high. They decided to go in and look around. In fact, they were there for a whole hour, going from one department to another, amazed at the variety of goods on sale. Afterwards, as they continued along Oxford Street towards the park, they told themselves that, perhaps they had underestimated the difference between Banbury and the nation's capital.

They found Hyde Park with little difficulty. Its northeast corner was there at the end of Oxford Street, as the man in the pub had said it would be. Immediately adjacent to it was Marble Arch and Harry was able to pass on to his companions a little nugget of information that he had read somewhere; that this was the site formerly known as Tyburn where, until the latter part of the century before last, criminals had been publicly hanged. The four looked around them silently for a few moments, as though to see the shadows of some of the miscreants who had been sent from here into eternity in days gone by, but there was too much hustle and bustle about them for this to be anything approaching a solemn moment, so they crossed the road and entered the park.

They found themselves in a paved area at the very edge of Hyde Park, called Speakers' Corner. As the name implied, it was here that people who were so inclined, came to make speeches. Provided one observed the laws against sedition, anyone could make a speech on the subject of his or her choice, serious or trivial. There were always plenty of people about, enough to guarantee an audience, who were usually good-natured, for just about everyone. This was all new to the four men from Banbury, and they stopped to listen to the three speakers who were there that afternoon.

The first was a pale, earnest looking young man, with unruly red hair and thick spectacles, who was standing on a wooden box, while a homely type of woman stood next to him holding a banner that told the audience that they were from the Vegetarian Society. The speaker seemed to be trying to convince the crowd of the evil of eating meat. Judging from the heckling, he was having little success, but the jeering was benign and no one bore the poor fellow any ill will, since in his attempts to introduce them to the delights of nut cutlets and in his increasing frustration at failing to make even one convert, he was providing them with some first class free entertainment.

The pals moved onto the next speaker, who was standing on an overturned crate, but they didn't stay more than a few moments because it was clear that he was a bible thumper, there to save souls.

That sort of thing makes people very nervous and even those who agree that perhaps their souls do need saving prefer to think of it as something that should maybe happen one day, but not right now, thank you.

The third speaker had by far the largest audience. He was standing on a purpose-made dais, which he had obviously brought with him, that enabled him to stand several feet higher than the crowd. A Union Jack was draped over the rail in front of him. He had maybe a hundred people around him and there was precious little heckling.

"The Germans marched into my country without the slightest provocation," he said. He had a foreign accent of some sort, but you could understand every word he said. "We were neutral, we had caused them no offence, but they ignored our neutral status, because that is the nature of the German."

A murmur echoed from the crowd.

"Treaties mean nothing to them. The word of the Germans is worth nothing, because they will break it to achieve what they want. And what do the Germans want?" He looked out over the crowd, waiting for an answer.

"To win the war," someone yelled.

"They want kicking up the arse," someone else called out, to the appreciative laughter of the crowd.

"Yes, they want to win the war," the man went on, "And to do so they have thrown aside the rules that are customary in war. They care nothing for humanity or justice. They just want to rule Europe."

More murmuring emerged.

"When they came to my village, they took all the men from the age of fourteen to sixty and herded them into the square. Then, they chose ten of these men at random and put them up against a wall, the wall of our church if you please, and they shot them."

The rumble from the crowd was anything but good-natured now.

"They shot them down in front of their mothers and their wives. They made these poor women watch as the men they loved were shot, murdered, in front of their very eyes. And for why? They did this as a demonstration of what the village could expect if anyone interfered with the German army, and when the village mayor protested, brave man, he too was shot. And before the Germans marched on, they did things to some of the women which I can not describe to you now."

"Bastards," someone yelled, echoing the indignation and even anger of the crowd.

"This is happening all over my poor Belgium and in parts of France too. The German pestilence is sweeping over the civilised countries of Europe. Is this what you want?"

"No," exclaimed the crowd. The four friends joined in as enthusiastically as the rest.

"The British Empire declared war on Germany in order to come to Belgium's aid. Was that the right thing to do?"

"Yes," somebody shouted just as loudly.

At this point, a man in the uniform of sergeant in the British Army, mounted the dais and stood beside the Belgian. He had a thick moustache and held a pace stick under his arm as he stood, ramrod straight.

"This gentleman," he shouted, in his best sergeant's parade ground voice. "'as told you of the hawful hatrocities what are going on in Belgium. Even, as we stand 'ere, 'elpless Belgian civilians is being murdered by the 'un."

"Shame," shouted someone.

"You're not wrong; it is a bleedin' shame and it's up to the British Empire to put a stop to it. Now, Lord Kitchener 'as asked for a 'undred-thousand volunteers for the British army, which is the finest in the world. Is he going to get 'em?"

"Yes," the crowd shouted. After all, how could anyone think otherwise?

"That's what I was 'opin' I would 'ear. I didn't think that the young men of England would turn a deaf ear when they 'eard their country callin' 'em. So, do you know what I'm goin' to do?"

The question must have been rhetorical, for he didn't give anyone a chance to answer.

"I'm now goin' to march to the recruitin' station and if there are any real men among you, you'll come with me and, when we get there, you'll take the king's shillin' and join the army for the duration to 'elp us put the kibosh on the Kaiser!"

This got a big cheer. The sergeant got down from the dais and the crowd parted for him.

"Now, 'oo's comin' with me? Who wants to be a 'ero? You, sir? An' you? An' what about you?" He looked directly at some of the young men standing near him. They all nodded. Then, he began to march away from the dais, every inch the soldier. Already, a group of men had fallen in behind him, much to the cheers of the crowd.

"Should we?" Bert asked his friends, voicing the question that they all were thinking.

"I'm not sure," admitted Harry

"You heard what the French fellow said," remarked Joseph. "We can't just let the Germans get away with it. We have to do something."

"He's right," said Sam. "I think we should do it."

"What about you, Bert?" Harry asked.

"Well, it'll beat working on that farm, I'll be bound. Why not?"

Harry thought for a moment. Sometimes the most important decisions in a person's life were made on the spur of the moment, with little or no thought.

"All right then. Let's go," he said.

So the four of them joined the swelling crowd, which was following behind the sergeant. Those who hadn't joined, mainly women and old men, watched and applauded.

"Well done! Well done!" shouted one old fellow, who had to be at least seventy, with a snow-white beard, tears streaming down his face. "I'm too old to go with you, so kill a German for me."

"We'll do that," called a youngster. "We'll kill loads of the bastards. But why not join us, Grandad? Lie about your age and join up with us."

This caused more laughing and cheering and contributed to what was almost a holiday mood. Bert saw a young woman, waving from an upstairs window and he blew a kiss to her. Joseph beamed at everyone; Harry and Sam too were carried along with the feeling of an adventure just begun.

At the recruiting office, Sam pretended to be fifteen years younger than he was, but of course he fooled no one and he was rejected. The other three were accepted and told to expect their orders in ten to fifteen days.

They didn't feel like doing any more sightseeing that day, so they made their way back to Marylebone Station and just had time for another cup of tea in the station cafeteria, before catching their train back to Banbury. There, the three successful recruits told their families about Wally's funeral, about Madame Tussaud's, and Selfridges, and about Hyde Park… and that they'd enlisted and were about to go to war.

Chapter IV

The Chauffeur

When Jimmy Hope had gone for his interview for the position of chauffeur to Lord Beckanhill, he had never driven a car before. He wasn't exactly sure why he was even applying for the job, except that cars fascinated him. He had a very good understanding of the workings of the internal combustion engine, gleaned entirely from reading every book and article on the subject he could acquire. He had never before worked as a member of the staff of a big house, but the sight of the sixty-four-room manor just to the north of London did not intimidate him as he approached it. He reported to the back door, of course, and was surprised that Lord Beckanhill himself was going to see him.

The butler ushered him into one of the drawing rooms. Lord Beckanhill actually stood up to greet him. Jimmy took a liking to him straight away.

"What do you know about automobiles?" was the first question.

"I know how they work, milord," said Jimmy.

"Have you driven many?"

"Not... many."

"How many, exactly?"

"None at all, milord."

Lord Beckanhill looked at the young man for a moment, then chuckled.

"Hell of a brass neck you've got, applying for the position of chauffeur when you can't even drive."

"I'm a very quick learner, milord."

Lord Beckanhill chuckled again.

"I have many automobiles. I bought my first one in the days when people were still referring to them as horseless carriages. Taught myself to drive. I have six of the things now. I still like to drive them myself now and again, but there are times when I'd prefer to leave the driving to someone else. Why should that be you?"

"Because I shall be very good at it," said Jimmy.

"Can't fault you for your confidence." Lord Beckanhill paused, "Right, let's start you off, see what happens. Uniform, room above the garage, fifty pounds a year, paid quarterly. Suit you?"

"Yes, milord, absolutely."

"Three weeks to teach yourself to drive. If you haven't managed it by then you'll be out on your ear."

"I won't disappoint you, milord."

Jimmy was delighted to be working for Lord Beckanhill. He discovered that, as well as being rich, the aristocrat also had the imagination to appreciate the inventions that had come so frequently in the last quarter of the nineteenth century and the start of the twentieth. Instead of retreating from them and declaring them a danger to his way of life, he positively embraced the thought of living in a world that included motor cars, telephones, electric light, the telegraph, moving pictures, phonograph records and, latterly, wireless telegraphy and aeroplanes.

"These are exciting times we live in, Hope," he said to his chauffeur more than once. "New inventions won't go away. There's no point in looking backwards. D'you know, you can go to the post office and send a telegraph to your uncle in Canada and he'll have it in his hand in a matter of hours? One day it'll be the same with telephones, you mark my words."

Jimmy didn't actually have an uncle in Canada, but he appreciated the example.

Another time, Lord Beckanhill enthused over moving pictures.

"Have you ever seen one, Hope? No? Well, you should. It will astonish you. I first saw one about fifteen or sixteen years ago, at a house in Kensington. Chap I knew, he had a projection apparatus. After dinner one evening he brought us into his drawing room where he had a sheet pinned to the wall. He switched the lights off and started up his machine, and do you know what we saw?" He didn't give Jimmy a chance to reply. "People walking across Blackfriars Bridge. Right there on the wall, clear as crystal, like a moving photograph. Men and women walking, and hansom cabs and omnibuses on the road. I felt I could reach out and touch them. I could hardly believe it. It lasted less than a minute. We made him show it over and over again, three or four times. Now of course they are much longer. A whole industry has grown up around them. I've seen countless ones. You should go see one on your evening off, Hope. Believe me, ordinary photographs are on the way out. They're obsolete."

Lord Beckanhill was not disappointed in his new chauffeur. Jimmy found that he was one of those people who had an almost natural understanding of the internal combustion engine. He could listen to a car idling for a few seconds and could tell exactly how well each component was functioning, which ones needed attention, adjusting or replacing, and which were working properly. Not surprisingly, his employer was delighted to have working for him someone who made sure that his half dozen cars were all in tip top condition, and who very quickly became an excellent driver as well.

So it was that in 1913 Lord Beckanhill bought his first aeroplane and learned to fly. He had a few untidy landings, one or two he was lucky to walk away from, but eventually he managed it. It seemed to him only logical that his chauffeur should also learn. Jimmy took to flying as though born to it. He soon qualified as a pilot and inside a year he had put in over a hundred flying hours.

Lord Beckanhill predicted war in the days following the assassination in Sarajevo.

"All this posturing," he said. "All these threats can only end badly. There'll be a war across the Channel and like as not we'll find ourselves dragged into it."

"Do you think aeroplanes will be used, milord?" Jimmy asked him.

"Makes sense, of course, being able to see far beyond the enemy's front line, but in my limited contact with military types, on manoeuvres with my territorial unit, I expect it won't be until the war after next that the usefulness of aircraft will eventually sink in.

War did come, of course. Lord Beckanhill held a commission in the local Yeomanry, and soon received his notice of mobilisation. Jimmy went to the nearest recruiting station and told the sergeant in charge that he knew how to fly and would like to join the Royal Flying Corps. He showed him his Aviator's Certificate, granted him by the Royal Aero Club. The sergeant scarcely bothered to glance at it, and Jimmy was assigned to a London regiment that needed to keep the numbers up: the 35th Middlesex.

Jimmy still intended to apply for a transfer to the RFC one day. He made a point of reading everything he could find about the various aircraft used, not only by the British army, but also by the French, Italians, Germans, and Austrians, and from the pictures and diagrams he saw, he could recognise most of them by sight. It was his belief that the aeroplane would be a very important weapon in this war, not only for reconnaissance, but also as a bomber, and with that, of course, would come the fighter, designed to protect other aircraft and destroy enemy planes. His fellow soldiers treated his ambition, and his opinion, as belonging to a good-natured eccentric. No one imagined for a second that Jimmy Hope would ever be transferred to the RFC. For the time being, at any rate, he was in the infantry.

Chapter V

The Office Manager

Edwin Marvell was possessed of most things that a reasonably successful man – one who was neither high born, nor low – could expect by the time he had reached the age of thirty. He had left school at fourteen and had gone to work straight away as an office junior with a firm that manufactured medical instruments, where the enthusiasm and diligence with which he applied himself to his work were rewarded with regular, well deserved promotions and the accompanying increases in pay, so that after sixteen years, he was a much respected member of the firm. While not yet appointed to the board of directors, it was generally believed that he would eventually reach one of the top, possibly the *very* top, positions in the company. He had a good salary which, if not exactly princely, was certainly not ignoble. This enabled him to keep himself and his wife in comfortable circumstances in a rented semi-detached house in Ealing, a reasonably pleasant district in west London. They didn't live in a grand enough style to have servants, but they did employ a charwoman three mornings a week to clean the house. That was the way things were and Edwin Marvell didn't see why anything would have to change. Being the sort of person that he was, he had managed to put away a small amount each month to provide for his wife and himself following his retirement, which he expected would be at the age of sixty-five. They had no children, but there was still plenty of time.

It was on this Friday that Edwin Marvell did something that no one could remember his ever having done before – he left work early because he felt unwell. Being unwell, in this case, meant that he had a raging headache. Of course, like almost everyone else in his office, and in the entire country for that matter, he'd had headaches before from time to time; but this was one of such severity that he had difficulty concentrating. He told himself that he ought to stay on for the remaining two hours of the day, but he found himself unable to work and he was afraid that, if he pressed on regardless, he'd make stupid mistakes with his paperwork that would give rise to twice as much work the following week for someone else, faced with the task of correcting them. So he went to see his employer, who unhesitatingly gave him permission to leave. This caused some remark among the staff, because no one had ever seen Mr. Marvell leaving early before. It was almost carved in granite that he was always among the last to go home each evening.

Edwin Marvell's wife Sophie, six years his junior and living very comfortably, would also have been surprised, had she known. She too was depending on her husband to stay at his office until half past five, as he did every single day of his working life, because as Edwin was making his way home by bus, from Wigmore Street to Ealing, she was entertaining her latest lover, an unemployed labourer who could not have been more than eighteen or nineteen, whom she had permitted to flirt with her as she'd walked by the river near Hammersmith one afternoon a few weeks earlier. She had brought him home that same day and had allowed him to bed her, an activity they had both enjoyed two or three times a week ever since. He was not her first and she knew that the affair would run its course, they would part, and then, when the urge became too great once more, she would find another lover. Edwin, meanwhile, would continue to be ever dependable, and she knew she would have the house to herself until his return each evening, at around six-thirty. As a result, she always made sure that her men left by five o'clock at the latest, giving her time to clean herself, straighten up the bedroom and get Edwin's tea ready.

Edwin was unable to telephone her to tell her that he would be home early, because they had no telephone. He had, in fact, suggested that they get one: he used one at work all the time and he considered it an essential, modern communication tool. Sophie, however, had never used one and she didn't like this newfangled idea of voices coming down wires from nowhere. It was far more civilised to write letters and, if something was very important, why, one could always send a telegram. So she had vetoed the idea, which was ironic as things turned out, because if the Marvells had owned a telephone, then their lives would not have changed so drastically that evening.

Sophie and her lover – who had told her his name was Tom, though she suspected he was lying, just as she had sometimes lied about her name to the men whom she had permitted to seduce her – were in the Marvell marital bed and, at the precise moment that Edwin returned home, Tom had just reached his climax and Sophie was about to reach hers. With the noise the two of them were making, neither of them heard the front door open and close.

Of course, as soon as he heard the sound his wife was making, Edwin knew exactly what was happening. He had never suspected her of having affairs; in fact, the idea had never even occurred to him, but that noise was definitely his Sophie, about to come. He realised she was being unfaithful and, in the space of a few seconds, he considered that, if she was being unfaithful, she had chosen the logical time to do so since, in the normal course of events, he was never at home in the afternoon. Then, as he began to climb the stairs, he wondered who the other man was and if it was someone he knew. Strangely enough, he was not very angry. He was far more sad. This was the end of his marriage, that was for certain. Forgiveness didn't even enter his mind. One thing though, which he was in no mood to appreciate, or even notice, was that his headache had vanished.

Evidently neither Sophie nor her Tom heard Edwin as he reached the landing and took the few steps to the bedroom door. They were too busy laughing and giggling, so they were both startled when Edwin opened the door. Sophie saw him first. She made a sound, somewhere between a yelp and a scream. Tom managed an "Oh God!" and sat bolt upright. Neither of them offered to explain. Sophie pulled the sheet and bedspread up to her chin to cover her nakedness, not that she had anything that either man had not seen before. The silence lasted maybe five seconds, but to all three of them it seemed a lot longer. It didn't take

Edwin more than a moment or two to size Tom up. He was little more than a boy – obviously not a serious prospect as a long-term lover for Sophie, more just the plaything of the moment.

"I think you'd better go," he said to the young man.

Tom couldn't believe his luck. He'd been imagining all sorts of unpleasantness, a vicious shouting match at the very least. Maybe violence. For all he knew, the wronged husband may have had a knife, or even a gun, in his pocket. This woman had been fun, but she was not worth getting hurt for.

"Yes," he muttered. "I'll get out right away, mate. You won't see me again."

He gathered up his clothes and shoes in his arms and scuttled out of the room, half bent over, as though he expected Edwin to hit him as he passed.

Once they were alone, the couple looked at each other. Edwin hadn't moved from the doorway and Sophie was still crouching in bed. She was pretty sure her husband wasn't going to do her any violence, but she was not absolutely certain, so she stayed quiet.

"Well, that's that, isn't it?" Edwin stated at last.

Strangely enough, Sophie had never even considered what would happen if Edwin found out. She had just assumed he never would. Good old dependable Edwin would never deviate from his usual schedule, so she'd always be safe in the daytime.

"What are you going to do?" she asked.

"I'm going to leave you. Just give me a few minutes and I'll be out of your life."

"Where will you go?"

"That is not something you'll have to worry about."

Another thought occurred to her. "What will happen to me?"

"And that, Sophie dear, is not something that I intend to worry about."

At this point Sophie realised that she was facing a big problem. She had never worked, she had no money of her own. She would be left high and dry.

"Edwin," she whined. "You don't have to be silly about this. I was wrong, yes, but we don't have to throw everything away for one foolish mistake."

He said nothing.

"And it wasn't really my fault anyway. He just started talking to me in the street when I went out to the shops. Then he followed me back here and just about forced his way into the house. I couldn't stop him."

Edwin continued to say nothing. She took this to mean that he was believing her story, so she went on, "In fact, I've a jolly good mind to report him to the police. He just barged in and had his way. So you see, it wasn't my fault. I was the victim here."

There was silence. She waited for him to say something. Eventually he did.

"I shall pack up some belongings and leave here tonight. I may send for some more things in the near future and, if I do, I shall arrange to have them collected. However, I shall not see you again after this evening."

In her mind's eye, Sophie saw a sad parade of humiliation, homelessness, penury, and disgrace approaching her.

"Edwin, you're not really going to be a bore about this, are you?"

He turned and went downstairs.

"Edwin," she called after him. "Edwin, come back. Don't be ridiculous. You can't throw away our marriage over one silly mistake."

None of this seemed to make the slightest impression on her husband. She could hear him moving around downstairs.

"I'd forgive you, you know, if the tables were turned," she shouted. "Anyway, how do I know you haven't been having your way with someone behind my back? It wouldn't surprise me at all. I don't know what goes on at that office of yours."

In her attempt to divert attention from her own sinning, she began to grasp hungrily at this infidelity of Edwin's that she had just invented. "So don't go getting all high and mighty with me, Edwin Marvell, if just once I do something you've probably been doing ever since we got married. It won't wash."

Quite what that washing phrase meant, she couldn't exactly say, but it sounded good to her. She stopped talking for a moment, to see if what she had yelled down the stairs had produced any effect on her husband, but since he didn't come dashing upstairs to tell her that she was forgiven, she fell back onto the pillow, considering what to do next. She couldn't think what that was, so she resorted to simply lying there, feeling sorry for herself.

After a few minutes, Edwin came back upstairs. He was carrying a suitcase he had taken from the spare bedroom and he began to pack as many of his clothes as he could into the one case, while Sophie watched him in silence. He then strapped the case shut and carried it downstairs. A moment later he came back up to the bedroom and he spoke to his wife for the last time in his life.

"I'm going now. I shall send word as to where I am so you can forward my post. You shall be hearing from my solicitor when I institute divorce proceedings, and I suggest that you instruct a solicitor of your own. There's no need to see me out. In fact, I don't think there's any need for us to have anything to do with each other ever again." Then he went downstairs. Sophie, meanwhile, had suddenly decided that her best course of action now was to resume yelling at her husband.

"Divorce? What are you talking about, divorce? That's just stupid. We don't need to divorce over this. And how am I expected to afford a solicitor? This isn't fair. You come back here right now. You can't leave me!" But it made no difference to Edwin, who gave no sign that he had even heard her.

"You swine," she screamed, louder than ever. "Why can't we give things another chance? I would if I were you. I'd forgive you if you made a silly mistake like I did, as you probably have, many times, I shouldn't wonder. This is rich, isn't it? The pot calling the kettle black." Perhaps she had now actually convinced herself of this. "Well, go on, then, get out. I don't need you. I never did. I just stayed with you because I felt sorry for you."

When she finally did realise that he was leaving, that he really was walking out on her, she suddenly changed her tone.

"Edwin, you can't leave me. I love you."

And the last he heard before closing the door behind him was, "What will happen to me?" He no longer cared.

He was carrying one suitcase containing clothes and washing things, and a briefcase into which he had put a number of important documents, such as his bankbook, his birth certificate and an insurance policy. The question now was, where to go. He took a cab to a bed-and-breakfast, close to where he worked and, having paid for a week in advance, he went straight to bed, not bothering to eat.

The next day he found, to his surprise, that he just could not face the thought of going to work – his office was open every alternate Saturday until 1pm. Now that he was no longer living at home and he was estranged from his wife, there didn't seem to be any point in continuing his life as it had been. So, he telephoned his office to say he was still unwell and after a very big, nourishing breakfast, he went out. One of the other guests at the bed-and-breakfast, with whom he had chatted over the fried eggs and bacon, had told him of his own plans for that morning and he had asked Edwin to join him. After thinking about it for a little while, Edwin had made up his mind and said he'd be happy to accompany his new-found acquaintance on his little expedition.

On the Monday morning, Edwin was back at work. His colleagues noticed there was something different in his manner, but no one could put their finger on what it was and, of course, no one asked him. He went to see the managing director and handed in his notice. One week only. Unfortunately, he couldn't guarantee his presence for any longer than that because, he explained, he had joined up and was expecting his orders to report for army training to arrive at the end of the week. He apologised profusely, but after all, there was a war on.

Chapter VI

The Officer and The Artisan

The Queen's Head was very busy. Victor Cadogan had tried his usual pub, The Anchor, a couple of streets away but that had been packed solid. Far too noisy and crowded, and he hated drinking standing up. Here, at least, he was able to sit at a small table in the corner, nursing a pint of mild and bitter, to a background of chatter and the comforting smoky fug that made a pub so welcoming.

The big question, the great matter that Victor was pondering, at a time when so many men were flocking to the colours, was this: should he, or should he not, stay in the army? Stay in, that is, at his present rank, in his current regiment.

He had joined one of the county regiments a few years before the old queen had died. He'd sworn himself to her and soon after had been sent to fight in the South African war. Attrition and his own abilities had seen him promoted to sergeant in just a few years, and a perceptive commanding officer had suggested that he put in for a commission. He did, and it was granted.

After the Boer War, promotion came more slowly, and all these years later he was still a lieutenant. That he would not have minded so much. He'd be promoted quickly enough at the front, as long as he wasn't killed. What he did mind was that they had received news that the battalion was shortly to be posted to India. Not to the war, but to India, to replace another battalion that was being recalled home to be made ready for the front.

To Victor Cadogan, this seemed almost like cowardice. True, they were ordered to go, but it still seemed as though they would be hiding from the war. He had been in a war; he had knowledge and experience that could be put to good use.

It wouldn't be put to good use in India, he knew that. The battalion had already served five years there. Some thought that India was the finest place to soldier in. Victor had hated it. Five long years in the barracks at Pushtali, a small, charmless town where nothing ever happened, many miles away from anywhere remotely interesting. The novelty of being somewhere far from home, in one of the Empire's possessions, had soon worn off and any sense of excitement Victor may have had at this posting was replaced by boredom and assaults on his sense of smell. The smells Victor noticed most of all, depending on which way the wind was blowing, were sewage, burning rubbish and ox dung.

Victor had spent five years of stultifying boredom there when, apart from morning parade and platoon inspection, there was frequently nothing to do all day. In the evenings he'd tried to make conversation with his fellow officers, who seemed to want to talk about nothing except horses, hunting and polo. There were long, earnest discussions about the merits of one type of bridle over another, the best feed for a horse, or which counties were the most advantageous to ride over in pursuit of foxes. Victor thought this was somewhat ridiculous, because it was an infantry regiment, and only officers above the rank of captain actually had horses there. He had tried to converse on other matters but had been rebuffed. Talk of politics, women or army matters (no shop talk in the mess was the rule) were not allowed. He had tried sitting quietly on his own, reading a book, but had been told that reading in the mess was looked down upon, so he confined his reading to his hot, cramped little room.

He welcomed the occasional military exercises that came along from time to time because they meant a break in the routine. Likewise, he enjoyed being officer of the day, because then he at least had a few tasks to occupy him.

And always that heavy, smothering heat; on occasion it was so hot as to be almost suffocating, the gentle movement of air provided by the *punkah wallahs* making little difference. What was just as bad, even if he kept his door and window closed, dust from the *maidan* would find its way into his room and cover everything.

The first time Victor saw a monsoon, he almost didn't believe it. He had heard of monsoons, of course, and the old timers had often spoken of them, but still, it didn't seem possible that it could rain so hard, and for so long. Day and night, for weeks on end. It was almost like a solid curtain of water. Anyone venturing away from shelter was soaked to the skin in a matter of seconds. The air went from being dry and dusty to unbearably humid and clammy, and his clothes and book bindings became mildewed.

The CO and several other officers spent monsoon season in the cool of the hills, on exercises, so the word was. In truth, they were all staying in bungalows they had rented. Victor could not afford to rent one himself, and anyway, subalterns were expected to remain in the barracks during monsoon season.

The only respite from this mindless existence was Aditi. He met her while he was walking through town one afternoon, during the fourth year that he was stationed at Pushtali. She was serving behind the counter of a small tea shop. Victor just glanced at the shop as he walked by. It was little more than a room under an awning, with two small tables. He had passed this way countless times before and had never given the place a second thought. There was never a shortage of tea at the barracks, so there wasn't any need to stop and order any at this place. What made that day different was that there was a woman serving a tray of tea to two customers at one of the tables. As Victor glanced at her, she'd looked back at him and their eyes met. She had the most beautiful big brown eyes that Victor fancied he had ever seen. He felt himself smile, and she smiled back at him before returning her attention to her customers.

It was a measure of the impression that this woman had made on him, even in the space of just two or three seconds, that Victor couldn't wait to go back into town to see her again. He did so after two painfully long days. As he approached the shop, he saw her walking through the door into the building. He sat at one of the tables and after a minute or two she came out again. She broke into a smile when she saw him.

"What can I get you?" she asked.

"Just a pot of tea, please. Local blend."

"Would you care for something to eat? Sweetmeats, perhaps?"

"Yes, alright. A selection of sweetmeats would be nice. Please choose for me. I trust you."

She smiled at that, and then went back inside, emerging a few moments later with his tea and snack. As she set them on the table she said, "I was hoping you would come again." Her English was accented but fluent.

"And I was hoping to see you here. That's why I came," said Victor, and they both found themselves smiling again.

After that, Victor went as often as he could to the tea shop. On his third or fourth visit he asked her to sit with him, but she had to refuse. It would not be proper, she explained, to be seen sitting with a customer in the shop where she worked, but he was able to prevail upon her to meet him after her day's work was finished, and together they walked slowly through the town, talking, and finding out about each other.

Her name was Aditi and she came from a town many hundreds of miles away. When she was very young her parents had married her off to a rich merchant and she had lived comfortably, if not happily, until recently, when her husband had suddenly died. The practice of *suttee,* burning widows on their husbands' funeral pyres, had been banned by the British for a century, but it still happened from time to time, and Aditi felt threatened and afraid. Her husband's family were very traditional, and she was by no means sure that a man-made law would stop them from carrying out what they saw as a religious duty. So, one night she'd packed whatever possessions she could, including a few items of jewellery, into a carpet bag and, with the help of a friend, she'd fled. She travelled by train to a town twenty miles away and then rode on an ox cart to Pushtali, a destination she had chosen completely at random, where she found a room to live and employment in the tea shop.

Victor listened in fascination, and he told her about his life in England. She was just a few years younger than him and was no naïve teenager. She had read a lot about London and the River Thames, and she loved to hear him describe Tower Bridge, and how it opened to let big ships pass beneath it. She could not, no matter how often she tried, understand what snow was like. Victor tried to explain repeatedly but the concept of frozen vapour was beyond her imagination.

They walked together many, many times, sometimes pausing to sit in what was referred to as a park, though in truth it was little more than a patch of earth where grass struggled to survive. Victor's military duties became nothing more than a means of passing the time between visits to Aditi. Their conduct was never anything even approaching intimacy. Their behaviour was at all times respectful and respectable.

Victor's experiences with women had been few and brief. He was not at ease in their company, not even paid company, but at last he had found someone with whom he felt completely comfortable This, he decided, was the woman for him. Of course, it would be complicated, and definitely not easy, but he was determined to take her with him, when the battalion returned to England, as his wife.

One afternoon soon after, the CO had called Victor into his office and bade him sit down.

"A word to the wise, old man," he said. "It doesn't do to be seen walking out with a native woman. Gives entirely the wrong idea to the men and the locals. The limitations we set on ourselves and on them are there for a reason. What's more, it could be taken as an insult by your fellow officers to be seen to prefer a native woman's company to theirs. No doubt you're saying to yourself that she is special, she is different, you and she could make a pukka couple."

Victor started to say something, but the colonel held up his hand.

"Let me finish, please. I've seen it all before, you know. Officers and men who try to make a go of it with Indian women, and it never ends well. Can't do, unless she's the daughter of a maharajah, and probably not even then. Take it from me, you can't carry on like this."

Then he'd smiled at Victor.

"Now, if you want to meet in secret, that's different. Having a bit of stuff on the side, behind closed doors, well, we turn a blind eye to that.

Quite natural; the men understand it. Perfectly excusable to have a bint in town to visit when you can. You wouldn't be the only one. The RSM, I believe, has two."

Victor couldn't think of anything to say that wouldn't get him into trouble, so he kept silent.

"So, are we all shipshape on that?" asked the colonel. "Jolly good. I'm sure there'll be no need to mention it again. So glad we've been able to straighten this out." And the conversation was over.

That evening he'd told Aditi what the colonel had said. She listened in silence. Victor hoped that she would be as outraged as he was, and that it would draw them even closer together, but when he went to the tea shop to see her two days later, he was told that she had left the town very suddenly the day before. He never saw her again. The battalion's remaining time in Pushtali passed with agonising slowness.

In the normal course of events, the battalion would not have been posted back to India so soon after its last tour of duty there, but of course events were not normal. There was a war on; a big war that might well get bigger. There was a battalion now in India that, for what reason they alone knew, the General Staff thought would be more useful at the front than Victor's own, and he could not stand the thought of several more years wasting his army career, and his life, in a place like Pushtali. He was a lieutenant in his thirties. In India he would probably not see promotion for a long time, if at all. Besides, there was a war to be won and he knew he could make a bigger contribution to winning it at the front line than by sitting about in a glorified hut, talking endlessly about bloody polo ponies.

It was simply the legality, or possible lack of it, of resigning his commission in wartime that made him hesitate. It could possibly be seen as desertion. Technically, he supposed, he could be shot for it.

"Is this seat taken?"

A fresh-faced young man, holding a pint mug, was pointing at one of the empty stools at Victor's table.

"No," said Victor. "Help yourself."

"Thanks," the man said, and sat down. He quaffed generously from his mug, then said, "Crowded, isn't it."

"Yes, it is," said Victor, because it couldn't be denied.

"Lots of soldiers about," remarked the man, and he was right; there were uniforms everywhere.

"That's true," agreed Victor. If it were not for the permission given to officers to wear civilian clothes when away from their barracks, he too would have been in uniform.

"I'll be a soldier too, pretty soon, I hope," the man said.

"Oh yes?"

"Yes. Grenadier Guards; that's the regiment I want to join."

"I see."

"I saw them at Buckingham Palace once, years ago. Changing of the Guard, it was. The way they did their drill, their movements, their marching, it was perfect. I've never forgotten it. Didn't think I'd ever be one myself, though."

"Well, I wish you luck."

"Thank you. My mum's tickled pink at the thought of me in a bearskin, guarding the King." The young man held out his hand. "I'm Percy Glass."

"Victor Cadogan." They shook hands.

"Are you from round here, Mr Cadogan?"

"No, my family are from Kent. I'm just in London temporarily."

"I see," said Percy, "I'm a London lad myself. Not this part; a bit more towards the East End."

"So, what brings you to the West End? Do you work here?"

"No, I work in Shoreditch. I'm a wood turner. It's a nice job. I like working with wood. It's very satisfying to take an ordinary length of wood, clamp it into the lathe and shape it into a tool handle or a stair rail or an ornate table leg or something. Pays quite well too. The reason I'm here is I'm going to the War Office to tell them I'm volunteering for the Grenadier Guards."

"Is that the best way to do it?"

"Honestly, I'm not sure, but even if it isn't, they're bound to tell me where I ought to go to join up."

"And you'll give up the wood turning?"

"I'll be sad to, but I have to. Way I see it, once Germany came marching through Belgium, we either had to do something, or else hang our heads in shame. I'm not one to let other people do the work while I lollygag about at home, so I'm off to do my bit. They're going to keep my job open for me for when it's all over."

Victor was very impressed by this nice young man. He admired his spirit.

"Would you care for another pint?" he asked.

"Very kind of you," said Percy, "But I'd better get on my way."

"Yes, I suppose I ought to get a move on too. There are things I need to do."

On the pavement outside the pub, the two men bade one another farewell and went their separate ways. Percy caught a bus to Whitehall. Victor nodded to himself, as though agreeing to his inner thoughts.

That sums it up perfectly, he thought. *Lollygagging*. He was a soldier after all, and he should be helping win the war, not lollygagging around in India.

His mind was made up, and he would worry about the legal side of things after the war. He made straight to the nearest post office and sent a telegram to his commanding officer at battalion headquarters.

I DO HEREBY RESIGN MY COMMISSION WITH IMMEDIATE EFFECT STOP CADOGAN LIEUT

Then he hailed a taxi and asked to be taken to the nearest army recruiting office, where he forsook Cadogan in favour of his mother's maiden name, and Victor Rangle (Vic to his mates) was sworn in as a private in the 35th battalion of the Middlesex Regiment.

Chapter VII

The Aristocrat

The Beacon Hotel was pleasant enough for the people who stayed there. It didn't have the class, of course, of the luxury hotels of Mayfair and its room charges were correspondingly much lower. It catered mostly to the middle class guest: businessmen, families visiting London, that type of person. It was not, and the management would shudder at the very idea, the sort of hotel that catered to commercial travellers. It was a cut above that sort of thing. It was, quite simply, a nicely run hotel, not far from the British Museum, where a reasonable price would get you a clean room, a superb breakfast and, if you had neither the money nor discernment to eat elsewhere, a passable lunch and dinner.

Because he was being frugal with his allowance for that month – he was not even sure that there would be any allowance for him next month – Lord Roland Selway was staying at the Beacon, which to his surprise he found pleasant enough, and he didn't miss the service that he would have received had he stayed in his family's house in Belgravia. However, he couldn't stay at the family home because he was in the middle of a huge argument with his father, and he wanted to distance himself from his relations as much as he could until it was all resolved.

Lord Roland was the third son of the seventh Duke of Dornoch. As such, he was expected, by his elder relatives and his father in particular, to abide by rules laid down both for his own good and that of the Selway dynasty, by his forebears. The family owned a very large estate in Scotland, some smaller properties in England, and interests in a number of financial and other similar concerns. They were rich, very rich, but since the duke honestly believed that no true gentleman ever knows how much money he has, he would have been unable to tell one exactly how rich – always supposing that one had the appalling bad taste to ask him in the first place. The routine of the family had remained unchanged for years – the Season in London, shooting in Scotland, annual visits to Monte Carlo and Baden-Baden – all the while the interest on the investments, and the rents on the many properties the family owned, rolled in to keep them as rich and prosperous as ever. The sons and daughters went to the right schools and colleges, made the right marriages, and lived the leisured life that they considered their birthright.

Or rather, most of them made the right marriages. This twentieth century had brought with it certain modern ideas that the duke and duchess and their contemporaries could only deplore, among them the idea that younger family members could marry for love alone. According to their lights, marriage was for joining families together and, if love went with it, that was a just lucky bonus. The duke's first son, Alaric, had married well enough, to the daughter of a viscount with little breeding, but an almost obscene amount of money and investments. The second son, Reginald, would never marry. The family referred to him as one of nature's confirmed bachelors, when they talked of him at all. He had been packed off out to the Malay States, where the family owned a number of rubber plantations for him to oversee.

Roland had finished at Cambridge in the spring of 1914 and when he returned home he was summoned to his father's study that first evening for a chat about 'the future', as the old man put it. In fact, whatever he may have called it, it was not so much intended as a chat, but more as a cross between a lecture and the issuing of instructions. They had begun with a few platitudes, the duke having the grace to at least congratulate his son on having obtained a first class degree in Classics. Small talk, though, was not the duke's forte. He wasn't that sort of man. He had told his son that he was now expected to court and marry the daughter of the Earl of a seat in southern England. No need to worry about the details – he had planned it all with the girl's father twenty years ago. It was all settled. The wedding would be in October, so he could permit himself a brief holiday to recover from his exams, if he wished, and maybe sow a few wild oats while he was at it, but he was to present himself at Belgravia in early August. After the wedding, he and his bride would honeymoon in Egypt for a month, then settle in their own home in London, which was to be a gift from the bride's father. The entire wedding settlement would be very substantial and this joining of families would be to everyone's advantage.

Roland, in spite of having moved in these circles all his life, was very taken aback. He had a few points of his own that he wanted to raise. He had hardly even heard of the girl until this evening, he knew nothing about her, so how on earth did he know whether he wanted to marry her? That was not really relevant, his father assured him. *He* had met the girl, found her to be personable enough, and judging from her family history, she'd probably be the sort who would be able to provide him with several children.

"How do I know that I'm going to fall in love with her?" asked Roland. "Or she with me? Surely we can't decide anything until we know that?"

"That isn't really important," replied his father. "What does matter is that this marriage is concluded by later this year. Look, Rollo, in all probability you'll end up learning to love each other as you spend your life together. Look at your mother and me – that's what we did."

Strangely enough, Roland wasn't placated by this line of reasoning. He'd argued with his father, and his father, who was not accustomed to being answered back to by his children, or his servants, or by anyone at all really, became more and more irate, until Roland stormed out of the room and didn't appear for dinner that evening. The following day, the two men had spoken again and the same argument ensued. The duke had called on his son to remember his duty to the family. Roland told the duke that he would choose his own wife, thank you very much, but not until he was good and ready. He had no intention of marrying just yet. Nothing was resolved.

Over the next couple of months, Roland did meet his putative bride twice. She was a very pleasant girl called Maude and, although they got on very well together, there was no spark there. In one of the few moments they had together, away from prying ears, they both agreed that given the choice, they would prefer not to have to marry each other. Maude, however, had been brought up to believe that her father's word was law and if he told her to marry someone, no matter what she really wanted to do, she would have to accede to his wishes. Roland wasn't so easily cowed. He told her not to worry; he'd see to it that they wouldn't have to marry. Then, he told his father that he was going to take a holiday and embarked on a tour of Europe, taking in Paris, Geneva, Rome, Heidelberg, and Brussels.

He had arrived home just as war was being declared. This, he told his father, would surely change things. He would have to take some part in the war, so he couldn't get married. The duke told him he could think again – the wedding was going to take place, though, of course, in wartime it would be bad taste to celebrate too lavishly and there would be no German wines served at the reception. As for taking part in the war, Roland could do his bit, in fact it was expected of him. The duke knew people in the Admiralty and he could pull a few strings to ensure that Roland gained a commission in the Royal Navy, just as his oldest brother and two of his cousins were going to do.

This led to another argument, another refusal by Roland to marry Maude and, this time, it ended when he stormed out of the house to spend the night at Claridges Hotel. He spoke to his father by telephone the next day. The conversation was not particularly edifying.

"You are to come home at once," said the duke.

"I will, if you agree to cancel this wedding."

"That is out of the question."

"Then I'm not coming home."

"If you don't come home, I'll stop your allowance."

The duke always threatened to cut off his children's allowances whenever they displeased him, but so far he had never carried out this threat. Even so, Roland could not completely discount the possibility that one day he might actually do it. The allowance from his father was all he had to live on, but he couldn't allow himself to cave in just like that.

"Do so," he said. "I am not marrying Maude and that is that!" He hung up the telephone.

He was angry at his father's refusal to budge but composed enough to realise that, without the allowance, he would have to conserve what money he had remaining. Luckily, the last month's allowance had only recently reached his bank account and he had hardly spent any of it. Still, staying in a place like Claridges was out of the question, which was how he came to move to the much more modest Beacon Hotel in Bloomsbury. He paid for two weeks in advance and sat in the small room, wondering what to do next.

While he was considering this, he spent most of his time walking, reading, or rediscovering the museums and art galleries in London, which he had not visited for years. He also saw a number of his friends who lived in town; the ones who could be relied upon not to tell his father where he was.

With a charming touch of irony, he met a woman with whom he did fall in love. She was quite unsuitable for someone of his background and that made no difference to him, because after knowing her for only a week, he decided he wanted to marry her.

He first saw her in the British Museum. He had been there two or three times, mainly because it was close to his hotel. He noticed her admiring an Egyptian exhibit and when she looked up and saw him looking at her, he resisted the temptation to look away and instead he smiled at her. She smiled back at him and he felt a strange tingling go down his spine, while his heart began to beat very fast. It took more courage than he thought he possessed, but he managed to get up the nerve to speak to her.

"Fascinating, isn't it?" he said.

"Oh yes, very much," she enthused. She had a foreign accent of sorts.

"I like to come here as often as I can to look around." It was all he could think of to say, but he didn't want to let the conversation come to a halt.

"And so do I. This is a most excellent establishment."

After that, it was quite easy to talk to her about the exhibits and they went round several halls, discussing what they saw. They even left the museum together. It had begun to rain; Roland had an umbrella, she didn't.

"I say, look here," he said. "You'll get soaking wet. Why don't I walk you to your destination and we can share my umbrella?"

She made a token protest, he insisted, and together they walked towards the Underground station, both sheltering under his umbrella. They had to lean towards each other to walk like that and their shoulders were touching – Roland liked that. After a few minutes they passed a small restaurant. Roland hadn't had lunch and he wondered if she had eaten. She hadn't, so he asked if she would allow him to buy her lunch. She was delighted to accept.

They sat at a table and ordered.

"My name's Rollo," he said.

"That's an unusual name." She definitely did have an accent.

"It's short for Roland, but all my friends call me Rollo."

"Rollo. I like it. My name is Erika."

A thought occurred to him about the way she spoke. "Are you German?" It wouldn't have mattered to him if she had been. She could have been from Outer Mongolia for all he cared.

"No, I am Italian."

"Italian. I see. I'm sorry, it's just that your accent, it made me think perhaps you might be German. Or at least a German speaker."

"I am."

"How do you mean?"

She laughed. She had long, light brown hair and green eyes. When she laughed her face lit up and, for a moment or two, Roland found it difficult to breathe.

"It seems that no one in England knows about where I come from. In the northeast corner of Italy is Trieste. It is part of the Austrian Empire, but there are many there who wish for it to be part of Italy. I was born not far from the border, where people tend to speak both Italian and German. My father was Austrian before he become an

Italian and my teachers spoke German, so that is the language I learned first, but in my heart I am and always will be an Italian."

"I never knew that," said Roland, "What brings you to London?"

"My father. He is a correspondent for one of the most important Italian newspapers. He was sent to London three months ago. My mother is dead and I am his only child. I did not wish to separate from him, so I came with him. Now, I work without pay as his assistant and secretary."

"I hope you are enjoying London."

"I like it very much. So many museums and interesting old buildings." she enthused.

"And we do have the best theatres in the world here too."

"So I am told. But my father has no interest. I do not like to go alone."

This was an opportunity being served up on a plate and Roland was not about to let it pass.

"Well, look, I know we have only just met, but would you like to come to the theatre with me tonight? I was going to see a show I'm sure you'd enjoy. I'd be delighted if you could go with me"

"That is so kind of you, but it will be an imposition for you to have to buy an extra ticket."

"No, no, not at all. In fact, I have two tickets already," he lied, "A chum of mine was going to come with me, but he had to cancel. I'd hate to waste it."

She allowed herself to be convinced, so they arranged a time and a place to meet, and, after the meal, he walked her to the Underground station, with a promise to see her that evening. Then, he hailed a cab and went to the theatre where the latest Bing Boys show was playing, buying two tickets.

They had a wonderful evening. He was smitten with her and asked to see her again. She said yes and they went out the following evening. And the one after. And the one after that. The next day, she invited him to have lunch with her and her father, who was delighted to meet him. The old man questioned him on his opinions of the current situation. He seemed convinced that Italy would enter the war in the next few months, and that this development would be their chance to settle some old scores with Austria.

"You have not joined your army?" he asked Roland.

"No, sir. There was some talk of my joining the navy, but I don't know how keen I am on that."

"You are not a pacifist?"

"No, no, not at all. I have just had a few family matters that have been occupying my attention recently, but I think they are about to be resolved."

He was right. A few days later, he asked Erika to marry him. She didn't hesitate to accept. This was when he told her all about his family, his title, and the proposed marriage to Maude. Roland told Erika that he'd quite understand it if she changed her mind. Erika took a very practical view. She asked him if he still would marry her, if it meant being cut off by his family. Roland told her that he certainly would and she said that, if it made no difference to him, it would make no difference to her.

They didn't want to wait, so they bought a special licence and arranged to be married in three days' time. There was also something else which Roland had to do. When he told Erika she became very solemn, but she said she quite understood. These were trying times for millions of people and she would put up with the disruption as best she could. She loved Roland and was behind him in everything he did, so that afternoon he sought out the place he wanted and took that very important step. They married three days later.

Their honeymoon was at the Beacon Hotel. Roland simply changed rooms and booked into a larger one, in the name of Mr. and Mrs. Selway. It was the best week of his life. At the end of the seven days, Roland found a telegram waiting for him at the hotel reception desk. Somehow, his father had found out where he was. Roland opened it.

RETURN HOME IMMEDIATELY STOP MARRIAGE MAUDE TO TAKE PLACE TWO WEEKS STOP FATHER.

He didn't reply straight away. The following morning, he and Erika left the Beacon and, as they were en route to her father's flat, where she was to live for the time being, he went into a post office and sent a telegram of his own.

REGRET UNABLE RETURN HOME OR MARRY MAUDE STOP HAVE MARRIED SOMEONE ELSE AND JOINED ARMY STOP ROLLO.

Chapter VIII

The Artist and The Labourer

When Colin Tunniford told his father that he wanted to make his living as an artist, the old man had taken a couple of puffs on his pipe, exhaled, looked over his son's shoulder and said, "Well, that's as quick a way as any to starve." The matter had then progressed from discussion to argument. The more Colin had insisted that he could make a good living by selling his paintings, the more his father had insisted that he couldn't.

"Paint for a hobby by all means, old boy," said Pa Tunniford, "but have a real job as well. Look at your two brothers. They've both made a go of it." And he was right. Both Colin's brothers, much older than him, had successful careers: one as a banker, the other as an architect.

"Well, they've both had a bit more of an advantage than I have," said Colin. What he meant was that his brothers had both been to Public School, which was a very good starting point for those who wished to establish themselves in one or other of the professions. But by the time Colin had reached thirteen, the Tunnifords had not been able to afford another set of fees, so he was sent to Grammar School. A very good Grammar School, in fact. His father had been to that same school and told everyone how much he had enjoyed it. He never wanted Colin to feel hard done by.

"I was in the same form as the chap who wrote *Three Men in a Boat*," he used to love telling people. "You know. Jerome. I never reckoned him above half, but the fellow knew how to write an amusing tale. I wrote to him at his publishers to tell him. He sent back a nice letter. Said he remembered me."

When Colin finished Grammar School, he gained a place at university and graduated with a respectable degree in geography. It was shortly afterwards that he had the discussion with his father about what he would do with the rest of his life. It did not go well. If voices were not exactly raised, they were certainly not subdued.

Eventually the two men, father and son, reached a compromise, an arrangement that Colin saw simply as a stop-gap. He would get a job to earn enough to pay for a roof over his head, keep food on the table and satisfy the occasional caprice and indulgence. For now, he would confine the painting to his spare time.

The stop-gap job, which his father found for him through a friend of a friend, was with an insurance company in Holborn. It wasn't a senior position – he was just one of many clerks sitting at a desk, but he was diligent and dependable, and his new employers were very pleased with him. In fact, Colin was informed that, all things being equal, he could look forward to promotion sooner rather than later.

To his delight, and his family's great surprise, Colin also made a success of his painting. When he was able to exhibit it, his work sold; not for huge sums, not consistently enough for him to be able to give up the job with the insurance company, but enough so that the two incomes enabled him to keep body and soul together very comfortably. It was with both satisfaction and smugness that he was able, on a visit to his parents, to tell his father that he had just sold a painting, a view of the St John's Wood roundabout, for fifteen guineas.

He met other artists, mixed in artistic circles from which he drew most of his friends. It reached the stage that he came to think of himself as an artist who did insurance work during the daytime, for pin money.

When war was declared, Colin shared the national mood that Germany needed to be taught a lesson for invading Belgium and in answer to Lord Kitchener's call for volunteers he, like hundreds of thousands of other young men, decided to enlist in the army for the five or six months that the war was expected to last; at the same time he could make use of his new experiences as inspiration for his painting. He could see that war art would be very much in demand for boosting morale and for propaganda.

Thus it was that one afternoon, after he had informed his employers of his decision, Colin was to be found in a long, jovial queue of young and not quite so young men outside an army recruiting office.

There was almost a holiday atmosphere. People were chatting away to each other. Someone sang a chorus of "Rule Britannia" to loud cheers. A few minutes later he did it again. The cheering was not quite as loud, but it was still substantial.

Two men walked out of the recruiting office, both smiling. They looked at the men in the queue and one of them gave a thumbs up. Some of the crowd applauded.

"They got in, then," said the man next to Colin.

"Looks like it," Colin replied. "I wonder how choosy they actually are."

"I reckon as long as you've got two arms, two legs and can see, you'll be alright."

Colin laughed. "Easy at that, do you think?"

"Maybe. Just as long as I get in. That's all I want."

Colin lit a cigarette, then he remembered his manners.

"Sorry," he said, "Would you care for one?"

"Ta very much," said the man.

When both cigarettes had been lit, Colin held out his hand.

"I'm Colin Tunniford."

"Nice to meet you." The man shook his hand. "I'm Hubert Snibley."

There was a pause, then Colin said, "I expect army life will be quite different from what we're used to."

"I bloody well hope so," said Hubert, "Sooner my life changes from what I'm used to, the better. Can't happen fast enough."

Colin wasn't sure if he should ask this total stranger to say more, or whether that would be prying. However, Hubert solved his dilemma by continuing to talk unbidden.

"Twenty-two years old next month, I am, and I still sleep on the floor in the two-room walk-up where my mum and dad live. Freezing in winter, noisy and hot in summer. Never had what you'd call regular employment. Just odd jobs here and there, a bit of labouring when I could find it. Never enough to pay my own way. My dad used to wait for me to get paid, then he'd nick the money off me for drink. Doesn't do that anymore. Not after the last time he tried it and I blacked his eye for him."

Colin didn't know quite what to say about this glimpse into a completely different world, so he just nodded to show he was listening.

"So now when my dad wants drink money, he rents out my mum. Ten bob a time. Sometimes more. I told her to stop doing it, but she said she doesn't want to let Dad down. He'd thump her too, probably, if she refused. 'Sides, I think she rather likes it, sometimes."

"That's awful," said Colin.

"Too right, mate. I've got a brother, couple of years older than me. He went, year before last. Upped sticks and left. Not a word from him since."

"Have you thought of leaving?"

"Well, that's what I'm doing now, you see. Joining the army. I got the idea when Germany walked into Belgium. I mean, that wasn't right. Not right at all. They need to be shown what's what, so here I am."

"Good for you."

"Then when it's all over, I'll have saved my army pay so I can find somewhere to live."

"They say this war will probably only last about six months," said Colin, "Perhaps even less. Home by Christmas, maybe."

"That'll suit me just fine. I won't need much. Just a room of my own and something besides the floor to sleep on. Don't know why I didn't think of this before. Should have done it years ago. I mean, you can still join the army, even if there isn't a war."

Soon they reached the front of the queue, went into the recruiting office, gave their details to a corporal behind a desk, then were given a cursory medical examination by a busy doctor in a white coat. Since they both had the requisite quota of arms and legs and could both see well enough to read the top three lines of an eye chart, they were passed as fit, and as part of a group of six they were attested, swearing allegiance to the King.

"Right then," the recruiting sergeant addressed them. "You are not the men you were when you walked in here. You are now soldiers in the British army, and subject to King's Regulations, which is the law governing the army. In a week or two you'll receive notice of where to report for duty, and when. That will not be an invitation or a suggestion; it will be an order, which you will obey. Failure to do so will be desertion, and the army will come and find you, and believe you me, you won't enjoy that one little bit."

Hubert was positively drinking in the military atmosphere already. Colin, even though he did not show it, was more amused by it than anything else. He told himself that he would do his bit, obey orders, be as good a soldier as possible, but he certainly would not allow himself to be seduced by the military mentality.

There were a few moments of silence, as the sergeant let his words sink in.

"Alright, lads," he said. "Off you go now. Well done."

"Thank you, sir," said Hubert.

"Don't call me 'sir'. Not ever. Make that the last time you ever address a sergeant as 'sir'."

"Yes, Sergeant. Sorry, Sergeant," said Hubert.

As Colin and Hubert walked out of the building, they could see that the queue was just as long and boisterous as they had left it.

"You going back to work?" asked Hubert.

"No, I'm off to see a friend."

"Friend, or girlfriend?"

"Well, sort of a girlfriend. We'll chat and have a beer or two. Want to come along?"

"Won't say no."

So the two new friends made their way together.

Chapter IX

The NCO

In the little garden of his friendly little house, in one of the quieter parts of Aldershot, in Hampshire, Fred Quill sat at a rusty wrought iron table, under the shade of an oak tree. He was reading his daily newspaper as he sipped tea from a china cup, bearing the willow pattern. What he read had caused him to frown and he was still frowning when his wife, Enid, joined him, bringing with her a plate of cucumber sandwiches, with the crusts cut off, and a plate of rich tea biscuits.

Enid saw her husband was exercised over something. The frown and the absent way he was chewing his sandwich as he stared at his paper were a dead giveaway. She was one of those gentle souls, who always believed in looking on the bright side, and so she tried to divert Fred's attention from whatever he was thinking of by saying something positive.

"Isn't it lovely out?" she remarked. "We don't often get the opportunity to have afternoon tea in the garden at this time of year."

Fred's reply was an absent, "Mm, yes," as he went on reading.

"More tea?" Enid asked, and when Fred nodded and held out his cup, she refilled it.

"This is a bad business," said Fred, after a few moments. Enid sighed. The war again – she knew that was what he was thinking about. Since this war had started, Fred's main preoccupation was the progress, or lack of it, of the British Expeditionary Force and he assiduously read the newspapers every day, noting how the war was going, following the front line and each battle on a map of Belgium and northern France, that he had tacked to the back of the kitchen door.

Enid hated the war, but Fred's interest was not surprising. He had been a soldier for thirty years. He'd joined the army as a boy, way back when Victoria was Queen, and had retired just a few years ago, having spent most of his time in the Dublin Fusiliers and latterly the Army Service Corps. He had left with the rank of sergeant. In fact, he had been promoted to sergeant no less than three times in his career, but twice he had been broken back down to corporal, both times for drunkenness. He had been off the bottle these last fifteen years and had managed to hold on to his three stripes since 1896. It was probably these two blots on his record that had prevented him from reaching the rank of Sergeant Major. He had still been a dependable NCO, much valued by his superiors. The army had been Fred's life and, even though he loved his wife and lived comfortably on his small pension, he missed the military life dreadfully.

If he couldn't actually be a soldier, the next best thing was to read about soldiers and soldiering, so he borrowed every book he could find in his local public library about the army and warfare. Some he had read several times over. When this war against Germany had broken out, Fred, like most people in the country, had been very enthusiastic. It was well past time that someone taught Germany a lesson. However, he was very perturbed when, instead of giving the Germans a bloody nose and pushing them back to Berlin, the British army, tiny in comparison with its enemy's, fought and lost two major battles and was, for a brief time, in retreat. Well, reasoned Fred, the British army had retreated before, even lost battles before, but it hardly ever lost wars.

What Fred did not expect, was for the war to bog down the way it had. From the Belgian coast, down through France, and right up to the Swiss border, the two sides, unable to outflank each other, had dug in temporarily, in an unbroken line of trenches. Temporary had become more or less permanent for the time being and, as winter approached, it was obvious that there would be no attempt at a large-scale offensive until the following spring. The two armies now faced each other from a growing network of front line, support, supply, and communications trenches. This, Fred thought, was not the way armies, especially his beloved British army, should fight, but if it had to, then it needed the best people in charge.

"A very bad business," he said again.

"Yes, dear," Enid agreed. She didn't know exactly which detail he had read about in the paper, but she knew that he considered the entire conduct of the war a bad business.

"The army hiding in mud holes and dodging snipers' bullets. That's not the way it should be."

"No, dear."

"What Field-Marshall French needs to do, is to direct the army at the enemy's weakest point and break his line. Send in the infantry first, the finest in the world, you see, and once the enemy's line is broken, the cavalry can pour through the gap and finish them off. That's the ideal prey for cavalry, you know, fleeing infantry."

"I see," Enid nodded. In fact, she had heard this several times over, but Fred did seem to need to voice his opinions out loud and she was his sole audience. She was only glad that whatever happened, her Fred was well out of it. "Would you like another sandwich?" she asked.

"What? Oh, yes, that'd be very nice." Fred reached out to take a little triangle of brown bread from the plate that Enid was holding, but a spasm of pain made him pull back.

"What's the matter?" asked Enid, worried.

"Phew! That fair took my breath away," Fred panted. "A touch of the old indigestion, I shouldn't wonder. I'd better not have anything else to eat, thank you. When we go inside, maybe you could look out some Epsom salts for me, to settle things down."

"Yes, if you're sure that will be enough. Wouldn't you rather go see Doctor McCann, just to be on the safe side?"

"See the doctor just on account of a spot of indigestion? Why on earth would I want to waste his time like that, when a glass of salts will do the trick marvellously?"

"Well, if you're sure."

"I am," he said. "Makes you wonder, though. When you think of all the strange food, the out and out muck I had to eat during thirty years in the Army, it's odd that I should have trouble digesting good old English food like cucumber sandwiches."

"Yes," Enid agreed. "Well, we're neither of us getting any younger, Fred."

"Mmm. But we're not too old just yet," said Fred and went back to his newspaper, while Enid wondered what he meant by that.

What Fred had meant was that he was considering, in fact had pretty well set his mind to rejoining the colours.

The Quills had only one child, a daughter called Doris, who had married a schoolteacher possessed of a pleasant disposition and myopia so acute, that he had been rejected on both occasions that he had tried to enlist. They had gone to live in some town in Wales with an unpronounceable name. Fred could never say it – a long name full of Ls and Ws and hardly any vowels, like so many Welsh place names. They wrote to their daughter every week and she wrote back just as often. She was expecting a child in a few weeks and the Quills were excited about impending grand-parenthood. That very day, Fred had posted the latest letter to Doris. He had written two pages and Enid had added a note of her own. Fred had sealed and addressed the envelope, but there were no stamps in the house, so he had set out to walk to the post office a few streets away.

No one seeing him would have had trouble guessing that he had once been a soldier. It was the way he walked – straight and confident, not slouching along like so many men did, who hadn't undergone military training. It was a bright afternoon and he enjoyed the walk, greeting along the way one or two neighbours who met him. He bought his stamp and posted his letter, but what made that particular walk so special was that he saw a poster on the wall outside the post office. It said: 'All retired Non-Commissioned Officers in the Royal Navy and Army are asked to re-enlist for the duration of the war', and it sent Fred's spirit soaring. From that moment, he knew he was going to go back into the army. He wouldn't feel so useless. Enid wouldn't be too pleased about it; in fact she'd be very upset. He decided he would have to choose very carefully the right moment to tell her.

"Enid." Fred looked up from his paper, after reading in silence for a few minutes.

"Yes?" Enid had been looking at the flowers she had planted in the garden, to great effect; they had made it such a pretty little place.

"They want people like me to go back into the service. Retired sergeants and such like."

"Oh Fred, why you? You've done your bit. Thirty years they had you for. They can't expect any more than that from you."

"They need every man they can get. My thirty years mean I have a lot of experience. I want to put that to good use, surely you can understand that?"

"What I understand, is that I don't want my husband killed. I thought all that was over, that I wouldn't have to worry about that any more."

"Oh, Enid, there's precious little chance of that. Look at me. Do I look like a fighting soldier to you? I expect they'll put me in an administrative post somewhere, filing documents and the like. Or training even. I could very well end up training recruits, right here in Aldershot and coming home to you each evening, most likely. There's nothing to worry about, dear."

Enid was quiet for a few seconds, then said, "You've made your mind up already, haven't you?"

"Yes, I'm going to do it. But it's all for the best, old girl." He patted her arm. "It's the right thing to do. You can see that, can't you?"

Enid couldn't see it, and as Fred was telling her about how he was going to sign on the dotted line the next day, she was trying not to cry.

Chapter X

The Bank Clerks

"You're sure you've got enough petrol?"

"Yes, for the tenth time. Stop worrying."

"I just don't want us breaking down in the middle of nowhere late at night."

"We won't."

"We did last time – we had to spend the night cooped up in the bloody thing, till someone came along the next morning to tow us to a garage. I'm not anxious to repeat the experience."

"Stop worrying. Everything's under control. I'll have you safe and sound at home, in your bed long before midnight."

"You sure?"

"Yes. Because that's when my car turns back into a pumpkin."

Johnny Winslow laughed at his own wit. He had always been the carefree one, the one who was instinctively inclined to take risks here and there, to do it now and worry about the consequences later. Usually it paid off. His oldest and closest friend, Wilfred Leuchars, was the cautious, down to earth one. He knew just how much to permit himself to be led on by his friend's enthusiasms and when to dig his heels in. Johnny was usually right, except on a very few occasions, such as the one a few months ago, when the two had driven to London for an evening out and, as Wilfred would never forget, ran out of petrol in a country lane and were effectively marooned there until after dawn. That was when he and Johnny discovered just how small the interior of Johnny's car was, as well as how unsuited it was for sleeping. Wilfred gave Johnny a rollicking when they got home. Johnny ruefully accepted his friend's scolding, and the two continued to be the greatest of friends.

They had known each other since childhood, had gone to school together and, after finishing their education, they had started work at the Rochester branch of the London and Kent Bank, both on the same day. Now, five years later, they were still there, both valued members of the junior staff. Johnny was still a teller; Wilfred had been promoted to a junior supervisory position. Neither had married; neither had even come close, though they had worked their way through a steady stream of girlfriends in the previous few years. The two chums spent most of their time off work together and were able to venture beyond the limited pleasures of Rochester, without being restricted by train timetables, because Johnny owned his own car. He had bought it second-hand and it had long passed its peak performance years, but it usually got him and his friend from A to B and neither of them would have given up the freedom of movement that the car afforded them.

That Friday, they were planning to motor up to London after work, to see a show and have a meal. There was no work the following day, so they could, in all conscience, stay up late that night. There would be three of them going. Johnny and Wilfred roomed together a few streets away from where they worked. It was a small flat, with three little bedrooms, the third being occupied by Eddie Ross, a co-worker of theirs from the bank. He led his own life, but sometimes he accompanied the other two on their evenings out – tonight was one of those occasions.

When work ended and the bank closed, the three men hurried home, got cleaned up and changed and, within fifteen minutes, were in Johnny's car, about to set off for London.

"Hang on," said Eddie. "Shouldn't we decide exactly where we're going first?"

"We have decided," replied Johnny. "We're going to London.

"Yes, but where in London? It's rather a big place, you know."

"No! Is it really? And there was I, thinking it was just a small village."

"Very funny. But that doesn't answer my question."

"We're going to see a show, aren't we?" asked Wilfred.

"Yes, but which one?"

"We are going," declared Johnny, "to the Metropolitan in the Edgware Road, to see Harry Lauder. Any objections?"

Neither Wilfred nor Eddie objected particularly to Harry Lauder, who was one of the biggest music hall stars of the time, so they both shook their heads. Johnny let in the clutch and started the drive to London.

It was an enjoyable, mostly uneventful journey. There was a bright moon, so the countryside was bathed in what was almost a colourless daylight. There was not much other traffic on the lanes and roads between Rochester and the outskirts of London. At one point, Johnny took a blind corner a bit too fast and almost collided with a farm cart being pulled by a mule, but that was the sort of thing you expected when Johnny was driving. Another time, a few miles on, they found themselves behind an army lorry, which was trundling along. The lane was too narrow for them to pass it, so Johnny dropped back a few yards, to where the lorry's exhaust was not quite so pungent, and they followed it at its own pace. The canvas awning on the lorry was hitched up and they could see two rows of men – soldiers – sitting in the back, facing each other. At one point, going up a slight gradient, the lorry slowed to a crawl.

One of the soldiers closest to the open flap, called out to them. "Where're you off to then?"

"We're going up to London," Johnny called back, "to see a show!"

The soldier laughed and gave Johnny the thumbs up. "It's alright for some, mate," he said with a grin.

"Someone's got to do it," Johnny called back.

Another soldier, next to the first one, had been glaring at the three friends in the car. He didn't join his comrade in chuckling at Johnny's comment. "And someone's got to do this," he shouted. "Where's your white feather, then?"

"What?"

But before the second soldier could shout back a reply, the lorry changed gear and accelerated, as the gradient flattened.

The three friends in the car were somewhat subdued by this last exchange, because they all knew exactly what the soldier had meant. Young men not in uniform were sometimes given white feathers in the street, often by young women, as a silent accusation of cowardice. They didn't say much to each other for a while and, after a couple of miles, the lorry turned into a field, containing several rows of tents in geometrically straight lines, where hundreds of soldiers were bivouacked.

After that, the road was clear and Johnny hit the accelerator, as though to put that incident behind them. Their spirits rose again and they reached London in no time. Johnny crossed the Thames at London Bridge and headed along the Embankment to Westminster, from where he made his way north to Hyde Park, round Marble Arch, and up the Edgware Road. It was busy on Friday night, of course, and they drove past the Metropolitan Music Hall and then turned off into a side street. Johnny parked the car in Penfold Street. Then, they walked back down to the Metropolitan's box office and bought three tickets for the next performance, which was about to start.

They got good seats, in the eleventh row of the stalls, one of them an aisle seat. Since Eddie, at six feet four inches, was the tallest of the three, he claimed it. It was a full house and there was a good atmosphere, a buzz of anticipation from the Friday night crowd, as they waited for the curtain to rise. A few people up in the circle were singing, and there was a general good nature, a lot of laughter and excited chatter. A few vendors were walking the aisles, selling flowers, snacks, and soft drinks. In the air, the smell of several perfumes and colognes mingled with tobacco smoke and the occasional whiff of something more pungent from the cheapest seats.

The main attraction of the evening was Harry Lauder, but of course he was on last of all and there was a full programme to sit through before he came on stage. The houselights dimmed, a frisson of excitement ran through the audience and the curtain rose on a pastoral scene, where a young man dressed in a blazer and straw boater, and a young woman wearing a gown more suited to the ballroom than to perching on a garden gate, sang love songs to each other. They weren't particularly good, but the audience enjoyed them – they were acceptable as an appetiser, though they would not have done for the main course. When the young man sang *The Honeysuckle And The Bee* he received applause far out of proportion to his performance. The girl then sang *I Love You Truly* and received even more applause. The couple took a bow and, since the applause was continuing, they took an encore, which consisted of the previous year's most popular song, *You Made Me Love You*. The audience joined in, or at least those who knew the words did. Others managed to 'la-la' along to the tune everyone knew so well.

More applause, another bow, and it was time for the next act, which the Master of Ceremonies introduced as The Amazing Santorettis from Italy. Most of the audience suspected that their real name was more likely to be Higgins, or Jones, or something just as British, and that the closest they had ever been to Italy was probably when they sat down to a bowl of spaghetti in a restaurant, but it didn't matter. They were an entertaining enough juggling troupe and were good value for money for the ten minutes or so that they were on. When their leader turned to the audience and announced, "Ladies and gentlemen, this-a next act is-a very dangerous! I must-a ask you all for the complete silencio," the audience gave an "Oooh!" of excitement, and then complied with the request. One member of the troupe was strapped to a vertical board and another threw knives at him, from a distance of about fifteen feet, each blade narrowly missing the man by a whisker each time. Most people had seen an act like this before, but there was always the possibility that it might go wrong, so the audience held its collective breath, hoping the act would all go without a hitch, but also thinking how deliciously dreadful it would be if they actually saw the victim being accidentally skewered, right there on stage before them. There was no skewering that evening and the Santorettis left the stage to loud applause.

They were followed, in turn, by a comedian, a man with half a dozen performing poodles, a knockabout slapstick act, and a band consisting of three banjos and a drum, which was a veritable assault on the eardrums. Then came a gang of clowns, who for some reason, failed to amuse the audience and there was a general restlessness until they finished. A polite smattering of applause followed, and then it was the interval.

The bar at the music hall was far too small to accommodate more than a fraction of the entire audience, which was why, in common with similar bars in theatres and music halls all over the country, it was called a 'crush bar'. By the time Johnny, Wilfred, and Eddie got there, people were standing five deep at the bar, and the three barmen were working as fast as they could to serve as many people as possible in the fifteen minute interval. By a combination of brute force and determination, Eddie managed to get to the front quicker than most people around him and he caught the eye of one of the barmen. He ordered three pints of their best bitter and the three friends moved into a corner of the room to drink in relative comfort.

"Not bad, this, is it?" said Wilfred.

"Yes, I'm enjoying myself," replied Eddie.

"See?" said Johnny, "Aren't you glad I chose the Met?"

"Yes, I'll give you that. It was a good choice."

"Have you noticed," asked Eddie, "how many blokes there are in uniform here?"

The other two looked round the room and, sure enough, there were several soldiers in khaki, some in large groups, others in twos and threes.

"Well, there're soldiers everywhere these days," Wilfred remarked.

"Yes," Eddie agreed. "It's hard to believe that, up till a few months ago, you never saw a soldier from one month to the next. Now they're all over the place."

"That's because there's more of them, so you're bound to be seeing them."

"Ever thought of joining up?" Eddie asked the other two.

"Yes, of course," replied Johnny. "I expect we will sooner or later. Just so long as we can stay together when we're in."

"And," said Wilfred, "providing that we get into a fighting regiment that's going to the war in France. I don't want to join up, just to get stuck counting boots and blankets in an army warehouse in India or Africa or somewhere."

"You can stay together," Eddie told them. "I've been reading about it. All these new regiments are being formed with that specific purpose. People from the same area staying together. My mate Eric, right, he's from Grimsby. He says there's a regiment called the Grimsby Pals. They know each other, most of them."

Johnny sipped his beer. "Did you hear what that soldier shouted at us from that lorry on the way here?" he asked, bringing up the subject for the first time.

"Yes," said Eddie. "He said it was alright for some, going to see a show."

"No, I meant the other one, who yelled at us just before the lorry pulled away. He said we ought to have white feathers. He seemed very angry that we were having a good time, while he had joined up."

The bell rang just then, to tell them that the second half of the programme was about to start.

"Well, I've heard it said that if they don't get the number of volunteers they want, or even if they do, they're going to bring in a law that will force people of our age to join up."

"I don't believe that'll ever happen."

"Maybe, maybe not, but if it does, you won't be able to pick and choose what regiment you join. You'll just go where they send you. Come on, drink up. Let's get back to our seats"

Apart from a comedian, who stood in front of the curtain and had a very risqué patter, which bought gales of laughter from the audience, and a girl singer, who was very pretty, very sweet, but not very good, the whole of the second half was given over to Harry Lauder, who was, after all, the one the audience had come to see. The Master of Ceremonies, at the side of the stage, began to give the Scotsman a long, extravagant introduction, and the audience could tell he was deliberately spinning it out, so they went along with the gag by catcalling, whistling, and shouting out to him to get on with it.

"So without further ado—" cried the MC.

"About bleedin' time," someone shouted back from the cheap seats, to general laughter.

"—I give you the greatest entertainer in the British Empire... Harry Lauder!"

To thunderous applause, the curtain rose and on came the diminutive figure in a kilt and tam o'shanter, carrying a gnarled walking stick. He bowed, the band struck up and he gave them *She Is My Rose* before the applause had died down, and then *I Love A Lassie*. The audience lapped it up. Johnny and Wilfred were applauding as wildly as everyone else. Eddie was slightly less enthused. Lauder had a habit of chuckling between the lines of his songs, which sounded very false to his ears, and it irritated him, but not enough to stop him enjoying the show.

If Lauder had wanted to leave the stage, the audience wouldn't have permitted it. They cheered and applauded each song, and he went through *Roamin' In The Gloamin, Where Shall We go Tonight?*, and a song many had heard before – which everyone was destined to hear many, many times in the coming years: *It's A Long Way To Tipperary*.

The curtain fell and the crowd groaned, but Lauder stepped from behind the curtain to the front of the stage and continued to sing two more numbers, from just before the footlights.

Then the curtain rose and the audience could see that there had been a scenery change. Gone was the backdrop of what was supposed to be a Scottish glen, or something similarly rural; in its place was a painted tableau, designed to signify The Empire. From left to right, there were totem poles, mountains, a stretch of African bush, an ornamental Indian castle with a tiger and an elephant in front of it, a Chinese junk on a lake, and a kangaroo. In the centre, on a raised dais, was a girl dressed as Britannia, a Union Jack above her. At this point, the orchestra started *Keep Right On To The End Of The Road* and as Lauder began to sing, he waved his arms to the audience, inviting them to join in, which they duly did. Behind him, from both wings, performers dressed in various uniforms marched onto the stage. There was a Canadian Mountie, a soldier wearing an Australian slouch hat, another in a turban, a sailor, a soldier in the red tunic and black trousers of the army of twenty years ago, and of course several tommies. In deference to Britain's allies, there was also a French poilu, in a light blue greatcoat and a Belgian soldier in dark blue, with a képi on his head. When the two marching lines met in the centre of the stage they turned to face the audience and marched on the spot until the song was over.

This got the loudest applause of the night. Lauder acknowledged the cheers, while the troupe behind him stood at attention. Then he stepped forward and called for three rousing cheers for the soldiers and sailors of the Empire; he got them. The orchestra then played *Rule Britannia* and the whole house joined in. After more cheering, all the performers of the evening came on to take their curtain call, except the performing poodles, and stood in line abreast across the stage, with Lauder in the centre, to take a bow together.

"Ladies and gentlemen," he called, "Thank ye for your kind applause. We're glad ye enjoyed our show."

More applause erupted.

"Will ye please stand and join us in singing our national anthem."

There was a rustling as hundreds of people got to their feet, a drum roll from the orchestra, and *God Save The King* was sung and, in some cases shouted, by the whole house. Then the curtain fell, the house lights came up, and the audience poured out of the theatre.

The three friends began to walk up the Edgware Road, but decided that, before they went home, they could do a lot worse than have another pint or two, so they popped into The Green Man, just north of the Old Marylebone Road and each in turn bought a round.

Then it really was time to go, so they walked back to Penfold Street, where the car was parked, but before they got into it, they heard the sound of music.

"What's that?" asked Johnny.

"Dunno," said Wilfred. "Sounds like a brass band."

"A military band, more like," was Eddie's opinion.

"At this time of night?"

"It's coming from the main road. Let's go see."

They retraced their steps, along the narrow side street and back to the Edgware Road. Sure enough, there was a column of soldiers, a full battalion preceded by their regimental band, marching down the street. People were waving to them and cheering from the pavement, from doorways, through upstairs windows. A gang of small boys were trying to march in step to the music alongside the soldiers.

"Don't they look marvellous?" an elderly gentleman remarked to Johnny, all reserve gone, on what was almost a festive occasion.

"Yes," Johnny replied, because it was true, they did. Not as splendid as they would have looked if they had been in scarlet, rather than the modern army's khaki, but their turn-out was excellent and their marching perfect.

"They're a Territorial regiment from north London. They're marching to Victoria station."

"Oh yes?"

"Yes, they're off to the front. Marvellous. Absolutely marvellous."

After the last ranks had passed them, Johnny turned to his two friends.

"I've been thinking," he began.

"I reckon we all have," said Eddie.

"So you know what I'm going to do then?"

"Yes. And I'm going to as well."

"Where do we go, do you know?" asked Johnny.

"Someone must know. We can always ask a policeman."

"Will recruiting stations be open at this hour, do you suppose? It's almost midnight."

"We can but try."

"Now hang on a second," said Wilfred, who hadn't said anything while the others had been talking. "We've had an exciting evening and a fair bit to drink. Don't let's make any hasty decisions right now."

"Don't you want to join us?" asked Eddie.

"Yes. Yes, I do. But," he added, "I don't know if that's just the drink thinking for me."

"What do you suggest we do then?" asked Johnny.

"Let's sleep on it. If we all three feel the same way in the morning, we'll all sign up together.'

"Fine by me," agreed Eddie.

"And me," said Johnny. "Now let's go home."

They went back to the car and piled inside. Johnny started the engine, but before he had driven even ten yards the car sputtered to a halt. It had run out of petrol.

"I just don't believe it," cried Wilfred. Eddie called Johnny something less than complimentary.

"Well, at least we're not in the middle of nowhere," said Johnny in his own defence.

Neither of his companions was prepared to concede that this was actually a good enough reason to look on the bright side, so they said nothing.

"Now," Johnny continued, "one of us will have to go and find some petrol."

They argued for a bit about who that someone should be and then they fell quiet. They realised how very tired they were.

"Sod it," said Wilfred. "Let's do it in the morning."

So, the three of them slept in the car. Johnny was the last to fall asleep and, as he was about to nod off, he saw a man walking past the car, looking rather furtive and holding what looked like a small clock in his hand, but before he could wonder what that was all about, he too was asleep.

They woke, stiff and aching, shortly after dawn. Before worrying about petrol, they decided, because they were very hungry, to have something to eat, so they had a fry up at a workman's café. Over the eggs and bacon, they discussed what they had almost done the previous evening and all three of them agreed that they were just as enthusiastic as they had been a few hours ago.

"At least, if we do it now rather than waiting until we're forced to, we'll have more of a chance of staying together," Wilfred pointed out.

They decided that they wouldn't wait till they got back to Rochester. They'd do it before leaving London, at the nearest recruiting station. Then they'd worry about getting some petrol and driving home. After they'd finished drinking their tea, that's exactly what they did.

Chapter XI

The Poet

Alec Millcross would have been the first to admit that Widdershins Publishing Limited had not been exactly what he had expected. The morning had gone so differently from the way he had imagined it would, that he didn't know whether he ought to feel elated or disappointed. Since his meeting with the managing director and, as far as he could tell, the sole employee of Widdershins, Alec had bought a ploughman's lunch and two beers, and now he sat in the autumn sunshine in Regents Park, relaxing in a deck chair. He was one of several people sitting in an approximate circle around the park's bandstand, listening to a military band. They had gone through a few patriotic songs and after *Three Little Maids From School Are We*, they were sticking to Gilbert and Sullivan and playing *I Am The Very Model Of A Modern Major-General.* Alec, however, was only listening in an absent way. He was once again mulling over what had happened that morning.

Alec was a poet; that's what he told people. It probably didn't surprise all that many people to discover that about him. There was something about his face – the Byronic curls, the Cupid's bow lips – that announced to all and sundry that here was an artist, and left them to find out whether he used a paintbrush and easel, hammer and chisel or, as it turned out, pen and paper. In fact, though, he had never managed to make a living at writing poetry. He'd had a few poems published in provincial newspapers and in obscure literary magazines that hardly anyone read, but that had netted him the odd two or three guineas here and there, if he had been lucky. Some of the more earnest publications even expected their contributors to furnish articles and poetry free of charge, for the privilege of seeing their lines in print and thus validating their membership of the intelligentsia. So, in order to pay for fripperies like food, clothing, and rent, without having to ask his family for help, Alec had taken several jobs of varying duration, but he had never given up the dream of being a full-time professional poet. He submitted his work to one publisher after another, in the hope of having the traditional slim volume published and sold to what, he had no doubt, would be a willing public.

The rejections had ranged from the impersonal, to the brusque, to the encouraging. Some were even very friendly, but, polite or otherwise, what they all had in common, was a refusal to publish his poetry. Alec, twenty-two next year, was informally engaged to a young woman of modern opinions from Primrose Hill, who was five years his senior. It was her progressive attitude to the conventions of society, that had dictated that their engagement be an informal one. Alec hadn't exactly proposed to her; rather she had told him that she had presumed that, after they had been seeing each other for a while and had slept together a few times, if they found that they still got on, they might as well get married and Alec, rather taken aback, but delighted by this, had agreed. No date had been set and Alec didn't want to take that step until he was at least able to pay his own way. Myrtle, his affianced, had told him that this was an old fashioned attitude, but had not gone on to tell him that she would be happy to support him.

Then, last week, at his home in Cricklewood – a room he rented from a very understanding couple, who had frequently allowed him a certain latitude in paying his rent on time – Alec had received a letter from a publisher, to whom he had sent several sample poems two weeks before. Bracing himself for the usual rejection, Alec was surprised and then overjoyed to read that he had been invited to meet a certain Wilson O'Toole, who was the managing director no less, of Widdershins Publishing Ltd. Alec had found Widdershins' name and address in a trade directory and had submitted his work to them without knowing anything about them, but that was not unusual; there were hundreds of publishers in London and only a relative few were in any way well known.

Alec was between jobs at the moment, so he had little cash to spare, but this was a special occasion. He withdrew a precious guinea from his bank and had his one suit carefully pressed. He wanted to make as good an impression as possible with the firm's managing director, and to be able to hold his own if, for example, he met other poets or authors there, so they would treat him as an equal, as one of their own – which was, of course, what he wanted to be.

Widdershins' address was in Covent Garden. All the most famous publishers seemed to be in Bloomsbury, but of course, Alec reasoned, there was obviously not enough office space to go around, in the square mile or so that surrounded the British Museum, and Covent Garden was just a little distance away. There were some very nice, smart buildings there, among the theatres and the opera house and, no doubt, several were suitable for a publishing house to choose for its London office. He made sure his hair was impeccably brushed, that his shoes were polished to a shine they had not seen since they were brand new, before setting off from his home with an hour in hand.

It was a good thing he had allowed himself the extra time, because he had the devil of a job finding the place. He had imagined an imposing stone building of perhaps four or five storeys, with a brass nameplate, possibly even a liveried porter to greet visitors and hold the door open for them. Once inside he expected to hear the sounds of 'people at work', namely ringing telephones, clacking typewriters, and a general bustle, all taking place under bright electric lights.

What he did find, eventually, was a dirty, squat brick building at the end of an alley, abutting what looked and smelled like a tenement. The front door was closed, and beside it was a nameplate – not polished brass, but simply a wooden board with a few names lettered in black paint, some of the older ones cracking and flaking away. Alec saw: Thos. Raggiter, Investigations; Halditch & Scrite; Bidford Button Co.; Zephyr Trading Ltd; and among them was Widdershins Publishing Ltd. He had arrived. He had used up all the time he had to spare in looking for the place, so he pushed open the door and went in. There was no lighting of any sort, but by the daylight coming through the open door he read a sign on the wall, which informed him that Widdershins was on the second floor. He started to climb the stairs and almost tripped over the recumbent body of someone who had chosen that staircase to take a nap – by the smell of him, he was sleeping off what he had been drinking the night before. The Alec Millcross who reached the second floor and knocked on Widdershins' door, was considerably less confident than the one who had set out from the room in Cricklewood an hour before.

There was no reply to his knock for some seconds, then he heard a man's voice inviting him to come in. He opened the door and was greeted with the sight, not of the busy headquarters of a publishing house as he had long imagined it – a central reception area, carpeted corridors leading to the individual offices of the senior executives, with underlings going hither and yon carrying messages, manuscripts, and the other tools of the publisher's trade – but instead, he found himself in a dingy room, which contained but one person, a middle-aged man, in a grey suit and a pair of pince-nez spectacles. Three of the walls were lined with bookshelves, upon which were piled files, stationery, papers, magazines, and even a few books in varying conditions. Most of the fourth wall was taken up with a window that had obviously not seen a washcloth for months, possibly years. Under the window was a low table, on which sat a telephone and a gas ring. A long table, which perhaps had seen service in a dining room earlier in its life, occupied most of the remainder of the room, and at the far end of this table, which was as cluttered as the shelves that surrounded it, sat the gentleman who had bade Alec enter. He stood up to greet his visitor.

"I'm Alec Millcross." Alec told him. "I believe I am expected."

"Come in, sir, do come in," cried the gentleman. He was short, plump, and had several chins, but little hair – such that he had was collected in two little clumps above his ears. Alec noticed that the cuffs of his shirt and the points of his wing collar were frayed. "You are most welcome!" He held out his hand and Alec shook it, noticing that it was cold and damp, but he overcame the urge to wipe his palm on his trousers, for fear of causing offence.

"Do sit down," the man said, and pointed to a chair on his right, which was covered with papers. Alec hesitated. "Oh, put them anywhere, sir. On the floor perhaps. Pray make yourself comfortable."

Alec complied, and sat down.

"I have an appointment at eleven o'clock, with Mr. O'Toole," he said.

"You see him before you, sir. Wilson O'Toole, at your service. I have the honour to be the managing director of this company. May I offer you a cup of tea?"

"Thank you, that would be very nice."

O'Toole turned to the gas ring on the small table behind him. On it there was a kettle, which he lifted and shook; there was the sound of water sloshing around inside it. He grunted in satisfaction and then felt in his pockets, but he obviously did not find what he was looking for, because he then began searching among the papers on the table before him. After a few moments, he turned to Alec.

"My good sir, I wonder if I might trouble you for a match. I seem to have used all of mine, and I have no other means of lighting the gas ring."

"I don't have any, I'm afraid."

"I see. In that case I shall have to ask you to excuse me briefly while I go out to purchase another box. It should take but a few minutes."

"Really, there's no need to go to all that trouble on my account. I mean, I don't mind if we don't bother with the tea."

"Yes, yes, you are quite correct," O'Toole agreed. "Business before pleasure at all times. Now, you sent me that very interesting novel about the nursery governess who falls in love with the cowboy, did you not? I have your manuscript here." He began again to shuffle among the papers and files in front of him.

"No, I sent you the poetry," Alec corrected him. "You said you wanted to discuss publishing it. Here's your letter." He produced it from his inside pocket and handed it to O'Toole, who took it and squinted at it for a few moments before handing it back.

"Ah yes, to be sure, the poetry. Of course. I remember now." He lifted a manila folder off the desk and opened it. "Poetry. Most certainly." He looked up. "You are Alec Millcross, are you not?"

"Yes."

"But of course. I remember now. You introduced yourself by name when you came into the room."

"Yes."

"You sent me a total of five poems. I have them here. *Gossamer Visions, Ode To A Full Moon, How Comes Your Heart?, The Peddler's Daughter,* and *Tears At Eventide.* I am bound to tell you that I found your poetry most interesting."

"Thank you."

"Do you have any more?"

"Oh yes, I have a great many. I just sent you those five to give you an idea of what I can do."

"Indeed. Well, they give me the idea that you are capable of producing the most pleasing of effusions. I see, though, that they are of varying lengths. *The Peddler's Daughter* is thirty-six verses long. Quite a story in itself. *Gossamer Visions* by contrast consists of only…" He rapidly counted them. "thirteen lines."

"It's fourteen lines actually. It's a sonnet."

"A sonnet, you say? Gracious me, I can't begin to guess how I missed that very salient fact. Yes indeed, it's a sonnet all right. As fair a sonnet as has been submitted to this office for many a long year."

"Thank you."

"My pleasure, sir. Praise where praise is due. Now, Mr. Alec Millcross, I am delighted to tell you, on behalf of Widdershins Publishing Limited, that we find ourselves in the happy position of being able to publish a volume of your poetry."

"Thank you!" Alec was delighted. "That's very good news indeed."

"To be sure. Now, we would hope to publish a volume of about one hundred pages, so I shall need from you every single one of your poems that you can lay your hands on. If that isn't enough, you shall need to write more. Can you do that?"

"Oh yes, I certainly can." Alec was so pleased at the prospect of being published, that he would have agreed to supply a treatise on trigonometry in Norwegian verse, if need be.

"Excellent. And can you supply them soon?"

"I can send them to you by post this evening."

"That is most excellent. We may not be the biggest publishing house in London, and I am sure that neither Chapman & Hall, nor Macmillan, for example, will be too worried about us just yet, but these are early days, sir, early days. Meanwhile, at Widdershins Publishing, we don't like to waste time when it comes to bringing out a new work by a promising young writer. Tell me, have you engaged the services of a literary agent?" O'Toole asked.

"No, I haven't. Do you think I should find one?"

"Oh no, quite unnecessary, in my opinion. Agents just get in the way and complicate matters, with their contracts and their endless haggling. You see, Mr. Millcross, people like you and me, the writers and the publishers, we just want to produce the works of art, that together we create, and offer them to a grateful public. Agents simply serve to slow up the process."

"Yes, I see. Well, I won't bother with one then."

"Quite right. Now, I trust that you will forgive me if I propose that we begin in a modest way, with a print run of five hundred. We can always print more if there is a demand. Which I am sure there will be," O'Toole added.

"Five hundred? That sounds a bit low to me."

"Trust me, sir, that is the number I always suggest to new writers. It is usually found acceptable and, of course, a higher number might be a strain, financially, upon their resources."

Alec didn't know what he meant, but there was something about that that he did not like the sound of. "I'm not sure I follow, exactly," he said.

"Ah yes. I see I have been slightly remiss. Here we are, talking about numbers of volumes in the first print run and I have not yet explained to you our standard financial arrangement with our writers. I am sure that is of great interest to you"

"Yes, it is."

"No doubt." O'Toole cleared his throat before continuing. "At Widdershins Publishing Limited, we do ask our writers to bear the cost of the printing and distribution of their works themselves. Of course, they can recoup all those funds, and more besides, when the books are sold to the public."

"Pay for it myself?" This was not what Alec had expected at all.

"Just regard it, my dear Mr. Millcross, as an investment. You speculate a little to earn a lot."

"How much do you mean by 'a little'?"

"Well, let's see… Setting, printing, binding, and distributing five hundred volumes of poetry, on good quality paper. Allowing for all the variables that we are prey to in this trade… I should estimate that we can offer the entire process to you for, oh, thirty guineas."

"Thirty guineas? I haven't got thirty guineas," Alec exclaimed.

"Can you raise it?"

"Maybe. I don't know."

"Do try, my dear friend. Just think, you will be seeing your work in print; hundreds of people carrying your poems home with them, to read and enjoy for the rest of their lives, if not later than that. This is how you make your mark on posterity!"

In spite of the disappointment Alec had just felt, he now began to get excited at the idea of being in print; he began to calculate how he could best raise the funds he needed. After all, this would transform him into a published poet. He'd get his foot in the door – the first step on the road to fame and fortune.

"I'll do what I can," he said. "I need to speak to a number of people."

"Of course. I hardly expected you to be able to conclude the deal right away. By all means, do whatever you need to do. Meanwhile, I shall alert some of my contacts in the book trade that Widdershins shall shortly be producing a book of verse, by one of the brightest new poets in Britain today."

Alec felt a blush rising in his cheeks. "That is excellent," he said.

"Now, don't forget to send me the remainder of your poetry – everything you have, long and short. We'll need quite a lot to fill a hundred pages," O'Toole said, standing up.

Alec realised that the meeting was over, so he stood too, thanked O'Toole again, shook hands, and left.

The vagrant was no longer sleeping on the stairs, as Alec made his way down to street level in the dark. Outside, in the sunshine, he still felt optimistic about what had happened. He hadn't expected to have to finance his own publication, but this was only his first book. He told himself it was all for the best.

He had arranged to meet Myrtle that afternoon, so he had a few hours to kill. He didn't fancy going all the way back to Cricklewood and it was a sunny day, so he walked in the direction of Regents Park, where he thought he could spend a couple of hours sitting in the sunshine. On the way, he had stopped at a pub for a ploughman's and two refreshing beers. He wondered what Myrtle would say when he told her. He had a feeling that she would be less than elated that he was proposing to pay for someone to publish his works. In the back of his mind was the suspicion that he had been exposed, not to a publisher's zeal, but to an example of salesmanship. That was how he suspected Myrtle would see it too.

The band concert ended, the bandmaster turning to acknowledge the audience's applause with a salute, and the musicians began to pack away their instruments. Alec pulled out his pocket watch and decided it was time to get moving if he was to meet Myrtle on time. She was seldom punctual but she also hated it if anyone kept her waiting, so he made his way out of the Park, into Albert Road, and up to the address in Primrose Hill.

Myrtle lived on the top floor of a four-storey house, in rooms which had comprised the servants' quarters, until the latest owner had decided that he just needed the basement to live in, converting the rest of the building into flats, all three of which were occupied by young, single people. Alec had met them all at Myrtle's. Myrtle was forever giving parties for her circle of friends, all of whom were arty types, and were divided into roughly two camps – those who had succeeded in their chosen artistic fields and those who had not. The former group tended to look down on the latter, whom they regarded as mere dabblers in what was, to them, the serious business of making a mark on the intellectual consciousness of the world. The latter, meanwhile, often adopted an outward distaste for fame and monetary gain, which were, of course, a betrayal of their art. Alec, after telling one of Myrtle's friends, a precious young man in a silk smoking jacket, that he had received thirty shillings from a provincial magazine for two poems, was surprised to be told in return that he was 'prostituting his muse' in accepting money for his work. It turned out that this creature was in the habit of writing long rambling screeds of Latin verse, which he then used to tear to shreds and throw into the Thames. This, he assured Alec, was the poet at his purest, creating from the innermost recesses of his heart and then giving his art freely to nature, by casting it upon the welcoming surface of the mother river. Alec concluded that the fellow was either off his head or else, had a chip on his shoulder that no publication wanted to pay good money for long poetry in Latin.

Alec let himself in – Myrtle seldom locked her door during the day. He saw that this afternoon, Myrtle had two guests. One was a young man he had met a few times before, who was trying not to let a bright career in an insurance office prevent him from becoming a successful artist. The other was a young man in workman's clothes, who looked out of place. Alec decided that maybe he was one of Myrtle's pets – young working class men and women whom she invited to tea, so she could regale them with an account of how they were downtrodden and how they should rise up against the ruling classes. She always enjoyed going on like that.

"Alec, my sweet," cried Myrtle when she saw him. She was smoking a cheroot, a habit to which she had been much addicted of late. "How did it go? Are you in business?" Before Alec could reply, she turned to her two guests. "This is my dear friend, Alec. Alec, you know Colin Tunniford, don't you?"

Alec and Colin nodded a greeting.

"And this," she said, indicating the young workman, "is Colin's friend. Do forgive me, I've forgotten your name."

"Hubert Snibley"

"Yes, of course. How mortifyingly forgetful of me. Hubert Snibley, this is Alec Millcross."

"How do you do?" enquired Alec.

"Good evenin', squire."

"Alec has just been to see a very important publisher about putting out an edition of his poetry," Myrtle explained. "One of the top names in Bloomsbury."

"Oh, jolly good," said Colin.

"Well, I don't know if I could quite describe it exactly like that," Alec admitted. "It wasn't exactly what I was expecting."

"How do you mean, my sweet?" asked Myrtle.

"It wasn't in Bloomsbury, it was in a slum in Covent Garden. And as far as I could tell, it is strictly a one-man affair."

"Well, what of it? Just because they haven't been sucked into the cabal of publishers which is trying to get a stranglehold on all artistic publishing in this country, for purely commercial purposes, there's no need to look down on them."

"I wasn't looking down on them. I was just saying that it wasn't what I had been expecting."

"So? Do they want to publish you?"

"Yes, they do, actually."

"Well done. I told you you'd do it eventually. Now, when's the book coming out and how much are they giving you?"

"That's just it. They won't be giving me anything. They want me to pay all the publishing costs."

"Vanity publishing? Oh, Alec," cried Myrtle. Both she and Colin looked as though they could suddenly smell something in the corner of the room that had gone off.

"They want thirty guineas for it."

"Do you have thirty guineas?"

"No, not nearly. I was wondering about borrowing it somewhere."

"Well, don't look at me my dearest one. I haven't got that sort of money to spare," said Myrtle. She had, actually, and a lot more besides, but she had no intention of lending any to Alec.

"Oh."

There was a pause, during which Hubert Snibley took the opportunity to fetch himself another bottle of beer from the kitchen.

"Do you know where the money in poetry is going to be?" asked Colin suddenly.

"No, where?" replied Alec.

"War poetry. Stands to reason. Men in their thousands joining the army, the war touching every household in the land. People are bound to be receptive to poetry about it. Patriotic stuff, all about how we're going to teach the Hun a lesson. Maybe a few poignant verses about losing one's nearest and dearest on the field of battle, all that sort of thing. It'll sell."

"I suppose you could be right."

"I'm sure I am. The war is a theme that is going to creep into every aspect of art, you mark my words. In painting too."

"So you're going to be painting that sort of thing now, are you?"

"Colin," said Myrtle, "is going to be the most famous war artist in Britain. Just you wait and see."

"I hope so," said Colin. "Anyway, I joined up today."

"You joined up?" Alec was surprised. He didn't see Colin as the sort of person to put on a uniform.

"Yes. I can't really expect to be able to paint war pictures if I'm stuck in an office in Holborn, can I? The war'll be over in a few months and the insurance company's going to hold my job open for me, they told me so. So I joined up today. That's where I met Hubert. We signed on at the same time, didn't we?"

Hubert Snibley nodded.

"I invited him along to meet Myrtle."

"I'll never turn down a free beer," said Hubert.

"Not that I completely agree with this war, of course," added Colin.

"No, of course not," agreed Myrtle. "No self-respecting member of the intelligentsia could possibly approve of it."

"But it's a chance too good to miss," Colin went on. "So, I'll be able to get all sorts of material for my paintings and I'll make sure that I maintain a proper, intellectual detachment from what is going on around me."

"That's the only way," Myrtle nodded.

What with the disappointment of the morning, for he saw it no other way now, and his lack of thirty guineas to spare, and the effect of the two pints of beer he had drunk over lunch, in addition to what he had just heard from Colin, who was, after all, a fellow intellectual, Alec found an idea taking seed in his mind.

"Where did you go to join up?" he asked Colin.

"The recruiting station near Marble Arch. We had to stand in line for a while, didn't we?" Colin said. Hubert nodded. "We both joined one of these new regiments that Kitchener asked for."

"Then that is what I shall do too," Alec announced grandly, as he stood up to fetch himself a beer. "And I shall write war poetry that will make my fortune, when this nasty business is all over. Myrtle darling, you are going to be so very proud of me!"

Part Two

Preparing

Chapter XII

Training

All these men, then. In themselves, not even enough to form half a platoon, but they joined the three-quarters of a million who volunteered in the first three months of the Great War, becoming part of a military machine that gladly received them. They went willingly and un-coerced, ready to wage what they believed to be a just war, against an enemy who had long been spoiling for a fight and who, after his actions in the occupied portions of Belgium and France, had placed himself beyond the pale.

These were the men of the New Army, the army created by Lord Kitchener to supplement the small – small by European standards, that is – regular force, that Britain had put into the field when the war had started. They knew they were not professional soldiers, nor did they pretend to be. They had simply suspended their civilian lives for the duration of the war, which most of them still believed would be over in a few months. To them, the war was a duty, a moral obligation and also a great adventure. All of them knew the risks involved. In war, people got killed or wounded, sometimes hideously, sometimes just badly enough to leave honourable scars. However, each man believed that it wouldn't happen to him; to his comrades, his mates perhaps, but not to him – he was going to come out the other side unscathed.

Some of them may well have believed that they would find themselves on the battlefield, within a few short weeks of joining up, but in fact, what lay ahead of them all was a long and arduous period of training, which was essential in order that these men, from all walks of life, from all areas and classes of England, could be turned into soldiers.

Soldiers who would obey orders instinctively, without hesitation. No matter what their backgrounds, or reasons for enlisting, they were not to be allowed to become merely willing amateurs.

When the new recruits received their orders, they were told to report to a barracks in Mill Hill. This was where they began the process of becoming soldiers. Many were excited at this new departure in their lives; a few were already regretting their impulsiveness in joining up, but they knew it was too late to do anything about it now.

They were broken down into companies and then into platoons, and they got to know the men who were to be their comrades in arms. Some friendships were made almost at once, some tentative steps towards friendship were taken by others, and there was at least one reunion.

Private Percy Glass was standing in a long line at the barracks stores, waiting to be issued with his uniform and kit, when he heard a voice behind him.

"I thought you were going to join the Grenadier Guards."

He looked round and saw a face that was familiar, though it took him a second or two to place it.

"I know you," he said. "The bloke from the pub."

"Yes. Vic Rangle. And you're Percy something."

"Percy Glass."

"So, what happened with the Guards?" asked Private Rangle.

"I couldn't get in. Not tall enough. I was rather disappointed. Still, this seems a good enough outfit."

"Yes. A nice lot of chaps to spend the war with."

Sergeants and corporals ordered the men here and there from reveille to lights out, chivvying them along, teaching them to drill, to march, to salute, never to call them 'sir'. They did their initial arms drill with obsolete Japanese rifles, but later they were issued with the British army's standard weapon, the Lee-Enfield Short Magazine .303 rifle, and bayonet.

"Your rifle is your best friend," said one of the corporals drilling 2 Platoon. "Look after it, keep it clean. Woe betide any soldier whose rifle is anything but pristine when it is inspected."

This corporal had a very strong Irish accent; as strong as a fake Irishman in a music hall comedy skit. Corporal Seamus O'Malley spoke that way deliberately. He wanted to cultivate the image of the jolly Irishman. In fact, he had a finger in every crooked pie going. Someone once remarked that he knew more ways of cheating at cards than anyone else in the British army. That may well have been true. O'Malley's method of pleasing his superiors, while he cheated those set beneath him, was to know army regulations inside out, and to be a very efficient NCO.

"Backs straight! Swing those arms!" he shouted at the men during drill. "Old Mother O'Malley would weep at how you're letting her wee boy down with such sloppy marching."

In fact, his mother was long dead. He had no memories of her at all, and he had never known his father. He had been born the unwanted son of a Donegal farm girl, who had been seduced and impregnated by the local parish priest, whose usual taste, according to the local gossipmongers who knew about him, was for adolescent boys, but who was probably attracted to the girl because of her flat chest and slim hips. When the girl had told the priest she was pregnant, he'd immediately confessed his sin to another priest, obtained absolution, and then was moved to another parish, where he was unknown, and where there was an ample supply of new altar boys for him to enjoy.

The girl, meanwhile, was deposited at the gates of a convent by her outraged parents, who wanted nothing further to do with her, and one wet night she was delivered of a son. The nuns looked after mother and son in a manner that afforded them the essentials of care and comfort but nothing over and above that. The mother was enjoined to confess her sins and to acknowledge her unworthiness every moment that she was awake. After several weeks of this bullying, she took her own life by slitting her wrists with a table knife that she had taken from the convent refectory. The boy was placed in a parish orphanage, where he and several other local waifs, were looked after as frugally as possible. His earliest memories were of being told that he was the product of sin. In this loveless environment, it was small wonder that he came to distrust everyone with whom he came into contact, and in him grew the conviction that he had to look after himself, because no one else would. He ran away from the orphanage at the age of thirteen, and no one made any great effort to find him.

"Did I sail across the Irish Sea just to end up with a useless crowd like you?" he said, more than once, on the drill square, even if the men's drill was perfect. Criticism always, praise never, was obviously his motto.

He never told anyone the real reason he had crossed the sea. After running away from the orphanage, he first went to ground in Dublin, where he worked at any casual labour he could find, and from there he stowed away on a ship to Liverpool, where he lived hand to mouth on the streets and fell in with a gang of toughs, who taught him all they knew about theft, burglary, assault, and extortion. By the time he had reached his sixteenth birthday, he had committed enough crimes to ensure that he would be put away for most, if not all, of his life. Luckily for him, he had never been caught. Then, one drunken Saturday night, he and two of his confederates murdered a shopkeeper and were observed by several passers by. O'Malley had enough sense to realise that he could not stay in Liverpool any longer and he caught a train to London. His two friends were caught, tried and, being of age, were sentenced to death and later hanged. O'Malley arrived in London unsure of what to do. Tired, cold, and hungry, he saw an army recruiting poster. In those days, the army still wore scarlet and policed the Empire. There was no chance of a general war, and no one wanted a conflict of any sort. So he joined up, intending to stay in the army only for as long as it took for the hue and cry over the murder in Liverpool, to die down. Then, he reasoned, he would desert. To his surprise he discovered that army life suited him. He found no difficulty with drills and regulations and, in return, he received a bed and three square meals a day, whilst also enjoying the benefit of being paid. What was more, he had an enormous supply of men to cheat in crooked games of poker, gin rummy, dice, and any other play that he could devise. Sometimes he amazed himself at the ease with which he relieved his comrades of their pay.

In due course, promotion came his way, twice, and he wore on his sleeve the two stripes of a corporal. So it was that he found himself in charge of a section in 2 Platoon.

"Lord save us!" he cried despairingly as the men under him executed several manoeuvres on the drill square absolutely impeccably. "Sure, an' I wonder if I didn't make a terrible mistake, picking this regiment."

In truth, of course, he hadn't done the picking. When the war came, his battalion was sent to France and at Mons a German rifle bullet had carried off a small chunk of the fleshy part of his left arm. He was sent back to England to convalesce and, after a recovery that he ensured was no more speedy than he could help, he was told he would not be returning to his unit, but instead would be joining one of the New Army regiments that were being formed, because they needed to be seeded with experienced men. He was assigned to the 35th Middlesex without having any say in the matter. He was very popular at first, but bit by bit the members of his company got the measure of the man. The regularity and skill with which he relieved them of their money at cards made that inevitable. Some were amused by him, some tolerated him, some took a big dislike to him, but they all knew they were stuck with him.

Early in 1915, the training for the 35th Middlesex, The St Marylebone Rifles, moved to Yorkshire, to a place called Swathdale, which the soldiers soon began to believe had been chosen because of its unrelieved bleakness, after which the actual front line would seem like a pleasant change. Here, they lived in tents, shed their civilian identities even more, drilled, marched, drilled, marched, shot at targets, marched, drilled, stuck bayonets into straw dummies, drilled, camped out in all weathers, before marching and drilling some more. Amidst the weariness, the blisters, the repetitiveness, the discomfort, and the cursing, they became what they were supposed to be – first class soldiers. Not as good as the Regulars who had made up the 1914 army, of course – nobody was – but good enough to fight the enemy. Those who had been afraid that the war would be over before they got a chance to take part no longer worried about that. The war that everyone thought would be a short one was proving them all wrong.

All through 1915, they trained. That year, Germany again proved, as if it needed to, that she had seceded from the list of civilised nations, when the first Zeppelin air raids on London took place. No one could pretend that this was a military action – it was carried out to terrorise and kill civilians. At the front, she also used poison gas for the first time. To the Allied soldiers, who at that stage had little or no protection against this new menace, this was a terrifying weapon, and serve the Germans right when the British and French subsequently used poison gas on them

Battles took place on the Western Front that year at Ypres, Neuve-Chappelle, Artois, and Loos. The casualty lists were long and depressing. In 1914, the two opposing sides on the Western Front had tried repeatedly to outflank each other, and each time had failed. Instead, they had dug in and by the end of the year a line of trenches, a very intricate network, stretched from the Channel coast to the Swiss border. Between the two lines was no man's land, in some places as much as half a mile wide, in many others less than a hundred yards. The two sides faced each other, the Germans having built a very strong, defensive trench system, with concrete reinforced dugouts, some even with electric lighting, and the allies knowing that the only way to win the war was to attack and overrun them.

At the end of the 1915, with neither front line having really moved at all, General Sir Douglas Haig became British Commander in Chief. A couple of months into 1916, the 35th Middlesex received orders to move to the front. Or at least to begin the process of moving to the front. They came south by train and were billeted at the barracks, in Mill Hill. Then, three weeks later, after much more drilling, marching, and endless kit inspections, designed to pass the time while they waited for further orders, they were moved to another, temporary, barracks in Lambeth and given forty-eight hours embarkation leave. Most of them took the opportunity to visit their families.

Chapter XIII

The Twins and The Colonel

Charles and Arnold Snow, both of them still second lieutenants, went straight to their family home in Berkeley Square. The butler opened the front door for them and they stood self-consciously in the hall, their new uniforms pressed, the leather of their belts and boots gleaming bright. Their mother was expecting them and, when she saw them, she did her best to hold back her tears. These two tall, handsome, grown-up soldiers were still her two sons and she hated the very idea, however worthy it may have been, that they were about to go to the place where thousands of men were killing each other.

She hugged them, told them how very proud of them she was, and saw to it that their bags were taken upstairs. Later, as they had afternoon tea in the drawing room, they told her about their training. Not all of it of course – training was very repetitive, so there was no point in going into details. Neither was there any point in dwelling on what they had been trained to do; best to leave that unsaid. So, they confined themselves to telling her a few stories about what they and others had got up to, making it sound more like a school romp than anything else.

They asked her if she had any news of friends of theirs who had also joined up, both before and after they did, who were in different units. There were a few items of this sort of news that she could pass on to them. Their cousin Geoffrey was in France already, his regiment having left England two weeks ago. The son of a good friend of hers was in the Navy. Another young man they knew, had applied to transfer from his Territorial regiment to the Royal Flying Corps. The cook,

Mrs. Corbin, had just heard the very sad news that last week, that her nephew had died from wounds received at Loos, so she had been given time off to go stay with her sister, the dead boy's mother.

When Colonel Hardy came home that evening from the War Office, he greeted the two boys no less warmly than their mother had done. At dinner, they talked of the war in generalities; to spare their mother's feelings, they stayed off the subject of the actual fighting in France and concentrated instead on the situation in the Dardanelles, and the debacle of Gallipoli.

After the meal was over and their mother had retired to bed, though, the three men spoke more frankly over brandy and cigars.

"This war isn't going anything like the way we thought it would," said the colonel.

"No, sir," agreed Charles.

"We never reckoned on this trench business. Armies are supposed to move, to manoeuvre, to attack an enemy, to outflank and pursue him – not to sit still in trenches, lobbing shells at each other."

"It can't go on like this indefinitely, can it?" asked Arnold.

"It could go on like this for years, until one side manages to break through the other's line. We'll just have to see who blinks first. It's still winter now. It's not attacking weather. Our next offensive will probably be some time in the middle of the year. That's what all you New Army chaps will be used for. However, if you and I can work that out, then so can the Germans, and they'll be ready for you. And don't make any mistake about it, the German army is practically second to none."

"Not as good as ours, surely?"

"Goes without saying, old man," the colonel replied. "I just wanted to make sure you weren't expecting a walkover."

"No, we're not expecting that, sir. However, we are expecting to win eventually," said Charles.

"Which we shall. There is no other possibility, but it does seem hard to believe now, that when you two first joined up, I really did think it would be all over before you got anywhere near the front line. And now, so many good men have gone."

"Plenty more to take their place," said Arnold.

"Yes, a great many. That's why we shall win this war – the quality of our young men. We'll be taking over the lead from the French, that is pretty certain. They're almost exhausted."

"They're holding their own aren't they, sir?"

"They are, but the cost is so high. They're losing men by the thousand at Verdun. The Germans are trying to drain from them the will to continue."

There were a few moments' silence.

"Of course," said the colonel, "I paint a much brighter picture when I discuss things with your mother."

"Of course."

"All I can do now is to wish you both God speed, and the very best of luck. I'm sure you'll both come home safe when it's all over. Now, I expect you'll think I'm being a worrisome old duffer—"

Cries of "No!" and "Not at all!" erupted from the twins.

"— but I think it might be a good idea if you both made your wills before you go. No need to tell your mother. You won't need them anyway, it's simply a precaution. Just pop round to old Bryson's office tomorrow morning. I'll telephone him and tell him to expect you. Makes it neater to get that out of the way."

The boys nodded.

"And, by all means, please do enjoy the rest of your leave. Pretty soon you'll have forgotten what good food and clean linen are like, and you certainly don't want to spend your precious free time with a doddering old fossil like me."

More protests followed.

"Thank you, but you ought to be with people your own age. I know I would be if I were in your shoes. So go out, see a show, get drunk, find yourself a popsy or two. Have fun."

The twins did what their stepfather had suggested. They did draw up their wills the next morning, at the offices of Bryson & Clogg, the family solicitor, and they did enjoy their last evening of freedom. They ate at the Ritz, saw a show, and while Charles did get drunk, allowing his brother to tip him into a cab and send him home, Arnold found himself a young woman plying her trade in Leicester Square and enjoyed her company for half an hour and fifteen shillings. She told him she liked young officers best, but he was astute enough to know that she probably told this, with variations, to all her clients – "Oh, I do like sailors/other ranks/civilians best of all!" It didn't matter to him. She was good at what she did and he carried a happy memory of her away with him.

On the day of their departure, they told their mother that she need not come to see them off at the railway station. It would be better to say their *au revoirs* then and there. They both used the French word, as if to stress that this was simply a temporary departure. Then, they took a cab back to the barracks, in Lambeth.

Chapter XIV

Fred and Enid

Fred Quill was feeling rather sheepish. He always did when he was around his wife these days; and well he might, he told himself. Enid, bless her, had never said one single word of recrimination, but he knew that she remembered their conversation as well as he did. Now he sat before the fire in their little sitting room, waiting for Enid to bring in the tea. It reminded him of their chat before he'd rejoined the army. It was too cold now, of course, to have tea in the garden, but that was the way it usually was in England. Besides, there was something so cosy, so comforting, so downright British, about tea and crumpets in front of a warm fire. Normally, he would have enjoyed it, but hanging unseen above them, like a malevolent spirit, was his glib assurance to Enid.

"Do I look like a fighting soldier?" – that had been his question, more by way of telling her something than of asking her opinion, and he had actually believed that he would end up behind a desk somewhere, or in a transport depot, or a training establishment. He had thirty years behind him – the army could put that to good use. But he also knew, from those same thirty years he had spent in uniform, that the army often, very often, did things that seemed to make no sense at all. Sometimes they didn't, but frequently they did, and Fred knew that he, as a sergeant, was in no place to second-guess his superiors.

"Do I look like a fighting soldier?" he had asked, and Enid had not answered. The truth was that to her, her Fred looked every inch the fighting soldier; he always had. He was her Hector and her Hercules. To her he symbolised courage, determination, everything that Britain needed in a soldier. She had married him twenty-five years before, and as she stayed at home with their young daughter, she had learnt to live with the worry that something would happen to him, that he would never come back again, or that he might return to her by way of an army hospital, wounded and disfigured, a shadow of the man that she had married. She had also learnt to put up with the long separations, when he had been posted to one or other of the garrisons, spread throughout the Empire. During the South African campaign she had been filled with foreboding. For reasons she could not explain, she had been sure that he would be killed, as so many young soldiers had. In fact, her Fred had almost been captured in 1899, when the armoured train he was on was derailed by Boers. It was the former First Lord of the Admiralty who resigned after Gallipolli, that Mr. Churchill, who'd saved him. Fred could remember seeing young Churchill – who was then a newspaper correspondent, not a soldier at all, even though he was carrying a pistol – running up and down beside the train, barking orders at the driver and fireman, organising the survivors, seeing that part of the train was able to escape with at least some of the soldiers who were riding in it, all while the Boers were shooting at them, with rifles and a pom-pom cannon. Fred was one of the few who got away. Young Churchill was captured, then escaped a few weeks later and rose to First Lord, though now it seemed that his career was over. Fred used to tell the story over and over again, but all that Enid could do was smile as she listened and try not to shudder at the thought of all those Boers, trying to kill her husband. When he had retired from the army, she had felt such a wave of relief sweep over her. After all that time, her Fred was safe, having suffered nothing worse than a few cuts and bruises.

Now their daughter had married and left home, and had become a mother herself, and just when Enid and Fred should have been relaxing in their old age, it was about to start all over again. The anxiety that had been a constant companion, from the day she had married Fred, until the day he had left the army, was about to reappear from the oblivion to which Fred's retirement had consigned it. She had believed, or had let herself believe, his assurances that he was too old to be sent into the actual battle zone. It had seemed highly logical that he would make a good instructor at an army training establishment. Someone had to train all those thousands of young men who needed to be transformed from civilians to soldiers. Who better than her Fred?

Maybe the army saw things differently, or maybe it was something as simple as an administrative error. Whatever the reason, her Fred was not going to spend the war behind a desk, or on a parade ground. He was going to the front, as a platoon sergeant, in one of those new regiments that had suddenly sprung up everywhere.

Enid didn't know if she could stand it. This war was not like the bush wars Fred had been in, or even the South African campaign. It was hard to believe, but the three years of the Boer War seemed almost halcyon days, compared to the catastrophe now taking place. The casualty lists were there in the newspapers every day for all to see. Men died by the hundreds. She almost hoped that Fred would be wounded – not badly, not enough to cripple or disfigure him for the rest of his life, but enough to put him out of the game

"Look, Fred," she said, after she had brought in the tea things and set them on the table, "Why don't you speak to your CO? Tell him that you've done your bit already and that it isn't fair to send you on active service. You could be a recruiting sergeant, or something like that. I expect you'd be excellent at it. Tell him, why don't you? You've said he seems like a good man. I'm sure he'll see to it that you're transferred."

"It doesn't work like that, old girl. They need me where they've put me." Fred wasn't sure that that was absolutely accurate. He might have been designated as fit for active service due to an army cock-up. Lord knew, he had seen enough of those in his time, but he wouldn't for a moment consider questioning his orders. It just wasn't in him. "But I'll be fine, you'll see. Good heavens, Enid, do you really think I've come this far just to let some German shoot me? We're going to win this war, then I'll be back home with you, safe and sound, before you know it."

Enid was not convinced, no matter how hearty Fred was, but she didn't cry. She didn't comment either, and Fred allowed himself to believe that he had said just the right thing to stop her worrying.

That evening they ate in a local restaurant. Even though his tummy trouble, for which he still had not seen a doctor, had been worse of late, causing him dreadful heartburn and shortness of breath, it didn't bother him that evening and he was able to eat well. Then they went to a show; not the sort of show one could see at one of the West End theatres in London, of course, but an amusing little play put on by the local rep company. There were a great many men in uniform in the audience. Enid noticed how so many of the young soldiers were deferential to her husband, who looked every inch the regular non-commissioned officer. What was more, she saw how two very young second lieutenants reacted to Fred. Of course, when Fred saw them, he stood to attention and saluted them. They seemed startled and their salutes in return appeared nervous, as though they were worried that the sergeant might not think that they were up to standard.

"Poor wee things," Enid remarked, when they were out of earshot. "They don't look old enough to be soldiers. They're little more than schoolboys." It was true, they had both looked terribly young.

"Well, that's it, you see," said Fred. "They need people like me to look after them. That's why they're sending me."

And as they walked home, Enid did begin to cry.

Chapter XV

Rollo and The Duke

The telegrams from his father had stopped arriving after the first few days of training. Roland Selway had welcomed the silence. For one thing, it was awkward for a soldier, a private at that, to receive a series of telegrams in an army camp. Most of his comrades had never received a telegram in their lives, and there he was getting three in the space of a few days, brought to him by a very disgruntled orderly room clerk, who clearly resented having to do this for a mere recruit. Said recruit was very well spoken, mind you, and the clerk wouldn't be at all surprised if he was used to having people do his bidding in civilian life. However, here he was just a recruit in training which, in the clerk's opinion, was undoubtedly the lowest form of life on the planet.

The first telegram had asked Roland to write a letter, explaining exactly what he had meant about marrying someone else and joining the army. Roland thought that his words had been well within the understanding of anyone, so he did not bother to answer. Another cable, two days later, indicated that the Duke of Dornoch did, in fact, understand what his son had told him. Obviously, he was resigned to that fact and was now trying to interfere in Roland's life in a different manner. He told his son to apply for officer training immediately. Apparently, the thought of his son serving as a ranker was too much for his patrician sensibilities. Roland ignored that one too. The third telegram repeated the instruction and ended with the phrase 'OR I SHALL TAKE STEPS', which Roland took to mean either that the Duke was threatening to stop his allowance again, or that he would pull whatever strings he could to see that his son was put forward for officer training – or both.

So, he gave in and wrote his father a letter, telling him that he was perfectly happy where he was, in the rank of private. But he knew his father, so to make sure, he requested an interview with his company commander, Major Henderson. That was his right, of course, but it was unusual for a recruit to make use of it so early on in his training. Company Sergeant-Major Bull told him as much, as he was marching him across the parade ground to the company office

"Not here five minutes and you think you can 'ob nob with the company commander."

Roland was wise enough to know not to reply to that comment.

"If you've changed your mind about joining up, then it's your own hard luck, sunshine. You're in for the duration. The Army's got you and it won't let you go now."

"No, Sergeant-Major."

"And don't think you can complain about your treatment 'ere neither. I know from your voice you come from a posh family. Don't go thinkin' you can be waited on, just because your mummy spoiled you."

"No, Sergeant-Major."

They reached the company office and Roland stood at attention, while the CSM knocked on Major Henderson's door and entered.

"Private Selway, sir, 'as requested an interview."

"Very good, Sergeant-Major, march him in."

Roland was ordered to march in, double time, then to take off his cap and stand to attention before the major's desk.

"Well, what is it?" asked the major.

"Sir, I do not wish to be an officer."

The major seemed taken aback, and Roland heard the CSM mutter something under his breath that he was pretty sure was less than complimentary.

"Is anyone asking you to become an officer?" asked the major.

"No, sir. But I want to make sure that no one can make me do it."

"No one can make you. You can apply for a commission in the fullness of time, if you want to, but you can't be ordered to become an officer."

"The thing is, sir, I'm afraid that my father might try to interfere. I'm happy to be a private, and I've told him that, but I think he might try to go over my head and pull strings at the War Office. He knows a lot of people."

"Really? Who is your father?"

"The Duke of Dornoch, sir."

That brought another suppressed expletive from behind him, while Major Henderson contented himself with raising his eyebrows.

"Really?" he enquired.

"Yes, sir."

"How extraordinary. Mind you, it's not unheard of, men from the officer class enlisting in the ranks, but that has come as a surprise, I must say. And you think your father might interfere?"

"I'm pretty sure he'll try to, sir."

"Well, he's welcome to try. You're probably the sort of person we'd like to see as an officer, but if you don't want to, then that's that. You'll stay in the ranks, father or no father."

"Thank you, sir."

"If I receive any gubbins from the War Office about you, I'll just say that you have not applied for a commission."

"Thank you, sir."

"I'll have to tell the colonel about you, in case anyone says anything to him about it."

"Yes, sir. Thank you, sir," said Roland, "But if it's all the same to you, sir, I'd prefer that as few people as possible knew about this."

"Well, I'm not going to go round the place telling everyone. Only those who need to know."

"Thank you, sir."

The major nodded. "Very well. March him out, Sergeant-Major."

"Sir!"

But before the sergeant could issue the next order, the major interrupted.

"Just a moment. Private, if your father is the Duke of Dornoch, that means your brother is the Marquis of Tain, doesn't it?'

"Yes, sir."

"How remarkable. He was my fag at Eton." He shook his head. "Remarkable. Carry on, Sergeant-Major."

The sergeant-major didn't say a word as he marched Roland back to his hut, but it was pretty obvious he couldn't wait to get back to the sergeants' mess, to tell his fellow NCOs exactly who was in the ranks.

Of course, a secret like that couldn't be kept in the army. Before long, everyone in Roland's company knew who he was and, as soldiers tended to do, they then conferred on him a suitable nickname. From then on, he was known as 'Duchess'. He didn't mind that at all. In fact, he rather liked it, and he told Erika about it in his next letter to her. He wrote to her most days, and she replied with equal frequency. He looked forward to her letters, and no matter how many he received, he could never get enough. He was less enthusiastic about the letters that began arriving from his father.

The first of these had arrived about three weeks into his training. It was most conciliatory. Roland read how his father fully understood that he did not want to marry Maude and, of course, he, the duke, would not dream of forcing anyone to marry against their will. Roland laughed out loud at that – didn't his father realise that he was already married? This business with Maude was purely academic now. The duke went on to say that he understood that Roland had needed to assert his independence, and he deserved a pat on the back for having joined the army in time of war, but now he needed to take stock of his situation, realise that no one from their family had ever served in the ranks, and that it was simply not on for the third son of a duke to be a private. What the duke proposed instead, was that he should use whatever influence he had in Whitehall, and in particular at the War Office, to get his son transferred to another regiment with a King's Commission. The Guards perhaps? Or maybe something in the cavalry? He'd make a damn fine officer, his father told him, and it would not be right to deprive England of his abilities in that department. Roland wrote back, repeating everything he had said in his previous letter. He went on to say he would refuse any commission offered to him and asked his father to leave him alone.

The next letter was not until six weeks later. Altogether more curt, it simply told him that Maude had married a young man of private means, who was exempt from military service on account of a heart condition. It went on to acknowledge, without comment, Roland's wish to serve in the ranks. They seldom wrote to each other after that, and when they did, it was simply to make a very superficial exchange of news. The duke showed no curiosity whatsoever about his new daughter-in-law and Roland found that hard to forgive.

Naturally, he spent his embarkation leave with Erika, but he did take a cab to the family house in Eccleston Square. He took Erika with him. The butler was surprised to find an army private standing on the front doorstep and did a double take. He was, after all, nearly sixty-five and his eyes were not what they had been.

"Lord Roland, is it?" he asked, squinting.

"Yes, it's me, Grimfield. Is my father at home?" Roland replied.

"Yes, Your Lordship, the Duke and Duchess are in the morning room."

"Fine. Don't announce me. I'll surprise them."

He took Erika's hand and led her across the hallway to the room he knew so well, opened the door, and stepped in.

"Hello Mother, Father," he said.

The duke started, and muttered, "Gracious." The duchess was more forthcoming.

"Rollo!" she cried, and got up from her armchair to embrace her son. It would be nice to report that it was a happy reunion, that his parents were delighted to see Roland and his new wife, but that would not be strictly accurate. Even the duchess, who was so pleased to see her son again, shared her husband's views on Roland's conduct and the unsuitability of his service. As a result, the conversation was stilted and uncomfortable.

Roland introduced them to Erika, but they did not know how to react to her. She was a middle-class girl from another country, and they treated her as though she had come from the moon. Roland was sure his two older brothers would have welcomed Erika to the family, but they were both away. They were both officers, the older brother in the Navy, his other brother in some colonial regiment out East.

The duke took Roland aside, while the duchess was talking to Erika about her home in Italy.

"Look here, Rollo," he said. "I know we got each other's backs up when we started discussing this after you joined up, but it's not too late to change things, you know. Bury the hatchet, and all that."

"What do you mean, Father?"

"I can still get you a commission in a good regiment. It's in the family blood. Selways have always been officers. There was a Selway commanding a battalion at the Alma, and at Waterloo, and at Quebec. There were two Selways, both captains, at Culloden Moor – on the winning side. You know it yourself, I'm sure, that you should be an officer. I can speak to old Dawlish at the War Office. We'll have you in the Guards with two pips on your shoulder, so you can be of more use to your country there, than you can as a private in that New Army rabble."

Roland stayed very calm. Inside, he was outraged.

"Father, I told you I wasn't interested over a year ago, and I'm still not. My regiment is about to go to France, to the front, and I am not going to run out on them now just to pander to your prejudices." The duke started to say something, but Roland held his hand up to stop him. "And what's more, my regiment is not a rabble, as you put it, but as fine a battalion of soldiers as you'll find anywhere. I am very proud to serve with them."

"You've broken your mother's heart, you know. There won't be any framed photographs of you in a private's uniform on her bedside table. And as for marrying her..." He jerked his head in the direction of Erika, who was still talking to the duchess.

"Don't say it, Father. Whatever you were about to say, don't, otherwise I shall never come back to this house again."

The duke frowned, but did not complete his sentence.

"You and Mother will just have to get used to the idea that I am married to Erika. I married her because I fell in love with her, and that is that. I would prefer that you accept her, but if you don't, it will be your loss, not hers. You won't drive us apart and, if you're honest, you'll admit that your objection to my being a private has nothing to do with my being of more use to my country as an officer. It's just snobbery on your part, isn't it?"

The duke still said nothing, but Roland could tell by the expression on his face, that his question had touched a nerve.

"Don't worry, Father. I may not be a private forever."

"You won't?" The duke brightened.

"No. I might make Corporal."

Roland and Erika booked into the Beacon Hotel, of course, for the rest of his leave. He could have afforded Claridges, or any other of the many more expensive hotels in London. After he had realised that his son was determined not to apply for a commission and that, by virtue of marrying Erika, he had made it impossible to marry Maude, the duke had given up all threats of stopping Roland's allowance. So, for over a year, the monthly payments had been accumulating in Roland's bank account and there most of the money had stayed, because he had had precious little to spend it on during his training up in Swathdale. On top of that, he had had his army pay, though that was considerably less than what he received from his father. Roland sent a monthly cheque to Erika, to cover her living expenses, but there was still a very healthy surplus left in the bank.

Even so, they stayed at the Beacon. It was where they had spent their honeymoon, after all. The proprietor remembered them, or at least he said he did, and at their request gave them the same room they had occupied in 1914.

Roland also had another reason for avoiding expensive hotels. As a private, he was under orders to wear his uniform at all times, even while on leave. Officers on leave could wear civilian clothes if they wished, though many of them chose to remain in uniform. There were bound to be many officers at all the posh hotels, and Roland did not fancy the idea of having to jump to attention every time one of them hove into view.

If his week-long honeymoon with Erika had been the happiest seven days of his life, the forty-eight hours of his embarkation leave with her were every bit as good. He felt euphoric every moment he was with her.

They went to visit her father, his father-in-law. The novelty of having such a relative had not yet worn off. The old man was delighted to see Roland again.

"You look taller and stronger than last time," he remarked.

"That's army training for you."

"I've been meaning to ask, do you have any Italian blood in you?"

"Not that I know of."

"I was wondering because you have that look. Dark hair, dark eyes."

"Black Irish," Rollo said. "According to my mother anyway. I know a branch of her family comes from the west of Ireland."

"I see. Now, please tell me, these new regiments, are they ready to take on the Germans? Of course, when I send articles to my paper, I say that the New Army of England will sweep the Hun right back into Berlin, but will they really be able to manage anything in an actual battle? You are all civilian soldiers, are you not?"

"No, sir. We are all soldiers. We all used to be civilians and, please God, we will be again, but for now we are all soldiers.,"

"Yes, of course. But are you as proficient as the regular army, or even the Territorials?"

"We've just had a year of training. I think we're every bit as good as the Territorials, or possibly even better. The regular army is superb; I don't think anyone is as good as them, and that includes the Germans, but we'll try to come as close to them as we can," Roland explained.

"And what plans for this year?"

"I'm only a private. No one tells me anything about plans."

"True. But everyone speaks of a big push later this year…"

"Obviously we are going to attack the enemy, some time or another, when the weather is suitable. But as to when or where, I'll probably be the last to know."

"That's good. That's very good. I am sure that this year, we will finish it. You will beat the Germans and we will settle things with those bastard Austrians."

As the old man had predicted, Italy had entered the war in the spring of 1915. Erika had written to Roland that she was both excited that her country was now involved in, what she and so many others, saw as a war between good and evil, and also very worried because her brother, a captain in the Italian army, would naturally be going into combat.

"We'll finish it," Erika's father went on, "and then you come home to my Erika. Make a home with her, make me a grandfather."

Roland smiled and blushed, his father-in-law laughed, and they moved on to discuss other matters.

The couple snatched one more night at the Beacon, the rest of the world temporarily cut off while they were engulfed in each other's presence. Then, it was time for Roland to leave. His orders, like those of all the other leave men in his regiment, were to report back to Lambeth by twelve noon. They would be marched to Charing Cross station that evening, to catch the train to Folkestone and, from there, to cross the Channel by boat.

"I'll be there to wave you off," Erika said.

"Oh, you don't have to do that."

"Maybe I don't have to, but I want to."

"But it will be so crowded and noisy. You wouldn't like it. And you might not even be able to find me in the chaos," Roland said. In fact, he wasn't so much worried that Erika would find it too noisy – he was more worried that saying goodbye to her in public would be too much for him, and he might weep or something – he'd never hear the end of that from his mates if he did.

"I'm coming. No more arguments. It's settled."

Roland kissed his wife. He had never known that it was possible to be that in love with someone.

Chapter XVI

A Party in Rochester

Somebody at the bank had organised a party. It was held in the function room, above the saloon bar of The Two Chairmen, in the centre of Rochester. The nice thing, was that everyone from the bank attended, including the manager. It was a good party, with plenty to drink, and various snacks to munch on. Someone was playing the piano in the corner. Johnny Winslow, Wilfred Leuchars and Eddie Ross were welcomed like heroes. Everyone was glad to see them again and they had brought two of their comrades with them, two men who had no family or friends to visit. One was Les Mosterby, an Ulsterman who had spent the previous two years of his life working in a factory in London and who didn't have time to visit his family in Belfast; the other, Matthew Clay, who didn't have any family anywhere, as far as anyone could make out, but then he hardly ever said anything about his background, so you never could tell.

The bank manager was enjoying himself and, like several of his employees, he'd had more to drink than he was used to, more than he could handle. After the first few pints, he could be found talking to Johnny and Eddie. Wilfred was across the room with Matthew Clay, where some of the young women who worked at the bank, taken on to replace men who had joined up, were listening with rapt attention to their tales of the training camp. True, these men had not actually been to the front yet, but they embellished their accounts of manoeuvres as best they could, to make it seem that, on many numbers of occasions, they had been inches from death.

"You're heroes," said the bank manager, putting an arm round Johnny's shoulder. Beer spilled from the pint mug in his other hand. "We're proud of you. The whole bank's proud of you, giving up your jobs, helping your country in her hour of need."

He swayed slightly, his stance as unsteady as his speech. The slur was quite noticeable and the two soldiers began to feel embarrassed. This was their former employer after all, who had been a figure of authority to them. It would be hard to take him seriously again.

"You too," he said to Eddie, probably not aware how loud he was speaking. "You're a hero too. My bank is full of heroes. We're all so proud." He tried to put an arm round Eddie's shoulder, but Eddie was too tall and the manager was a short man. He didn't manage and he stumbled, spilling more beer on the carpet. Johnny was too embarrassed to say anything, while Eddie muttered a word or two of thanks.

"Your jobs are safe," the manager cried, although it was more like, "Yourjbsrsff," instead. "When the war is over and you come back from the front," he went on, but then he paused for a moment, thinking about what he had just said. "Back from the front... Thass funny. I made a joke!"

This produced two pained smiles from his audience.

"When you come back, your old jobs will be waiting for you. You have my word on it." For emphasis, he slapped his chest, approximately in the region of his heart.

That was worth knowing. Neither of them, nor Wilfred either, for that matter, intended to stay in the army after the war was won, so a firm offer of employment was very valuable.

"I tried to join, you know," the manager went on. "Stood in line with all the other young men, but when my turn came they gave me the once over and said they didn't need me. Too old, they said. Now, I ask you, is that fair? Too bloody old... Do you know how old I am?"

Both Johnny and Eddie knew that the manager was fifty-two. Neither of them felt inclined to say so, but neither did they want to make the pretence worse, by suggesting that they thought he was much younger. He certainly looked his age. So they both shook their heads.

"I'm fifty-two. Thass not old. And I know, I bloody well know," he slurred, as he wagged a forefinger at his audience for emphasis, "that I look younger. I could pass for the same age as most of those young whippersnappers who were in the queue with me. I could have been ready to go to the front, like you two."

For a moment, a faraway look came into his eye and he was imagining himself in uniform, ready to do or die for his country. Then he recovered.

"Still, they didn't want me, and that's that." He shrugged. "So, now it's up to you, and the thousands of others. I'll be here waiting at the bank for you, once the war has been won," he repeated.

"And we're glad of the offer, sir," said Johnny. He swept his hand across his forehead. He used to have a lock of hair that he brushed back in an unconscious mannerism. The forelock had fallen victim to the army barber when he joined up, but he still held onto the mannerism, albeit unknowingly.

They chatted a bit longer on a few other topics, mainly about how things were going at the bank. Now that he had said his bit, the manger had calmed down. Conversation was possible without a lot of arms round shoulders, or beer spilling.

Across the room, another of their friends from the platoon was sitting quietly by himself. His name was Les Mosterby. He was a tall, imposing, heavyset man, whose appearance alone was enough to intimidate anyone of a mind to enter into an argument with him.

He was a good soldier and popular with his mates. He had a talent for singing and could remember the words to more songs, both highbrow and low, than anyone else in the battalion. It was a talent he seldom used, because he was, and had been from early childhood, painfully, agonisingly shy. Doing several circuits of an army assault course, with full pack, did not worry him at all, but the thought of talking to strangers terrified him. There were several people in the room he wanted to talk to, especially the young woman serving behind the bar, to whom he had taken a fancy. He kidded himself that he would go and talk to her, after he had finished his pint. Then he lit a cigarette and told himself that he definitely would go up to the bar and talk to her once he had smoked his fag. So far, he had promised himself five times that he would introduce himself to the young lady, and five times his nerve had failed him. So there he sat, a big, powerful man looking out at the room from under dark, bushy eyebrows, seemingly too forbidding to be shy, yet he truly was so.

One of the women at the party had noticed him. She found him somehow rather intriguing. Now, she was the complete opposite of him; petite, while he was larger than life, outgoing while he was shy, and full of self-confidence with strangers, a quality he lacked and could not even understand.

As she walked towards him, Les felt pleasure and trepidation in equal measure.

"Hello," she said.

"H'lo," he replied.

"I saw you sitting here alone; thought I'd come and say hello."

"Mm."

"I'm Dora," she said.

"Les," he mumbled.

"Sorry?"

"I'm Les. Les Mosterby." He was thrilled that she was talking to him and he cursed himself for being so tongue tied.

"You don't work at the bank, do you?"

"No."

"Didn't think so. Are you from round here?"

"No."

"Where're you from, then?"

"Ireland."

"Oh, that's nice. I've got an auntie lives in Clonakilty. Do you know it?"

"No."

"What part are you from?"

"The north. Ulster."

"Oh, is it nice?"

"S'alright."

"Is your family back there?"

"Yes." Les was the oldest of four children. The other three still lived with their mother, who was struggling to make ends meet following the death of her husband, their father, the year before. Les had made sure that part of his army pay went straight to her.

"What did you do over there?" asked Dora.

Les wished he could force himself to talk in actual sentences. He could chat away nineteen to the dozen with his army mates, but a strange woman terrified him. The words were there – he could almost feel them – but he couldn't make himself say them. Dora would have been interested, he was sure, to hear about how he had left school as soon as he was able and had followed in his father's footsteps, going to work at the shipyard of Harland and Wolff. In fact, he had been one of the hundreds of men to work on the *Titanic* and her sister ship the *Olympic*, and he, and so many of his colleagues, had felt a sense of personal loss when the so-called unsinkable ship had sunk on her maiden voyage on that cold April night in 1912. But all he managed to say was, "This and that, you know."

"I see," said Dora, still making an effort, "How did you end up in a London regiment then?"

That too was a story he would have told if this pretty woman's presence had not deprived him of the power of speech. She would have heard how building ships was not enough for Les. He wanted to sail in one, or in several. He loved to read about faraway places, and his ambition was to circle the globe, seeing as many countries as possible. By turn, he considered joining the Royal Navy, the Merchant Navy, and the Army. Unable to decide, he had made the first move, the first small step, on what he hoped would be a long, exotic voyage, when he left his job and his family in Belfast, taking a ship to Liverpool, and a train, third class, to London. Here, he reasoned, was the centre of the world, so it was here that he would be most likely to find an opportunity to see the world.

What he'd found was a series of casual jobs, which he needed in order to keep body and soul together. He was still looking for a way of travelling whilst also getting paid, when events made up his mind for him. War was declared and, after finishing a job on a building site, he volunteered for the army, one of his original three choices. He ended up in a battalion that was being recruited from part of North London, but he didn't mind. He was after all living in rooms in Paddington, at the time. So, he became a private in the St. Marylebone Rifles. Les condensed this tale to just a few words.

"That's where I was at the time," he said.

"I see. My brother's in a London regiment, the Royal Fusiliers. Do you know them?"

"No, sorry."

Les desperately wanted to keep talking to her, to ask her all about herself, her family, her work, but the words wouldn't come.

Dora nodded and said, "I hope you're enjoying the party."

"Yes," said Les. For a moment it seemed that he was about to say more, but he didn't.

"Well, it's been nice chatting to you," said Dora, and with a last smile she walked off to speak to someone else, leaving Les watching her, wishing she would come back so he could have one more chance to talk to her. But he was on his own.

Wilfred Leuchars and Matthew Clay were having a better time of things. Both were good looking men, both were in uniform of course, so naturally they had an admiring group round them – women who worked at the bank, and women who had come as guests of some of the male bank workers, all of whom were competing for their attention. The two soldiers were trying to answer questions about their year in the army, in a way that would make them sound brave, their lives glamorous, even though they had not been in combat, or heard a shot fired in anger.

"We marched for another hour," Clay was saying, "and another five or six men dropped out. Just collapsed by the roadside. Then we were stopped for a five-minute break. That's all they gave us, just five minutes."

There was a chorus of appreciative cooing from the young women. Clay had his eye on one in particular, a tall girl, with freckles and light brown hair. She wasn't saying as much as the others, but she was listening just as attentively as her friends.

"Five minutes? Is that all?" asked a plump blonde, who had obviously taken a shine to Clay, though he was not very interested in her.

"Five minutes," he confirmed. "Then they got us back on our feet and they marched us for another hour, along those country lanes in Yorkshire, a lot of going up and downhill. All the while, it was pouring with rain."

"I've never been to Yorkshire," one of the women remarked. This irritated Clay, since she seemed to be missing the point of what he was telling them, but he managed not to show it.

"You're not missing much," he said. "Anyway, after another hour we were all in. That made a total of five hours we'd been marching. And you know, we weren't actually going anywhere; we were just being marched round the same few square miles over and over again."

"Whatever for?"

"To toughen us up," said Wilfred, who felt it was time he added something. "To get us used to marching."

"Yes," agreed Clay. "To break us in. And to break in our boots, too."

Some laughter ensued.

"No, seriously. Our boots were still quite new. We had to get used to wearing them. You know what it's like to break in new shoes?"

There was nodding.

"You never saw such blisters," Wilfred said, to appreciative laughing.

"When we're at the front, in the actual front line, we'll have to keep our boots on all the time."

"Even when you're asleep?" asked the blonde.

"Even then. In case there's a surprise attack. You can't waste time putting your boots on if Fritz is coming at you."

"That doesn't sound very hygienic to me," commented the woman who had never been to Yorkshire.

"Probably it isn't," said Clay. "Anyway, as I was saying, we'd been marching for five hours, and most of us weren't used to walking more than a few hundred yards at a time, if that. We're all Londoners, don't forget."

"Not all of us." It was a pointed comment from Wilfred.

"Well, fine, most of us. We are the St. Marylebone Rifles, after all, and we weren't used to this. A few more men dropped out and this bloke next to me, he started to stagger, and I thought he was going to collapse. So, I put an arm round his waist and held him up. 'Never mind, mate,' I said, 'I'll carry your rifle for you. Just stick with us.' And I suppose I encouraged him, because after he handed his rifle to me, he was able to keep going. I ended up carrying four rifles that day, plus my own, but at least I helped four of my mates to keep on until the end of the march."

The women listening almost burst into applause. Wilfred would have said something to deflate Clay, if he could, but he couldn't, because the story was absolutely true. Clay noted, with satisfaction, that the freckled girl, the one he particularly liked, seemed as admiring as the rest, if not more so. He smiled at her, she smiled back at him. He was encouraged.

"Another thing they taught us was bayonet drill," he continued. "You know, how to stick an enemy with your bayonet if it gets to hand-to-hand fighting."

This drew a chorus of noises from their audience, indicating that the act of sticking ten inches of steel into a man was just too awful to think about.

"Not pleasant, I know, but sometimes war is like that. It's a question of survival – kill or be killed. I don't want to kill anyone but I will if I have to." He tried to look suitably solemn. This had the welcome effect of making the glances from the other women all the more admiring. One would have thought that Clay had already dispatched half a dozen Uhlan lancers with his bayonet, instead of a selection of straw dummies. The freckled girl especially, looked as though Clay was her hero. He was very pleased with the way things were going. He wanted to slip away with this girl, and he didn't even want to steal from her – he just wanted her for himself. If she had somewhere they could go, so much the better. If not, he'd find an empty building, or a barn, or anywhere else, even a field, if it wasn't too cold.

"I hope it won't come to bayonets," said Wilfred, almost breaking the spell, "but I was good with a rifle."

A rifle – now, that was a soldier's weapon. The girls turned to him.

"In fact, I won a couple of prizes on the shooting range. Before joining up, I'd never held a gun of any sort in my life. I suppose I must have a natural bent for it 'cause I got my bullet on the bullseye almost every time. So, if the opportunity arises, they're going to use me as a marksman. A sniper."

Now, it was Wilfred's turn to pull the admiring glances. Clay was none too pleased at this, so he immediately took charge of the conversation again, turning the attention back to himself, sending a special smile to his chosen girl while he was at it.

Across the room, Johnny and Eddie had freed themselves from the bank manager, who had realised he'd had too much to drink, wisely excusing himself before he could make a further exhibition of himself in front of his employees. The two friends noticed what was going on at the other end of the room.

"Look at that Clay," whispered Eddie to Johnny.

"Why? What's he doing?"

"He's flirting with them all. Quite unashamedly."

"What's so wrong with that?"

"That tall girl he seems to be after, that's my sister Joy, you ass!"

"Is it?" Johnny peered at the two men and their entourage. "Oh, yes, so it is. I didn't notice."

"That's typical of that Clay, trying to pick up a girl at an occasion like this. I never liked him."

"No?"

"No. And if he thinks he's going to get his paws all over my sister, he's got another thing coming."

"Maybe it's Wilf who's after her?"

"No, look at them. It's Clay. You can see it all over his face."

Johnny couldn't actually see anything on Clay's face except a very easy, assured smile, but perhaps that was what Eddie meant.

Eddie didn't waste any more time watching. He strolled across the room, greeting his comrades and their audience heartily.

"Hello, Joy," he said to his sister. "Are Wilf and Matthew keeping you and your friends entertained?"

A number of twittered affirmatives erupted from the women.

"Jolly good, jolly good. Always a good storyteller, is our Lance Corporal Clay." He clapped his hands to indicate that small talk was over, now it was down to the serious stuff. "Well, it's getting on a bit. We have to get back to our barracks in London by noon, so we'll be making an early start. Joy, I'll walk you back to Mum and Dad's now. That'll give me another chance to have a natter with them before they go to bed."

He looked expectantly at his sister, who, a little reluctantly let it be said, left her friends and took her brother's arm. Eddie waved goodbye to everyone else and the two of them left the party. Clay looked at his comrade's retreating back with venom. He'd guessed, quite correctly, why Eddie had extricated his sister. He didn't like being foiled, and he certainly did not like being made a fool of. He especially did not like hearing remarks like 'no joy for Matthew', from the likes of Wilfred Leuchars. That look he had given Eddie's back, it did not bode well for Private Ross. Clay was one rank higher than him, after all.

He spent the night at the flat Johnny and Wilfred shared with Eddie, trying to make himself as comfortable as possible in a rather threadbare armchair, while across the room Les Mosterby snored away happily on a battered but cosy sofa. On the train journey back to London the next morning, Clay did not speak to Eddie once.

Chapter XVII

A Letter

A-Company
35th Bn, Middlesex Regiment
28th February, 1916

A. S. Hawkins, Esq.
Managing Director
Redfield & Hawkins Ltd.
Diadem House
Wigmore Street
London W.

Dear Mr. Hawkins,

I was very sorry to miss you when I visited the office of Redfield & Hawkins yesterday afternoon. They told me you were away seeing clients in Birmingham and would not be back in the office until today. I trust that your trip to Birmingham was successful – knowing you, I am sure it was.

It was very enjoyable to see my former colleagues again, after all this time. Mr. Oakley and Mr. Farjeon made me feel very welcome and allowed me to call on my old friends who were in the building. I understand that Mr. Jameson retired some months ago, and that Miss Pilger is now married; it was but a little surprise to learn that both Mr. Wood and Mr. Law have joined up. These days, one expects that most young men have done so. Now that conscription has been introduced, of course, they will all be going. I was delighted to see that Mrs. Green is still your secretary. It would be hard to imagine the office without her there. However, I suppose that even she must be contemplating retirement eventually. She seemed almost old enough to retire when I joined the company, all those long years ago.

It is hard to believe that I have been in the army since the year before last. I rather suspect that, when I joined up, I thought I would be sent to the front in a matter of weeks. It never occurred to me that it would take this long to become a soldier. However, that is exactly what I am now. I have undergone the most extensive and rigorous training, and I can honestly say that I am as much a soldier as any man who has ever worn the king's uniform. To my delight and surprise, I find that I enjoy army life very much indeed. At first, I found it hard to take seriously the regular soldiers' obsession with even the smallest matters of military discipline and courtesy, such as saluting, drilling, spit and polish &c. Now, of course, I can see that it is all vitally necessary, every last detail of it, if we are to become efficient soldiers. A regiment is a unit, not unlike a machine or, if you will, a precision made watch – in order for it to function, every piece must work correctly.

I belong to the 35th Battalion of the Middlesex Regiment. This is one of the new battalions that was formed when the war started. Our unofficial name, but the one we like to use among ourselves, is the St. Marylebone Rifles. The battalion was first raised, and paid for, by the Mayor and Borough of St. Marylebone, before it was taken over by the War Office. Indeed, most, though not all, of the recruits come from that part of London. I like to think that I qualify as a man of St. Marylebone, because that is where I worked for twelve happy years – and, I trust, will work again, once this war has been brought to a successful conclusion.

Shortly towards the end of our training, I was given the happy news that I was to be promoted to the rank of lance corporal, which is one rung above private on the army ladder. That means I shall be leader of a section within my platoon. Our company is made up of four platoons. Each platoon is under an officer and a sergeant and consists of four sections, each containing several privates and an NCO. In the case of my own section, that NCO is me. That means that I have a single stripe on my sleeve, a little bit more money each week, and can give orders to privates when necessary.

Our platoon officer is 2nd Lieut. Arnold Snow. Normally, I would not mention his first name, but in our company we have to, because there are two 2nd Lieutenants called Snow. They are twin brothers, though they are not identical. We can tell Mr. Arnold Snow from his brother, Mr. Charles Snow, who is in charge of another platoon, with no difficulty. Our platoon sergeant, Sgt. Quill, is an interesting man. I should imagine, to judge from his age, that he has had many years of experience in the army and, in other circumstances, would no doubt be a very interesting man to talk to. Of course, chit-chat between sergeants and lower ranks is not encouraged. I will say that his age has obviously not affected his vocal cords, or his ability to spot breaches of army discipline. However, even though he is very strict, he is also very fair. The same can be said for our Company Sgt-Major Bull, and the chief NCO in the battalion, RSM Callow.

The men are wonderful. I enjoy their company and have become friends with several of them. Luckily, the gulf between lance corporal and private is very small and does not inhibit friendship in any way. One man in my company was a hospital porter before joining the army, at the Middlesex Hospital. I told him that I worked for a firm that made medical instruments and he was most interested to hear that, though the name Redfield & Hawkins did not mean anything to him. As he said, however, in his position, he would not have known anything about who supplied the hospital's equipment; his job was just to move it from one place to another. Another of my chums, Colin Tunniford, wants to become a war artist and hopes that eventually he will be transferred from our battalion to another unit, where he will be able to paint war scenes. This has not stopped him from becoming a most efficient soldier, however. He is friends with a man in our platoon, Private Millcross, who has actually had a few poems published in various periodicals. I do not know much about poetry, so I am unable to tell you whether his poems are any good or not, but at least I do know that the ones he has shown me do all rhyme, and I suppose that is half the battle.

He intends to have a notepad and pencil with him at all times while at the front, so that he can jot down any lines that may occur to him.

In fact, almost all my comrades are characters in their own way. Private Snibley, for example, entertained us a few evenings ago by playing the spoons, which is something I had heard about, but had never actually seen before, and Private Marren, who is from Oxfordshire, likes to tell us city-bred fellows all about country life. There are two others from the same village in our company and, they too, are fine chaps.

We shall be going to France very soon and, unfortunately, I shall not be able to visit the office again before we depart, so we shall not be able to meet until I next return to London on leave, whenever that is. However, I should be very pleased to hear from you, or anyone else at Redfield & Hawkins, should you care to write to me. I am sure that when we are all in the front line, letters from home will be most welcome.

I shall leave you now, with my very best wishes to you, and to everyone at the old firm. I trust that I shall be able to rejoin you all at Diadem House before too long.

Yours sincerely,
Edwin Marvell

Chapter XVIII

A Surprise for Alec and Colin

At the start of his leave, Alec Millcross stayed with his family in Ewell, just to the south of London. He reached home towards the middle of the afternoon and went for a long walk through the fields with his parents and younger sister. It was a crisp winter's day and they could see their breath as they walked, their feet crunching on the fallen leaves, made brittle by the frost. They didn't say much to each other; they were just happy to be all together again. Alec's enlistment had come as a surprise to them, even though it was something that hundreds of thousands of young men were doing all the time. They had told themselves that he would do it sooner or later, all the while thinking that later was the preferable, and probable, option. They had never quite known what to make of their son. He had received a good education, doing well at the local grammar school. Mr. Millcross was a skilled draughtsman and, without it ever having been said, he assumed that his son would one day follow him into the profession, but when Alec had left home and tried to make a living out of writing poetry, he had kept his own council. He had assumed that his son would work that ambition out of his system; then, his life would follow a more secure path and, had it not been for the war, that may well have been how things would have turned out, which would no doubt have come as a great relief to the would-be poet's parents.

They were also worried about the sort of people their son sometimes mixed with in those modern artistic circles in which he liked to move. From that point of view, Mr. Millcross regarded the army as a safer place for Alec than the bohemian drawing rooms which he imagined were waiting to ensnare his son.

They were walking along a pathway that ran down one side of a field, their house visible a few hundred yards away. It was slow going, the muddy surface frozen, uneven, and pitted, which meant walking carefully to avoid the risk of a twisted ankle.

"We'll go on ahead and put the kettle on," Mrs. Millcross announced, and she and Alec's sister began to walk straight across the field, taking the most direct route to their front door. Mr. Millcross kept to the path and Alec, who suspected that this might have been planned, stayed with him.

"We'll be along presently," Mr. Millcross called after the women, as he and his son walked on in silence.

"How are you finding the army?" he asked, after a couple of minutes.

"It's fine. I thought I'd hate it. I mean, there are some things I don't like at all, but, by and large, I'm enjoying it. I don't regret joining up in the slightest, if that's what you mean."

"I didn't think you would. Your mother was taken aback when you joined up. In fact, we both were. I don't think we ever saw you as a soldier, so we were very surprised. We've been imagining you, drilling on a parade ground, marching for miles in all weathers, firing rifles at targets, doing sentry duty in the middle of the night."

"I've done all of those things, and more. But you take the rough with the smooth."

"What's the smooth?"

"Comradeship, a sense of purpose, doing something for my country, the whole experience of being a soldier. I wouldn't miss it for the world." explained Alec.

"Well, I'm glad you're enjoying it so far, Alec, but it's bound to be different at the front. Your mother is very worried. So am I."

"It'll be different, you're right, but do try not to worry. I wouldn't be surprised if I'm out of uniform by this time next year."

"As soon as that?"

"Very possibly. Everyone knows that later this year we'll be launching a big push at the Germans. We'll be using all the New Army regiments that have been training during the past year. The Germans won't be able to withstand that – hundreds of thousands of men, hurled against them in one go."

"I'm sure they won't, but we do worry, all the time. The casualty lists in the paper seem to get longer every week. Mrs. Twist's boy, the one who used to do odd jobs for us, he was out in France in a Territorial regiment and was killed just before Christmas."

"I remember him. I'm sorry to hear that."

"And Mr. Golightly from the post office. He was called up as a reservist at the start of the war. He was killed at Neuve-Chapelle."

"It's a war, father. Some people will be hurt, killed even. But most of us won't. So don't worry, please."

Mr. Millcross said he wouldn't worry, but, of course, he knew he would, right up until the day the war ended. They walked on a bit more in silence.

"Do you still write poetry?" Mr. Millcross asked, after a minute or two.

"A bit. Not much, though. I intend to write a great deal when I get to France. I expect the papers will be eager to print poetry written by men who are actually at the front. It'll help me make a name for myself."

"I daresay you're right." There was another pause. "Do you ever think about after the war?"

"Yes, sometimes, but it has a rather unreal quality about it. I'll have so much to go through before then."

"But, even so, you have thought about it?"

"Yes, but I've not reached any conclusions about what I want to do. Obviously, my first choice would be to make a living writing poetry."

"Yes, that would be nice, but how many poets are there who can actually earn enough to live on? Without taking a second job, I mean?"

"Not many, I should imagine."

"Quite. So, I was wondering if you'd give some thought to training as a draughtsman, as I did?"

Alec had been waiting for that. The thing that worried him most about being asked that question, was that his father's idea made such good sense. He knew he would probably make a decent draughtsman and his educational qualifications certainly indicated this. The trouble was, he dreaded the idea of pursuing such a career. The very thought of it made him want to yawn from boredom. He knew what he wanted – to write poetry, to be paid handsomely for doing so, and to enjoy the fame and fortune it would undoubtedly bring, but even he could admit to himself that it was an unlikely prospect. He decided to take advantage of the war when he answered the question.

"It's not out of the question, I suppose," he said. "I had hoped to do something else, but we'll just have to see how that goes. At any rate, I won't be making any decisions till the war is over."

His father knew that was as good an answer as he was likely to get, so he contented himself with a nod and a half smile.

"Very well, old man," said Mr Millcross. "Let's go in to tea."

Later, whilst sitting in front of the fire with his parents and sister, relaxing after sandwiches, cake, and several cups of tea, Alec told his family that he'd be heading up to London the following afternoon.

"I thought you didn't have to be back at the barracks until the day after tomorrow," his mother said.

"I don't, but there are a few people in town I'd like to see before I go to France, so I thought I'd take a train after lunch tomorrow and spend the night in London."

"Some of that wild crowd you run with? Poets and artists and the like?"

"They're not wild. Well, most of them aren't. It's just that they are friends of mine, so I'll be spending an evening with them."

There was a sad silence. Alec's parents were thinking about how much they would have liked the extra twenty-four hours with their son and, like them, Alec was thinking the unspoken thought – that perhaps this was the last time that they would ever see him.

The next day, he took a train up to London, and a bus to Primrose Hill. He had almost reached the house containing Myrtle's flat, when he saw another man in uniform coming towards him. As he got closer, he realised it was Colin Tunniford.

"What are you doing here?" he asked and, from Colin's expression, it was clear that he was wondering the same thing.

"I've come to see Myrtle. Same as you, I imagine."

"Is she expecting you?"

"No. You?"

"No. I just got here. I spent last night with my family."

"So did I."

Both feeling rather uncomfortable, they walked up the stairs to the top floor flat.

"At least we'll give her a nice surprise," remarked Alec, as he knocked on the door.

For the longest moment there was no reply, then the two men heard the shuffling of footsteps and a voice, tired but obviously Myrtle's, asking who was there.

"Two of your favourite admirers," called back Colin and, a few moments later, the door opened.

Myrtle blinked at them for a second, then registered who they were.

"Good God, how extraordinary to see you in those uniforms. Well, you'd better come in."

She turned away and left them to shut the door behind them.

"I'll make us some tea. Do sit down." She went into the tiny kitchen to light the gas ring, as the two soldiers sat in the living room. "What time is it?"

"Almost two o'clock," Colin answered.

"Two? My God. Still, I didn't get to bed till six-thirty, so it's not surprising I suppose. One of those wild nights, you know. War or no war, there are still some pretty good parties."

"Did you get my letters?" asked Alec.

"And mine?" Colin chimed in.

"Darlings, I received so many letters from both of you," she said, as she brought in the tea things and set them out on a small table. "I was utterly delighted you were both thinking of me so much. I would have replied more often, but I just had so much to do, what with the anti-war campaign, and poetry readings, and all that sort of thing. Last night, I saw this fascinating modern poet, from somewhere called Omaha. That's in America, isn't it?"

"Yes," said Alec.

"I thought it was. Cecile Gravely swore that it was in Japan, but she wouldn't know a Jap if one bit her on the thigh. Anyway, this chap – Butch, his name was; isn't that too quaint for words? – read several of his poems to us. It seems he had a technique of just opening the dictionary at random and copying down words, seven to a line. He says that's the only way to express oneself, free from the shackles of grammar and syntax. Simply casting at the listener a series of words, to demonstrate that thoughts can communicate themselves, without ordered language. It was too moving for words. We stayed for hours listening to him. Poor Geoffrey Sinclair was moved to tears."

"Geoffrey's not in the army yet?" asked Alec. He remembered the man in question: always on the point of writing a great novel, that would throw into sharp relief the inequities of modern society; always dressing like a dandy, or at least the way he fancied a dandy would dress; and always short of money.

"What, Geoffrey? Not him. He says he sees that German imperialism in Europe must be stopped, but he prefers to offer moral support, rather than take part in the grubby business of doing any actual fighting. Besides, he says he owes it to the people not to risk being killed. When he writes his novel, it will cause such a stir that the very fabric of British society will be rent asunder. He has to survive the war in order to fulfil his destiny. He received his conscription summons a little while ago, but has asked to appear before one of those tribunals. He's going to tell them that his future work is vitally important and that he's far too valuable to risk his life in battle, so he should be exempted."

The strange thing was that in October 1914, both Alec and Colin would have nodded in agreement at hearing this. They may even have said that sort of thing themselves, or something similar. The artistic crowd often used to talk like that to each other. But in February 1916, neither man was particularly impressed.

"Well, I doubt those tribunals will fall for that sort of guff. If he's trying to avoid being called up for a flimsy reason like that, it won't work," said Alec. "We'll just have to hope he manages to avoid getting killed, won't we? Or else the world will have to do without his great novel."

Colin smiled. Myrtle looked put out.

"I can see army life has left its mark on the two of you," she remarked. "Damn, I've left my cigarettes in the bedroom." She turned to face the open door and called out, "Darling, be a dear and bring me my cigarettes. And put something on – we have company."

Before either man could react to the idea that Myrtle had not slept alone – which meant that, of course, she had not been faithful to either of them – they saw, entering the room, wearing a bashful smile and what was obviously one of Myrtle's dressing gowns, their comrade, Private Hubert Snibley. Somehow, he was managing to look both sheepish and smug, at the same time. He handed Myrtle her cigarette case and deposited himself on the sofa next to her.

"Mornin'," he greeted his friends.

"What are you doing here?" asked Colin. It was, of course, a superfluous question, but it had to be asked, and Myrtle chose to be the one to answer it.

"Hubie's been writing to me too. He's been a very faithful correspondent, in fact, so I told him to come and stay with me when he had leave."

Snibley nodded. "Got 'ere yesterday," he said.

"Yes," Myrtle went on. "We went to the poetry reading together."

"We did," agreed Snibley with a rueful grin at the two men, while making sure that Myrtle didn't see. Neither Colin nor Alec were ready to share a humorous moment with him just yet, so they looked back at him blankly.

"Don't you have family in London?" Alec asked him.

"Yes, but I'm buggered if I can be bothered with them. My father's probably drunk and my mother was on the game last time I saw her, which was the day before I joined up. I wasn't going to waste precious leave time with them, so I came to stay with Myrt, like she asked me to."

"I'm so glad you did, precious," said Myrtle, blowing him a kiss wrapped in cigarette smoke. "Colin, I really have to thank you for introducing us. I knew from the first time we met that we'd have a grand fling. But what about you two? Alec, have you found the love of your life yet?"

This, from the woman who had informed him that they would one day get married.

"I thought I had," Alec answered her. "But obviously I was mistaken." He stood up to leave and Colin followed suit. "Well, nice seeing you again but I've got to be on my way. Things to do this evening, and tomorrow we're off."

"Me too," said Colin.

"So soon?" Myrtle seemed genuinely surprised. If she realised the awkward situation the two young men were in, she gave no hint of it. "I was hoping to hear how your painting was going, Colin. And what about that book of poetry, Alec? Was it ever published?"

Neither man felt inclined to discuss the lack of progress on their respective artistic fronts, so they mumbled platitudes and left, with peremptory pecks on the cheek for Myrtle and brief nods of farewell for Snibley – not farewell for too long, since they'd be seeing him the next day.

Out on the street, Colin and Alec stood about feeling awkward for a moment, both still smarting from what had happened upstairs. Then, Alec asked Colin if he fancied a drink, Colin said he did, and they strolled down the road to the nearest pub.

"You know, I was in love with that woman," said Alec, when they were both installed at a table, in the corner of the saloon bar, each holding a pint of bitter. "Right up until five minutes ago, I was convinced she was the one I was going to marry. She told me we would."

"She told me the same thing," said Colin.

"What, that she was going to marry me?"

"No. That she and I were going to get married one day."

"Shit." Alec didn't swear very often but he felt this merited an expletive.

"She probably tells everyone that. She's probably telling Snibley the same thing even as we speak, I shouldn't wonder."

"All that time, and Snibley never said a word. The thing is, it's so bloody obvious. I wrote to her two or three times a week, all through training. She replied to me perhaps five times in total. Quite a heavy hint there, wouldn't you say?"

"Spilt milk, old man," said Colin. "Don't waste time worrying about it. I thought the same thing. In fact, I was very jealous of you, as you knew her too."

"And I of you."

"Which is why, I suppose, we never spoke of her." Colin shook his head. "And all the while she was after old Snibley."

"Well, good luck to them both, and sod the pair of them."

"Couldn't agree more." And they toasted the sentiment with large gulps of beer.

Both Alec and Colin, finding that their plans had been suddenly changed, spent the remainder of their leave with their respective families, who were delighted to see them again. They were wise enough not to ask any questions about the sudden change of schedule, but simply to enjoy it.

Chapter XIX

An Evening at The Red Lion

The men of Banbury all went home for their leave. They took a train from Marylebone Station, all three of them remembering that it had been from here that they had begun their circuitous walk to the recruiting office, all those long months before. They arrived at their home station in the middle of the afternoon. A pony and trap took them to their village, which was a few miles out of town. They went to their various homes, arranging to meet later that evening at the Red Lion, their customary watering hole in the days before the war, when they had marked the end of each day with a pint or two.

Harry Travis, the oldest of the three and no doubt the wisest, in his opinion anyway, found his wife hanging washing on the line, outside their little cottage.

"Hello, Ivy," he greeted her.

His wife looked up at the sound of his voice, and she saw him standing before her, a warm smile on his face.

"It's so cold today, this lot'll never get dry out here," she said. "Like as not I'll have to take it all into the house later." Then she burst into tears and fell into his arms.

"Hey, don't take on so," said Harry, holding her tight. "There's nothing to cry about. I'm here now, that's good news."

Ivy took that as a cue to cry some more.

"I didn't think I'd ever see you again," she sobbed. "I was sure the Germans would get you."

"The Germans? Lovey, I've been training in Yorkshire. I haven't come within a hundred miles of a German."

"Yes, I know, but they bombarded Scarborough, didn't they? And they could've done it again when you were there."

"Pet, I was nowhere near Scarborough. And didn't I write to you every chance I got, so you knew I was alright?"

"Yes, you did." She blew her nose on a handkerchief she kept up her sleeve. "But I was expecting a telegram at any moment, to say you'd been blown up."

Harry regarded his wife for a few seconds, then shook his head and chuckled.

"You silly thing, you. You wont be gettin' any telegram on account of me. Not ever."

Ivy sniffed and attempted a smile.

"Now let's go inside, lass, and you put the kettle on."

Bert Giddington's wife adopted a completely different attitude when she first saw her husband. She was talking to a couple of her friends in the village square, on her way to the grocer's shop, when she saw Bert walking towards her, a grin on his face.

"Bert!" she yelped, dropping her shopping basket.

"Hello, Alice," Bert called back.

"Bert, it's you!" she screamed again, and started to run towards him. Bert waited till she got to him and then swept her up in his arms, swinging her round, before putting her down. They embraced and kissed passionately, like the newly-weds they had been five years before. Someone watching them from the doorway of the post office said something about that sort of behaviour in public being unseemly, but everyone else smiled upon the couple. Most people had a husband, son, brother, or lover in uniform, so they quite understood.

When Bert and Alice at last separated, they gazed into each other's eyes for a moment, lost for words.

Alice spoke first. "You look ever so handsome in your uniform, Bert."

"And you're prettier than ever, Alice."

"Why didn't you tell me you were coming?"

"Wanted to surprise you, love. Anyway, it wouldn't feel right, sending a telegram." He was right. Telegrams were bearers of bad news, harbingers of grief. He had been wise not to scare her with one.

"But I've not got anything prepared for you."

"Never mind, girl. A warm bed with you in it, that's all I want."

"Bert!" she squealed in delight.

Bert smiled back at her and she took his arm as he walked her home. The shopping would have to wait.

Joseph Marren got to his cottage at about the same time. His sister was washing dishes and saw him through the kitchen window as he opened the garden gate, and she ran out to meet him, not even bothering to dry her hands.

"Hello, Mavis," he greeted her, giving her a hug.

"Hello, Joe. My, it's grand to see you."

"You too. It's nice to be home."

They went into the cottage together.

"Davey's at work," Mavis said. "Won't be back till this evening."

Joe nodded. "How's Mum?"

Mavis made a face. "The same. Come and say hello."

They went into the tiny living room, which contained an old sofa and an armchair, leaving very little room for anything else. In the chair, sat an elderly lady. She had never been particularly large to begin with, and now she was shrunk with age. She had a rug over her legs and was reading a newspaper by the light that came through the window behind her.

"Hello, Mum," said Joe.

The old lady looked up, then folded her newspaper slowly and put it on her lap.

"So, you've decided to come home."

"Yes, Mum. I'm on leave. It's called special embarkation leave."

"Very fancy, I'm sure, all this army talk. Whatever they call it, it means they've let you out. And you've remembered you have a family; that's very nice of you."

"Of course I've come home, Mum. To see you, and Mavis, and Davey."

"So, you decided this is your home after all. I suppose we should feel honoured, what with you gallivanting all over the place in the army. Do you know how long it is, since you upped and went?"

"Mum, we've been through all this before. I did what I thought was right. You wouldn't want me to do otherwise, would you?" Joe asked.

"What you thought was right? You'd never been further from your home than Oxford before all this war business started." She seemed to have forgotten his trip to London, but then Joe remembered that was where he'd enlisted and decided not to remind her. "What do you know about such things as armies, and what is right?" she continued. "You belong here, not in France, or wherever it is you've been."

"It wasn't France, Mum. It was Yorkshire. I told you all about it in my letters. You did get my letters, didn't you?"

"I expect I did. I don't know as I have time to go reading letters from people who forget where their home is."

"We did get your letters, Joe," said Mavis, "and we did read them. You remember, Mum? I read each one aloud to you."

"Perhaps. Anyway, what are you doing back here? Your army chums not good enough for you all of a sudden?"

"I told you, Mum. It's embarkation leave. We've all got forty-eight hours, because we're off to France the day after tomorrow."

Joe took a step closer to his mother, who continued to regard him without the slightest suggestion of a smile. He bent forward and kissed her on the cheek.

"And seeing as I had the time, I came back to be with my mum."

"Very grateful, I'm sure."

"We're so pleased to see you, Joe," said Mavis, "and I know Davey'll be thrilled when he gets home."

"We almost lost your brother too, thanks to you," said his mother.

"What do you mean?"

"What do I mean? I mean that a few weeks after you ran off to play at being a soldier, your brother tried to do the same. He sneaked off to Oxford and tried to join up there. He knew he wouldn't manage it if he went to the recruiting office in Banbury, because someone there was bound to know him."

"He's too young."

"I know he's too young, that's how I managed to stop him. When I found out what he'd gone and done, I went to find Constable Thurber and told him what Davey was up to. He managed to get a message to whoever deals with these things in the army, and they cancelled Davey's enlistment. Of course, he wasn't pleased and sulked for days. All your fault, you see."

"Well, I'm glad he didn't get in. The army's no place for someone his age. But don't let's quarrel, Mum. It's ages since I was home. I've lots to tell you, about what I've been up to, and all my new chums."

"I'll make us all a nice cup of tea," said Mavis. "Then we can hear all your news."

"I don't think I've time to listen to a lot of chit chat," said Mrs. Marren. "And anyway, I haven't finished reading my paper." She picked up her newspaper, gave it a couple of bad-tempered shakes, and resumed reading it. She took no further notice of her son.

As arranged, they all gathered that evening at The Red Lion Inn. It was a scene that had taken place – and would continue to take place – thousands of times across the country during the course of the war. The juvenile, the old, the infirm, the exempt, and the female, meeting to greet and celebrate local young men in uniform who were home on leave, relaxing amongst their own, before joining or rejoining the war. Sometimes it was a joyful, optimistic occasion, especially at the start of the war. As the casualty lists lengthened, but the Allied gains did not, it became possessed of a grim foreboding, one that needed more and more effort to ignore.

This evening, however, was reasonably merry. Bert, Harry, and Joe were not the first men from the locality to go off to war by any means, but this was their evening and they were the centre of attention. One thing was for sure – they didn't have to put their hands in their pockets all evening. Everyone there, or almost everyone, felt it an honour to buy a drink for the three men. There were admiring glances, and even a bit of gentle flirting from some of the women. The men were quick to congratulate the three soldiers and a few, both young and old, felt more than a little touch of envy.

In the face of such attention, the three men sat together for safety, the centre of a circle of admiration. Sam Barker was with them. He had tried twice more to join up and had twice been rejected, so he endured the hardships of his friends' army training through the stories they told.

"I tried to join up with these brave lads," he would tell anyone who would listen, "but they wouldn't take me on account of they thought I was too old."

Ivy Travis, Alice Giddington, and Mavis Marren sat with the three men. Mavis had always had a crush on Bert Giddington and, as such, cast unrequited glances his way, but as the only single man of the three it was Joe who was attracting most of the flirting. His mother sat close by, silent and malevolent, sipping a port and lemon, next to her younger son Davey, who, having failed to enlist, was full of admiration for his elder brother. You could tell that he was counting the days until he was old enough to join up himself.

Portly Mr. Benson, a civil servant of sorts, and a respected member of the village community, bought a round of drinks for the three men, their women, and the assembled hangers-on, of whom there seemed to be more and more, as people realised that there was a party going on.

"But tell us," he asked, after distributing the drinks from a tin tray and keeping a brandy and soda for himself, "what led you to join a London regiment? Most lads round here have joined the Ox and Bucks."

Harry smiled patiently. They'd had to explain that several times before. "We were in London when we joined. We went there for Wally's funeral, remember? So they put us in a battalion that was being formed there."

"Yes, I see," said Benson. "Any chance they'll let you transfer to another regiment?"

"No, not at this stage. Besides, we wouldn't want to leave the St. Marylebones'."

"You wouldn't?"

"No," said Harry, and his two comrades nodded in agreement.

"Not even to join your mates in the Ox and Bucks?"

It was probably true that a lot of young men of their acquaintance had joined the Oxfordshire and Buckinghamshire Light Infantry, and perhaps it would have been nice to serve alongside them, but it was not possible. Nor did the three men want it to be.

"We're with our mates now," said Harry.

"Never thought of that."

"What're they like, those London people?" asked Mavis. Although it was only sixty miles away, and trains ran there and back several times a day, Mavis had never been to London, which was not at all unusual for someone who lived in a rural community like hers. Most people seldom went further afield than the nearest market town – a few of the more adventurous went to Oxford occasionally – but, for most of them, London might as well have been on the other side of the world, as remote as India or New Zealand.

"They're good men," answered her brother. "Just like you and me, really."

"'S'right," agreed Bert. "They wouldn't know a plough from a harrow, but you can't blame them for that, bein' city folk and all."

"And they're not all from London. We've got people from all over the place in our battalion."

"So, are you going to win the war this year?" asked someone on the edge of their little group, a man whose married status had, thus far, exempted him from conscription and he was not averse to trying to belittle what the other three had done.

"Win it? I don't know about this year," Bert said. "But we'll do our best, whatever we're told to do."

"I can't tell you when we'll win this war," agreed Harry. "I'll tell you one thing though – we'll never lose it."

"But how much longer can it go on, Harry?" asked his wife. "It seems to have been with us for so long."

"Only a year and a half, pet."

"They say there's going to be a big push this year," ventured Davey Marren. "Everyone's talking about it."

"The Germans must be very pleased about that, us telling them what we're going to do," said Harry.

"You know what I mean. It's just the rumour going round."

"You shouldn't pay attention to rumours or gossip. It never does any good, you know."

"But there's going to be an attack, isn't there, sooner or later?" Davey insisted. "Something has to happen."

"Sooner or later, of course there will. The war has to keep moving. And that's all I, or anyone knows, 'ceptin' General Haig, and he hasn't got round to confiding in the likes of me just yet," said Harry.

They left the question of the big push alone for the time being and a moment of silence blanketed the party. The fire in the grate crackled, one or two people sipped their drinks audibly, someone coughed.

Davey Marren, though, was not about to waste the chance to find out as much about army life as he could from his brother and his friends. He may have been unable to join up, but if he couldn't be in the army, he wanted to know as much about it as possible.

"Have you ever seen an aeroplane?" he asked.

"Once or twice," answered Bert. "There was an airfield not all that far from where we did our training. We used to see them fly past on occasion."

"I'd love to go up in one of them," the young man enthused.

"Stuff and nonsense," his mother said, the first time she had opened her mouth, except to drink, all evening. "Men flying about in machines. I just don't know what they're thinking of. Ought to be back on the ground doing a proper job, instead of all that flying about. Not getting the harvest in and not winning the war neither, that's what they're doing."

"The aeroplane's a new weapon, Mum," said Davey to his mother, who snorted in disgust. "You know, I read about where our planes have dropped bombs on the enemy, right inside Germany."

"And they did the same to us," said Mr. Benson.

"Those were Zeppelins, not aeroplanes," Davey answered. "Not the same thing. Their planes won't be able to bomb us because of the Channel, something about flying across water. I read it in the paper, their bombers will never be able to reach us, so they use Zeppelins, which we can shoot down."

Harry and Bert wondered what paper Davey had read that particular gem in, but they felt that life was too short to argue over things like that, so they both nodded absently and sipped their beer.

"That's what I want to do," Davey went on, "when I'm old enough to join up. I want to join the Flying Corps and shoot down Zeppelins. I'd make a good flyer, I know that."

"We've got a private in our mob who's always going on about flying," Bert said.

"Yes, Jimmy Hope, you mean," said Joe, with a nod.

"He knows all about aircraft, he does, so he says he ought to be able to fly for the army, and he wants to apply for a transfer as soon as he can."

"Don't you have to be an officer to fly planes in the army?" Davey wanted to know.

"Dunno. I can't say as I see our mate Jimmy as an officer though. Still, there's all sorts being officers these days, so I suppose stranger things have happened."

"And all sorts of people not being officers," remarked Harry.

"Yes," Bert chuckled, "Like our Duchess."

"What?" His wife sounded surprised. "You've got a duchess in the army?"

"A duke, more like." The three soldiers chuckled.

"Son of, you mean," said Harry.

"What are you talking about?" Alice wanted to know.

"One of the lads in our platoon, is the son of a duke."

"Not really?"

"Yes, really. The genuine article. And so we call him Duchess."

"What's he like?"

"A really good man," said Harry.

"No side to him at all. Everyone likes him," agreed Bert.

The chat continued, more drinks were bought and drunk, a dull rain fell outside. One young man trying to impress the soldiers, who had hardly even noticed him, by drinking double brandies, staggered outside to be sick. Mrs. Marren nodded off.

Davey Marren was the most curious about the St. Marylebones' and the war in general, so he asked the most questions, but several others chipped in, with queries and remarks of their own. The conversation touched on such topics as poison gas (a foul weapon, they all agreed, but something which they had no choice but to use, especially now the Germans had introduced it to the battlefield), army food (it could be better, but it could be a lot worse), promotion prospects (it was too early to think about promotion), the military capabilities of France (doing their best, but needing British help), Belgium (a gallant little country), the Turks (who would have thought they'd be able to hold off the invasion at Gallipoli?), conscription (a very good idea, which should force the shirkers to do their bit), women working in men's jobs (to be thanked; as valuable, almost, as the men at the front), and what to do with the Kaiser after the war was won (hang him, probably, or at least exile him like they did to Napoleon).

The talk then turned back to the question of the big push later that year, which everyone seemed to know would be coming. In fact, it was not a hard deduction to make. The war could not be won by standing still, so it was obvious that the Allies would have to attack decisively, at some point. Since no one knew any details, of course, they could only discuss it in general, hypothetical terms. Joe, who like everyone else there present, had not been anywhere near the front line yet, was talking about how to get through the enemy's barbed wire as easily as possible during a gas attack and was saying how they would soon no doubt be issued with new respirators, which would be the best that science could make. At this point his mother emerged from her slumber with a noisy snort, and interrupted her son.

"Poison gas! Barbed wire! I never heard the like. You have no business going off from your homes to join a war. I don't know what you are all thinking of. Why did you have to leave here? What for?"

"Because it was right, Mrs. Marren," said Harry. "Because it was the honourable thing to do. I know we told you how we joined up after we heard a crowd-pleasing orator, telling us the tale of Belgium being invaded, but that doesn't mean we were hoodwinked or tricked in any way. We joined because it would have been wrong to sit by and let Germany trample over Belgium and France, and just take whatever she wants. And if we turn our backs, and let Germany squash Belgium and France, then how long will it be before she turns on us and tries to do the same thing to England? It just would not be right to pretend we can't see what has to be done."

No one said anything, so he continued, "We may not enjoy everything we have to do, but we are doing our rightful duty with a clear conscience. Training was hard, but we came through it. I expect that life at the front will be harder than anything we have ever experienced before. It may be frightening, it may be downright ghastly, but we'll not let that stop us doing what we have to, as best we can. Pray God, we'll all of us come home safely, but if it should be otherwise, then that is how it will be. We may even have to take the lives of some poor German lads – this is a war, after all – but we'll not run scared on that account and neglect to do our duty. I know you miss having Joe around and it isn't easy for you, not having him there, but he has another duty now. It doesn't mean he thinks any the less of you, but he has to do what he knows is the right thing. We're going to win this war one day, and the only way we can do that is for people like us to do what we have done and are about to do. Joe is a good man who can't sit back and let evil triumph, Mrs. Marren. Be proud of him."

No one said a word for several moments, and they could hear the rain outside, the crackling of the fire, and the ticking of the clock on the wall. Everyone in the pub had stopped to listen to Harry, even those not in their group.

Then Bert murmured, "Well said, Harry," and, all at once, everyone in the Red Lion was applauding. Several people cheered, a couple thumped the bar with their beer mugs, and Ivy Travis beamed at her husband, beginning to weep. More drinks were bought. Then someone, no one could remember who later on, began to sing *Rule Britannia*. Only Mrs. Marren looked unimpressed. She shrank back into her chair and said not another word the whole evening.

The next day, the three men caught a morning train back to London. They still had plenty of time left to spare, so for old time's sake, they made their way to Oxford Street and enjoyed the hospitality of several pubs there, before going back to their barracks.

Part Three

Into The Maelstrom

Chapter XX

Kit Inspection

"Corporal O'Malley!"

"Yes, Sergeant."

"What're you doing?"

"Just showin' the men some pictures of me home in Donegal, Sergeant."

"Pictures of your home?"

"Indeed, yes, Sergeant."

"Pictures of your home, my arse! You were trying to get a poker game going, weren't you?"

"Wouldn't that be against regulations? You'll not catch me breakin' the rules, Sergeant."

"One day, I will."

"Always with your little joke, Sergeant."

"There's a full kit inspection in half an hour, you know."

"Yes, Sergeant."

"Well, hadn't you better see to it that the men in your section are ready, instead of bothering the rest of the platoon with your cards?"

"My section are all ready, Sergeant. They'll put the rest of the platoon to shame, sure they will. And it was photos from home I was showin' the men, Sergeant, not cards."

"Go on, you bent leprechaun, sod off back to your hut."

Fred Quill could not find it within himself to be angry with the little Irish corporal. In a way, he was rather fond of him.

"I'm off, Sergeant. We'll be ready for the inspection in my section, and you'll find nothing wrong with any of us," said O'Malley, and left the hut.

Fred Quill was right about the inspection. The commanding officer had announced that he would hold a full inspection of the entire battalion that afternoon, before they marched from Lambeth to Charing Cross station, to take their train to Folkestone. So Arnold Snow, the subaltern in charge of 2 Platoon, A-Company, had ordered his platoon sergeant, Fred Quill, to have his men ready for his own inspection, one full hour ahead of the lieutenant-colonel's. If the C.O. was going to find fault with anyone, it was not going to be with someone in his platoon. All the other platoon commanders in the battalion had the same idea and, as a result, everyone in every platoon was ready for two inspections that afternoon.

The barrack huts were really quite comfortable; 'comfortable', of course, being a relative term. Compared to the tents they had lived in for all those months during their training, the wooden huts, each with a stove at one end, were luxurious, especially in comparison to the perpetual draughts they had become accustomed to. They were still getting used to the delight of a bed, albeit a small army cot, each. This unaccustomed comfort had put them all in a good mood, so no one resented this inspection. They had been through inspections many times before, of course, but this was by way of being their last in England, and they were all determined to put on a good show.

A battalion in the British Army, at full strength, consisted of just over one thousand men, comprising headquarters staff and four companies. Each company was divided into four platoons, made up of four sections, under a junior officer and a sergeant. So it was found that 1 Platoon, A-Company was commanded by Charles Snow. His brother, Arnold, was in command of 2 Platoon, assisted by Sergeant Fred Quill, upon whom he depended a great deal, as most second lieutenants would upon a sergeant with thirty years' service. No. 1 section of 2 Platoon was led by Lance Corporal Edwin Marvell. Lance Corporal Matthew Clay was in charge of No. 2 section. Corporal Seamus O'Malley led No. 3 section.

That afternoon, Arnold Snow inspected the kit of every man in his platoon, with the exception of himself and Sergeant Quill. To his surprise and delight, he found nothing out of order anywhere. Every buckle and button shone as never before, every inch of leather was polished as if by experts. Beds were made perfectly, sheets and blankets drum tight and not a crease to be found. Personal kit was laid out with geometric accuracy. There was not a single speck of dirt on a single rifle or bayonet. Arnold was very pleased with his men.

"Not bad, eh, Sergeant?" he remarked, after the inspection.

"No, sir. They did well."

"As well as regular soldiers could manage?"

Fred Quill thought for a second.

"You can't rule it out, sir," he admitted, which, from him, was high praise for the men under him. He wouldn't tell them, of course, but he was very pleased with the men in 2 Platoon.

The entire battalion acquitted itself well when the Commanding Officer inspected them, an hour later. They were drawn up on the barrack square and Lieutenant-Colonel Wintergrass made a point of actually looking carefully at every man under his command, rather than walking swiftly down the ranks. He had been a regular soldier in the Boer War and had retired on half-pay until the outbreak of hostilities in 1914, when he had been brought back to command a New Army battalion. As far as he was concerned, the distinction between Regular and New Armies would be blurred beyond distinction in the front line, and it was the professionalism of men, such as his, which would achieve that.

Before dismissing the parade he mounted a small dais, at the edge of the square, in order to address the battalion.

"You men," he called, "represent all that is good about England. When the need arose, you put down your pens, and your hammers, and your ploughs, and flocked to the colours. I have watched you turn yourselves from civilians into a skilled fighting unit. We'll be leaving England today for the front. What fate has in store for us, no one can tell, but I have every confidence that every last one of you will do his duty and that England will be very, very proud of the St. Marylebone Rifles."

The men were then dismissed and were ordered to be back on the parade ground in one hour, to march out.

****

A Coy, 35 Btn, Middlesex Regt.
1st March, 1916

Colonel & Mrs. H. Hardy
- Berkeley Square
London W

Dear Mother and Colonel Hardy,

Well, here we are in Folkestone! I haven't been here since that outing we all took when Charles and I were very young. Not that I would recognise the place now anyway. I seem to remember a shingle beach, wooden breakwaters draped with seaweed, and the smell of the sea – and the sound of the ocean, of course. But, where I am now, there is no sight of the sea and certainly no sound or smell of it either! I am in the railway station canteen. Our train arrived a while ago and we are waiting for our turn to board the troopship that will take us across the Channel to France. The men are waiting in a goods yard across the road from the station. The C.O. thought it best not to allow them to wander off, even though we do have a wait ahead of us. The last thing anyone wants is for the ship to be ready to sail, and half a dozen men lost in the dark somewhere!

The train journey here was quick and uneventful. I shared a compartment with Charles and a few other subalterns, and we alternately chatted, read, and watched the scenery go by until it got dark. The part of this journey I shall never, ever forget is the part in which we marched from our barracks in Lambeth, to Charing Cross Station. Of course, as a battalion we have often marched before. At times it seemed as though we never did anything else. This time, though, was different. This time, it was as though we were on public display, and I think we did ourselves proud!

I don't think we took the shortest route. In fact, after discussing it with my fellow subalterns, I am sure that our C.O. chose the route. You see, we marched across Westminster Bridge, when it would have been easier, surely, to cross the river further east. But our route of march took us right past the Houses of Parliament! There were people on the terraces as we crossed the bridge and although, of course, I have no way of knowing, I like to think that perhaps the Prime Minister or the Minister for War was among them and saw us go by. They would have been exceedingly impressed, of that I have no doubt!

At our head, on horseback, was the CO, Lieutenant-Colonel Wintergrass. He cut such an impressive figure that every officer and man who followed him, no doubt, stretched his abilities to look as martial. Here was England at war! Behind him came the Second-In-Command, Major Fullerton, and the adjutant, Capt. Case, both on horseback. Everyone else was on foot.

The battalion staff were next and then the rest. We marched in order of companies, so my company, A-Company, was first. Brother Charles was ahead of me, of course, since he leads 1 Platoon, but my platoon, which I fancy is the finest in the entire regiment, came immediately after. I am sure that upon seeing us, no one would have been able to guess, unless he knew already, that these men had, until the outbreak of war, been civilians, who had never marched in step, worn a uniform, or held a rifle. We marched as though to the manor born, and we showed those who fate and elections have set above us, what sort of men are about to go to the front to fight for Britannia's freedom.

Our battalion musicians played us all the way from the barrack square, to the forecourt of Charing Cross Station. Of course, in the actual front line, they are our stretcher-bearers. For the time being, though, they put fire in our veins with Soldiers Of The Queen, The British Grenadiers, Heart Of Oak, *and several others. I have never felt so proud in all my life as when we crossed Westminster Bridge in the late afternoon light and, in the shadow of Big Ben, we right wheeled onto the Embankment, before progressing to Charing Cross Station. The people cheered us and I was reminded of* Henry V. *In truth, we are a band of brothers and, of those who have yet to join us, they shall indeed think themselves accurs'd and hold their manhoods cheap.*

When we reached the station, we found our train waiting for us at the appointed platform, ready to depart. It is not easy to take a battalion of about one thousand officers and men, not to say anything of their weapons, and equipment, and other impedimenta, and see that they board a particular train in a crowded, noisy station, but we managed it. At least, our sergeants did. What a magnificent body of men our sergeants are! Our Regimental Sergeant-Major, Mr. Callow, oversaw the whole process, and the other sergeants under him carried out his orders. It seemed to me that we were all aboard in a matter of a few minutes, though I am sure it must have taken a bit longer than that. At any rate, I was soon to be found in a compartment reserved for subalterns and, with brother Charles and six others, I rode down to Folkestone in happy comfort.

The adjutant has taken the RSM with him, and two of the company sergeant-majors as well, to find out about the boat crossing. The men are waiting outside the station and I have taken these minutes to write to you. No doubt we shall be moving off presently, but I wanted to take this opportunity to assure you that I, and Charles too I'm sure, have never been so happy and so sure of the rightness of what we are doing. I do not know what the future has in store for me, of course, but I know I shall face whatever happens with courage and unshakable confidence in the justice of England's cause.

With fondest wishes from,
Your loving son,
Arnold

Chapter XXI

The Channel Crossing

When it finally happened later that evening, the Channel crossing was uneventful and reasonably swift. The 35th Middlesex crossed from Folkestone to Boulogne on a ferry of many years' service, which had been commandeered for the duration of the war by the Admiralty. They shared it for just over an hour and a half with another New Army battalion from the Midlands. Lieutenant-Colonel Wintergrass chatted to his counterpart in the other battalion on the foredeck, and the two men shared the latter's hip flask. The other officers remained at deck level, talking among themselves or else staring, either back towards the White Cliffs, wondering when they would see them again, or forwards, towards where the French coast lay, feeling a mixture of emotions, ranging from eager anticipation, to out and out dread. It was dark and the ship was running without lights, as a precaution against being seen by enemy vessels.

The NCOs and men were below decks. They were crowded in, but that didn't matter much because it was to be a short journey. Some sat on whatever they could – bunks, benches, stairways. Others stood, or leaned, against bulkheads. A few managed to find out of the way spots where they could lie down for a while. The atmosphere below decks soon transformed into heavy fug: a mixture of sweat, tobacco smoke, and damp sea air.

In one place, a few of the 35th Middlesex were talking about what lay ahead, smoking cigarettes and pipes, each trying to conceal his nervousness at the thought that, after all the training, they were finally on their way to service overseas. The front was about to become real for them.

"The thing we have to worry about," said Harry Travis, "is submarines. The way I see it, there's not much likelihood of one of them German battleships having a go at us. But their submarines are everywhere."

"I thought they stayed out of the Channel," ventured Wilfred Leuchars.

"Don't know who told you that," replied Harry. "But they didn't do you no favours. That's rubbish. Submarines can get just about anywhere they want.

"So what 'appens if we get 'it by a torpedo then?" asked Hubert Snibley.

"We drown, that's what." Matthew Clay was never one to look on the bright side, if he could help it.

"Leave it out, Corp," Harry protested. "If we gets hit, then we keep our heads, go up on deck in an orderly manner, and man the lifeboats."

"Just like what the CSM told us," someone agreed, and a few others nodded.

"That's as maybe," Clay said. "But if we do get hit, and I'm not killed or wounded too badly to move, then to hell with orders, I'll be up them stairs and onto the deck before the rest of you can even blink."

"D'you think we will be hit?" asked Bert Giddington

"Nah," said Clay. "The navy patrols the Channel so thickly, they won't show their noses here. There's at least two destroyers screening us right now, for example."

"But that's just the point. They don't show their noses, or anything else for that matter. They stay underwater and the first anyone knows about it is a torpedo up the bum."

"What I'm trying to say," Clay persisted, "is that the Germans don't send their submarines to the Channel. It's too dangerous for them, and there are richer pickings for them elsewhere."

"Like the Lusitania," said Joe.

"Yes, exactly, like the Lusitania. And that wasn't here, was it? That was off the coast of Ireland, miles away from here."

"U-boats," said Hubert Snibley.

"What?"

"U-boats, Corp. I 'eard that the Germans call their submarines U-boats."

"Yes, they do."

"What does the 'U' stand for, then?"

"Dunno."

"Underwater, I'll bet," said Joe.

"Don't be daft. How can it be underwater? It's got to stand for a German word."

"Why is the second half of the word 'boat' then, if they're talking German?" countered Hubert

"Good point," agreed Wilfred.

"I reckon," said Hubert, "that boat is one of them words that means the same in German as what it does in English."

"Such as?" Clay wanted to know.

Hubert thought for a moment. "Like Kaiser," he said.

The men were in a companionway, on what was the starboard side of the ship, though that was a term that most of them had never heard of and of the few who had, most did not know what it meant. They leaned against the bulkhead, which they would have referred to as a wall, so as not to obstruct the companionway, or passage, as they would have called it. Two of their number, Les Mosterby and Matthew Clay, were sitting on a wooden crate that had been stowed there, the Ulsterman and the Londoner sharing a cigarette. Most of them smoked, as was the custom, and their discussion was not designed to increase the sum of their knowledge, but rather to pass the time. There was a lot of that in the army, they had discovered – long periods of inactivity while they waited for instructions, or for something else to happen – and conversation was how they made the hours go by faster.

Corporal O'Malley was suddenly among them. He was not in a good mood. He had tried to find a place to lie down, but all the best spots had been taken. He had then taken the opportunity to join a poker game, organised by some of the men from the other battalion, but the game had been legitimate and most of the other players were too canny for O'Malley to risk being caught cheating, so he quit after losing almost four pounds. He needed to do something mean and spiteful, protected by his rank, to feel better. When he saw this little group chatting away, a good-natured debate going on, which they all appeared to be enjoying, he decided to put a stop to it.

"Private Mosterby," he snapped.

Mosterby looked up in surprise. "Yes, Corp?"

"On your feet, Private," O'Malley ordered.

Les Mosterby stood up.

"Now, move out of my way." O'Malley pushed forward to take Mosterby's place on the crate. He sat down and leaned back with an exaggerated sigh of comfort. The bulkhead was damp with condensation, although he didn't let that spoil his pleasure. Mosterby looked surprised, but said nothing.

"Ah, now that's better," O'Malley almost purred. "And I'm sure you'll be agreeing, will ye not, that no corporal should have to stand while a private is restin' his arse sittin' down?"

"I suppose not, Corporal."

"Especially not a private from some broken down Belfast slum, am I right?"

"Whatever you say," Mosterby sighed. He knew O'Malley was baiting him, not for the first time.

"Whatever you say, *Corporal.*" O'Malley reminded him

"Whatever you say, Corporal."

"Better. We'll be makin' a soldier out of you yet, Mosterby. Probably too late to do the army any good, mind, but better than leavin' ye as ye are." And he chuckled. His ill-natured intervention in the group had killed the jolly conversation stone dead, but that was what he had intended. In a few moments, he'd suggest a game of Crown and Anchor. That was forbidden by army rules, but that didn't seem to make much difference in the ranks – people still played it, up and down the army. O'Malley had a board and a set of dice, which he had bought from a rather unpleasant little man in Walworth, during his embarkation leave. They had cost nineteen shillings and sixpence, but O'Malley didn't mind paying that much, since he was sure he would be able to recoup his outlay many times over, considering that the dice were weighted.

As it turned out, there wasn't enough time. Company Sergeant-Major Bull appeared a moment later.

"We'll be in Boulogne shortly," he announced. "Corporal O'Malley, Lance Corporal Clay, you'd better see that your sections are ready to disembark as soon as the order is given. Anyone delaying things because he hasn't got all his kit about him, will be answerable to me. So will his section leader." He moved on. O'Malley didn't mind. He was certain there would be dozens of opportunities to relieve his fellow soldiers of their money.

When they reached Boulogne, they were formed up on the quayside and when all the men, officers, horses, weapons, and baggage had been unloaded – no mean feat in itself – the battalion marched to the edge of town, where the officers were billeted in civilian houses and the men bivouacked in a field. There were three other battalions in the same brigade as the 35th Middlesex and they would not be arriving in France until the next day.

Some of the men had wondered if they would find themselves in the front line that same evening and they felt a mixture of relief and disappointment in roughly equal measure that they were to be under canvas that night. The next day, after reveille and breakfast, they struck camp and formed up by the roadside. The men were ordered to stand easy and they then waited. After almost two hours, they heard the sound of marching, and the three other battalions in their brigade approached, fresh off the boat that morning.

As they passed, men waved greetings to each other, and the officers and NCOs turned a deaf ear for a few moments, as the men exchanged salutations and comments.

"How good of you to join us."

"Thought you was never coming."

"Nice of you to turn up."

"Alright for some, sleeping out in a field till lunchtime."

After that, it was all business again, and the 35th Middlesex fell in behind the third battalion as it moved past, before the entire brigade marched out of Boulogne. This was not the short march of the day before, from Lambeth to Charing Cross. This was the sort of march that they had become used to during the long months of training. Marching four abreast, with officers in front and NCOs behind or alongside them, ready to order the men to close up ranks, pick their feet up, or to keep moving. This was the sort of march that went on for hours – fifty minutes marching and ten minutes resting. This was marching that began with the men in good spirits, chatting to each other as they were permitted to do when the order to 'march easy' had been given. Sometimes they would sing, other times they would continue in silence, lost in their thoughts, but as the march continued, they felt their webbing belts dig into them, their equipment became heavier, and their muscles began to ache. After the first fifty minutes, the men sat and chatted, some smoked, and enjoyed their ten minutes' rest, before tackling another fifty minutes on foot. But after some hours, when the order to fall out was given, men would shrug off their packs and collapse at the side of the road, exhausted beyond conversation, many of them falling asleep the moment they lay down.

Lieutenant-Colonel Wintergrass had announced, before the men marched off, that he expected the 35th Middlesex to reach its destination without a single man falling out – not a one. So it was that as never before, the men helped each other. If a man appeared to be near collapse after the first few hours, two of his comrades would hold him at each arm. Perhaps another would carry his pack for a while, and another his rifle.

On the whole, Sergeant Quill was very proud of the way the platoon was showing itself. They were marching like regular soldiers, as was only right and proper after all those months of training. He saw Private Vic Rangle, at the end of the first rank. Now, he looked as though he had been born into uniform. A strange one was this Vic Rangle, however. He was friendly, cheerful, got on very well with his fellows, and never had any trouble with the NCOs set above him. He was an efficient soldier, who underwent training with the ease of a man to whom none of this was new. He never, however, talked about his background to his comrades and, so it was that, after having him among them for over a year, not one of the other men in the platoon knew a thing about him, other than what they had seen since they had all joined up. Sergeant Quill could tell, almost at once, that this was not Rangle's first experience of military life, but he kept his own counsel. Most people who rejoined the army, after having spent time in Civvy Street, at least mentioned it to their comrades. Not Private Rangle. A friendly question from one or other of his mates about his background, was invariably met with an apologetic smile and a non-committal answer that told them nothing.

So there he was, in the 35th Middlesex, about to accompany his fellow soldiers to war. As far as he was concerned, Vic Rangle, the officer, was now just a distant memory, and he was quite happy for him to stay that way.

Further back, Private Snibley, at the end of a rank of four, began to stagger. Almost at once, Sergeant Quill was at his side.

"Private Snibley, you are not to fall out!"

"I can't go on, Sar'nt."

"Course you can, son. You never dropped out in training now, did you?"

"No, Sar'nt."

"Then you shouldn't be allowing a little stroll like this get the better of you."

"No, Sar'nt."

"You heard what the C.O. said. No one is to drop out. You heard him, didn't you?"

"Yes, Sar'nt."

"Well then, that's how it's going to be, see. No one is dropping out and, if they do, they bloody well won't be from my platoon."

"Sar'nt."

"You'd be letting your mates down if you did."

"Yes, Sar'nt. I'll do my best."

"It better be bloody well good enough. Private Ross!"

"Yes, Sar'nt?" replied Eddie Ross, who was marching next to Hubert Snibley.

“If Private Snibley looks like dropping out again, give him a swift boot up the arse.”

“Yes, Sar’nt!”

Fred Quill resumed his position behind the platoon. He didn’t suppose for a second that Eddie Ross would actually deliver the boot in the arse, as ordered; rather, it would prompt him to help Snibley, with either verbal encouragement or by carrying something, possibly even enlisting others to help too. By and large, Quill thought his platoon was a good one and he felt sure that no one would drop out, if they could possibly help it.

Of course, no one had told the men where their destination was, so they had no idea how long they would be marching, and they wouldn’t know where they were going until they got there. In fact, they were not headed for the front, not just yet. They’d be there soon enough, but first they had to spend time at a place called Étaples.

Chapter XXII

Étaples

Étaples was not a place of joy. It was not where men went when they wanted to laugh, to enjoy the pleasures that life could offer them. It was a vast, barren expanse, outside the town of the same name, ringed by tents and wooden huts, a cemetery in one corner, a railway line cutting through another. Étaples was a vast training camp through which, among others, new recruits freshly arrived from Britian passed, being sent to the front. On top of the many months in England, in which they had been transformed from civilians to soldiers, the men had to undergo two weeks of this. Their own officers and sergeants were billeted elsewhere and they were entrusted to the care of the camp staff – officers, who had come out of retirement for this purpose, dug out of civilian life and referred to as 'dugouts', and NCOs, who wore yellow armbands to denote their status and were given the contemptuous nickname, 'canaries'. The men who passed through the camp went on to the front, while the instructors at Étaples stayed where they were, safe and fed. They knew they had a cushy billet, and they realised that the men they were training knew it and, as such, resented it. They countered this resentment with a vindictive bitterness that the men had not encountered before in the army. Every order was given, it seemed, in bad temper. Every command accompanied by an insult. The men felt more like criminals than soldiers about to risk their lives at the front. For the first time, the men, well used to the rough edge of a sergeant's tongue, as all soldiers are, became angry and resentful at the treatment they received. Some even felt betrayed by the army they had joined.

The routine was the same every day; up at five-thirty in the morning, training for an hour and a half before breakfast, eaten, like all meals at Étaples, in crowded, filthy huts which smelled of sweat, rotten food, and unwashed soldiery. The first day set the tone for the rest of the two weeks. A-Company was entrusted to the care of a canary called Sergeant Mildman.

"I have never seen such a useless shower of nancy boys in my life," was how he introduced himself to them, as they stood to attention in perfect ranks before him, in one corner of the camp. "Words fail me!"

Then he made a liar of himself by speaking again, almost immediately.

"You may have had it cushy up till now, but you're in for a rude awakening, let me tell you. You're going to the front line soon and it's my job to see that you're ready."

The men felt that after more than a year of training, they were ready. No one said anything.

"Right, you worthless lot, the soft times are over. Now you're goin' to learn to become soldiers, like what the King pays you for."

He paused for a moment, scowling at A-Company.

"Bayonet drill," he yelled. "I suppose you do know how to fix bayonets?"

"Yes, we bloody do," came a disgruntled voice from the ranks.

"'Oo said that?" Mildman roared. "'Oo was that talkin'?"

A-Company stood rigidly to attention, every last one of them, in perfectly dressed ranks. Nobody said a word.

"Ten seconds. That's 'ow long 'oomsoever was talkin' 'as to own up. Otherwise, the 'ole company will be punished."

Still silence.

"I'm waitin'. If no one owns up, I'll 'ave the lot of you runnin' on the spot, in full kit, till you get 'eart failure. It won't trouble my conscience one little bit. Now, 'oo the bloody 'ell was it that answered back?"

"It was me, Sergeant," called one of the men.

Sergeant Mildman approached the man in question and stood in front of him.

"What's your name?"

"Private 935 Winslow, Sergeant."

"Right, Private Winslow, you've saved your mates from punishment, but not yourself. You will report to me right 'ere, in full kit, at 19:00 hours. Understand?"

"Yes, Sergeant."

"And p'raps you'll learn to keep your useless gob shut in future."

"I hope so, Sergeant."

"Right," Mildman continued, not quite sure if Johnny Winslow was baiting him or not. "Let's get on with it." He gave the order to fix bayonets, and the Company spent the next ninety minutes repeating something they had done many times over before, during their previous training. They took turns to charge at sacks of straw, hanging from a beam. Each sack represented a German soldier, and they had to despatch him in the approved fashion – run at him while giving a good loud scream, thrust the bayonet into his belly, twist it, pull it out. Fighting with blade and point had, of course, been the business of war since long before the days of ancient Egypt. In this war, bayonets would account for less than one percent of all battle deaths, but soldiers still had to know the thrust, twist and pull that their predecessors had used at Alma, Waterloo, Dettingen, Blenheim, and countless other battles.

The 35th Middlesex knew what to do, but they practised it still, each man wondering if this was something he would actually have to do, in the heat of battle. Shooting someone, or hurling a grenade at the enemy, that was all very well, but standing within a couple of feet of a fellow human being and actually thrusting a steel blade into his belly, seeing the agony on his face as the blood gushed; that was something else entirely. Mind you, most of them reasoned, if the other bloke was about to kill you, or one of your mates, then you'd just have to spit him first – fair's fair.

Bayonet drill, square bashing, food, more drill, and more square bashing. The soldiers' day at Étaples ended in the early evening, with a meal and a little free time, but there was not much to occupy the men in the way of entertainment and, anyway, most of them were too tired to think of anything but sleep.

Johnny Winslow, however, had a special evening ahead of him that first day. He reported to Sergeant Mildman, as ordered, at 19:00 hours. He was carrying a full pack and his rifle. Mildman arrived at the appointed spot, on the dot of seven o'clock.

"You brought this upon yourself, Winslow," he said.

"Yes, Sergeant."

"Only yourself to blame."

"Yes, Sergeant."

Then, Sergeant Mildman had Johnny march, back and forth, across the parade ground at the double, his rifle held at high port. After half an hour or so, he ordered Johnny to march on the spot.

"You think this is enough?" he asked.

"Sergeant," Johnny replied, avoiding a yes or a no.

"You think I'm a bastard, don't you?"

"Sergeant.'

Mildman set Johnny marching across the parade ground again, to and fro. After twenty minutes or so, he gave the order to halt, not because he took pity on his victim, but because he was bored.

The sleeping arrangements at Étaples were less than luxurious. In fact, most of the men quartered there felt that they were terrible. The men slept in round bell tents, in lots of twelve, their heads at the outside, their feet towards the central wooden pole. Since Johnny was the last in that evening, he, by default, got the worst position of all, which was to lie with his head by the tent flap. If there was a breeze, which there usually was, he was the one who felt it most. Any time anyone had to leave the tent to use the latrine, Johnny was the one who had to move to let them out, and back in again. Twelve men to a tent was a very tight fit, and no one had been at all consoled when Corporal O'Malley had told them all that he could remember times when he had been one of twenty-two men squeezed into a tent that size.

Johnny tried to be as unobtrusive as possible when he opened the flap and stepped into the tent, but even so, he managed to disturb several of his comrades, and he was greeted by the smells that rose from eleven unwashed men, along with several growled comments.

"Shut the flap!"

"Be quiet!"

"Watch what you're doing, for God's sake!"

"That was my fuckin' leg you just trod on!"

And so on, with many more in the same vein. All part of the rich comradeship of army life.

Soon enough though, Johnny was in his own bedroll, lying as the twelfth slice of that particular soldier cake. When you have several lines of tents, with a dozen men sleeping in each, you are bound to get all sorts of sleeping noises. So it was in this tent. Some of those who had not woken up at Johnny's entrance were merrily snoring away, but not all of them were asleep. Eddie Ross was particularly uncomfortable, being six foot four inches tall and unable to stretch out fully. He had to lie with his legs slightly bent and, as such, hadn't managed to fall asleep yet. Les Mosterby, almost as tall, was having the same trouble.

Apart from the snoring, moaning, and other noises of men asleep en masse, there was another sound, clearly audible in the tent, the distant rumbling of artillery. Not a barrage, just rather like thunder over the horizon, but with a sharper edge to each crack.

"Ours, do you reckon?" someone asked.

"Yes, probably," another someone replied.

"Nah, I reckon it's Jerry's guns," said Harry Travis.

"No, definitely ours." That was Vic Rangle.

"How can you tell?" Travis challenged.

"Those are guns firing, but we're not hearing the sound of the shells actually exploding. So, they have to be ours. They're being fired here and then landing over in German occupied territory."

"You heard artillery before, Vic?"

As usual, Vic Rangle avoided answering any questions about his past life. Because he didn't want to lie to his comrades, he contented himself with, "It's just common sense really, when you think about it," which was a good way of not answering.

"Yes, I s'pose so."

They lay there, listening for a few moments more.

"People're getting killed by that lot, you know."

"Better them than us."

"I suppose we'll end up under something like that sooner or later." Hubert Snibley could be so pessimistic at times.

"Yes, probably."

"Shut up. I don't want to hear that sort of defeatist talk." Edwin Marvell took his responsibilities as a lance corporal very seriously.

"Sorry."

"You should be. Now can we get some kip please? It'll be time to get up before you know it."

In fact, it was several hours before they had to get up, but it seemed a lot less to the men who had slept in that cramped tent. The rest of their fortnight at 'Eat Apples', as the British soldiers came to refer to the place, consisted of more of the same. They relearned many of the drills and techniques they had acquired during the long months of training, in Yorkshire. They learnt new ways to fight, as well. They were taught how to kill with their bare hands, how to gouge out an enemy's eyes with their thumbs, the best way to cut a throat with a dagger. They had it dinned into them that they had to be ready to kill the enemy any way they could. War was not a game where you gave your opponent a sporting chance. This was life and death.

After two weeks, it was over. Not one man in the battalion was sad to say goodbye to the place. They marched out to the war, without a single regret that they were leaving. They never wanted to see the place again, and most of them didn't.

Chapter XXIII

A Train Journey

It was as though Étaples had tried to break them and had failed. In spite of the canaries and the dugouts, they were still the St. Marylebone Rifles, still proud and intact. Volunteers they may have been, civilians until only a year and a half ago, but the battalion that marched out of Étaples were soldiers to their bootstraps. Now they were again under the command of officers and NCOs who were not destined to sit protected in the rear areas, safe from harm, but were instead positioned by men, who would share their every danger and would survive or perish with them, as the fates of war would dictate.

No long, exhausting march awaited them this time, as A and B Companies headed for their new destination, with the other two companies to follow the next day. A railway track cut through one corner of the camp, and it was the matter of but a few minutes to reach the platform of the local station. While the men stood easy, the adjutant went to find the station's transport officer, a nervous, harried man, like most of his ilk. He first claimed to have received no notification that two companies of the 35th Middlesex and its headquarters staff were due to leave Étaples that day, but after a frank exchange of views with Captain Case, a telephone call or two, and a search through a stack of dockets on the table, in the corner of the small room that served as his office, their train was identified and they were directed to the end of a spur line, half a mile away, where their train, consisting of cattle cars and passenger carriages, waited for them. At the front, was a locomotive with steam up, giving off dyspeptic rumblings from inside its iron belly and occasionally letting off jets of steam in loud spurts. The engine driver, sullen and unshaven, in shabby blue overalls, watched the soldiers march up and wait to be given the order to board.

The carriages were for the officers, with the C.O. and senior officers in the one carriage marked '*1ère Classe*'. Lowly subalterns, like the brothers Snow, and the senior NCOs, had to make do with more spartan accommodations. The cattle cars were for the other ranks. The men of 2 Platoon climbed into the one designated for their use – a brown painted wooden box on wheels, with a sliding door in one side, no windows, and no furnishings, or seating of any kind, inside.

"So, this is what I have to put up with on my chauffeur's day off," remarked Johnny Winslow, as he climbed aboard.

"It doesn't look very comfortable," agreed Wilfred Leuchars.

In the scrimmage outside the door, Harry Travis saw the legend painted on the side of the car: '*8 chevaux où 40 hommes*'. He turned to Rollo Selway.

"Duchess, you've got lingo. What does that mean?"

"That, means that this delightful conveyance has been deemed suitable for either eight horses or, as in our case, forty men."

"But not both," remarked Johnny Winslow.

"I reckon," said Harry, after he had climbed in, "that it's only ever been used for horses. Or cattle. Look at the state of it."

The others saw what he meant. The wooden floor was worn and pitted, with some gaps showing through the planking. Straw was scattered about and the stink of horse and cow dung had permeated the wooden boards. In fact, more solid evidence of the previous occupants was still lying about, having been overlooked, or ignored, by whoever had been responsible for sweeping the wagon out.

"Never mind, Harry," said Bert Giddington. "You'll be fine, as long as you don't sit in it."

"I don't imagine anyone's going to be doing much sitting in here," said Alec Millcross. "Not the way they're packing us in."

He was right, of course. Forty men, complete with packs, inside of a cattle car, left very little room for manoeuvre.

"How long d'you think we'll be in here?" asked Joe Marren.

"Could be hours, could be days," replied Alec. "You've been in the army long enough to know that. Or maybe we'll all just stand around here for a few hours, then they'll have us all off again and marching somewhere."

"Just as long as we don't go back to Étaples."

"Amen to that," said Les Mosterby.

In fact, Alec Millcross was partly right. The train stayed motionless on the track for about an hour, then, all of a sudden, it gave a lurch forward, and there was a succession of clangs and bangs, as the couplings between the cars took up the slack. Inside the car, several men were thrown off balance, knocking into each other, cursing and crying out. Then, with a flurry of steam and noise, the engine began to move off, pulling its load behind it. Someone tried to slide the door shut but his comrades further inside the car shouted at him to leave it open. It was hot enough as it was without sealing them in.

They had all of them been on trains before, of course, but never in cattle cars, and never on one as slow as this. This train seemed incapable of reaching a speed faster than a leisurely trundle. It was a bright, sunny day and, if the car had been less crowded, it could actually have been a fairly pleasant journey.

After a short while, the men began to organise things, largely at the direction of Lance Corporal Edwin Marvell, who took charge of the situation.

"Right." He raised his voice above the general hubbub. "We could be in here for a while, so we may as well make things as comfortable as we can."

"Where're we going, Corp?" shouted someone.

"How long till we get there?" from someone else.

"I don't know," Edwin replied. "General Haig has not chosen to confide in me on this occasion. It could be a while, though, so I suggest that we all pile our packs up at that end of the wagon." He pointed to the end furthest from the door. "We can sort them out when we get to wherever it is that we're going."

A suggestion by a lance corporal had the force of an order, so the men began shucking off their packs and dumping them at the indicated end of the cattle car.

"Neatly, for God's sake," shouted Edwin. "Not just any old how. The more orderly you pile them, the more room there is for us."

Not wishing to be overshadowed, the other lance corporals began chivvying their men along. Except Lance Corporal Matthew Clay, who thought there were enough junior NCOs being officious.

"Nice work, Edwin," he said.

"Thanks. It's probably a good idea."

"It is." Clay looked round. "Have you seen O'Malley? He doesn't seem to be with us. Any idea where he is?"

"God knows. Probably sharing a compartment with the C.O., knowing him."

At that moment, Private Eddie Ross asked, "Where do we pee, Corp?"

"Out the door or down your trouser leg, take your choice," was Matthew Clay's answer. Not very helpful, of course, but then Clay never wanted to do anything that would make Eddie's life any easier; he had not forgotten being foiled in his attempt to seduce Eddie's sister at the party in Rochester. And it was certainly true that there were no toilet facilities at all in their wooden box.

While Eddie Ross was contemplating this answer to his question, and seeing if there were any particularly wide cracks in the floor he could pee through, the object of Matthew Clay's curiosity, Corporal Seamus O'Malley, was in another carriage. Maybe Edwin Marvell had overestimated the corporal's ingenuity, because he hadn't inveigled his way into the first class carriage with the senior officers, but he had managed to secure a seat in a third class compartment, with a group of platoon sergeants. All the other corporals were in the cattle cars with their men, but O'Malley, the old soldier, had endured his fill of travel like that over the years, so he had managed to organise a poker game with a group of sergeants before they left Étaples, and he had made sure that he lost just enough that they would want to continue the game on the journey to wherever it was. He regarded the loss of a franc or two, now and again, as nothing more than his train fare; besides, he'd get it back from them as the journey neared its end.

Sergeant Fred Quill was the only one of the five sergeants in the compartment who was not taking part in the game. He had wanted to boot O'Malley out, but his fellow sergeants had protested and then the train had begun to move, so O'Malley had ended up staying where he was. Now, they sat on the wooden benches of the compartment, facing each other, with one of the sergeant's packs on the floor between them, pressed into service as an improvised card table, a small pile of notes and coins in French currency resting upon it.

"You must be mad to play cards with this bloke," said Sergeant Quill, not for the first time.

"But it's me that's losin', Sergeant," O'Malley protested.

"I'll believe that when I see it."

"Such a suspicious nature must be a terrible burden, Sergeant."

"Call," said a sergeant from B-Company.

"Two fives," O'Malley showed his hand.

"Pair of nines," the sergeant crowed.

"You're too canny for me, Sergeant Brodie," remarked O'Malley, as the victorious sergeant scooped up the pot. "I'll be bankrupt before this train journey's over."

"Ha," cried Sergeant Quill.

He knew perfectly well that O'Malley had initiated this game as an excuse to travel in relative comfort, and he had spotted O'Malley's technique, which was to fold almost immediately at the start of most hands, leaving the four sergeants to battle it out between them. That way, he hardly lost a thing. Every so often, he would win a hand and recoup most of what he had lost and occasionally, just for show, he would play a hand, for not very high stakes, and lose, loudly.

The next hand, O'Malley folded almost at once, even though he had been dealt two tens. He was relying on instinct to tell him when the journey was nearing its end. Then, he would win two or three hands, in succession and recover most, or all, of his losses. Meanwhile, he sighed loudly in defeat as he placed his cards face down in front of him and shook his head sadly. A few minutes later he muttered admiring noises, as Sergeant Brodie again won a fairly respectable pot on the strength of a pair of sixes and some rather unsubtle bluffing. Fred Quill watched, puffing on his pipe. He knew O'Malley was a cheat and would probably pull a few strokes before the game was over, but as long as he wasn't affected, he was just going to enjoy the spectacle. He had warned his fellow sergeants and they had elected to take no notice. Now, three of them were several francs down and one had a modest pile of winnings in front of him – for the time being. So be it. Fred Quill relaxed and turned his gaze to the French countryside, which was slowly passing by the window.

Closer to the front of the train, in a compartment not much more comfortable than the one that Corporal O'Malley and his victims occupied, Charles and Arnold Snow sat with six fellow subalterns, all of them platoon commanders in the battalion. They were watching the same countryside roll by them and they were discussing where they were going. Their company commanders had told them that they were destined for a place called Lesmurs, but none of them had ever heard of it. Obviously, then, the discussion about the nature of the place was pure speculation, but those among them who had been to France before felt they were in a position to offer more informed opinions.

"Cobbled streets," said one. "All these villages have cobbled streets. They call it *pavé*"

"Do many of them speak English?" asked another.

"*Mais non!* Hardly any and, for some reason, a lot of those who do, pretend they can't."

"They've never forgiven us for Waterloo, you know," remarked another, a tall lieutenant, with red hair.

"That was a hundred years ago," protested Arnold Snow.

"A mere blink of an eye in the French folk memory, old boy," said Red Hair. "We stopped them from owning all of Europe and, no matter how cordiale the entente may be, it still sticks in their throats."

"Well, I found the French perfectly nice to me when we came here for a holiday two years ago."

"You've been here before?"

"Yes," said Charles. "The Boy and I spent a few days in Paris, the summer before all this started."

"What did you do there?"

"Saw the Louvre, went up the Eiffel Tower, visited Notre Dame and Sacré-Cœur."

"Well, there you are then. You were tourists, and they were nice to you while you were spending money there. Not like the real French at all."

"And how do you know?" asked Charles.

"My step father has a little place near Le Touquet. We pop over to spend time there three or four times a year, or at least we did before the war started. It's in a little village and the locals have never made us feel welcome. Most of them don't even throw a smile in our direction."

"Well, I think it's all jolly exciting," said a second lieutenant from B-Company, who didn't look old enough to shave yet., "I've never been to France before. Never been out of England at all, actually, except to the Isle of Wight."

"The Isle of Wight is part of England, Jeremy," said Red Hair.

"You know what I mean. It's the only time I have ever had to cross water by boat to get somewhere, until now. I'm looking forward to meeting more French people. I met several when the men were at Étaples and we were billeted nearby. They seemed nice enough."

"Is it true," another asked, "that the French government is actually charging the British army rent for the trenches we are occupying?"

"I've heard that rumour. Don't know if it's true."

"Well, if you don't know if it's true, then it's best not to repeat it," said Charles. "It's not the sort of thing to do the men's morale much good."

"Certainly. But I'll tell you one thing I'm pretty sure of, and that's that they are making us pay for every train that the army uses. Including this one."

"Are you sure?" asked Arnold.

"Absolutely sure. My brother-in-law works in Whitehall. He's actually in the department that deals with the payments. He told me."

"I see. Well, I hope they're not charging too much for this one. We don't seem to have been able to go faster than a walking pace so far."

At that moment, in the first class carriage, the C.O. was saying something similar, to his second in command.

"At this rate," said Lieutenant-Colonel Wintergrass, "we would have been better off marching. Is this sort of thing normal, Basil?"

"I really can't say, sir," replied Major Fullerton. "But it does seem rather slow."

"Slow? My Aunt Dolly could walk faster than we're going, with a fair wind behind her."

A joke by the battalion commander is always funny, and everyone in the compartment dutifully chuckled.

"I thought you'd been to France before, Basil."

"Yes sir, several times, and I don't think I was ever on a train this slow. They all seemed to be almost as good as ours, as I recall."

"I once made a journey by train that lasted for days," said the C.O. "Not because it was slow, but because of the distance."

"Indeed, sir?" said Captain Case. "Where was that?"

"It was after I retired from the army. Or at least thought I had," said the colonel with a rueful smile. "We went to visit my wife's people in Victoria, in British Columbia. Boarded a train of the Canadian Pacific, in Montreal. We had a sleeping compartment, of course, because we were on that train for days."

"How marvellous," remarked Major Fullerton.

"It was. The prairies were so utterly flat, they seemed to go on forever and, let me assure you, gentlemen, you have never seen such big, open skies in your life. Then, you come to the Rocky Mountains, which are spectacular. We stayed at Banff for a few days, before continuing on to Vancouver. It was a wonderful trip. If I come out the other end of this war in one piece, I'd like to do it again."

Silence fell on the compartment for a few moments, and then they felt a change in the train's movement.

"Hello, are we stopping?" asked the Colonel. "We can't be there already, surely?"

Major Fullerton opened the window and leaned out.

"No, we're not, sir. We don't seem to be anywhere in particular. We've probably stopped for signals or something."

"Well, I hope it doesn't take too long, whatever it is."

No one on the train knew why they had stopped, except the engine driver, and he wasn't telling anyone. Down in the cattle truck where the members of 2 Platoon were travelling, this delay was taken as something of a godsend, by at least one of the soldiers.

Private Eddie Ross had been experiencing increased distress due to his need to urinate. It dawned on him, eventually, that Lance Corporal Clay's suggestion of peeing out of the open door was not completely out of the question.

"Alec," he called out to Private Millcross. "Hold my trouser waistband at the back will you? I'm going to pee out of the door and I don't want to fall out."

"Yes, of course. Just as long as it doesn't all blow back in at us."

They got into position for this little manoeuvre, watched by several interested comrades, who offered ribald advice and similarly unhelpful comments, when the train slowed to a halt.

"Now what?" someone complained.

Eddie Ross, though, saw the answer to his problems, which would save him from having to urinate like that in front of his comrades – something most of them would have done without batting an eyelid. About twenty yards away from the train track was a small clump of trees, at the edge of a field.

"Just what I want," he said to no one in particular, and he jumped out of the car.

"Better hurry, Eddie," Alec Millcross called after him.

But Eddie Ross had only one thing in mind. It took him but a few seconds to reach the trees, stand behind one so that he was relatively screened from the train, unbutton his flies, and start to pee. This was what he had been waiting for and the relief was luxurious. He stood there with his eyes shut, a grateful smile on his face, as the seconds, many of them, passed.

It was at this point, when Eddie Ross was in mid-stream, that the inevitable happened. The locomotive gave a deep sigh and started to move again, slowly at first, before accelerating to a crawl.

"Eddie," yelled Alec. "You better get back here now!"

"Come on, Eddie," shouted Johnny Winslow.

As every man on the face of the earth knows, there is a point during urination when things can not be stopped, no matter how urgent the reason. Eddie had passed that point so, for several seconds, he had to stand helplessly, peeing away, as he saw the train judder into movement.

"Eddie, for God's sake," Alec shouted.

Eventually, their friend appeared round the trees and began to run after the train which, meanwhile, seemingly out of a sense of perversity, was going a bit more rapidly than before, and Eddie had to run as fast as he could to get to the car. Meanwhile his friends were encouraging him with applause and yells.

"Eddie! Faster!"

"Hurry, Eddie!"

"Almost here! Come on, Eddie!"

Eddie Ross did manage to reach the open door of the wagon, where several willing hands reached down to grab him and help pull him in.

"That was close," Eddie remarked to his chums.

Lance Corporal Marvell had seen all this, and he reckoned that Private Ross had had enough of a scare in almost being left behind, so he forbore to reprimand him at length. "Do your flies up, man. You look like a vagrant," was all he said.

With that little bit of excitement behind them, the men settled down as best they could to enjoy, or endure, the remainder of the journey, dependent on how comfortable they had been able to make themselves. The luckiest group were the men who were sitting in the open doorway, their legs dangling over the edge. The train was not going fast enough for this to be dangerous and the lance corporals did not interfere. As though to join them in their joy at having left Étaples, the sun shone down on them – this was a day of brightness and celebration.

Harry Travis looked up and saw an aeroplane flying over, inaudible above the noise of the train.

"What's that one, Jimmy?" he asked Private Hope, who was sitting next to him. All aircraft looked the same to Harry, just grey shapes in the sky, but Jimmy Hope could usually tell one from another.

Private Jimmy Hope looked up at the aeroplane that Harry Travis had pointed out, squinting slightly against the sun.

"I think it's a BE2. Can't be absolutely sure, but that's what it looks like. Eyes like a hawk, me." It was true that Jimmy Hope had a very piercing gaze when he looked at anything, as though he were sizing it up, under hair so thick and resistant to organisation that Sergeant Quill once told him, using the imagery of the war, that he was bringing his own barbed wire with him.

"More importantly," said Percy Glass, "Is it one of ours or one of theirs?"

"One of ours."

"That's a relief then."

Harry Travis grinned. "Jimmy will be up there in one of those one day soon, won't you!"

"That's right. I'll be in the Royal Flying Corps, flying my plane in the clouds, while you lot are all stuck in some muddy trench somewhere. And will I feel sorry for you?"

"Most probably not," said Percy. They all liked Jimmy Hope and there was no malice in his comment. They all trod gently round his ambitions, not wanting to damage them in any way.

They fell silent for a bit, then Jimmy said, "It looks nice, France, doesn't it?"

"Yes," replied Johnny. "And very peaceful. You wouldn't think there was a war on, just to look at it."

"I've never been abroad before," remarked Harry, which did not surprise any of his friends, because there was nothing unusual about that.

"Neither have I," said Johnny.

"What about you, Vic?" Harry asked Private Rangle, who was sitting in the doorway with them and, true to his usual form, was not saying much. "Have you ever been abroad before?"

"Oh, once or twice, yes."

"Really? Where to?"

"India, Egypt, Malta, places like that. I wonder how much longer this journey is going to take."

This was taken by his comrades, correctly, as signal not to probe any further and the little group in the doorway fell silent again, quietly enjoying the ride. Behind them, inside the car, men chatted, rested, read, tried to sleep, or just sat quietly with their thoughts. Rollo Selway re-read, not for the first time, his latest letter from Erika. Alec Millcross, clutching a pencil stub and a sheet of paper, attempted to write a poem about train travel but he couldn't concentrate because behind him Privates Marren and Tunniford were arguing with a group of men from 1 Platoon about whether, in a mechanised war like this, they would actually have much use for their bayonets.

"You can always use your bayonet as a tin opener, I suppose, when they bring up the rations," said Colin Tunniford.

After a few miles more, the train began to slow again to a walking pace and then, for no reason that anyone could see, it came to a halt in the open countryside, to ironic jeers from some of its passengers.

They remained there for ten minutes, then twenty, and still there was no movement. The locomotive sat at the front, groaning and exhaling steam.

"What's going on, Corp?" Bert Giddington called to Lance Corporal Clay.

"How the bleedin' hell do I know?"

"Just wondered."

"Do you suppose we'll still be on the train tonight? Will we have to sleep in here?" asked Alec Millcross.

"I don't know. If we do, then we do, and that's that."

"Sufficient unto the day," remarked Rollo Selway.

"Yes," Matthew Clay agreed, not knowing what that meant. Private Selway was always coming out with things like that. It came from having had a posh education, he supposed.

The train had come to a halt alongside a field of growing corn, and a dirt track ran down the side nearest the railway, and along this track, to appreciative cheers and shouts from the soldiers further along the train, came three attractive, young French girls, leading a donkey cart. The oldest must have been about twenty, the other two a few years younger. When they came alongside the car where 2 Platoon was riding, the soldiers joined in the good natured shouting.

"Parlee voo! Parlee voo," shouted Harry Travis.

"Say *oui, cherie!*" called Colin Tunniford.

"Look at the blonde one," said Bert Giddington to Johnny Winslow. "I wouldn't mind that at all."

"You're a married man, Bert."

"I know, but there's no harm in looking, or imagining."

"Leave them for us single men."

Maybe the shouting and applauding from the men of the platoon was more inviting than that from the other cars, or maybe it was more flattering. For whatever reason, the French girls brought the donkey cart to a halt and waved back at the men, who cheered even louder. They tried to shout something back, but they couldn't make themselves heard above the good natured din.

"What's that, my darling? Is it me you want?" shouted Bert Giddington

"*Je t'aime*," shouted Johnny Winslow, which was almost the full extent of his French.

"I like that little one with the ribbon in her hair," said Joe Marren, to no one in particular.

"Oh, cruel fate, to dangle such beauty before us," said Colin Tunniford.

"Why don't you paint their picture, Tunniford?" jeered Lance Corporal Clay.

In the cart were several wicker baskets and they appeared to be full of green apples. Pointing at them, Colin Tunniford shouted: "Throw us an apple, darling."

The French girls giggled and smiled, but did not move off.

"Right," said Colin. "This is too good a chance to waste." And the next thing, he was out of the train and running the few yards to where the girls were.

"Apple?" he said to one of them, pointing at the basket of fruit, then miming eating one. "Apple *pour moi?*"

"*Ah, vous voulez une pomme,*" said the oldest.

"Yes, that's right. *Pomme*. Can I have a *pomme*?"

"*Mais, bien sur*," said the girl, and she reached into one of the baskets and handed Colin Tunniford an apple.

"*Merci, cherie*," cried Colin, and kissed her on the cheek, while she smiled and giggled, the watching soldiery cheering. Then, all of a sudden, it was as though once Colin Tunniford had joined them and was chatting to them, a barrier had been broken and several more of the men decided that they didn't want to be left out. The girls were surrounded by soldiers who had jumped out of the train. Nothing was going to happen with the girls, but they still wanted to be close to them, to talk to them for a few minutes. Vic Rangle, though, sat in the doorway of the wagon, smiling bleakly at his chums.

"My name's Harry," Harry Travis told the girls, pointing at his chest. "Harry. *Moi* Harry."

"'Allo 'Arree," replied the oldest girl. "*Je m'appelle Blanche*." She used the same identification technique as Harry, pointing at her chest. "*Blanche*."

"Nice to meet you, Blanche. This is Colin, and this is Johnny." Harry indicated his friends.

Joseph Marren, meanwhile, was trying to make himself understood to one of the other girls, a dark haired beauty, who was staring uncomprehendingly at the strange man in the strange uniform.

"What I'm trying to say is, I think you're very pretty. Have you ever been to England? I come from a town called Banbury; well, just outside it really."

Johnny Winslow was having more success telling Blanche what he thought of her.

"I think you're beautiful. Tell her, Duchess," he called to Rollo Selway, who was standing in the wagon doorway, watching them.

"*Il dit qu'il pense que tu es tres belle*," Rollo shouted to Blanche, who smiled and laughed, looked a bit bashful, and said, "*Merci*," to Johnny, before planting a kiss on his cheek, to cheers and laughter from all present. Johnny put both his hands on his heart, sighed, and looked up at the sky with a big smile on his face, which was greeted with more laughter.

"'Oo the bloody 'ell gave you permission to get off the train?" a voice roared, and they all turned to see Company Sergeant-Major Bull striding towards them. They had noticed this little get-together from the compartment where the senior NCOs were riding and, to save Regimental Sergeant-Major Callow getting involved, CSM Bull had volunteered to deal with it.

"What do you think this is, a bloody charabanc, 'oppin' on and off whenever you want? Stop all this malarkey right now! Any man back not on the train in ten seconds, I'll be taking his name for company defaulters, do you hear me?"

They did, of course, and no reply to this question was expected.

"Well don't just stand there staring at me like a lot of wax dummies – move!"

And they did.

"'Arree, 'Arree," Blanche called, and when Harry Travis turned, she thrust a basket of apples at him.

"*Pour vous. Bonne chance!*"

"Oh, *merci*, lass," he replied, and got back on the train.

CSM Bull walked back to the carriage where the NCOs' compartment was, hoping to get there before the train started moving again, so he would not be forced into the indignity of running after it.

He need not have worried. The train sat motionless for at least another fifteen minutes. The moment had passed, though, as far as Blanche and her sisters were concerned and they moved off along the dirt road, their patient donkey pulling the cart with its load, minus one basket of apples.

After this little incident, the men were more subdued. They waited for the train to start again and some of them munched on the apples they had been given. Eventually, with much noise and steam, the engine came back to life and they were off again.

This time, they managed to achieve a respectable pace, the sort of speed they had come to expect from trains, and the men sitting in the doorway retreated back inside the wagon.

The train stopped several times more before they reached their destination, but no one got off again. In the car where the poker game had continued, uninterrupted since they had pulled out of Étaples, Sergeant Quill remarked that, by his calculations, they ought to be almost there by now, though he didn't say where 'there' was. The next hand, Corporal O'Malley found himself in possession of three sixes. He knew that Sergeant Brodie had a pair of sevens and that one of the other sergeants had two twos and two fours. With much grumbling and predictions of financial ruin, he allowed the other two to drive up the value of the pot, each convinced that he held the winning hand, until someone finally called and he showed what he had.

"And there was me certain that you had a full house at least, Sergeant," O'Malley said as he scooped in the pot. "D'ye think we have time for one more hand? It looks like my luck may be beginning to change, and not a moment to soon, let me tell you." Before anyone could say anything one way or another, he dealt out another hand.

As they began to bet, and one of the other Sergeants hesitated, before raising the pot by a franc, O'Malley remarked: "Oh, you've got to watch Sergeant Brodie, Sergeant. He's a born poker player down to his fingertips. He'll have the shirt off your back before you know it."

Sergeant Brodie, flattered into carelessness, bet far too much on a weak hand and, a few moments later, O'Malley was scooping the pot in, again expressing surprise that he had won.

"Right, put the cards away, Corporal," said Sergeant Quill. "The game's over. We're probably almost there."

O'Malley was happy to do that. In the last hands, he had won back almost all that he had lost. The way he calculated it, he had paid just over one franc for a seat in a passenger car. Once they were settled into camp, wherever it was, he would begin the serious business of winning at cards and Crown & Anchor, against the men.

The men were surprised when the train actually stopped at a station. They had resigned themselves to spending the night in the cattle car, but all of a sudden their officers and NCOs were ordering them off and into the courtyard outside the station, where they formed up in ranks of four, by platoon.

Lieutenant-Colonel Wintergrass was at the head of the column and, like all officers above the rank of captain, he was on horseback. Major

Fullerton gave the order to move off and the men began to march. It was dark by now and, after a couple of miles, they came to the town of Albert, the largest town in that sector of the front. There was plenty of activity within the town, with men on passes spending the evening there, supply wagons, lorries, and even horse drawn artillery trundling through. They saw several examples of the sort of damage that artillery could do. Every so often, a burned out or demolished building presented itself, but life seemed to go on as normal around the ruins. They all saw for themselves the golden statue of the Virgin Mary, leaning precariously from the top of the steeple of Albert cathedral, where a German shell had pushed her, early on in the war. She had already found her place in military legend – it was said that when she finally fell, the war would end. Every one of them, from the C.O. downwards, looked up at her as they marched past, but she showed no sign of falling.

There was plenty of noise in Albert, of motors, marching feet, voices both soft and raised, orders being shouted, hoof beats on the cobbles, and in several places they heard music. And they could also hear, in the distance, the rumble of artillery and the crackle of small arms fire.

"We march to the sound of the guns," said Alec Millcross.

In fact, they didn't march that far. After they had passed through Albert, they found themselves on a dirt road, lined, like so many roads in France, with poplar trees. Four miles down that road and they came to a signpost, that told them they were entering the village of Lesmurs. As far as they could tell, it was a small collection of houses and it appeared to be fast asleep. Just the other side of Lesmurs, they came to a field. The order to left wheel was given, and they marched into what was going to be their home for the time being.

Pioneers had erected long, geometrically perfect lines of bell tents; the battalion cooks, who had gone on ahead, had set up their stoves and had a warm meal ready for them to eat. NCOs walked to and fro, giving orders, making sure that each platoon was allotted sufficient tent space, that equipment was stowed, and sentries posted at the gate. The senior officers, satisfied that the men were all fed and accommodated, rode back to the village, where billets awaited them. Eventually, after meals had been eaten, duties posted, inspections made, and all men were accounted for, A and B Companies of the 35th Middlesex settled in for the night. It had been a long day and, except for those men who were detailed for sentry duty, they presently fell asleep, rising when roused the next day, to breathe in the moist morning air as they dressed for duty. Rooks were cawing in a clump of trees at the end of the field, artillery was still rumbling in the distance, and they took a closer look at this place where the war had brought them.

Chapter XXIV

Pompette's

The village of Lesmurs was set in farmland, to the west of a small ridge that each morning briefly delayed the arrival of the first sunlight. As their ancestors had done for centuries, the villagers rose early to man the little village shops, tend the crops, to sow and to harvest, to feed the livestock and, once a week, to take their wares to market in the town of Albert, a few miles down the tree-lined road, past the wayside Calvary erected in 1872. It had been blessed by the local bishop, to replace the one that had been destroyed when the Prussians had swept through two years before. At night they retired with the sun, to rest before the labours of the next day. Half a mile away, behind a stone wall and at the end of a very long drive, stood an eighteenth century château, quite small as such things go, previously the home of minor aristocracy and owned, since 1895, by a Monsieur Barsadot. Barsadot was a rich industrialist who, since becoming a widower three years before, seldom visited the place, but still kept up a staff of four locals to look after the building, inside and out. As an absentee landlord, he was one of the major employers in Lesmurs. On Sundays, the villagers attended mass at the church of Ste. Agnes, which they shared with the neighbouring village of Eséreé. This had been the way of life in Lesmurs since the Bourbons had ruled France, through the reigns of both Napoleons and through all three republics. At first, the coming of a war did not seem to the villagers to be reason enough to change their solid, comforting, and undemanding existence.

Or so they may have told themselves, but the war came to Lesmurs and the life of the village changed drastically. Now, with the conflict nearly two years old, almost all of the young men of the area had gone to be soldiers, and several of them would never be coming back. The village curé, Père Desfelles, had been able to offer comfort as best he could to grieving parents on several occasions, and he was sure he would have to do so again many times before the war ended. People were beginning to wonder who would be left to work the land in the future.

The front line was just a few miles away, but they were fortunate that this was a quiet sector. They heard artillery quite often, alongside the crackle of small arms fire. Once in a long while, an enemy shell landed in one or other of their fields and, occasionally, they saw aircraft flying overhead, but there was nothing in Lesmurs to attract the attentions of the Germans and, if they tried hard enough, they could pretend for a short while, now and again, that things were as they always had been.

True, soldiers of the French army had come. The officers had stayed at the château, which M. Barsadot had put at the disposal of the government for the duration of the war, while the other ranks lived in tents erected in neat lines, in fields requisitioned for that purpose, in return for compensation that, the farmers grumbled to each other, was not generous enough. The officers told their men to behave, the curé warned the villagers from the pulpit of the dire consequences of liaisons between the visiting soldiers and the young women of the area, and life in Lesmurs once again found its own equilibrium, as the soldiers by turn did duty in the front, support, and rear sectors, with rest periods in between, in and around the village. In this quiet sector, live and let live was the tacit understanding between the French and German armies. Even with the carnage of Verdun to the south, the attempted exsanguination of France, here life in the trenches was placid, as such things go, and Lesmurs continued its slumberous existence.

Things began to change in the spring of 1916. France needed more of her soldiers at Verdun and, as they moved out of Lesmurs, they were replaced by British troops, who came in large numbers in preparation for the coming offensive – the big push, that everyone had long been talking about. Among them were regiments of the New Army, and thus it was that the 35th Middlesex Regiment was eventually posted to

Lesmurs. This latest development was not a cause for joy among the villagers. Not only were these soldiers from a foreign army – allies, yes, but not French – but their presence had aroused the interest of a hitherto quiescent enemy, who had decided to welcome the new arrivals with more frequent artillery fire, to both the front and rear areas.

The British had been in possession of this sector for some months by the time the 35th Middlesex arrived. As such, the villagers of Lesmurs were, by now, used to their allies from across the Channel, whom they greeted with either a guarded welcome or with sullen indifference. Not a few of them were quite happy to let the Germans keep whatever parts of France and Belgium they occupied, just as long as their lives were no longer subject to upheaval. Others found themselves able to use the presence of foreign troops, in large numbers, to good advantage. Farmers could charge rent for fields that were lying fallow, making them available for battalions to bivouac, rent that was higher than that paid by the French government for the same purpose, and thus the local farmers welcomed the British presence. In one such field, were the St. Marylebone Rifles quartered.

The field was surrounded by a tall hedgerow that had been there for longer than anyone could remember; since before the time of Richelieu probably. High and impenetrable, it formed a natural barrier to anyone trying to enter or leave the field by stealth. At the gate, two sentries were on duty, and the men lived in the same round bell tents they had all come to know and hate. Officers, the rank of captain and above, lived in billets in the village, but lowly subalterns, like Second Lieutenants Charles and Arnold Snow, had to make do with small tents; although at least they slept one to a tent, not twelve.

During the days, the Tommies drilled, cleaned, marched, attended lectures, and, with the exception of those who found themselves on duty, were permitted to sample the delights of Lesmurs in the evenings, provided they were back inside the camp by 11:59 pm. This was all very well, except that Lesmurs, which as a rule tended to go to sleep early, had very few delights to sample. There was a small bar, with enough room to seat maybe ten people, but this was the haunt of local regulars, who were not about to let the British soldiers displace them. The Tommies, meanwhile, had little to do other than wander the streets, buy wine or beer to drink outside, and generally loiter about – unless they were lucky enough to be able to hitch a ride in an army lorry, or from some friendly local with a car, or more likely a horse and cart, into Albert. Even then, there was always the risk of not being able to get back to camp in time to avoid punishment for being absent without leave. Some men, having sampled everything that Lesmurs had to offer, did not even bother to leave camp of an evening. Those men who had been hoping to partake of *la vie Parisienne*, were severely disappointed by Lesmurs. In fact, some of the prominent citizens of Lesmurs had made representations to senior British officers that they were less than delighted to have soldiers in quantity, wandering aimlessly about the village every evening, their hobnail boots scraping the cobblestones, at a time when all good citizens were trying to sleep.

That was when Monsieur and Madame Pompette came into their own. It was M. Pompette's idea; he had been to Albert several times since the start of the war, and he had seen the many estaminets which had sprung up for the refreshment of the soldiery. Some were well appointed, well stocked bars, complete with hot food, and sophisticated cabarets. These were usually the territory of officers only and, when seating space was in short supply, senior officers had priority. In the army, it was ever thus. Others – and it was these that M. Pompette saw, marked, learned, and inwardly digested – were larger, noisier, and had less of a variety of drinks available. Some confined themselves only to beer and wine. These were where the other ranks went to relax, paying inflated prices for whatever drinks were on offer, and enjoying a change of scene from inside the camp.

There may have been laws in France, regulating the condition and operation of catering establishments. If there were, M. Pompette knew little of them and cared even less. These were different times, after all. Certain aspects of life, normal in peacetime, were naturally overlooked in the confusion of war. He owned two huge barns, and he really only needed one for the smooth running of his farm, so he decided that the other one would make an excellent estaminet. Nothing sophisticated –

just the swept interior of a barn, with stone flags for a floor and a wooden roof and walls, which, in spite of the clean-up, still harboured a vague hint of cow manure in the air, as a reminder of what the building had previously been used for – with long tables and benches, like a dining hall, which could be fashioned out of unseasoned planking. Likewise there was a counter across one end of the barn, to serve as a bar.

It took him, and the two of his four sons who had not yet been called up for military service, two weeks to convert the barn into an estaminet, which he named *Le Repaire des Lions* – The Lions' Den – out of deference to his British customers, and one Tuesday evening he opened for business. With a stroke of marketing genius, he positioned one of his sons, driving a horse and cart, outside the gate of the field where the closest British battalion was bivouacked. As soldiers left the camp that evening, looking for a diversion for a few hours, the young man greeted them, with what little English he had learned, just for this occasion.

"'Allo Tommy! You come drink? I take you. Nice bar, I take you."

This, not surprisingly, immediately aroused the interest of the soldiers who heard him.

"What bar, mate?"

"Nice bar. Good drink. Beer. I take you now."

"Where is it? Albert?"

"No Albert. Lesmurs. Five minute. I take you."

"A bar in Lesmurs? For us soldiers?"

"Oui, Lesmurs. Bar for Tommy."

"Alright, matey, that sounds good. Let's go have a butcher's."

Eight soldiers clambered aboard the cart, and a few minutes later they were delivered to the barn, where M. and Mme. Pompette, their youngest son, their daughter, and one of M. Pompette's farm workers, were waiting to greet them, offering beer and wine at a low price. The other son, meanwhile, took the horse and cart back to the camp and, in no time, had found another cartload of willing customers.

In time, a very short time, the reputation of The Lions' Den spread among the British battalions camped in and near Lesmurs, and the place was always packed in the evenings. It was crowded, noisy, smoky, usually good natured. The soldiers themselves tended to eject troublemakers when necessary; they had no wish to jeopardise their one place of entertainment. The special low prices of the first few evenings did not last long, of course, but that did not seem to worry the soldiers. M. Pompette still had one or other of his sons at the camp gates every evening, to bring customers in, and at 11:30pm, the cart was available to take any soldier who did not feel like walking, back to camp – for a small price, of course. After a couple of weeks, he arranged for a second horse and cart to bring in soldiers from another battalion, encamped just outside Esérée, a couple of miles away. Once a week, M. Pompette went into Albert to deposit the takings at his bank and to buy more supplies. What was more, he had a friend who knew someone, who knew someone else, who knew how to get hold of cigarettes, in bulk, at a very good price. Not one hundred percent legal, of course, but this bothered M. Pompette not at all, neither did it the soldiers who gladly bought them from him.

By the time the 35th Middlesex arrived, Pompette's – no one ever called it by its real name in spite of the red lettered sign hanging over the main door – was well established, successful, and ready to welcome them and their money.

That first evening, after everyone had settled in at camp and every inspection had taken place, several members of the St. Marylebone Rifles walked out of the camp looking for an evening's diversion from their duties. They had but a few days before they went up the line, and they had no intention of wasting their precious free moments. Ten of them walked out, to be greeted by one of the young Pompette fils, anxious to show the new arrivals where all the fun was. By this time, he knew a bit more English and had his routine down pat.

"Good night, Tommy. If you want beer, come with me. I show you a good bar to go."

This was enough of an invitation to the soldiers of A-Company. Somehow all ten of them managed to get aboard the hay cart, and they were transported to Pompette's. A few minutes later, Privates Travis, Giddington, Marren, Selway, Ross, Winslow, Leuchars, Glass, Hope, and Millcross walked into the estaminet.

It was already full, crowded with soldiers from the 35th Middlesex and from a territorial unit camped near Eserée, but the gang from 2 Platoon managed to squeeze themselves onto the benches at the end of one of the long tables. The Pompette daughter saw them arrive and came over to take their orders.

"Beer, wine for you?" she asked.

"Do you have any brandy?" asked Wilfred Leuchars.

"Beer, wine for you?"

"That's all you have?"

The girl had exhausted her knowledge of English and just stared back at the men, her eyebrows raised in enquiry. A lance corporal in the Territorials sitting next to them, broke their impasse.

"You won't get a brandy here, mate. Strictly beer and wine, this place."

They thanked him and ordered eight beers, and red wine for Alec Millcross and Rollo Selway.

"Beer's alright," said the lance corporal. "You can see them open the bottles and pour it. But you'll never actually see them open a bottle of wine. They bring the bottles in from the back, already opened."

"So?" asked Percy Glass.

"Well, they obviously water it, of course. Makes it go further."

Mlle. Pompette arrived at this point, with a large tray bearing ten glasses and set about distributing them.

"D'you water down the wine, love?" asked Harry Travis, only to be answered by a smile and a nervous giggle, before the girl walked back to the bar.

"Doesn't understand," said the lance corporal.

"Nice, though," said Johnny Winslow, watching her retreating back.

"Out of bounds. Old man Pompette'll have your balls for breakfast if you try anything with her."

"If he finds out."

"He'll find out. And he can make life very difficult for you. I've heard he slips a few francs to the military police every so often, to make sure there's no official interference here, and they'd be only too happy to pin some bogus charge on you that'll have you locked up for a long time. That or duff you up some dark night. No, if you want any of that sort of thing, you have to go to Albert. A few brothels there. The stories I could tell you." He noticed Rollo Selway sipping his wine. "Well, am I right? Do they water it?"

Selway took another sip and, playing to the gallery, frowned slightly and looked at the ceiling. Then he sniffed his glass, took another sip, licked his lips and opined.

"Hmmm," he said.

"He knows his wine, does Duchess," said a grinning Joe Marren.

"A light little wine," said Selway. "With an understated bouquet and less body than one would perhaps hope for. Not one of the great vintages, of course."

"Of course," laughed Johnny Winslow.

"But in my humble opinion, based on just this one sampling, I find myself irresistibly drawn to the conclusion that there has been an addition, since the bottle was opened, of H2O."

"Of what?" asked Bert Giddington.

"Water," said Alec Millcross, the only other wine drinker in the group. "I thought so too. I'll probably stick to beer in future."

"Water or no, it's not completely unpleasant," said Selway, looking round. "This place seems to be doing a very good business."

"Yes. They say old Pompette is getting rich as Croesus because of this place," said the lance corporal. "Don't know if it's true, but it wouldn't surprise me."

"Have you been here long?" asked Alec Millcross.

"About half an hour."

"No, I meant here. Lesmurs."

"Oh, just over a month. We've done one stint up the line so far. We came out three days ago."

"What was it like?" asked Alec, posing the question they all were wondering.

"Very different from what we expected, I can tell you that much. Much dirtier, much more uncomfortable than anything we experienced in training. Food's worse, everything's worse."

The lads nodded, but this was not too surprising.

"And then there's the rats."

"Rats?" Johnny Winslow shuddered.

"Yes, millions of the fuckers. They get everywhere."

"Oh, I don't like rats," shuddered Percy Glass.

"Well, you better get used to them. You can't escape them. Them and the lice."

"Lice? Oh, God."

"You'll be lousy after being up the line. Can't be helped."

"Isn't there a delousing procedure or something?" asked Percy Glass.

"Yeah, there is, when you come out of the line, for all the good it does. If you listen carefully, you can probably hear the lice laughing.

Well, rats and lice; not pleasant, but no doubt they would learn to live with them. They weren't here for a holiday, after all, but this wasn't what they really wanted to know. This was all peripheral to it.

"Yes," said Bert Giddington. "But what's it actually like?" What he meant, of course, was what was it actually like, being in the trenches?

"Could be worse," the lance corporal said. "At the moment there are Saxons in the opposite trench, not Prussians, so you can be glad of that. They aren't especially aggressive, but they won't let you go taking any liberties. They probably know the big push is coming, somewhere or other, and they've got the wind up a bit."

"Was anyone in your battalion killed?" Joe Marren wanted to know.

"Lord, yes. We lost several to shellfire and mortars – mortars are right bastards. You can hear them coming and if they're headed for your bit of trench, then that's it. There's no taking cover from them. And then there are the snipers. No matter how relaxed things are, they'll shoot you given half a chance. We lost quite a few men to snipers."

He noticed Eddie Ross, sitting at the end of one of the benches. "How tall are you, mate?" he asked.

"Six foot four."

"Strewth. You'll be lucky if you last a day. The tall ones are always the first to get it. They forget to crouch and pretty soon, bang!"

"I'm sure Eddie will remember to be careful." Johnny Winslow didn't like the turn the conversation had taken. "Any words of advice for us?"

"Yes. Don't go to the latrine during the daytime. Don't go at all if you can help it, but definitely don't go during the daytime."

"Why not?" asked Alec.

"Flies, mate. A trench latrine isn't much more than a plank over a hole in the ground, so it's best avoided anyway, but it's always full of flies. As soon as you sit down, you disturb the flies and they rise in a huge black swarm."

"But flies don't sting or bite, do they? They can't harm you?" said Percy Glass.

"No, but the Germans can, mate. They can see the sudden cloud of flies from back in their trench, and they'll send over a shell, or a mortar, to blow up the latrine and whichever poor sod's using it."

"I can't believe—"

"Well, you better believe it, 'cause it happened to a mate of mine. Blown to bits while having a crap. And I've heard of it happening on many other occasions."

"They never told us about that in training."

"Listen, half of what you were taught in training you can forget. The other half you can adapt to circumstances. But you can be absolutely sure, the front line won't be much like you were told to expect."

This rather sombre note didn't match the jolly atmosphere of Pompette's and no one at that end of that long table said much for a few moments, each lost in his own thoughts, but then Mlle. Pompette appeared to take their order for another round of drinks. Same again – eight beers and two red wines, watered down or not, and someone asked the lance corporal what he wanted. He gladly accepted a beer from them and, sensing that they wanted no further talk of being killed by the Germans, went on to tell a few stories, real or imagined, about what he had got up to at his favourite brothel in Albert. There are few things more boring than listening to another man boasting of his conquests, especially his paid conquests, so the group from 2 Platoon found their attention wandering. Some of them began talking among themselves. After a few minutes, Rollo Selway saw Les Mosterby and Hubert Snibley walk into the place and, as they stood in the doorway, bewildered by the mass of khaki humanity crammed onto the benches, he stood up and waved to them.

"Les! Hubie!" he called to his chums, and they made their way over. "Shift up, everyone," he said and, somehow, they found enough room on the benches for two more.

"What took you so long? asked Harry Travis.

"Couldn't get away," said Mosterby. "That bastard O'Malley kept finding things for us to do. Last thing was, he had me inspecting tent pegs, making sure they were all hammered into the ground at the correct angle."

"Bloody bastard," muttered Bert Giddington.

"He is," agreed Hubert Snibley. "I stayed behind to keep Les company."

Someone signalled to Mlle. Pompette and they got in beers for the two late arrivals, before everyone settled down again for an evening of serious drinking. There was a piano in one corner of the barn, something M. Pompette had bought cheap, probably because it was not exactly in tune, and it was there for anyone who could play it and wanted to. Soldiers liked to sing. German soldiers, for all their militarism, liked sentimental songs. British soldiers, especially at this stage in the war, preferred jolly, up tempo songs, that they could sing to raise their spirits, at rest or when marching. Sometimes they adapted existing songs to their own purpose, often with words they would never dream of singing back home, among their loved ones, and sometimes they sang songs that had been composed by members of their own ranks, though usually their origins were impossible to determine. This evening, a corporal from another regiment sat on the upturned barrel that served as a piano stool and started to play. Everyone in the place recognised the tune and joined in – *Pack Up Your Troubles In Your Old Kit Bag*. They sang chorus after chorus, with even old Pompette and his wife managing to hum along to it. They had heard it enough times since the British had been in Lesmurs. Then the pianist started on *Are We Downhearted?*, and again everyone joined in. The mood of the place was one of cheer and optimism. The men there from the 35th Middlesex were apprehensive about what was shortly to come, yes, but they had not experienced the loss of a single man yet, and in the hearts of each one of them was the certainty that, whatever might befall him during the coming weeks, months, or even years, whatever might happen to his mates, he would survive.

And so ended the evening. The men drank more together. Either their constitutions were very strong, or maybe M. Pompette did water his wine a lot – or maybe even both were true – but Alec Millcross and Rollo Selway were both almost as sober as they had been when they'd arrived. The rest, the beer drinkers, varied in condition. Harry Travis gave no signs of having drunk more than a glass or two, while Johnny Winslow needed to be helped back to the camp by his friends.

They arrived back safely before midnight and went to sleep in the bell tents that they had at first despised, but were now becoming used to – tents which were far more comfortable than anything they could expect in the front line, where they would be going in a few days.

Chapter XXV

The Trenches

The trenches – two words that encapsulated the war on the Western Front, then and ever afterwards. No need for a man to say he had been at the front, or had taken part in the Great War; he simply had to say he had been in the trenches. There was nothing new about trench warfare, of course. Soldiers had fought and suffered in trenches in Crimea, and in the American Civil War, for example, but this was the first war where one main front consisted of nothing but trenches. No matter what diversions took place at sea, in the air, in Gallipoli, in the sands of Mesopotamia and Arabia, in Russia, in Africa, or in the Italian Alps, the High Command in London realised that this was the front where the war would be fought and won.

The trenches stretched from the English Channel, four hundred miles through Belgium and France, to the Swiss Frontier. Two sets of trenches in which British and Empire troops, French, Belgian, and Portuguese faced the Germans. They lived, stood watched, ate, slept when they could, became infested with lice, fought, were wounded, and, at an average rate of many hundreds of souls a day, they were killed.

The 35th Middlesex knew all about the theory of trenches. They had been lectured on them more times than they cared to remember, during their training at Swathdale. They had seen diagrams, photographs, and written descriptions. Out on the Yorkshire moors, they had dug small sections of trench and had manned them for days and nights at a time. It was here that they had discovered that each side occupied not one, but at least three trenches – front, support, and rear

– running more or less parallel to one another, joined by communication trenches. In fact, the system was so complex that trenches had to be named, mapped, and signposted.

They had also learnt that trenches were not dug in straight lines, but in a dog-tooth design, like the battlements of a medieval castle. This involved much more digging, but the reasoning behind it was sound. It broke the trench into sections a few dozen yards long, separated by square-cornered bays, and had the effect of containing the blast of any shell that might land inside, while in the event of an enemy attack, the Germans, who dug their trenches to exactly the same design, would be unable to enfilade them for more than a few yards. The communication trenches were narrower, some with scarcely room for two men to pass, and followed a zig zag pattern.

So, in the safety of Yorkshire, they had dug trenches as their instructors told them, six and a half feet deep at least, with a parapet and a fire-step on the side facing the enemy, wooden duckboards running along the trench floor, with a drainage ditch underneath them. In front of the trench, they had hammered wooden and iron stakes into the ground and, between them, had strung length after length of barbed wire. They hollowed out dugouts for officers to sleep in, to serve as Company H.Q., and larger ones for the medical officers to use as aid posts. Their instructors had surveyed what they had done and pronounced it good. The men performed duties in these trenches, learnt to keep watch, to sleep as best they could in such conditions, to bring up rations and ammunition at night, along communication trenches. They endured both good and bad weather and, at the end of it, they were sure that they knew what trench warfare would be like. In fact, they'd had something of an idea, but there was one enormous difference between the trenches they dug, maintained, and lived in in Yorkshire and the real trenches waiting for them in France – in training, no one was trying to kill them.

Now, after over a year's training, a Channel crossing, the two week ordeal at Étaples, and a few days bivouacked in Lesmurs, they were about to experience the real thing. They were relieving a New Army battalion from East Anglia, and this was to be done on a company-by-company basis; A and B Companies were to go up the line one night, with C and D to follow twenty-four hours later.

That evening, after everyone had eaten a hot meal from the field kitchens – the C.O. had been very insistent about that – the two companies formed up in ranks of four and marched off towards the front line. They did not march in one continuous column, as they were used to doing, because the possibility of enemy action was very real, so they were spaced out to minimise the effect of any attack; one hundred paces between platoons and four hundred paces between companies. The C.O., Major Fullerton, and Captain Case were scattered along the column and, in A-Company, Major Henderson walked with 3 Platoon, while his second in command, Captain Huntingdon-Roberts, at his own request, marched at the very head of the column with 1 Platoon.

The men were marching easy, and they had not been ordered to keep silent, though they had been forbidden to smoke or light matches.

"This is it, then, Sar'nt," Private Millcross remarked to Sergeant Quill, who was walking alongside the front rank of 2 Platoon.

"This is it, Millcross. This is what you joined up for."

"It's rather exciting, really."

"Yes it is. You just keep your head, remember what you've been taught, and you'll be alright."

"We'll all be going home again in one piece, eh, Sar'nt?" said Private Ross.

"God and the Germans willing, yes we will."

"We just have to make sure the Germans don't go home in one piece," said Private Selway, who was also in the front rank.

"That's right, lad." Sergeant Quill knew nervous chatter when he heard it. He had been in this situation – the last moments before going into danger – more times than he could recall. If the men were not ordered to silence, then some talk like this could lessen the tension.

"Someone said they are Saxons in the opposite trench, not Prussians," said Private Ross. "That must be to our advantage, eh, Sar'nt, not to be up against Prussians?"

"It can't hurt, Ross, but remember this: Prussians or Saxons, we're better than they are."

"We'll soon have them on the run," said Private Millcross.

"Going to write a poem about it, Alec?" asked Private Ross.

"I might, if I get a chance."

"I'm not sure how much time you'll have for writing poetry, Millcross. You may very well have to wait till we get back out of the line."

"I expect you're right, Sar'nt. That's what I'll do. I'll just store up all the memories and impressions of trench life that I can while we're in the line, then write about them later."

"You do that, lad. I'm sure they'll be well worth reading."

There was a silence for a few minutes and the men were left with the sound of their own footsteps, against the distant rumble of the war, then Private Ross asked: "Can we sing, Sar'nt?"

There had been no actual orders given about whether or not singing was allowed, so Sergeant Quill hesitated for a moment, but Second Lieutenant Arnold Snow, walking just ahead of them, looked over his shoulder and answered the question for him.

"Best not to, Private. You can talk if you want to, but there's no point in advertising our presence more than we have to."

"Yes, sir. Very good, sir," Sergeant Quill answered for the men.

Further back, Lance Corporal Clay had noticed an aeroplane ahead of them, flying parallel to the trenches, in the evening sky.

"What's that one, Hope? One of ours, or one of Jerry's?"

"Can't see what it is, but it's probably German."

"How can you tell?"

"He's over the rear German trenches, flying a patrol along their lines, looks like."

"Can he see us?"

"Probably."

"Then why aren't our lads trying to shoot him down, if that's the case?" Private Leuchars wanted to know.

"Our pilots can't be everywhere at once, you know."

"Trust you to stick up for them."

"Well, I'll be one myself, soon enough. Just you see."

In one of the rear ranks, Private Winslow was asking Lance Corporal Marvell if he knew how far away the actual entrance to the trench was.

"We'll be there soon enough, Johnny, don't you worry."

"I'm dying for a smoke, Corp."

"You're probably not the only one, but you know the orders."

"Yes, I know. I was just commenting."

"Now you've got me thinking about smoking, Johnny," said Private Tunniford. "Thanks a lot."

"Always happy to oblige."

"Try thinking about something else," suggested Lance Corporal Marvell.

"Like what?"

"Like a nice pint of beer," suggested Private Giddington.

"Oh, yes. That would go down a treat just now." agreed Private Tunniford.

"I'll miss Pompette's. It's a good place."

"We're not going up the line forever," said Edwin Marvell. "We'll be back out in a couple of weeks, you know."

At this point, they heard the noise of a car approaching them from the opposite direction, headlights ablaze. As the orders were given all along the column, to stand aside to let the vehicle through, the men, platoon by platoon, rank by rank, were brilliantly illuminated. After the car, containing two middle-ranking staff officers, receded into the distance, Private Winslow turned to Lance Corporal Marvell.

"Good thing I didn't smoke, Corp," he said. "Someone might have seen us."

"Hush, Johnny." In the circumstances, Edwin Marvell couldn't bring himself speak more harshly than that.

"You can have a fag once we're in the line," said Bert Giddington. "We all can."

"Well, let's hurry up and get there then."

Suddenly, they heard the whoosh of approaching shells. These had been fired from field guns just a few miles away and, because the sound of the gunfire was followed almost immediately by the sound of the shell exploding, they were known among British troops as 'whizz-bangs'. A light-hearted name for something that was anything but amusing. Before anyone had a chance to react, one shell landed in the field to their right and, a moment later, another exploded among the trees beside the road, up by the head of the column.

"Cover!" yelled Sergeant Quill, as did officers and NCOs from up and down the column. Everywhere, men ran to throw themselves flat in the grass by the side of the road, some even jumping into the ditch. Two more shells landed in the field to the left of them, then all was quiet – the uncertain silence that followed the explosions was almost as unnerving as the cataclysm that had preceded it.

Lieutenant-Colonel Wintergrass judged that it was safe to continue, and he stood up in the middle of the road.

"Fall the men in again, George," he said to Captain Case, whose shouted order was taken up by officers and sergeants in all the platoons of both companies. In A-Company, Major Henderson hurried to the front of the column. He could see that 4, 3, and 2 Platoons were unscathed, but the second shell had gone off next to 1 Platoon.

"Anyone hurt?" he called out, as he covered the hundred paces between the two leading platoons. The commander of 1 platoon, Second Lieutenant Charles Snow, turned to face his company commander. There was mud on Charles's face, where the shock at what had just happened had etched new lines, and his uniform and hair were in disarray. In the few minutes since the shell burst, Charles Snow had checked his platoon for casualties and had received a report from his sergeant. Things could have been a lot worse, he told himself if the shell had landed in the road itself instead of next to it, but this was bad enough. His first experience of violent death and mutilation had shaken him. For once, the boyish smile was missing.

"Two men killed from 1 Platoon and three injured, sir, and Captain Huntingdon-Roberts is dead."

Major Henderson was a professional soldier, and he had seen death many times in the South African war. It didn't leave him unmoved but, as a soldier, he was able to give that impression. It was just what an officer had to do.

1 Platoon were standing in numbed silence, as two of their number lay dead in the road. One wounded man had been propped against a tree, his legs a bloody mess, and two others, with lesser wounds, were standing next to him.

"Right," said Major Henderson. "Lay those two by the side of the road. You two," he called, addressing the walking wounded, whilst also indicating towards the seriously wounded man, "stay with him until the M.O. arrives."

Their comrades laid the dead men on their backs on the grass verge. Someone placed their helmets over their faces to cover them – a small act of decency amidst the clinical business of war.

"Now," he said to Charles, "where's Captain Huntingdon-Roberts?"

"Over here, sir." Charles showed the major where the captain's body lay in a ditch. He was on his back, his eyes open, and the top of his head was missing.

"Dear, oh dear," sighed Major Henderson. "Poor old Roy. It should have been me, you know."

"Sir?"

"He was very keen that he should be the one to be at the head of the company when we went into the line for the first time. Practically begged me. I let myself be persuaded."

"I suppose that's war, sir," said the young, green subaltern to the experienced professional.

"Yes, you're right. You never can tell what's going to happen to any of us. Anyway, see that he's put with the other two. I'll report back to the C.O. and tell the Medical Officer he has some customers."

"Very good, sir."

"And fall your men in. We'll be moving off again any moment."

The late Captain Huntingdon-Roberts was retrieved from the ditch and laid alongside the other two corpses, and his face, or what was left of it, was also covered. Then, 1 Platoon fell in and the column marched on.

One hundred paces behind, 2 Platoon took a minute or two to reach the same spot. They were greeted with the sight of the three dead men lying side by side on the grass verge. Not a man among them, including Second Lieutenant Arnold Snow and Sergeant Fred Quill, could prevent himself staring at them as they walked past, Arnold being greatly relieved that his brother was not among the casualties. These were the first men of the 35th Middlesex to be killed in action. This was the starkest of all reminders that they were actually going to war.

"They look as though they're just sleeping," said Private Mosterby.

"A sleep they won't ever wake up from," remarked Lance Corporal Clay.

"They seem smaller, somehow." Like a lot of the men, Colin Tunniford had never seen a dead body before.

"Poor buggers," said Harry Travis, and most of them made a muttered comment of the same sort to their comrades.

"Come on, lads," said Sergeant Quill, who had, of course, seen it all before. "No use dwelling on it. We've got a job to do."

Vic Rangle said nothing. He had seen it all before too, and he knew they would be seeing a lot more of it.

So the column walked on, until 1 Platoon, at its head, reached the entrance to the sector of trench that they were to occupy.

When the trenches here had first been dug, there had been just a front line, then support and reserve lines had been added later, alongside a warren of communication trenches to link them to each other. Originally, the way into the trench system had been down a set of steps, cut into the earth, into a communication trench. This had not lasted long. Thousands of feet walking up and down them, and the effects of the weather, had transformed this improvised staircase into a muddy slope. Some attempts had been made at re-cutting, but the same thing had happened each time, so in the end a couple of posts were driven into the ground, with a rope strung between them to form a sort of banister. This muddy slide was the maw that waited to swallow the St. Marylebone Rifles.

When 1 Platoon, at the head of the column, reached this spot, they came to a halt and waited for 2 Platoon to catch them up, and in turn they waited for the remaining two platoons. A middle-aged corporal had been detailed to act as their guide, and he stood, hands on hips, till all of A-Company had arrived.

"Are you our guide?" asked Major Henderson.

"Yes, sir."

"Right, well, you'd better carry on."

"Sir!" Officers and superior NCOs notwithstanding, the corporal was in charge of this part of things. "You'll be going into the trenches single file," he shouted. "When you're in the C.T. –"

"The what?" someone shouted from inside the ranks.

"C.T. – communications trench. When you're in it, you'll see nothing but mud walls either side of you and the sky above you. It is very easy to get confused and lost in there. Keep sight of the man in front of you at all times. If messages are passed back to you, pass them on behind you at once."

He looked round, to see that they had all understood. This was the real thing. They were all taking in everything he said. No one was larking about.

"Right, let's get moving. Follow me."

He started to climb down the slope, but then there was the sound of voices from the trench.

"Just a moment. Gangway!" Two soldiers appeared, from the battalion whom the 35th Middlesex were about to relieve, carrying a third, who had blood streaming from a wound in his head. As they climbed the slope and passed 1 Platoon, one of them said, "Sniped," to no one in particular. The men took that lesson to heart straight away. They had been warned about enemy snipers since the early days of training, but this was the first time they had actually seen what such people could do.

The wounded man was borne off down the road by his comrades and 1 Platoon, one after the other, entered the trench. A few minutes later, they were all in and it was the turn of 2 Platoon. One by one, they held onto the rope and walked carefully down the mud slope. Some almost fell, but only one member of the platoon actually did. Private Tunniford felt his legs slide from under him and next thing, he was flat on his back in the mud, with his friends showing their sympathy by laughing.

"Get up, Private Tunniford, quickly now," said Sergeant Quill. "No one told you that you could have a lie down."

There was no point in disciplining the man, for it had obviously been an accident, but the line had to keep moving. Private Tunniford got to his feet and squelched into the trench, followed closely by his fellows.

The trench smelled of damp mud and the chill of the night pinched their nostrils. The corporal had not been exaggerating when he had told them that all they would be able to see in the communication trench, would be the walls and the sky. The men tramped along – fifteen feet in one direction, a zig to the left, fifteen feet more, and a zag to the right. If a man lost sight of the soldier in front of him, it was easy enough for him to believe that he was on his own.

From the entrance of the communications trench to the front line, past the reserve and support lines, was less than half a mile, but it took the men over two hours to make the journey. Messages were passed back twice. At one point, just ahead of the support trench, several strands of barbed wire sagged down to below head height, the result of German shelling. Very nasty for anyone to walk into. The hushed warning of "Barbed wire, watch out!" was passed back from one man to the other. A little further on, where a duckboard had broken, each man warned the one following him against tripping on the splintered wood.

This trench system seemed far more complicated than the ones the soldiers had seen mapped out for them on paper and on blackboards during training. This was an entanglement of trenches, so complicated that they were signposted, and many of them named – Oxford Street, Piccadilly, Watling Street, or, ominously, The Road to Nowhere – which gave them an air of permanence. When they did reach the front line, A-Company turned left, so that they would be occupying the northernmost stretch of the section of trench manned by the 35th Middlesex. The battalion they were relieving was in no mood to linger a moment longer than they had to, and as soon as the company had arrived, they moved to the support trench, their company commander pausing only briefly to hand over to his counterpart, Major Henderson.

The men, meanwhile, once they had been allocated positions, were left to contemplate their new surroundings.

"It sounds like pigeons flying over us," was how Joseph Marren described it.

Les Mosterby wasn't sure about that, but it wasn't like any sound he had heard before. They were talking about the noise that the German bullets made as they flew above the trench, a few feet above their heads. They had heard innumerable gunshots before, during training in Yorkshire, at Étaples, and, at a distance, when they were encamped at Lesmurs, but these were the actual reports as rifles and machine guns were fired. They had never heard the sound of bullets in flight before.

It may have been dark, but that didn't stop either side from taking pot shots at each other. Machine gun fire appeared to sweep the trenches at irregular intervals, while rifles would be fired into the night, in the hope of hitting someone. Both sides tried to cheat the darkness by shooting magnesium flares into the sky, to cast an unforgiving white light on the landscape.

Both A and B Companies were now settled, if it could be described that way, into the front line trench. A-Company H.Q. was a dugout near one of the communication trenches, linked to the rear by telephone cables, buried six feet deep in the mud, that ran all the way back to Lesmurs. Platoon commanders had their own dugouts, as did sergeants. The men slept where they could – on the fire-step, on the trench floors, in little funk holes that they scraped out of the trench walls, although these reportedly had a habit of collapsing from time to time.

The next morning they stood to arms – the morning stand to – just before dawn. The entire battalion stood ready. Their bayonets were fixed, to repel a German assault, because this was deemed one of the most likely times for the enemy to attack; when the sun had just risen above the horizon and was shining, from low in the sky, into the eyes of the British defenders.

After stand down, they had breakfast, and then those who were not on sentry duty were free to rest, sleep, or, most likely of all, be given other tasks to do. On that first morning, Privates Millcross, Glass and Leuchars were ordered to dig out a stretch of one of the communication trenches. Part of the wall had collapsed overnight and they had to clear out the debris. The three men, armed with long-handled shovels, made their way to the designated spot.

"Right," said Alec Millcross. "Let's get it over with."

So they set about the job in hand. As explained to them, the task was very straightforward – dig out the fallen mud and heave it out of the trench, onto the ground above. Not much to it really; but earth, especially wet earth, is heavy, and soon the men's arms began to ache, just as their good natured banter, with which they had been seasoning their task, slowly died away. Chatty conversation was replaced by monosyllables and grunts. Then, just as Percy Glass had flung yet another shovel-load of earth over the top, they heard a high metallic clang, followed by the whine of a ricochet. Percy Glass dropped his shovel.

"That bloody hurt," he cried out..

"Are you hit?" Alec Millcross asked him.

"No, but his shovel has been," said Wilfred Leuchars. "Look at that!"

There, on the back of Private Glass's muddy shovel blade, was a round, shiny dent where a German bullet had struck it.

"Cheeky buggers!" he said. "That's not bad shooting." Then as if in tribute to the enemy sniper, he laughed. Percy Glass had the loudest laugh in the platoon. "You'll scare Jerry half to death, making a noise like that." Johnny Winslow had once told him.

Someone else used that identical description of the Germans later that morning, for an entirely different reason. The men posted as lookout, at fifteen yard intervals, watched no man's land through periscopes. At one point, one of them, Lance Corporal Edwin Marvell, suddenly burst out, "Well, I'll be. Cheeky buggers!"

What he had seen, and what sentries either side of him had noticed, was that the Germans had hoisted a blackboard above their trench, upon which were the words: "Hallo 35 Mittelsex. We give you warm German wellcome!"

The other lookouts had noticed it too, much to their amusement.

"They must be Saxons. I can't imagine Prussians doing anything so informal," Edwin went on. "Hubert, go and fetch Mr. Snow. He ought to see this."

When he arrived a few moments later, Arnold Snow was equally surprised, and grudgingly amused.

"How did they know, sir?" asked Edwin Marvell. "We only arrived here last night."

"I have no idea, but they obviously do know."

"Spies, sir?"

"Who can say?"

At that point, a number of men in 3 Platoon, to their right, began taking pot shots at the blackboard, and one or two of Arnold's men climbed on to the fire-step to join in.

"Stop that," Arnold shouted at them. "That's exactly what they want you to do!"

His men stopped at once, as ordered, but in 3 Platoon they kept on shooting for a few moments more, until the Germans, who had been expecting this, fired back at the men exposing themselves above the parapet, killing one and wounding another.

"I don't know how they know who we are," Arnold told the men of 2 Platoon who were within earshot. "And it doesn't really make much difference to anything. We are here and they are there. Our sole purpose is to kill as many of them as we can. If they know the regiment of the men who are killing them, then good for them, but in the end, it makes no difference. Is that understood?"

The men nodded.

"The officer asked you a question," barked Lance Corporal Marvell.

"Yes, sir," shouted several of them.

Arnold nodded. "Carry on, Corporal," he said to Edwin, and he went back into his dugout.

While 2 Platoon may have ignored it from then on, the German blackboard had yet to claim another victim.

During the men's training at Étaples, the junior officers in the St. Marylebone Rifles had done forty-eight hours' duty in the front line trenches, as guests of another regiment, to get an idea of conditions and routines before commanding their own men there. Now, two subalterns from another New Army battalion, whose rank and file were training at Étaples, were attached to A-Company. Major Henderson introduced Arnold to Second Lieutenants Ambrose and Payne. After a few friendly words of introduction, and handshakes all round, the company commander left the two men in Arnold's charge. Second Lieutenant Ambrose was older than most subalterns that Arnold had encountered. As they were making conversation, he told them he used to be a schoolmaster in Brazil, teaching English to the sons of the wealthy, and he had returned to England, at his own expense, when war had been declared, joining up the day that he had arrived back in London. Second Lieutenant Payne looked too young to be a soldier at all. He was full of the fizzy enthusiasm of youth, having joined the army as soon as he had finished his last term at Charterhouse.

Arnold was in the strange position, after two days in the trenches with another regiment, and one night with his own men, of appearing the seasoned veteran. The other two men, equal to him in rank, appeared to defer to him. Every bit of advice he gave, they acknowledged with solemn nods. Whatever he pointed out, they inspected intently. It happened that, at one point, he told them about the Germans' message of welcome on the blackboard.

"Really? Fancy that," said Ambrose. "I must see that." And he got up onto the fire-step, peering over the parapet at the blackboard for a couple of seconds, before jumping down again. "That really isn't on, is it," he said, shaking his head and smiling.

"Let me have a look too," said Payne, and he stepped up to look out from where Ambrose had just been.

"Not the same place!" Arnold shouted in warning and he made to grab Payne's tunic and pull him back, but it was too late. There was a sharp, damp thud, the like of which would become all too familiar to

Arnold and his men over time, and Second Lieutenant Payne fell back dead, with a sniper's bullet in his brain.

"Oh, glory," said Arnold with a sigh. "You'd better stay here while I send someone to inform Major Henderson."

He left a shocked Second Lieutenant Ambrose standing over the dead body and walked off to the company HQ dugout. He was a bit surprised at his own reaction; he was sorry that the young man was dead, of course, but he was also very annoyed with him for having got himself killed. Still, this was the real war and they were in it now, to the end.

Chapter XXVI

The Listening Post

Night. A quarter moon. Blackness, punctured by occasional gun flashes and flares. Three figures crawled under the barbed wire in front of the British trenches, making themselves as flat as they could. They had been told the least difficult way to go, but it was still awkward and fraught with hazards. One of them managed to sustain a small gash on the back of his neck. His instinct was to cry out and swear, but the discipline of his army training stopped him. The three men only needed to move about forty yards, but even so, it was a long and dangerous journey.

A couple of hours before, Major Henderson had called Second Lieutenant Arnold Snow to the A-Company H.Q. dugout.

"I've got a little job for you, Arnold," he had said.

"Yes, sir."

"It seems that Brigade have got it into their heads that Fritz is up to something. I've no idea why they think that, but then I'm but a mere mortal. I expect they know what they're talking about."

"Of course, sir."

"Anyway, if the enemy is up to something, we need to know about it."

"Yes, sir."

"We're sending aircraft over every day to see what we can see behind the German lines, but I've no doubt that they'll be using other means, far more surreptitious than you and I can imagine."

"Spies, sir?"

"Well, evidently, you can imagine them." The major had smiled. "Yes, spies and all that cloak and dagger business. However, that need not concern us. What does concern us is that Brigade require our help. I want you to go out to the listening post and spend a few hours there, see what you can hear."

"Very good, sir."

"I understand you speak some German."

"I took it for a couple of terms at school, sir, but I think it's probably a bit rusty now."

"Well, it will have to do. We've had the order from Brigade, so we're going to have to do it."

"Yes, sir."

"Take two men with you, no more than that. Are there any other German speakers in your platoon?"

"Private Millcross speaks a bit, sir, I think."

"Fine, take him. And take someone who is good with a rifle."

"Private Leuchars, sir. He's the best shot in the platoon." Arnold explained.

"Excellent. Now look, you go out there at midnight, stay till three. The artillery have been ordered not to fire during that time, except in emergencies, to keep things quieter."

"Very good, sir."

"Take a Verey pistol with you. If you're rumbled, send up two green flares and we'll put down covering fire while you get back here. Got that? Two green flares."

"Yes, sir, I've got that."

"Jolly good." The major had taken a silver cigarette case from his breast pocket, opened it and offered it to Arnold. "Care for one of these? Turkish. You can still get them, war or no war."

"Thank you, sir." Arnold took a cigarette and lit it from a candle. Both men had then smoked in silence for a few moments.

"Ah, the simple pleasures," said the major.

"Yes indeed, sir."

"Look, Arnold, I don't know how useful this exercise will be, if at all, but we've got this big push coming up and if the Germans are doing anything at all to scupper it, we have to know. Even the smallest details can be useful."

"Yes, of course, sir."

"So keep your ears open out there, and I'll see you shortly after three ack emma."

"Yes, sir."

"Good luck, old chap."

"Thank you, sir."

The two men had shaken hands and then Arnold had left the dugout, to tell Sergeant Quill to fetch the two men he had chosen to accompany him into no man's land.

Which is why, a short time later, he and two of his platoon were making their way, silently and painstakingly, to the listening post. Creeping under the wire was the hardest part, with the attendant danger of laceration, and once that was over, the three men, as quietly as they could, stood up and walked at a crouch to their destination.

The listening post was an opportunist location. It was, in fact, a large shell hole, that had been designated for that use by a liaison officer from the Intelligence Corps. Some time previously, a working party had strung barbed wire round the edge closest to the German trench. It was a certainty that the Germans knew exactly where it was and what it was used for, and they probably had the range of the place, so if they suspected anyone was in the hole, they would shell it.

Arnold and his comrades arrived at the post and jumped down into it, laying quietly for a few minutes, waiting. There wasn't anything much that they could do to protect themselves if the Germans did start shelling, except hope that their aim was off.

Nothing. So far so good, thought Arnold. He had given his instructions before they had left the trench, so that the need to speak to each other was minimal. He and Alec Millcross, who admitted to having learnt some rudimentary German in school, were there to listen; Wilfred Leuchars knew to start shooting if they were spotted by a German patrol.

There was no technology to help them, no devices they could use – all they could do in the listening post was listen. As Major Henderson had promised, the British artillery in their section was not firing at all, but there was still plenty of noise. Arnold had with him a small notebook and a pencil to write down anything they heard, if there was light enough to see; if not, they were forbidden to light matches or to use an electric torch.

Sound travels further at night, so they were able to hear a variety of noises that distance would have completely obscured during the day. Arnold noted them all; he reckoned that more information than necessary was preferable to not enough. The people in intelligence, who would end up getting his notes, could decide what they wanted and discard the rest.

00:26 – Sound of footsteps in Ger. trench
00:31 – Sound of feet stamping in place. Cold feet?
00:40 – 2 voices. Unintelligible
00:42 – One voice says he is cold. 2nd voice says the rations were late. 1st voice says that is not unusual.
00:51 – Voice telling someone to stop leaning against the trench wall
00:54 – A bullet passes over the L.P.
00:58 – 2 voices. Unintelligible
01:06 – One voice asking where Johannes is
01:09 – Shots fired close to L.P. but not at us
01:13 – One voice unintelligible, then laughter

After this, Arnold became a bit more discriminating about what he reported, as he had almost two more hours to go and only a finite number of pages in his notebook. Some things, though, demanded inclusion.

02:26 – One voice says his leave has been cancelled. 2nd voice unintelligible. 1st voice says goddamned corporal is an arsehole. 2nd voice unintelligible. Laughter.
02:47 – Footsteps and several voices. One man addressed as "Herr Hauptman" Officer's inspection? Footsteps. One voice says the nights never seem to get shorter.

Arnold did not include in his notebook the fright that all three men experienced, shortly before their assigned time in the listening post was over. There was a rustling from the tufts of long grass near the lip of the crater and all three men looked up, expecting to see a German, but there was no enemy soldier. Instead, they saw, looking down at them, the biggest rat that any of them had ever seen. Rats flourished in the front line and in no man's land, what with all the dead bodies available for eating. For a few seconds, men and rodent stared at each other, then Arnold Snow threw a pebble at it, hitting it on the flank. The rat took no notice, regarding them for a few more seconds before shuffling off into the blackness. To Wilfred Leuchars, before he told himself he was being fanciful, it was as though the rat was committing them all to memory, so that it would recognise them again, when the time came to feast on their corpses.

At a few minutes after three o'clock, according to the watch on his wrist, Arnold gave the signal to the two privates to start moving back to the trench. He had filled several pages in his notebook and, while he was sure a lot of it would be discarded as being of no use at all, he knew that some of it would be useful. The parts about the rations being late, for example, and the soldier's leave being cancelled; an underfed, discontented enemy was always an easier opponent than one with steel in his backbone and food in his belly.

As they went back to their own trench, they had their backs to the Germans. For all of them, this was far more frightening than the outward journey three hours earlier. When approaching the listening post, they had been able to see the distance that they had to cover shrink. Leaving it, they all imagined German sentries levelling their rifles and preparing to fire into their backs. Alec Millcross found he was tensing his back muscles in anticipation, as though that would offer any protection. The temptation to flinch at each gunshot was hard to overcome, even though they knew, had had it dinned into them all through their training, that if you heard a shot from the enemy trenches, the bullet had already gone past you. As the morbid, but absolutely accurate, saying had it: you never hear the one that gets you. Arnold had the Verey pistol in his hand, ready to fire the first of two green flares in case they ran into any kind of trouble, but as it turned out, it wasn't necessary. They got to the British wire and Arnold called out the password, before some nervous sentry took a shot at them.

"Withdrawal." It was just an everyday English word, but it held within its three syllables several traps to confuse a German tongue. "Withdrawal. Patrol coming in."

They crawled back under the wire with no difficulty, save a small rip in Arnold's jacket and, in a few moments, were safely in the trench. Arnold thanked and dismissed Privates Millcross and Leuchars, before making his way to the company H.Q. dugout. Major Henderson was waiting, sitting in a shabby armchair that had been looted from an abandoned French farmhouse by some previous occupants of the trench. He was reading a book by candlelight and when Arnold pulled back the sacking that hung in the entrance and came in, he was deliberately casual, so as not to give away the fact that he had been on tenterhooks since the patrol had gone out at midnight.

"May I come in, sir?" asked Arnold.

"Yes, of course, Arnold," replied the major, putting his book down and standing up. "Good to see you back. I didn't hear any commotion out there, so I assume everything went smoothly."

"Piece of cake, sir."

"Jolly good. Now, what do you have to tell me?"

"Here, sir." Arnold handed him the notebook. Major Henderson began to flip through the closely written pages.

"Gracious. You managed to hear quite a lot, didn't you?"

"Yes, sir. I hope it's of some use."

"I'm sure it will be. I'll have it taken over to the intelligence people. I'm very pleased, Arnold. Well done."

"Thank you, sir."

Major Henderson took out his cigarette case and opened it.

"Here, have a cigarette."

"Thank you, sir."

"No, take two."

Chapter XXVII

Private Mosterby and the Dead German

Two days before the end of their stint in the front line, the St. Marylebones' were caught up in the after effects of a trench raid. Raiding was a practice that both sides indulged in, much to the regret of those who had to take part. In the dead of night, an officer and several men, one of them usually an NCO, would blacken their faces and creep across to the enemy trench, where they would take prisoner the first soldier they could find, dragging him back with them and killing any others who tried to stop them. Their prisoner could then be interrogated and, with any luck, give out all sorts of useful information. Trench raiding was essentially an activity best carried out by stealth, so raiders were loath to use guns or grenades, if they could avoid it. Instead, they carried with them a variety of knives and clubs, some of them army issue, others that they had made themselves or otherwise procured.

In theory, a trench raid was a very straightforward procedure. Put into practice, it was frequently anything but. If the enemy was alerted to their presence, or was even waiting for them, the raiders themselves could be killed, wounded, or captured. On some occasions, the niceties of the customs of war, regarding the treatment of prisoners, were not observed for captured trench raiders. If a raid ran into trouble, the raiders' own side would open up with machine gun or artillery fire, in an attempt to give their own men cover in the retreat to their own lines.

That is what happened on the night in question. The Germans had attempted a raid to the left of the St. Marylebones' position. It was shortly after midnight and, in 2 Platoon's little stretch of trench, Privates Marren and Winslow, and Lance Corporal Clay were on watch. As their comrades attempted what passed for sleep on the fire-step or in funk holes, the three sentries stood, head and shoulders above the parapet, their rifles pointed into no man's land, as they peered into the dark.

Nights were never completely silent. There was always the rumble of artillery fire here or there, rifle shots and, sometimes, the rip of machine gun fire. In an attempt to create light, both sides would shoot magnesium flares into the sky, which drifted down on little silk parachutes, soaking the ground beneath in a frigid, white light. Anyone out in no man's land became a target, until the flare fell to earth and fizzled out.

"Did you hear something?" Clay asked the other two sentries. He was tired and bored, calling to his comrades mainly to relieve the tedium.

"Like what?" Private Winslow called back.

"I don't know. I just thought I heard something."

"Just the usual."

"What's the shouting about?" Sergeant Quill was not asleep.

"I thought I heard something, Sar'nt."

"What?"

"Probably wasn't anything."

"Right. Well, there's no need to yell like that."

"No, Sar'nt."

Just then a magnesium flare went up from the trench to their left. As Private Marren watched it start to drift earthwards, Sergeant Quill saw his head tilt back as his eyes followed it.

"Don't look at the bloody thing, Marren! How many times do we have to tell you? Don't go looking directly at a flare. You've gone and ruined your night vision now, haven't you?"

That was true. Private Marren looked out into no-man's-land, but all he could see was blackness.

"Sorry, Sar'nt."

"Right, I'll stand with you for a few minutes, till you get it back."

"Thank you, Sar'nt."

"Just don't do it again."

"No, Sar'nt."

Silence fell again in their little part of the front line, punctuated by the never ending sounds of the trenches at night, the irregular pops and crackles of firearms. Staring into the darkness for a full tour of duty as a sentry, when nothing was happening, was soporific. Men tended to spend the first part of a night on sentry duty with their nerves on edge, ready to see the enemy behind every blade of grass, sensing the start of an attack in every windblown shift of the barbed wire. Then, for the second half of their duty, they would be trying to stop themselves from falling asleep. This was very wise – officially, sleeping while on watch, in wartime, carried the death penalty.

Sergeant Quill knew all about that. He had stood watch at night more times than he could remember over the years. When he sensed that Private Marren was getting drowsy, he gave him a nudge.

"Pay attention, Private." His tone was firm but not harsh.

"Sorry, Sar'nt."

"You haven't done anything to apologise for yet. And see to it that you don't, because if you do, apologising won't help you."

"Yes, Sar'nt."

"Right, I'll leave you to it for now."

"Thanks, Sar'nt."

Sergeant Quill was about to climb down from the fire-step and continue his rounds, when there was a burst of firing from their immediate left, in a section of trench held by a Territorial battalion.

"What the hell?"

A magnesium flare rose into the sky and, by its light, they could see the figures of several Germans trying to cut their way through the wire in front of their neighbouring battalion.

"Raid!" yelled Sergeant Quill at the top of his voice. "Raid! Stand to! Stand to!"

At once, the sleeping men of 2 Platoon, who hadn't been all that fast asleep anyway, were awake and up on the fire-step, rifles loaded and ready. The firing from the left became more frenzied.

"What's going on?"

"Are they attacking?"

"Who are they shooting at?"

"Keep your mouths shut and your eyes open," Lance Corporal Clay shouted.

Whatever was happening, it was centred about a quarter of a mile to the left of 35th Middlesex's section of trench. The Territorial battalion there seemed to be bearing the brunt of it, as both sides exchanged artillery and machine-gun fire, but, of course, the St. Marylebones' stood to, just in case the Germans tried anything in their sector.

"What is it?"

"Can't tell."

"Are they attacking?"

"Don't know. Don't think so."

"It's a raid."

"A raid gone wrong."

"Theirs or ours?"

"Don't know."

"Stop that yapping and keep your eyes peeled!"

"Yes, Sar'nt."

The firing to their left increased. Whoever was under it was having a very hard time of things.

"Poor fuckers." Private Mosterby kept his voice low and his feeling to himself.

"Steady, lads," said Sergeant Quill. "It's just a trench raid that's been scuppered. They're a lot more frightened than you are."

"Then they must be bloody terrified," remarked Private Tunniford to Private Leuchars.

"Shut it," barked Lance Corporal Clay.

"Fuck," someone cried out as a stray shell whooshed overhead, exploding somewhere behind the support trenches. Instinctively, several of them ducked.

"Hold your positions," yelled Sergeant Quill. The men looked sheepish. Ducking was an instinctive reaction, but quite useless. By the time you had heard a shell whoosh over like that, it had already gone past you.

For some reason, there was a brief lull in the shelling and small arms fire, lasting less than half a minute. Brief though it may have been, it was long enough for Private Marren, with his young ears, to hear something above the other sounds. Like the Germans, the British had hung empty tin cans along their barbed wire, to act as makeshift alarms if anyone tried to penetrate the wire defences. Now, Private Marren heard the sound of someone disturbing them, causing several cans to rattle.

"Sar'nt, there's something in front of us!"

At once, three or four men fired their rifles into the darkness.

"Hold your fire! Wait till you can see what's there!"

At that moment, another magnesium flare rose into the sky to their left and the bright, cold light was enough for the St. Marylebones' to get their first sight of an actual German soldier.

He must have been a member of the German raiding party and, in the confusion and firing after the raid had been discovered, he must have lost his bearings in no mans land, and instead of finding his way back to his own lines, he had gone parallel to the British trenches and blundered into the St. Marylebones' wire. When he had felt the barbs snag him, panic must have overtaken him, making him thrash about this way and that, because when the 2 Platoon saw him he was caught by his sleeves and legs, with no hope of freeing himself. They could see that he had blackened his face and had lost whatever headgear he had set out with.

Several men fired at him, a few of the bullets striking home. It was Private Tunniford's that actually killed him, but, of course, it was impossible for anyone to know that.

For a few moments, amidst the chaos of war, Lance Corporal Clay and Privates Marren, Giddington, Tunniford, and Winslow stood isolated from what was going on around them, transfixed and struck silent by what they had done. The first enemy they had seen up close, and they had killed him. This was what they had been trained to do, this was what their country expected of them and paid them to do. But still, but still…

Sergeant Quill had seen it before. Men were often taken aback like this the first time they saw death close up, especially death they had caused. He needed to snap them out of it.

"Now then, now then! That Jerry's dead and he can't do you no harm, can he? It's his mates you need to worry about. No one told you to stop keeping a lookout."

A few mutters of, "Yes, Sar'nt," and the men collectively pulled themselves together, each trying not to stare at the dead German, their very own dead German, lying just a dozen yards or so in front of them. Just then, Second Lieutenant Arnold Snow came round the bay, from the next sector of trench.

"I heard shooting, Sergeant."

"Yes, sir. One of the German raiding party got caught in our wire. The lads put paid to him." Sergeant Quill gestured in the direction of the corpse.

"I see. Good show. Well, carry on."

"Sir."

The men were given the order to stand down an hour later, to grab what rest they could until the dawn stand to. As usual, both sides exchanged artillery fire then – 'the morning hate', as the men called it. That morning, the St. Marylebones' escaped almost unscathed. One shell landed in a section of trench manned by C-Company, killing three and wounding four men severely enough to put them out of the war. A shell also landed in the belt of wire just in front of 2 Platoon's line. It was a low calibre shell from a field gun and, apart from frightening the men, it did no one any harm. It didn't even harm the dead German; it just jostled him a bit. What it did do was leave a small crater, just to the left of the corpse, and the raised lip of this crater effectively masked a couple of yards of British trench from the Germans facing it.

It was Private Millcross who saw it first. After the morning hate, once the men had been stood.down, he was one of the men on watch. During the daylight hours, of course, it was extremely dangerous to expose yourself, even for a second or two, above the parapet. Daytime sentries in this section of trench made use of a series of crude periscopes, each one little more than a couple of angled mirrors at each end of a rectangular box. Private Millcross, through his periscope, had a perfect view of the dead German, and while he tried not to stare, tried to be alert to anything in his field of vision that a sentry should be on the lookout for, his gaze kept returning to the corpse. Luckily, the exploding shell at dawn had shifted the body, so it was in a prone position, and Alec was spared the sight of the lifeless face. Then, he saw it.

Private Selway was resting on the fire-step, just a few feet away from him.

"What do you make of that, Duchess?" asked Private Millcross.

"Make of what?"

"Here, have a look."

Private Millcross stood aside so that Private Selway could look through his periscope. Strictly speaking, this was against regulations, but they risked it. Private Selway wasn't quite sure what he was supposed to see.

"What am I looking at?" he asked.

"You see the dead Jerry?"

"Yes, of course."

"Look at his belt."

"What about his belt?"

"Look what he's got on it."

Then Private Selway saw what his friend meant. Attached to his belt, so that it would hang at his waist, ready for him to draw whenever he needed it, was a dagger. Not just a run of the mill dagger, mind you. This had a blade of some six or seven inches, and, even at this distance, they could see that the knife was ornately decorated. Little sparkles of light betrayed that it was studded with something – beads, maybe precious or semi-precious stones, who could tell? There was also some sort of criss-cross pattern chased into the handle. This was no army issue dagger – this was something special. Possibly something the Jerry had bought, or even stolen. Maybe it was a family heirloom, or an antique? Whatever it was, the fellow had no further use for it.

"What's going on?" asked Private Travis, who had just joined the two men.

"Here," said Private Selway. "Take a look at the Jerry's dagger."

Private Travis peered through the periscope. "Oh yes, I see. That ought to fetch a few quid."

Private Rangle was on watch a few yards along the trench. He wondered what his friends were looking at, but he couldn't, wouldn't, leave his post to join them.

"What are you looking at?" he called to them.

"Our dead Jerry from last night. He's got a fancy knife on his belt," Harry Travis called back.

Private Rangle lost interest. He was a soldier through and through and his orders were to keep watch. Two or three others, though, were interested, and they drifted over to Private Millcross's position.

"Let's have a look," said Private Mosterby. "That should be worth a bob or two."

"What should be worth a bob or two?" No one had seen Corporal O'Malley approaching.

"The dead German, Corp.," said Private Travis. "He's got some kind of posh dagger on his belt."

"Let's see," said O'Malley, elbowing Private Mosterby aside. He peered through the periscope. "Now, isn't that a real beauty." Suddenly the brogue was much stronger. "That ought to fetch me a good price when I'm back home on leave."

He straightened up.

"Private Selway."

"Yes, Corporal?"

"Go get me that German's dagger."

"Now, Corporal?"

"Right now."

"But it's broad daylight!"

"And I'll not lose that dagger to some scrounger in a wiring party tonight. That dagger's mine. Go get it."

"Why don't you get it?"

"Don't you fockin' dare talk to me like that, Selway! Go get it now!"

"You want me to leave the trench and go get a dagger from a dead German, so I can hand it over to you and you can sell it. Is that correct?"

"Yes it is. Now, do as you're ordered before I put you on a charge."

"With the greatest respect, Corporal, I think I had better check with Sergeant Quill first. I'm not sure if your order, in this instance, is not *ultra vires*."

"Ultra what? Don't give me any of your toffee nosed chat, Selway. Do as you're told!"

"You don't have to, Duchess," chimed in Private Travis, one of an interested knot of spectators.

"Shut up, Travis, or you'll be on a charge too."

The sight of the little Irishman getting worked up was all very entertaining, but they all knew that it would be wrong to underestimate his vindictiveness. He may have been issuing a questionable order, but he was perfectly capable of putting Private Selway on a charge, with the facts suitably embroidered, to ensure that he was believed and that the private was punished.

It was at that point that Arnold Snow appeared.

"What's the commotion, Corporal?"

"That dead German, sir."

"What about him?"

"I'm organising someone to recover his personal effects. For intelligence, sir."

Arnold looked through the periscope. He saw the dagger and guessed what was at the bottom of things.

"No need to bother, Corporal," he said. "If he was on a raiding party, you can be sure his pockets are empty. German raiders never carry anything that could remotely be of use to the enemy. Neither do ours. I don't want a member of my platoon risking his life for nothing."

"Sir." O'Malley stood ramrod stiff.

"Carry on, Corporal."

"Sir."

As Arnold Snow continued along the trench, the knot of soldiers around Corporal O'Malley and Private Selway began to disperse.

"Ration party'll be along soon," said someone.

"'Bout time," said someone else.

"Right then," said O'Malley. "Who's going to get me that dagger?"

"Didn't you hear what the officer said?"

"Yes I did. So I'm not ordering anyone to get it. I'm asking as a favour. And then, when I sell it, I'll give whoever fetches it part of the money."

"How much? Fifty-fifty?" asked Harry Travis.

"Fifty-fifty? You mad?"

"I'll get it," announced Private Mosterby.

Everyone turned to look at him.

"Private Mosterby," O'Malley crowed. "You'll go fetch me my dagger will you?"

"Yes."

"And there was me thinking that a useless Belfast Protestant like yourself would be the last person to do me a favour."

"Don't do it, Les," advised Private Selway. "It's not worth it."

"Shut up, Duchess. My old pal Mosterby is about to do something worthwhile, for once in his life."

"Les, it's not worth the risk," said Private Travis.

"Don't worry, Harry," said Private Mosterby. "I'll be careful. And do you know something? When I recover that dagger, it'll be entirely mine. I'm not getting it for anyone else. I'm getting it for myself."

"That's my fockin' dagger," O'Malley squawked.

"In that case, Corporal, please feel free to go fetch it yourself."

"You go fetch the dagger, Mosterby, and then we'll talk."

"We'll talk about how nice my dagger looks; we can do that."

"We'll talk about how you'll hand the bloody thing over to me."

"Maybe you'd like to ask Sergeant Quill to join us for the discussion, Corp. I'm sure he'd have plenty to say on the subject of men being ordered to get a dagger off a dead Jerry, right after the platoon commander said it wasn't allowed."

Corporal O'Malley knew when he was beaten – for the time being at any rate. Let Mosterby go get his prize, he thought, and he'd work out some way of relieving him of it.

"Go get the fockin' thing if you're going to," he grumbled, then walked off down the trench, so he wouldn't actually have to watch someone claim what he thought of as rightfully his.

Private Mosterby stood on the fire-step, placed his hands flat on the parapet and bent his knees slightly.

"Les, be careful," cautioned Harry Travis. "It's not worth getting killed for, just to cock a snook at that little bogtrotter."

"I'll be alright, Harry, never you mind. Besides, I could do with the money." He smiled at his comrade, then, in one quick jump, he pulled himself up and over the parapet. He lay flat on the ground for a few moments, then began to crawl under the wire, towards the German corpse.

The German snipers were very good. So were the British snipers, but there was a feature of the Germans' deployment that worked very well to their advantage. British snipers were members of a battalion, and so they moved with their battalions, from the front lines to support lines, to reserve areas. The German snipers, on the other hand, stayed permanently in one place. Each one was responsible for his own section of trench, just a few hundred yards wide. That way he could literally memorise every feature of his own little acre – every mound of earth, every tree stump, the silhouette of the British parapet, the lie of the barbed wire – so that he would notice any change immediately.

Now, one of them lay out in no man's land, watching the line of earth that was the lip of the shell crater, which had appeared overnight, in front of part of the British trench that was his assigned area. He knew the fact that this crater masked a few yards of their trench from the Germans, would make the British soldiers behind it feel safer and that, eventually, one or more of them would be careless, and he would have them.

He had been lying motionless for over an hour, staring at the mound at the lip of the shell hole. Sooner or later, he knew, he would see something. And he was right. He wasn't surprised, because he was a trained sniper, and he knew his prey, but he did permit himself a half-smile of satisfaction.

What he had seen was Les Mosterby, or at least part of him. Mosterby had just reached the dead German and had managed to unhook the dagger from the dead man's belt. It was a beauty. The blade was steel, with an ornate pattern engraved on it, and the handle appeared to be carved ebony, with stones of some kind, possibly even precious ones, embedded in the pommel. Heaven knows why the German had taken it with him on the raid. Maybe it was a family possession, or a good luck token. If it was, it hadn't done its job. *Anyway*, thought Mosterby, *that will fetch a few francs from a souvenir hunter.* And the rear echelons were full of them. More money, he decided, that he could send home to his mother.

It was his big mistake to linger, even for a few seconds, admiring his trophy. Those few seconds that he remained still, were all that the sniper needed to aim his rifle and very gently squeeze the trigger. Although one could constantly hear the sounds of isolated rifle shots and bursts of machine gun fire, meaning that the sound of this shot was just one of the many to Private Mosterby's comrades, what they did hear was the noise of the bullet hitting their friend in the side, just below the left armpit. They also heard Mosterby's cry of pain, and he half stood, twisted, and fell. At once, several of his friends were up on the fire stepfire-step, peering over.

"Les!"

"Les, stay down!"

"I'm coming to get you, Les. Hang on," shouted Harry Travis, preparing to climb out of the trench.

"Get down, you bloody fools," yelled Vic Rangle, the old soldier in him, again, coming to the fore. "There's a fucking sniper out there with our trench in his sights. Do you want him to pop the lot of you?"

That was enough to bring his comrades to their senses. They ducked below the parapet, but continued to call to the wounded Mosterby.

"Come on, Les. Nearly here."

"Just a bit more, Les. Come on!"

The mortally wounded Mosterby was not giving in without a struggle. Grunting with pain, he crawled slowly back to the trench. He had just a few feet left to go, when the sniper shot him again, the bullet this time passing through his right thigh, ripping open his femoral artery. Mosterby managed a scream before pulling himself over the lip of the trench, where his comrades were able to grab him and pull him in. They could see he had been hit, and he was badly wounded.

"Stretcher-bearers," yelled someone.

"Hang on, Les," said Private Travis. "We'll get you to the aid station. You'll be alright."

Mosterby's response was to groan loudly, and more blood poured from his wounds, soaking his uniform.

"Where are those bloody stretcher-bearers?" Private Travis asked. But wherever those bloody stretcher-bearers were, it didn't matter. Les Mosterby gave a final shudder, a sigh, and then he died.

As for the dagger that had been the cause of all the trouble in the first place, that was lost. When Private Mosterby had been hit the first time, as he twisted round and fell, he had dropped the dagger into the shell hole, and it had fallen to the bottom. Out of sight, no one gave it another thought and, in time, it was covered with earth, as the sides of the shell hole collapsed. Probably it is there to this day. Meanwhile, they covered Les Mosterby's body with a greatcoat and buried him that night, in a hastily dug grave, just to the left of one of the communication trenches.

Chapter XXVIII

Rehearsals

The best laid plans. Sometimes, the best plans aren't even laid, before they are undone. General Haig wanted to attack the German lines in the far north. On a front that had no flanks, the only option, since the autumn of 1914, had been to launch frontal assaults against defended positions, and that had been against every military planners' deepest instincts. Therefore, Haig decided he would create a flank by attacking at the northern end of the line, where the trenches met the sea, with the Royal Navy bombarding the enemy rear. A successful attack there would turn the German line, and the stalemate of trench warfare could have ended.

It could have. The plan may well have worked, but no one would ever know, because it never took place. British troops were needed elsewhere. At Verdun, to the south of the British positions, France was dying. The Germans had launched an attack, with the express intention of bleeding France to death. Men perished at a rate hitherto unparalleled in any European war. German losses were very substantial too, but France was exsanguinating as though from an opened vein. The French general staff planned an attack in the Somme region, to take pressure off Verdun, and they requested British help. Haig acquiesced and, in order to make enough men available, the intentions for an attack in the north were shelved.

Meanwhile, as the meat grinder of a battle at Verdun consumed more French lives, but showed no substantial German gains, it became clear that the French could not sustain a defence there and also mount an attack elsewhere. The strategy was changed. Now, the attack was to be a mainly British affair, with French assistance. No bombardment from the sea, no flanks, no rolling up the German lines – the big push that everyone knew would take place some time in 1916, that everyone had been talking about, would be another frontal assault, against very well defended positions.

This had been done before, with varying degrees of failure, but no substantial success. The British high command was determined that this time would be different. They wanted to make sure that this time, men would not be hurled against a secure enemy, able to fight back. In this attack, before a single British soldier left his trench, the enemy line was to be blasted to oblivion – both his trenches, and the wide belts of barbed wire in front of them.

C-Company had been filling sandbags in preparation. The C.O. and the adjutant had gone to watch them for a while. The purpose of those sandbags, many thousands of them, was to build a replica of the trench system, spanning several fields, which mirrored the British front line trenches in the sector that the 35th Middlesex were occupying. These trenches weren't dug, but were instead represented by sandbags, piled to a height of about four feet. In front of them, white tape had been strung from posts, to show where the barbed wire was in the real front line. Across the fields of green grass, which served as no man's land, more white tape represented the German trenches – the finish line.

On a day when the sun blazed down to the accompaniment of a light breeze, the entire 35th Middlesex were assembled, in companies, behind the mock trench system. Major Fullerton, on horseback, addressed A-Company, passing on the instructions that he himself had received from the planners, not long before.

"All men are to proceed at a walking pace. No one is to run. No one is to stop for the wounded. Do not get ahead of the men either side of you. The first wave will advance in one extended line. The artillery barrage will destroy the enemy's wire and his trench system. Your job is to mop up survivors, if any, and to occupy what is left of the enemy trench."

So on he went. He described the ideal result of the first action of the big push, before it was then time to put it into practice.

The men lined up behind the sandbag breastwork, as they would in the real trench on the real day. What with the sunshine and the atmosphere, there was almost a carnival mood, no matter how much the NCOs and the staff officers in attendance tried to stifle it.

"Silence there!"

"Stop that bloody laughing!"

"Pay attention!"

"Private Winslow, this isn't a sodding day out at the seaside!"

Then a staff colonel blew a whistle and, instead of climbing the six foot ladders they would have to use on the day itself, the men clambered over the sandbag wall and began to walk towards the white tape that stood in for the enemy front line. As far as the planners could tell, they had made their own version of no man's land exactly as wide as the real thing.

"Walk," yelled one or other of the sergeants. "You were told not to run."

The men threaded their way through the gaps in the white tape that represented the British wire.

"Jolly good," said a staff captain, holding a clipboard and a stopwatch. "Through the gaps, quickly now, but don't run."

The men crossed the fields, reaching the other side of the notional no man's land, and found more white tapes.

"Through the gaps in the German wire, if there's any of it left in one piece," shouted one of the sergeants assisting the staff officers.

When they were all past the line marking the Germans' trench, whistles blew, and the order to halt was called up and down the line. The staff officers converged on their colonel, notes and timings were compared, opinions sought and exchanged, before a staff major turned to the 35th Middlesex and yelled, "Again!"

Back to the sandbag line they had to go, with no restriction on running this time.

"Hurry up there!"

"Run, you lazy shower.'

"This isn't a stroll in the park."

"Get a bloody move on. The war'll be over before you lot get back at this rate."

So back they trotted, to wait behind the line of sandbags until the whistles blew once more, and again they vaulted over the top, walking to where the notional enemy was waiting to be wiped out. The staff officers conferred, lieutenants and captains reported to majors, who spoke to colonels, and the shouted order was given: "Again!"

This happened five times. Not because the men were doing anything wrong, but because the planners wanted to be satisfied that, on the actual day, every man would know exactly what he had to do. On paper it was a very good plan. This attack, which General Haig had found foisted upon him by circumstances and the French, was not going to be like previous attacks, which had been so costly in lives, wiping out so much of the Regular Army and the Territorial Force. This time, they were not simply going to hurl men, in quantity, against the German machine guns. This would be different. The attack would be preceded by an artillery bombardment, unprecedented in its intensity. It would last for days, with high explosive and shrapnel shells in a non-stop barrage, to destroy the enemy defences and barbed wire. On the day of the attack, the British would explode several mines under the German lines, just before the end of the bombardment at 7.30am, the precise moment that tens of thousands of soldiers, along a twelve-mile front, would climb out of their trenches and walk in line, abreast, across no man's land, through the pulverised barbed wire defences, into the ruins of the German trenches, to kill or capture any Germans who may have survived the seven days of the barrage. After that, it would be up to the cavalry, so far very underused in this war, to pour through the gaps and pursue the beaten enemy. The stalemate of trench warfare would be over; a war of movement and manoeuvre would begin, which would lead to victory.

Unfortunately, as it turned out, none of those things went to plan.

Chapter XXIX

Fatigues

A-Company was officially enjoying a rest period. That was the theory. They were out of the line, camped in the same tents, in the field outside Lesmurs, and in the evenings, many of them passed an hour or two at Pompette's. However, there were obviously several different ways of interpreting the concepts of enjoyment and rest. There was something, in the official mind, that abhorred the very idea of men being idle, which meant that resting, even to their lights, had to be an exhausting activity. Besides, there was always work to be done.

On a day of bright, warm sunshine – one more suited to inactivity than labour, had they but had the choice – 2 Platoon had been ordered to unload several army lorries of supplies, destined for use by the Royal Engineers. Under the eye of an R.E. corporal, they had to remove several hundred wooden crates, containing heaven knows what, from inside the lorries and pile them up at the edge of the field in which the trucks were parked. It sounded straightforward enough, and it seemed a fairly simple task, if one really had to do it. However, life is seldom simple, and as 2 Platoon and soldiers everywhere, since time immemorial, had discovered, if there was a way to complicate an uncomplicated task, someone in authority would manage to do it.

For what reason 2 Platoon could not tell, the lorries and the site where the crates were to be stacked were at opposite corners of the field. That meant that every crate had to be carried over a hundred yards and, to show that it was entering into the spirit of the occasion, the field itself lay on a slight incline, which meant the men had to bear their loads uphill.

The crates themselves were another matter. Made of un-planed, unvarnished wood, and marked with the broad government arrow, together with several stencilled letters and figures that obviously meant something to somebody, each one sat, ready to thrust splinters into the ungloved hands of the unwary. Whatever they contained made them very heavy, but such was the size and shape of the crates, that while one man alone could not lift one, there was scarcely enough purchase for two men to hold one securely. It was only with a lot of cursing and grunting, and a lot of trial and error that the men were able to work out, for themselves, the best way of completing this task. They still didn't have it absolutely right, and Private Percy Glass was only just in time, jumping back as a crate fell off the back of the lorry, onto the soft earth below.

"That was almost my bloody foot, Colin," he exclaimed.

"Sorry, Perce," said Private Tunniford. "It just got away from me."

"Be careful, for Gawd's sake," yelled the R.E. corporal.

"Sorry, Corp."

"That's valuable stuff in there."

"It won't happen again."

"See that it doesn't."

"Yes, Corp."

"They ought to have given us padded gloves, like the ones wiring parties use," Bert Giddington remarked to Matthew Clay. Clay was as hot and uncomfortable as the rest of them, and hypothetical suggestions did little to change his demeanour.

"Yes, they should have but they didn't, so we just get on with it."

"Yes, Matthew, I was just making conversation."

"You can make conversation when we have a rest break. This isn't the time for chatting."

And so the long day wore on. There were six lorries in all to unload, each one full of crates. No matter how uncomfortable the work, or how badly their hands were cut by splinters, they did not let up. After about half of the crates had been moved across the field and stacked, the corporal blew on his whistle.

"Right, take a break. Smoke a fag, have a piss. You've got ten minutes."

2 Platoon moved over to the side of the field where the grass was longer, and they began to relax in the shade of a clump of trees. Some sat, some lay back, a few of them making use of the talent they had acquired as soldiers, being able to fall asleep instantly, when even a momentary rest was offered. Many of them lit cigarettes.

"What do you suppose is in them boxes?" Percy Glass asked no one in particular.

"Ammunition, I reckon," said Joseph Marren.

"No, that's probably not it," said Rollo Selway. "This stuff is for the Royal Engineers, not the artillery."

"That's right," said Edwin Marvell. "The Sappers don't use ammo. They're probably going to build something, and this is stuff they need for that."

"You could always ask that corporal."

"That miserable sod? He won't tell us, I'll bet you."

"He probably doesn't even know himself."

In the middle distance, to their left, a single German shell landed in an empty field. It was testament to their experience of being front line soldiers that they spared the explosion a momentary glance, and their reaction to it was conversational, rather than agitated.

"Missed," said Percy Glass

"What was all that in aid of?" asked Alec Millcross. "They can't be aiming at us, surely. Not at this distance."

"They're not," Vic Rangle assured him. "That's probably just a test shot. Setting a new gun into position. That, or else they're just banging a shell over here at random because they're bored. That was a howitzer, many miles away. They have no idea we're here." No one ever argued with Vic Rangle when he made pronouncements like that. He seemed to know exactly what he was talking about.

A ten minute break never seemed to last very long, but it was always a welcome respite from the tiring work of fatigues. Battalion commanders always resented having to order their men to spend their rest periods exhausting themselves with unending physical labour when out of the lines, so that, when they went back into the trenches, they were already tired out. Ideally, they should have been able to catch up on the very many hours of sleep that they missed when they were in the trenches, but supplies had to be moved, trenches dug, ammunition piled up, and there was far more work to do than the labour battalions could manage, and no one was more available than front line soldiers who were out of the line.

Lieutenant-Colonel Wintergrass was keeping a weather eye on his men. There was no real reason to do so, but he was not a man to sit still, and he wanted to satisfy himself that the men were not being ill used. He and the adjutant, Captain Case, were on horseback. Earlier, they had watched a number of men from D-Company unloading artillery shells from a train, a backbreaking job, and he had given them a few words of encouragement, though, as he did so, he realised that words of encouragement from a man sitting comfortably on horseback, to hot, grubby, perspiring men on the ground, in the middle of an exhausting task, may not be taken too well. So he decided not to make any speeches when he went to see 2 Platoon at work. Besides, if he made himself known to them, they would have had to stop what they were doing, in order to come to attention.

So it was, that Lieutenant-Colonel Wintergrass and Captain Case were watching from the other side of the clump of trees, beneath which 2 Platoon were resting. They sat on their horses in the dappled sunlight, hoping to remain unobserved.

"That looked like very hard work," said the colonel to Captain Case after a while, absently swatting at an insect as his horse munched contentedly on the grass.

"Yes, sir. They do seem to have accomplished quite a lot already."

"They do, but it appears that there are still three lorries yet to be unloaded."

"I wonder what's in those crates."

"No idea. No one bothered to tell me. Just told me they needed some of my men to shift them."

Suddenly, there was a burst of laughter from the men, and both officers looked over to see what the reason was. Nothing was immediately apparent – they just saw a group of men who appeared to be in good spirits.

"No need to have any concerns about morale then, sir," said Captain Case.

"I never have had any, George. Never had even the slightest concern about it with my men."

"No, sir. Of course not."

Just then, the men began to sing. If someone had suggested it, the officers hadn't heard. All they heard was a collection of voices, some good, some less so, all at once singing a slow, rather sad little song, that had gained a wide currency among British soldiers.

"Far, far from Wypers, I long to be,
Where German snipers can't get at me."

They gently lilted on to the last line, about the singer waiting for whiz-bangs to send him to sleep.

The colonel smiled affectionately.

"Bless their hearts, they sing that, but they haven't been anywhere near Ypres."

"Nice song, though."

"Yes, very. It's always good for the men to sing. Reminds me of when I was a company commander, my men singing before Colenso."

"That must have been something, sir."

"It was, it was. Many of them were Welsh. Wonderful singers."

"Come on, Percy," they heard one of the men yell, and they looked over to see Percy Glass stand up, to the cheers of his fellow men.

"Now what?" said Captain Case.

The two officers watched, wondering what to expect. *Pack Up Your Troubles* perhaps, or a chorus of *Tipperary*. Percy Glass began to sing.

"The thing above the Sergeant-Major's bollocks
Is something he should never have to hide.
It makes his uniform seem rather shabby,
Compared to what is hanging down inside.

Now, the Colonel's got a lovely one he sure knows how to use,
And when he gets it out no mamzelle ever can refuse.
But the thing above the Sergeant-Major's bollocks
Is the one that every girl round here has tried.

"The thing above the Sergeant-Major's bollocks
It fills us all with regimental pride.
We also do admire the Privates' privates,
And some are grand, it cannot be denied.
We think the padre's got one but to say more would be wrong.
The Corporal's got one too, but it is only two stripes long,
But the thing above the Sergeant-Major's bollocks
Is the one that keeps the French girls satisfied."

As the last line died away, to the cheers and laughter of the men, Lieutenant-Colonel Wintergrass, who had been staring at the ground during the song, slowly shook his head.

"Extraordinary," he said.

"I don't think I've heard that one before, sir."

"Neither have I. I wonder where it comes from."

"Where do any of them come from, sir?"

"Who knows?" said the colonel. "Some of the men's songs almost seem to appear out of nowhere and spread throughout the army at a speed that's almost frightening."

"It would be nice to think that someone might write them all down, as a memorial. Be a shame for them to be lost."

"Yes," the colonel reflected. "Mind you, I'm not entirely sure that absolutely all of them need to be remembered."

The two men lapsed into silence for a while, each of them simply enjoying the sensations of the warm day – sunshine, lots of green, countryside scents, insects buzzing, and the creaking of their leather saddles. On the other side of the clump of trees, the corporal was telling the men that their rest break was over, and they were getting to their feet to address the task of unloading the remaining three lorries.

"I suppose we should make ourselves scarce, don't you think?" said the colonel.

Of course, when your C.O. asks a question couched in those terms, it is only a courtesy. There is no expectation of disagreement. It was simply an order, dressed in politeness, and Captain Case didn't miss his cue.

"Yes, sir."

"We can go and see how C-Company is doing."

C-Company had been detailed to unload supplies from a train. This was taking place about a mile to the other side of Lesmurs, and the two officers turned their horses and trotted away, still unobserved by the men.

Over the other side of the field, 2 Platoon sweated and swore and, very efficiently, managed to move three lorry loads of heavy, unwieldy crates, one by one, to where they were being stacked. When it was all done to the satisfaction of the R.E. corporal, Lance Corporal Clay told them to take ten minutes' rest before marching back to camp. Privates Winslow and Glass strolled over to the clump of trees to have a pee, while most of the others just sat on the ground, by the lorries, and many of them lit cigarettes.

"Look at the state of my hands," said Eddie Ross, holding them out so everyone could see how grazed and bruised they were. The hours of holding and lifting un-planed wood had taken their toll

"Terrible," said Wilfred Leuchars, whose hands showed just as much wear and tear. "You may never play the violin again, my son."

"When we get back to camp, you can ask the M.O. if he's got anything to put on them," suggested Rollo Selway. "He's bound to have a salve or something."

"Yes, but maybe it would be best not to bother him."

"I expect you're right."

"You city people are just too soft," Bert Giddington chimed in. "Comes of spending your working lives sitting on your arses in an office. Not like being on a farm. That'd show you what real work is like."

"Soft, did you say?" asked Eddie Ross.

"Yes, soft. Absolute softies."

"Just for that you can give me a cigarette."

"Me too," said Wilfred Leuchars.

Bert Giddington passed out two Woodbines without protest or resentment. He struck a match, lit Eddie and Wilfred's cigarettes, then blew it out, before striking another to light his own. It hadn't taken the St. Marylebone Rifles long to take on board the superstition that had been born in the trenches – to take the third light from a match was very bad luck. Wilfred nodded in approval.

"What do you suppose they'll have us doing next?" Bert asked them all.

"Digging trenches," suggested Hubert Snibley.

"Filling sandbags," said Harry Travis

"I don't know," said Rollo Selway. "But whatever it is, we can be pretty sure that it will involve lugging heavy objects, in great quantity, from A to B."

"I predict," said Alec Millcross. "That the C.O. will call us all together and reward us for our labours, by telling us that all fatigue orders are null and void."

"Yes, of course he will," said Rollo. "And then he'll tell us we can all go to the Ritz and sign the bill on his account."

"With second helpings of everything."

"I don't know much about eating at the Ritz," said Lance Corporal Clay. "But I wouldn't mind a really slap up meal in an ordinary café. Just bacon and eggs, with all the trimmings."

"With chips?" asked Eddie.

"Yes, chips of course, and fried onions, and beans."

"Don't forget to order toast."

"I hadn't forgotten. Two slices of toast, dripping in butter."

"Stop it, I can't stand it," someone protested.

"And I'll wash it down with a cup of tea, made with water that doesn't stink of chlorine."

There was a moment or two of contented silence, as the men imagined the feast, so far removed from what they were fed in the trenches.

"There's something I'd like more than a slap up meal," said Joseph Marren.

"A woman, I'll be bound," said Clay.

"No, not a woman. I'd like a comfortable bed with clean sheets, and I'd like to be able to sleep in it for at least ten uninterrupted hours."

"You're right, Joe. That sounds like real luxury," said Johnny Winslow. He had just returned from the other side of the field. Percy Glass was some way behind him, strolling unhurriedly towards them.

"Got to wait till we're on leave before we can sleep that long again," said Joe.

"Yes. When do you suppose that will be?" asked Johnny.

"Not soon," replied Rollo.

"Not with the big push coming. They wont be letting any of us go home. They need us all at the front," said Alec.

"Just when is this big push going to be? That's what I want to know."

"Don't worry, Joe, they'll let us know when they're ready. You won't be left out."

Vic Rangle had called it a random shot, or possibly a shell fired out of boredom. Maybe it had been, the one that had exploded some hundreds of yards from them earlier that morning. So, very possibly, was the shell that now landed in the field they were occupying. Just one sudden explosion, the whoosh that preceded it giving them scarcely enough warning to do more than look up in alarm.

Luckily for 2 Platoon, the shell exploded across the field, leaving them shaken but unharmed.

"Shit," said Johnny Winslow.

"That was close," was Bert Giddington's obvious, but accurate, comment.

The earth thrown up by the explosion fell back to the ground, while the dust and smoke were dispersed by the wind, and the men became aware of a high pitched screaming. Private Percy Glass was lying on the ground and, even as his comrades ran to him, they could see he was badly hurt. He was on his back, and his tunic was soaked with blood. He screamed again and arched his back.

"Help me! It hurts!"

"It's alright, Percy," shouted Harry Travis. "We'll get help." But even as he tried to reassure his friend, he wondered exactly how they could do that. They were out in a field, a mile away from the nearest encampment, with no telephone or other means of summoning help.

Percy Glass screamed in pain again.

"Help me!"

Lance Corporal Marvell, at least, had an idea.

"Does anyone know how to drive a lorry?" he asked

"Yes, I do," said Harry Travis.

"Right, go and ask the corporal if we can use one of those lorries to take Percy back to camp. If we move fast enough, we might be able to get him to the battalion aid station in time."

Harry Travis ran across the field, to where the corporal was watching the goings on from a distance.

"Corp, can we borrow one of those lorries? To take our mate to the MO?"

"You what?"

"We need to get Percy to the aid station. He's badly hurt, and we want to use one of those lorries."

"You can't do that. Anyway, the drivers aren't here."

"I know how to drive one of those sodding things, Corp, we just need your permission."

"Out of the question, mate. I can't give you permission for that without my sergeant saying so first."

"For fuck's sake, Corp, he's going to die if we don't get him to the doc."

"And I'm telling you that you can't just stroll off with one of our lorries, not until I get proper permission to let you. Besides, your mate, he's going to die anyway. Sorry, but it's true."

It was an unfortunate argument, and a fruitless one. The corporal was an old soldier with twenty years' service, so he had seen war before, and he knew what he was talking about, even though what he said made Harry Travis very angry. Before either of them said anything more, there was another, even louder shriek from Percy Glass.

Edwin Marvell and Alec Millcross were reassuring him that everything would be alright, as soon as they got help, and the rest of 2 Platoon could do nothing but watch. Percy Glass gave no signs of having heard anything his friends were saying to him. He moaned loudly, rolling onto his side, and what his friends saw then, made them realise that there was no hope. The shell had exploded behind him, and Percy Glass's tunic and shirt had been burned off his back. His friends just saw blackened flesh and, in a couple of places, bone was showing through. Blood poured from where the shell fragments had cut him, and it was obvious that Percy Glass was not much longer for this world.

"Oh, my God!" Johnny Winslow couldn't help himself. He also realised that if he had been a just a few seconds slower walking across the field, he would have been dying too.

Percy Glass rolled back onto his back and screamed even louder this time. Then he lifted his head and vomited blood, an enormous quantity of blood, down his front, before he fell back and moaned loudly. Then he was dead.

Mrs. Edna Glass
38 St. Cyprian's Road
Hackney
London, E.

Dear Mrs. Glass,

By now, I expect you will have received the telegram informing you of the sad death of your son, Percy. I am writing today to offer you my deepest sympathy for your loss.

Percy was a very welcome member of the platoon, and since the day he joined us, he showed us how lucky we were to have him with us. He was unfailingly cheerful, hard working, and uncomplaining in the face of discomfort or adversity. He was very popular with his fellows and his superiors alike, and he will be sorely missed.

The end came when Percy was the unfortunate victim of a single enemy artillery shell, which detonated close to where he was standing. I should like to assure you that Percy can have known nothing about it. His death was instantaneous, and he did not suffer at all.

Again, on behalf of the men of my platoon, and myself, I send you my sincerest condolences.

Yours sincerely,

A. Snow, 2nd-Lieut.
Officer i/c 2 Ptn, A-Coy, 35 Middx.

Chapter XXX

The Battalion Sports Day

The C.O. wanted to hold a battalion sports day. Other battalions had held them, and they were generally popular. They gave morale a lift and, when the men were out of the line, it gave them something other than fatigues and the war to think about. Now, if you were a lieutenant-colonel in command of an army battalion, there was a very easy way to set about organising a sports day for your men, and it was this method that Lieutenant-Colonel Wintergrass used.

The 35th Middlesex had just completed their second, twelve-day tour of duty in the trenches and were back in Lesmurs. 2 Platoon, A-Company had suffered no casualties this time, other than the usual cuts and bruises that were inevitable when living and working in such conditions. The battalion as a whole had got off lightly, with ten men killed, including one officer, and twenty-nine wounded. The colonel knew that the next time they went into the line would be for the big push. It was time for a diversion. He spoke to the adjutant about it.

"George," he said. "I've been thinking about a battalion sports day."

"Indeed, sir?" replied Captain Case, who guessed at once what was coming.

"Yes. They seem very popular. Get the men competing for the fun of it, company versus company, platoon versus platoon, that sort of thing."

"Yes, sir."

"I know we have limited facilities and all that, but even so, I'm sure we can put on a damn good show. Maybe even get the Brigade Commander to come down and watch."

"Good idea, sir."

"Yes. We can have running races, tug of war, even horse races perhaps. Enough to make a good day of it. Dish out a few prizes to the winners."

"Yes, sir, that sounds excellent."

"I think so. Anyway, George, I'll leave it in your capable hands, shall I? Jolly good. Let's make it a really memorable occasion."

"Very good, sir."

"Fine. Well, keep me posted."

And that was how lieutenant-colonels organised battalion sports days.

To his credit, Captain Case managed very well, in just a few days, to organise the sort of occasion the C.O. had in mind. He let the platoon commanders know that the sports day was going to take place and that the men were required to take part in the events.

Second Lieutenant Arnold Snow spoke to his platoon.

"There's going to be a battalion sports day. I shall expect this platoon to carry off all the trophies. My brother tells me that 1 Platoon will be the most successful. Well, we are going to prove him wrong. Those of you who want to take part, and I expect that to include all of you, give your names to Sergeant Quill."

The sergeant found several volunteers and, with a bit of cajoling, arm twisting, and the odd threat or two, managed to get enough participants to make sure that 2 Platoon could put up a good fight in every event.

The weather, on the day, was very co-operative; sunny, bright, but not too hot. Captain Case had managed to procure the use of a wide, flat field, a couple of miles from Lesmurs, where lanes had been marked out with army issue white tape. A wooden platform draped with bunting had been erected at one side, where the guest of honour, Brigadier General Whitcroft, sat with Lieutenant Colonel Wintergrass, Major Fullerton, the M.O., the padre, the company commanders, and one or two prominent citizens of Lesmurs. Captain Case was bustling here and there, making sure everything ran smoothly. The battalion band played martial music and a medley of popular favourites before the sports began.

When the senior officers were settled, Major Fullerton gave a signal to Captain Case, and the first event began. It was a hundred yard dash. Four men were running, one from each platoon in A-Company, with Joseph Marren carrying the flag for 2 Platoon. The RSM, suitably neutral, was the starter.

"I shall say 'To your marks', followed by 'Go!'," he told them. "At which point you will start to run, and not before. Any man who runs, before I give the word, will be disqualified." Then, in his best parade ground voice, he gave them the off.

Everyone cheered the runners on, the men loudly and without inhibition, especially those in A-Company. The senior officers were more restrained; when Joe Marren beat his nearest rival by half a second, they clapped politely With commendable neutrality, the officers were equally as polite during the races between the platoons in B, C, and D-Companies. The final race, consisting of the four winners, was far noisier. This time, Joseph Marren was running on behalf of the whole of A-Company, and he managed a very creditable second place, just behind the runner from D-Company.

Then there was a two-hundred yard race, this time with Eddie Ross representing 2 Platoon, but, in spite of his long legs, he was beaten into second place. This was followed by an 880, which involved two circuits, of a measured track, round the edge of the field, with sixteen men running. Rollo Selway had not wanted to take part, but had permitted himself to be cajoled into it, and to nobody's surprise greater than his own, he won.

In lieu of a shot put, there was a grenade throwing contest – unarmed grenades of course. A lance corporal from C-Company, who had played cricket for his county before the war, was the easy winner.

Then came the subalterns' horse race. All sixteen platoon commanders in the battalion had been informed that the C.O. expected them to enter into the spirit of the occasion and to take part in this event. This was, of course, the equivalent of an order, never mind that some of the second-lieutenants in question had never ridden a horse in their lives. In fact, four of them hadn't, and six had only ridden occasionally. In one of his more flippant moments, the colonel had remarked that a broken collar bone or two would not be the end of the world, as long as the subalterns put on a decent show. Then he corrected himself, saying he didn't want anyone to take any unnecessary risks, before he went on to say that he expected every platoon commander to take part, which again placed all their collar bones at hazard.

The race was very simple. The four subalterns of each company were to gallop across the field, go round a post driven into the ground and marked with a red flag, gallop back across the field, round a second post, followed by a third crossing of the field, round the first post, then back across the field, to the starting point. First past the post would be the victor, with the RSM standing at the finish line to decide the winner. In the event of close finishes, his word to be final – not that any mere second-lieutenant would dream of arguing with the regimental sergeant-major.

The first race consisted of the four subalterns from A-Company, including the two Snow brothers. Even though they didn't keep horses themselves in London, they had both ridden often when visiting friends who lived in the country. The other two had never ridden until a few days before, when they had tried to learn how, in time for the race.

The four subalterns sat on horseback at the start line, as the RSM addressed them, in a voice that brooked no nonsense.

"Gentlemen, I shall give you the command 'Go', and you are to race over the course as it has been laid out, twice across the field, and back again. Mr. Hooper, sir, control your mount." One of the horses appeared nervous and its novice rider seemed even more apprehensive. "Give the men a good show, gentlemen, just like the colonel is 'opin' for." Then he took one pace back, regarded the four young men for a moment, before he barked, "Go!"

Three of them started at once, including the two Snow brothers, but the fourth was a few seconds late, following at a stumbling trot, appearing to clutch the saddle for dear life. To the cheers of the entire battalion, the three other riders raced for the post at the far side of the field, but form will always tell, and the two Snow brothers, with their experience, pulled ahead of the novice. The fourth rider, meanwhile, to the delighted cheers of the men, managed to achieve a brief canter before falling off his mount, hurting little more than his backside and his dignity. The race proper, was now just between Charles and Arnold Snow, and as they crossed the field for the third time, Charles managed to pull significantly ahead of his brother, and by the time he reached the finish line, to thunderous cheers, he was almost two lengths ahead.

So, honours were given to 1 Platoon, with no disgrace to 2 and 3 Platoons. The Commander of 4 Platoon was telling anyone who was listening, that horse riding wasn't really his strong point, but he was glad he had given it a go, for the men's sake, and what a shame it was they weren't going to have a fencing event, because he was really jolly good at that.

Corporal O'Malley was running a book on the final of the subalterns' horserace, and he was glad to see Arnold Snow eliminated. Several men had bet on him. He had given odds of 10-1 on both Snow brothers, and there had been a number of takers, but the strongest riders in the battalion were in C and D-Companies, with O'Malley having no doubt that one or other of the subalterns who had been riding horses since early childhood, would win. There were two of them and he was offering odds of 2-1 on them both, although if either of them won it would leave him with a tidy profit. This was entirely against army law, but on an occasion like this the colonel and the other officers all turned a judicious blind eye.

Sure enough, after an uninspiring race by the subalterns of B-Company, in which the four riders scarcely achieved more than a fast trot, the two favourites won the C and D-Company races, and there was a brief pause before the final. A few more men placed bets with Corporal O'Malley, including a couple of reckless optimists, who bet on the B-Company rider at odds of 50-1. Then, four riders formed up at the start line.

"Right, gentlemen," said RSM Callow. "As before, I shall give you the command to go. Good luck to you all." He stood back and allowed himself a dramatic pause, that lasted for five, then ten, seconds, as the subalterns' nerves tightened, and then, after he'd decided he had tormented them enough, he gave them the off.

This time, the race was between four skilled, experienced riders and the entire battalion was involved, not just a single company. The men cheered themselves hoarse, and the officers permitted themselves to join in somewhat.

By the time the riders were crossing the field for the third time, the clear leader, to almost everyone's surprise, was Charles Snow. As he led his nearest rival by almost two lengths, the whole of A-Company was on its feet shouting, "Come on, Charlie Boy!" while the senior officers pretended not to hear such familiarity. Round the pole they went and the rider from C-Company managed to close the gap a little, but Charles Snow stayed in the lead long enough to finish in first place, to cheers, yells, and shouting, from just about everyone below the rank of captain. The RSM, ever on his dignity, applauded politely as he bestowed a benign smile upon the winner. The brigadier-general made some approving comments, which Lieutenant-Colonel Wintergrass acknowledged with thanks and then agreed with. The only person in the battalion who was less than happy, was Corporal O'Malley, who was going to have to find a way to pay out on all the bets that had been placed on Charles Snow.

There followed a few more sprints, an egg and spoon race, a sergeants' pillow fight, staged on a plank over a shell hole full of dirty water, and the tug of war, with honours distributed more or less equally between the companies. The brigadier-general made a speech, exactly the same sort of speech that most of the officers and men had heard at school sports days during their youth, congratulating the winners, consoling those who had not won, and pointing out that taking part and giving of one's best, was more important than actually winning – in other words, playing the game for the game's sake. Lieutenant-Colonel Wintergrass made another speech, making sure that it was shorter than the brigadier's, saying very much the same things, but in a way designed not to steal his superior's thunder. Prizes, ranging from a box of cigars, to a bottle of whisky, to a crate of beer, were presented to the winners. Then the adjutant called for three cheers for all the competitors and, as the band oom-pahed away, the men were formed up and marched back to the camp outside Lesmurs.

The officers retired to their billets, Lieutenant-Colonel Wintergrass and Major Fullerton accepted the Brigadier-General's invitation to dinner at brigade headquarters, and the men relaxed, many of them spending part of the evening at Pompette's; a pleasant end to an enjoyable day.

Chapter XXXI

The Censor

In the field where the St. Marylebone Rifles were encamped, in row upon row of bell tents, only two permanent structures had been erected. Two wooden buildings, which could only be described as flimsy, had been constructed. One was the guardhouse, by the entrance to the field. The other was the orderly room. In fact, it was two rooms really – a large one, where the battalion clerks sat and worked, and a smaller one, where each day's orderly officer worked and, since the tenure of the post lasted twenty-four hours, could rest upon an army cot. Among other things, the orderly office was where the mail to and from the battalion was delivered and collected.

Something that was truly remarkable, but which everyone took for granted, because it quickly became part of the routine of the soldier's life in France, was that, between them, the Army and the Post Office managed to organise an excellent postal service for the troops. A soldier at the front, even in the front line trenches, could write a letter, or postcard, and expect it to be delivered to its destination in Britain, in probably little more than forty-eight hours. Most soldiers wrote a lot of letters – it was a way to keep in touch with home and loved ones, as well as being something to do – and they welcomed and treasured every letter, card, and parcel they received.

One warm, languid Sunday afternoon in June, when the birdsong was loud enough to be noticeable, the men of 2 Platoon found themselves unusually unoccupied. 3 Platoon had been detailed to unload artillery shells from railway wagons, a couple of miles away, and the whole of D-Company had been co-opted into taking part in a welcome parade for a couple of Portuguese generals, who were visiting this part of the front, but the rest of the battalion – at least those who did not have specific duties – were able to take advantage of this unaccustomed freedom, and many of them took the chance to write back home.

Arnold Snow wondered how many letters he would be reading that afternoon. While officers' letters were not censored, the men's always were, and as today's orderly officer, he had drawn that duty. He always tried to detach himself from his task when censoring mail, but, even so, he could not help feeling a frisson of embarrassment, as the words he read hinted at the real emotions, fears, hopes, and private thoughts of the men set under him. Still, someone had to do it and he knew that, shortly, the orderly room corporal would present him with a pile of mail, which he would have to go through carefully, censoring anything that, in his opinion, could possibly be of use to the enemy, if the letter in question fell into the wrong hands.

He finished his own letter to his mother – a couple of pages of vague news, full of cheerfulness and the assurance that both he and Charles were fit and well – and dropped the sealed envelope into the wire basket, which served as a post office for officers, knowing that it would probably fall onto the doormat, in the house in Berkeley Square, in a couple of days. He decided to permit himself the luxury of a cigarette, so he got up, went and stood in the open doorway of the orderly office, and lit a gasper.

Outside, he could see men relaxing in the sun – the lucky ones who had not been detailed for duty and the ones who had not gone into Lesmurs; not that there was much to do there at this hour, because Pompette's didn't open for business until the early evening.

In the shade of a tree across the field, he could see several of his platoon sitting on the grass. They appeared to be passing objects around, and it took Arnold a moment or two to realise what they were doing; they were sharing out the contents of a couple of food parcels. That was always the way. Some men received food parcels, sent by friends or family, quite frequently; others less often, and some never. However, it was the unwritten rule in the battalion, and across the whole Army, as far as he knew, that the men who received parcels shared the contents out with their mates. Arnold couldn't be sure who the recipients had been of the parcels now being shared. Private Selway, he knew, often received parcels and, since he was the son of a duke, they tended to contain high quality food. From Fortnum's, probably. He couldn't help wondering what Privates Snibley and Marren made of Gentleman's Relish. Due to that strange process, by which news managed to filter through the whole battalion, Arnold knew that Private Ross had an aunt, who had organised her friends into a knitting circle, and she regularly used to send Eddie parcels full of thick, woollen socks, which were distributed among his grateful friends.

The men looked happy. Arnold was glad of it. He finished his cigarette and went back inside. The orderly corporal had evidently been and gone, and there was a pile of mail awaiting his attention, so he got to it. The tools of this job were a pot of black ink and a small artist's paintbrush, with which he could obliterate any offending words. If there were too many, he would have the letter returned to the soldier who wrote it, with instructions to rewrite it if he wanted it to be approved.

He picked up the first letter and read it. There was nothing sensitive in it – no place names, no accounts of military activities, nothing an enemy would be interested in. He put the letter back in the envelope, initialled the back flap and put it aside, the first of what would become a pile of approved letters, which the orderly corporal would collect later, seal, and then mark them as approved by the censor with a rubber stamp. He went onto the next envelope.

As he went through, he saw several letters from members of his own platoon.

Out in France
in June 1916

Dear Mum and Mavis and Davey,
Just a quick word to tell you that everything is well here and I hope you are all in the pink as I am, so are Harry and Bert. We are all in good spirits and we really do have a lot of good larks in between the training and going to the front and my pals and I

like to go to Pompets which is like a sort of French pub (not like the Red Lion, ha ha) which is just outside a nice little town where we are all camping in tents, Mum those tents are the round ones I told you about you remember, we are squashed in like sardines. Speaking of sardines my pal Rollo he is a duke, no I am not pulling your leg, he has food parsels and shares them and often there are sardines in them. Of course I am grateful for the parsel you sent me last month and again Mavis that cake was the cat's wiskers. I don't know what the future holds because in our training we have ██████████ so maybe we will be on the move very soon who can tell? I will write again as soon as I can and give you all the news, meanwhile I hope this finds you as it leaves me.
With love
Joe

****

A Coy, 35 Bn Middx. Regt
On active service, France
20th June, '16

Shadrack, Dawes & Co.
13A Chandlers Alley
London E.C.

Dear Mr. Dawes,
In reply to yours of 17th inst., I am writing to confirm that I have no knowledge of the whereabouts of my estranged wife, Sophie Edna Marvell, née Potts. I have not seen or spoken to her since October of 1914. As far as I know she left our rented home at 141 Roundell Terrace, Ealing later that month but I have had no communication either from her or from anyone acting on her behalf. I expect to be released from military service later this year or early next after the successful conclusion of our next big offensive and I would like divorce proceedings to be under way by then. If you need to engage the services of an investigator to find my wife, please do so.
I have written my will in my service paybook, and in the unlikely event of my being killed in action, all my property, including my life savings, will go to my mother. I do not wish my wife to be able to make any claim against my estate.

Yours faithfully,
E. Marvell

****

A-Company, 35 Middx
B.E.F. France

Wightwick Publications Ltd.
Sanger Road
Ipswich

Dear Sirs,
Please send me a copy of your illustrated publication 'The Wonder of Aircraft' to the above address. I am on active service but it will reach me wherever I am posted. I enclose a postal order for one shilling and fourpence.
Yours faithfully,
James Hope, Pvt.

There were many from members of other platoons, writing in differing moods, with different concerns.

...Surely you can see he is no good for you, Lorna. Yes, he may be in an important position with the County Council and I am sure he is very impressive with his fancy office and telephone, but it's not right Lorna that I am out here doing my bit and he comes creeping round you like a reptile. I don't blame him for that because you are a very beautiful woman but Lorna I can not bear to think that you might leave me for him. Think of the children and consider how it will be for them if you leave their father high and dry while he is stuck out here in France fighting for his country...

****

...though I can't say I think much of our sergeants. Some of them seem so thick. Maybe that's what makes them good soldiers. Our platoon went on a route march the other day and our sergeant got us lost. He couldn't find ████ on the map and we wandered round until he found a road sign. I knew exactly where it was but I wasn't

going to tell him. He has the stripes so let him do his job. What is more, he has very bad breath, but of course we can't tell him that. I am disappointed and astonished that they haven't even made me a corporal, when you see what sort of an oaf can become a sergeant. Still, that is the battalion's loss not mine. I'll just do what I'm told and no more...

****

...I enjoy this outdoor life. Such a change from back home and with all the training and what have you, I'm in very good health. This is much better for me than sitting in a stuffy office all day! So I was thinking, I may stay on in the Army after the war. I enjoy being a soldier and when all the other volunteers return to civilian life I'm sure the opportunities for promotion will be more than ample...

It was with a sense of comfort, that he found more from his own platoon members. Most of them, he read without taking in the contents, although one or two did give him reason to pause for thought and to decide that some men needed keeping an eye on – he'd have a word with Sergeant Quill about them.

...I don't know if Colin has done much painting recently. He never talks about it. I have written a poem or two but I don't know how good they are. I sent one off to 'Poetry Today' but so far I haven't heard back from them...

****

... What with the big push coming up and all the increased training in ███████ ███████████ I just don't seem to have the time to paint. It doesn't seem as important as it used to, somehow...

****

...carnt wait till I get a spot of leave to see you Myrt but I hope we dont' waste it on pottry readings again! Lets just stay in bed for a few days like last time eh! I went to a brothel near here last month like you said I should feel free to experince the French

girls, it was alright but she wasnt like you Myrt and she didnt even speke English. I wont go there again Myrt, I will save it all for you when I get some leave and I hope you are strong enough!!…

****

…These are all grand fellows, Enid. I know I keep telling you, but I am very proud to be part of this regiment. I have helped to turn these civilians into real soldiers. Now I know you were sad when I re-enlisted, but I don't think you need worry for much longer. We have the big push coming up soon. It's supposed to be a secret but everyone seems to know about it. I am sure that this will be what wins the war for us. So you see, old girl, I only have one more battle and then I'll be coming home to take part in the victory parade! Afterwards, if you like, we can think about moving to Wales, to be near our Doris…

****

…Oh Mother, I am in the most frightful funk. The other chaps are taking it all very well, even when fellows in our platoon were killed, but all I can do is stop myself running away. If I do that they'll find me and I'll be court martialled and shot. All I can do is hide what I feel inside and put on a brave face so no one knows. It would be letting my pals down to show I'm afraid. Just let me get through the big push and then we can win the war and all go home. I don't even mind if I am wounded. I just don't want to die…

The job took him about an hour. He still had lots of ink left in the pot for the next orderly officer. That was probably a good sign – the men were becoming more careful about what they said in their letters. Now, the mail would be sent off to brigade headquarters and from there, by whatever route it took, to England, at no charge to the senders. Each man was permitted two letters a week, postage free. Arnold nodded to himself as he thought of that. It was the least the Army could do for the men.

Chapter XXXII

The Barrage

The big push, the attack into which so many New Army battalions were being thrown, that was supposed to deliver the knockout blow to a dazed and stunned enemy, was planned for the twenty-ninth of June, and because of various delays in preparation, was postponed until the first of July. The first stage of the offensive that had been forced on General Haig, was an artillery barrage. This was not unusual. Attacks across no man's land – and, of course, no other form of attack was possible on the Western Front – were usually preceded by artillery barrages for an hour or two, or even a bit longer. This one, though, would be unlike any operation of artillery that had ever been seen in this war, or any other. It would last not for a few hours, but for seven whole days – a continual bombardment of the German lines, without interval, that was designed to smash the enemy's trenches to rubble, destroy his dugouts, and wipe out everyone in them. It would also obliterate all trace of the wide belt of barbed wire in front of their trenches, leaving the attackers nothing to do other than walk across no man's land, in their thousands, mopping up the occasional pocket of survivors, thus forcing a gap in the enemy lines, to let the cavalry through to chase the enemy back to Germany. It was, as many a red tabbed general was wont to observe at the time, so very simple really.

A previous offensive at Loos the year before had faltered and failed because of a lack of artillery shells. The subsequent scandal had contributed to the downfall of the government, its replacement with a coalition, and the appointment of a new prime minster. This time, there was to be no shortage. Munitions plants had been working twenty-four hour shifts, and hundreds of thousands of shells had been imported from Canada and the United States. Over one and a half thousand field guns, howitzers, and heavy guns faced the Germans, along a front of twelve miles, and at exactly the same moment, on the twenty-fourth of June, they all opened fire, with the first of over ten million shells, of various calibres, hurled at the enemy.

To British observers, behind the front lines and able to observe without the risk of being shot by snipers, this was like nothing they had seen before. Watching an artillery barrage, one expected to see a series of explosions – flashes, smoke, earth and debris thrown skyward – but this was more like one continuous explosion. It was not possible to mark the individual detonations, because they followed so closely, one upon the other. One newspaper correspondent tried to count the explosions that he could see from his vantage point, but there were too many of them. He then attempted to blink his eyes in synchronisation with the explosions, but there were still too many, too rapid. Finally he made his teeth chatter, and only then did he approach the frequency with which the shells landed – and this was just one part of the sector of the front line that he could see, from where he watched. It was but a sampling of what was happening, along the whole twelve miles.

To the British soldiers in the trenches and in the rear areas, the barrage was a source of both amazement and comfort. No one had seen anything like it before. Most of them wouldn't have believed that such an intense bombardment was possible. For an hour or two, maybe, but this was going on day after day, without let-up. The destruction to the German side of no man's land must have been enormous. It was hard to see how anyone, or anything, could survive. And that was their source of comfort; they knew that their job, when the time came to climb out of their trenches, was simply to deliver the knockout blow, to an enemy dazed, demoralised, and reeling, if not actually dead already. They just had to look at the destruction going on, not to mention the noise, to know that there would be no sleep for Fritz these days. In fact, when the wind was in the right direction, the sound of gunfire could be heard as far away as the English coast.

The Germans called it *Trommelfeuer* – drumfire. Not because it was like the thumping of a bass drum, but because it was more of a never ending drum roll. Their trenches were on higher ground than the British, and their shelters and dugouts were cut deep into the chalk hillsides, some of them as much as forty or fifty feet down, or more, and there they sheltered, safe from almost anything except a direct hit. Even so, to the Germans, it was as though hell had been unleashed. Men were crammed together in crowded holes, deep underground, lit by flickering candles or oil lamps, or in some cases in the dark. It was impossible to bring rations up to the lines during the barrage, so they had to make do with whatever food and water they already had, and it was too dangerous for anyone to leave the dugouts to use the latrines. The air grew foul, the vibrations from the explosions constantly juddering through them, as though to shake loose their very innards; the noise, even this far down, was deafening and unceasing. Fear and claustrophobia, and a feeling of complete helplessness, combined to bring several of them close to panic. Some of them had to be restrained by their comrades from running screaming out of the dugouts to take their chances – which was really no chance at all – in the open air. Some men even saw their unwelcome companions, the trench rats, climbing the dugout walls in terror, trying to escape.

They watched the maddened rodents frantically looking for a way out of this torment, and they knew just how they felt. What's more, they all knew that this was in preparation for an attack, and that, when the shelling stopped, they would have to rush up the dugout stairs to the trench and try to stop the British overrunning their lines. What they didn't know was how long the barrage would go on for. After several days, which seemed to some of them as though it had lasted forever, and even though they were safely burrowed beneath the surface, they were still dying in their hundreds. A direct hit would cave in a dugout, or the unending vibrations would bring the roof of one crashing down, killing the lucky ones straight out, but leaving the wounded and merely terrified to suffocate in the darkness.

In their rest area, behind the lines, the 35th Middlesex waited. No more trips to town, no more evenings at Pompette's until after the attack, or perhaps ever. They checked and re-checked their equipment, and at night they tried to sleep, with all the noise of the barrage going on, to their own surprise, succeeding. As more than one of them remarked to his comrades, you can probably get used to just about anything.

One feature of any attack these days, was the retention behind the lines of what was termed 'minimum reserve'. In case a battalion was severely depleted by high casualties, a core of soldiers was kept out of the attack, to form the nucleus of the regiment when it was rebuilt. This was, naturally enough, not something one could volunteer for. The officers just picked a number of names at random from the battalion roll, and those who were selected were ordered to stay behind. One of those so detailed was in 2 Platoon.

It was the evening that the men were about to move up to the trenches. The barrage was now in its sixth day. The men were about to spend the night in the support lines, then move up to the front line at dawn, ready to go over the top. There was a lot of nervous chatter, shouting of orders, yawning, fidgeting, and laughter that was a bit too loud to be natural. Platoon sergeants were finding the men chosen for minimum reserve and falling them out. Sergeant Quill gave the news to one of them.

"Right, Private Ross, fall out. Go stand with those others over there."

"Sar'nt?"

"You heard me, Private. Fall out now. It's your lucky day; you're in the minimum reserve."

"I'd rather stay with my mates, Sar'nt."

"And I'd rather be beside the seaside, beside the sea, but I'm not, so I do as I'm told, and so will you, Private. Fall out."

"Yes, Sar'nt."

Private Ross's reluctance was genuine. This attack was what they were there for. It was, when you thought about it, the reason they had all joined up in the first place, to deliver the knock-out blow to the Hun. Now, all of a sudden, his invitation to the party had been revoked. His friends, several of whom had less than twenty-four hours to live, had they but known it, tried to console him.

"Not your fault, Eddie."

"Luck of the draw, Eddie. Your turn now, one of us next time."

"We'll see you afterwards. Get good and plastered."

With a quick cheerio to his companions, Eddie Ross walked across the field, to where about forty other men were standing. Some of them looked very crestfallen, a few even appeared to have been stunned by the news. Others, though not many, were doing their best not to look smug.

"Well," Private Ross remarked to the man next to him, someone from D-Company, "if this big push does end the war, we won't ever have the chance to be in an attack. All that training for nothing."

The D-Company man said nothing. He was watching his platoon across the field, particularly his younger brother, who was laughing and sharing a joke with his mates.

So, with Private Ross wishing he could be with them, they formed up as a platoon, within their company, within the battalion, as they had done many times before, and they marched towards the trenches. Overhead, the shells still flew by the thousand, to land upon the enemy trenches that were the object of the next morning's attack. Each man carried a pack that had been loaded down with extra supplies. It was assumed that crossing no man's land to the devastated German lines would be so easy, that carrying a pack, weighing fifty pounds or more, would not present a problem. Every man carried extra grenades and ammunition, some carried signal flags, or wire cutters, or even a roll of barbed wire. Because the men's orders were to walk across no man's land, not to run, the powers that be had decided that the extra weight would not be a hindrance.

Conversation on the march to the trenches was permitted, but was very subdued. The men were still optimistic, but the holiday mood had dissipated, to be replaced with a grim determination.

"No more rehearsals," said Private Selway.

"No," replied Private Leuchars.

"Funny to think this is what it's all been leading up to," mused Private Giddington.

"Yes," replied Private Travis. "It seems so long ago that we joined up. I can't really remember it."

"Home before the end of the year, do you reckon?"

"If tomorrow goes well, I don't see why not."

Their guide was waiting. They had done all this before so they didn't need to hear his instructions about keeping closed up, loose wires, and so on, but they listened anyway.

"If the barrage means Fritz is keeping his head down, sir, it would be a lot quicker if we walked along the top," Major Fullerton remarked to Lieutenant-Colonel Wintergrass. "We'd be at the support trench in no time."

"You're probably right, Basil," the C.O. replied. "But best do what we're told. Causes far less trouble in the long run."

Once in the support trench, the men had very little to do but wait for the following morning. The subalterns and sergeants made sure that the men had all of their equipment, uttering words of encouragement as they went. Overhead, the barrage continued to drop tens of thousands of shells on the German lines, with such a ferocity that some officers even entertained the hope that their platoons, or companies, or even battalions, would reach their objectives the next day without loss.

The ration parties arrived exactly as scheduled, and the men ate hot food, washed down with hot, sweet tea. The tea tasted of chlorine, of course, but they were used to that by now. Many of them didn't even notice any more. A chap could get used to anything, after all. Later, the men settled down to sleep as best they could. The first wave, which included all four platoons in A-Company, slept in the support trenches, while the other three waves slept in the reserve trenches. Officers and sergeants had dugouts to sleep in. The men slept anywhere they could find a few feet to stretch out in, or somewhere they could curl up.

This was it. The last big battle of the war, and Fred Quill had come out of retirement to take part in it. One last big push to knock the Hun back on his heels, and then flat onto his back. To Berlin, victory, and back home, to resume his retirement. This was the war to end all wars, so he wouldn't have to fight again, he thought. Enid would be happy and, in spite of how she'd felt, she would be so proud of him now, especially with how he had helped to turn his platoon from soft civilians into fighting soldiers, who were about to be tested in battle. They were a good bunch – he was sure they would do him proud. In a few hours, they would be moving from the support trench to the front line, ready to go over the top in the morning. It was hard to believe that there could be any Germans left alive under that bombardment, not after a whole week of it. He almost felt sorry for them. Funny how you got used to the noise – for long periods, he hardly even noticed it.

Right ho, Fred, he said to himself. *Get a bit of rest and you'll be ready for anything in the morning.* He wasn't getting any younger, that was for sure. He had the most dreadful indigestion again. It was really burning, up in the top part of his stomach; almost hard to breathe at times. This had been happening quite a lot recently. Fred didn't have much time for army doctors and, in his opinion, not a few of the ones he had met during his long years of service had been useless quacks, but he supposed that once this big attack was over, and they had reached their objectives and consolidated their new positions, he ought to go and see the medical officer; see if he could give him some pills or something, to put a stop to this gippy tummy. Not only that, but he fancied he was getting arthritis, or something; he kept feeling nasty pains in his left arm and shoulder recently. There was certainly no joy in growing old. Still, when he got home he would have Enid to look after him.

Fred patted his upper chest with his left palm as a spasm of pain almost knocked the breath out of him. Whew! That was a nasty one. Definitely a visit to the M.O. after the battle. Still, a little rest and he would probably be as right as rain in a few hours, ready for the fighting to come. Fred stepped into a dugout. Someone was asleep in an old armchair, in the corner. There was a plank resting across two crates along one wall. That would do. He lay down and tried to relax. The old soldier in him knew that, even with the noise of the barrage and the comings and goings of his own men, he would be able to fall asleep. The earth smell of the dugout was somehow comforting. Fred Quill rolled onto his side, turned his face to the wall, and slept.

To a man in the trenches, especially during a long, drawn-out barrage, three or four hours' sleep was little short of a luxury, yet most of the men of the St. Marylebone Rifles managed it, or at least something like it. Arnold Snow, in a dugout with several other subalterns, including his brother, was curled up in a broken armchair, looted months before, from the ruins of a French farmhouse. In spite of the noise and discomfort, he managed to drift off into an uneasy sleep. As his eyes closed, he remembered the speech that the C.O. had given them a few hours earlier, as the whole battalion had mustered in full battle order, in their familiar tent-filled field. Unlike so many senior officers, Lieutenant-Colonel Wintergrass always managed to speak to the men eye to eye. No guff. No pompous nonsense. His speech, brief and to the point, was what the men expected to hear: he was proud of them and had complete confidence that every last one of them would do his best. A good speech, Arnold thought; it reinforced the close-knit nature of this battalion.

Outside, trying, and in most cases succeeding, to sleep on the fire-step, on the duckboards, or in the entrances to communications trenches, the men were getting what rest they could.

"'Ere, Vic." Private Marren nudged Private Rangle, who was huddled next to him on the fire-step. "Do you reckon it will be alright tomorrow?"

"I expect so. It should all be very straightforward, that's what they tell us. You should always trust your officers, Joe."

"Yes." There was a pause. "You've been in battle before, haven't you, Vic? We all reckon you have, and you never let on, like."

"You could be right about that, Joe. Now, shall we try and get some sleep? It'll be time to move up to the front line before you know it."

"Yes, Vic, alright." Private Marren pondered for a few moments, then nudged Private Travis, who was the other side of him.

"Harry. Vic reckons it will go alright tomorrow."

"That's good, Joe," Private Travis managed with a bleak smile. "Now let's get a spot of kip."

"Back in Banbury by Christmas, eh, Harry?"

"Let's hope so, Joe. Now shut up, there's a good lad."

And they slept. It was a fitful, shallow sleep, but it was sleep, and it showed, as much as anything, how they had become soldiers, that they could make themselves as comfortable as possible in the open air, sleeping in a trench cut into the mud, under a dark sky, that for the sixth night running, was ripped asunder by the passage of thousands of artillery shells.

Dawn came good and early at that time of year, and barrage or no barrage, the whole front was awake for the dawn stand to. No one expected the enemy to attack that day, but they stood ready and prepared anyway, as they had done every day since the opposing armies had dug their trenches and hunkered down for a war of attrition.

After stand to, and before the breakfast rations arrived, Arnold Snow made another check on every man in his platoon. It gave him the chance to wish each one of them luck, and to make sure every one had his pack, his rifle, any extra equipment he needed, and a full water bottle.

"Use your water sparingly," he told each one. "There's no way of knowing when you'll get any more."

Some men replied with a quiet, "Yes, sir," or even simply, "Sir," while others made a cheerful retort of some kind. Arnold was left reflecting, yet again, at what wonderful chaps his platoon were.

"Good luck, sir," said Private Millcross.

"Thank you, and good luck to you too, Private," Arnold replied, just as he heard Lance Corporal Clay calling him.

"Sir. Mr Snow, sir."

"What is it, Clay?"

"I can't wake Sergeant Quill, sir."

"Has he been hit?"

"Don't think so, sir. He just won't wake up."

"Where is he?"

"In a dugout, sir."

"I see. Well you'd better show me."

"Sir."

Arnold followed Lance Corporal Clay to a dugout, a few bays away. Some of the platoon watched them walk by, but most were preoccupied with their own thoughts, as they waited for the order to move up to the front line trench.

Fred Quill was lying on the makeshift plank bed, on his right side, his legs bent and drawn up under him. Arnold Snow shook him by his left shoulder.

"Sergeant! Sergeant Quill!"

Nothing.

Arnold pulled on Fred Quill's shoulder and rolled him onto his back. One of his eyes was slightly open, his face white, his lips a strange shade of blue. Arnold knelt down and put his ear to Fred's chest.

"Nothing there," he said. "He's dead alright. There's not a mark on him. Must have pegged out in his sleep, poor chap."

"Yes, sir. Shall I organise a burial party?"

"No, we don't have time. We'll just have to leave him here; they can bury him after the battle. I'll notify Major Henderson later. There's nothing else we can do."

"Yes, sir."

"Right. Back to your section, Clay. We'll be moving up the trench any moment."

"Sir."

The two men went out of the dugout, leaving behind the body of what had once been Fred Quill.

The 35th Middlesex moved up to the front line trench before it was fully light, to relieve the battalion that had been there for the previous seven days. The few hundred yards, along the zig-zag of the communications trench, did not take them long and, once in the front line, they spread out, platoon by platoon. The attack was to be in four waves and, for the St. Marylebones', the C.O. had decided that the simplest way to deploy was one company per wave, in alphabetical order. So A-Company had the honour of kicking off for the battalion.

Zero hour was to be seven-thirty that morning. The barrage was to start creeping forward, as the men left their trenches and walked across no man's land, a wall of steel moving ahead of them as they took the enemy positions. At six-thirty the barrage intensified. The men who sheltered beneath it, would not have thought such a thing possible, but it happened. Each heavy gun, howitzer, and field piece fired more rapidly. Gun barrels glowed red hot, as more shells, making more noise than at any time in the previous week – in all of history, in fact – flew overhead, to bring destruction to the Germans.

During the previous weeks, special crews of British soldiers, many of them coal miners, had tunnelled under no man's land, right under the German lines, hollowing out large caverns, which had then been packed with high explosives. Just before seven-thirty, seventeen of these mines were detonated simultaneously, ripping huge holes in the enemy lines, as the earth and debris, thrown up by the enormous explosions, reached hundreds of feet into the sky. The shock wave knocked the breath out of the watching British, across no man's land. Many were jolted off their feet. The blast was heard in south-east England; it rattled the windows of the prime minister's study at 10 Downing Street, in London.

When they got their breath back, the British reflected that this was more evidence that the enemy would be pounded into oblivion, what with the barrage and the mines. They would just stroll across no man's land and mop up any resistance, if there actually was any that needed mopping up.

That was the plan. But those who had formulated it did not take into account the depth and strength of the German dugouts, way down in the chalk. Cramped, noisy, and stinking of fear they may have been, but the majority of them had withstood the barrage. The men inside were frightened, hungry, dazed, but they were still able to fight.

The planners were also convinced that the barrage would obliterate the wide belt of barbed wire, that lay in front of the German front line trenches. Granted, it had blasted some gaps in it, but, for the most part, the shells had just bounced the wire up and down, tangling it in some places, leaving it more or less intact in others. It waited, a malevolent obstacle to the British.

What was more, through mistakes in planning, or a mistake in communications, or perhaps some other unknown reason, the barrage ended five minutes too early. Five long minutes, while the British waited in their trenches for the attack to begin, where the Germans were able to climb out of their shelters and man the machine guns they were shortly to put to very effective use against the attackers.

The 35th Middlesex did not know this, of course, and as the officers blew their whistles at seven-thirty, they climbed out of their trenches and made for the German lines, to start winning the war.

The Attack

The razored edge of day creeps from the east
And all of us with arms and courage wait
And wonder what will be the end that fate
Will give to each, before the day has ceased.

From farm and cottage fair we came, from port
And town and village, each a volunteer,
And with our comrades we did stand to cheer
The victory that valour will have bought.

As soldiers now, we're ready to go forth,
And some will make triumphant that advance
While some as clay embrace the soil of France;
A sacrifice that fate will say is worth.

The warming light of day now shines upon
Twelve miles of men, about to cross dread ground
And duty do, to which we're gladly bound,
Nor shall we cease till victory is won.

Alec Millcross, 1892 - 1968

Chapter XXXIII

Lance Corporal Clay

Here we are, he thought. *After all the preparations and rehearsals and exercises and all the talk of the big push, here we all are, waiting in the front line to go over the top in the first wave. My luck to join a battalion that's going over first! No use complaining at this late stage. We're here because we're here because we're here. Just have to do the best we can.*

This, though, he surmised, *is definitely not what Old Mother Clay had in mind for her only son. Claybourne, I mean! It's funny – I tend to forget for the longest time what my real name was. It's as though all that business, that I don't like to think about, happened to someone else. In a way it did. I'm Matthew Clay now. One stripe on my sleeve and paid by the king to be a lance corporal in his army. When it's all over, if I survive, I suppose I'll go on being Matthew Clay. No one to go back to in my old life, with my mum and dad both being in lavender long ago. What am I talking about – if I survive? Of course I'll survive. I'll be coming out at the other end of this war. Find a nice job; no need to go back to that old business. There must be other things that I'm good at. Maybe even stay in the army. They'll need good NCOs. I could be sergeant or something, in a good regiment. Maybe get a posting somewhere in the Empire – nice and warm in winter, I'll be bound.* He liked this idea. *And it will keep me far away from anyone who is still investigating that other business; which I don't like dwelling on. It was all a mistake. I didn't mean it.* He shook his head to clear it. *Strange, though – I dreamed about poor Amy just the other night. It happens from time to time. She was sitting back in her armchair with her arms hanging down at her sides. Just looking at me. I was waiting for her to say she forgave me but she didn't. Just stared at me. It made me feel very uneasy and when I woke up it took me a long time to put it out of my mind. Well, maybe I haven't, seeing as*

I'm thinking of it now. Poor Amy. But it really wasn't my fault. Anyway, no use thinking about that, is there? Other things to do today. Won't be long now.

Bloody hell! My God, would you look at that. We've set off a mine, right under the enemy lines. I've never seen anything like it. That explosion must be thousands of feet high – right up to the sky. Nothing could live through that. Oh my. Even this far away, the blast well nigh knocked us off our feet. Poor sodding Jerry. There won't be much left for us to do now, except mop up and let the cavalry through.

The barrage has lifted, he realised. *That feels strange. A week it's been going on, day and night. I never heard such a noise, but it's odd how you can get used to things. I wonder how many shells we fired over at Jerry. Hundreds of thousands, I shouldn't wonder. Tell you what – I wouldn't mind owning a munitions factory right now. They must be making a bloody fortune; probably millions from our barrage alone. I wonder if the Germans got used to it, what with actually being under it.* He paused, thinking of them all, buried underneath the debris. *I can't really believe anyone lived through that. It's more than you can expect a person to survive. Lucky for us, though – our first big attack, and it'll be against an enemy trench where they'll all be dead already. Or at least most of them. Probably a few wounded lying about the place, too. It's hard not to feel a bit sorry for them.*

There. Mr. Snow is looking at his watch. Can't be much longer now. The lads all seem game. I'll be first up this ladder, Private Rangle to come after me. He's a good man. Knows what he's doing.

He glanced around again. *Not much longer now, surely. The barrage has been over for several minutes. Major Henderson's staring at his watch, and he's put his whistle in his mouth. He'll be blowing it any moment now. There. Thought so."*

"Come on, lads, time to go," he shouted, climbing up his trench ladder.

That wasn't as easy as it was in the practice exercises, he thought. *My pack's much heavier than it was then. Makes a difference, but not enough to stop me, of course. How far away is the German front line? Two, three hundred yards maybe?* He kept on walking towards the German trenches. *Should be there in no time. You've got to hand it to the working parties who went out last night. They've managed to get a path cut through our own wire, and they've marked it with white tape, clear as you like. I suppose Jerry was too busy, keeping his head down under the barrage, to do any mischief. Still, you can't take it away from them. They've done a wonderful job. This is all going exactly to plan, just like we were told.*

Right, now we're through the wire, we need to spread out. One long line, not all bunched up. And walking but not running. Not too slow, mind. We don't want the second wave too close behind us. He checked around him. *Good. Everyone seems to know what he's doing. We look like soldiers. Which is what we are, of course. The platoon is putting on a very good show. The colonel will be pleased.* He glanced round as he heard a voice. *Who was that who shouted out, 'Next stop Berlin'? This isn't a bloody carnival.*

"Shut up and keep moving," he shouted.

Nothing wrong with the men being in good spirits, he told himself, *but they mustn't think this is all a lark.*

Beautiful day for it, though. Hardly a cloud in the sky. Some of the men were a bit windy before we went over the top. Can't really blame them. I was too, if I'm honest with myself. But it looks as though this will be little more than a walk in the sunshine.

Ah, I see we've started shelling the German rear area now. Poor sods. We must have blown the shit out of them this past week. And that sounds like the patter of our machine guns. Strange; I didn't think we were carrying machine guns in the first wave.

It was then that he realised the reality of the situation. *Oh my God! Those aren't our machine guns, they're Jerry's. Fuck! We weren't expecting this. Oh God, oh God. What do we do? Think!* He tried to clear his head, to stop himself from panicking. *Yes, all right. No bunching up. Keep the lads line abreast. Please God, don't let us all get hit. The men will all want to take cover. If they do, the attack will stall. Keep them moving.*

"Keep going," he yelled. For a brief moment, the sound of his own voice, raised in command, offered him a small measure of comfort. Not for long, though.

Oh shit! Those fellows in 3 Platoon have been hit. They must have walked right into the enemy machine gun fire. God, there are hardly any of them left on their feet.

The Company Sergeant-Major is yelling something. Can't hear it above all the din. If I signal to him, maybe he'll shout again. I need to know what order he's giving. Yes, he's seen me, but I still can't hear what he's saying. Maybe if – There was a loud explosion. *Oh fuck, no. He's hit. Get up Sar'nt, please get up! God, it must be bad, the way he's writhing about. Poor bastard. I thought he was indestructible. How long has he been in the army?* He realised he was lingering too long. *Doesn't matter. Mustn't think about that now. Just keep on, keep the men moving.*

He looked around, to check on the other men. *Where's the platoon to our left? There's no one there. They can't all have been hit, but I can't see any of them. Are they behind us? No... can't see them. Yes, I can. Oh God, they're all down. All lying in a row. They can't all be shot – they must be taking cover, that must be it. But they don't seem to be moving. They can't all be dead; they just can't be.*

He tried to focus on the job at hand. *Got to get to cover. There's something there ahead, a shattered tree stump or something. That'll do. We're supposed to walk but never mind that, I'm bloody running.* He ran as fast as he could, jumping over several bodies of his dead comrades. *There! Lie flat behind it, flat as you can, boy. They can't get you here. It's not as big as I thought it was, but if I press myself really flat to the ground, that should help.*

Shit! That bullet hit my pack. Was that by chance, or have they spotted me? Lie still, old son. No need to give yourself away. Just wait till Jerry finds something else to shoot at. Not that it seems to be happening. Where have all these Germans come from anyway? How did they survive the barrage? They must have had some very deep shelters here. Just our luck that it should be in our sector. God, suppose it's like this along the whole front. It can't be – that would mean the whole attack is a fiasco. I can't believe that. This must just be a local difficulty. I expect the cavalry is already through the enemy front line, on either side of us. They'll be mopping up from the flanks soon, putting paid to this little lot.

I suppose we should do our bit, then, he realised. *The army's not paying me to lie down all day. On your feet, boy, you've got a trench to capture. Strewth, easier said than done with this heavy pack. Right, onwards and upwards. There's enough of us still standing, looks like.*

"Keep moving lads," he shouted. "Look for the gaps in the Jerry wire."

He looked around, to see who was following him. *I think they heard me. Yes, that was Private Snibley waving acknowledgment. I can't make out who's with him. The platoons are probably all mixed up now. The companies too, I expect. We need to get to the wire and find a gap. There must be lots of them, after all that shelling. Then, rush through the gap and into the trench, overpower them, and wait for the second wave. Just like we were told to.*

Oh God. Now the Jerry artillery has started up. Must lie down. We are really fucked. Machine gun fire, and now shelling. How on earth can we go on through this? How many of us are there left? Shit, that was close. A little more to the left and I'd have had it, that's for sure. He tried to pull himself together. *Right. Got to get to their trench. More shelter in there, and it's what we came here to do anyway. The last place we want to be is stuck out here, in the middle of no man's land. How can I rally the men? Maybe if I stand up and yell something. They might hear me over the shelling. This bloody pack – it's so heavy, makes it so much harder to stand up. Now, where is everyone? I can't see anything for all the explosions. It's got much more intense now, shells landing everywhere. If I didn't know better, I'd say they were all aimed at me personally. The enemy wire's not far off. So many shells! Got to find a gap in it. Then I can —*

Chapter XXXIV

Private Tunniford and Private Winslow

On that day, when so many men perished before the going down of the sun, some died quickly, others died slowly, by painful degrees; some died well, others badly. Two, among the many thousands who did die, were Private Colin Tunniford and Private Johnny Winslow.

For all his talk to Myrtle, and his other artistic and literary chums, Colin Tunniford had not managed to maintain the intellectual detachment from the war that he, and they, had thought was a *sine qua non* for participating in it. No matter how different he considered himself from his fellow soldiers, no matter how lofty the arty plane he felt he occupied, he was, in the end, a soldier, just like them. It came almost as a shock to him to realise that, those who fought with him, and those set above him, regarded him as just another ranker. Put men in uniform and what you get is uniformity. Once he came to terms with the fact that he was completely in the army, Colin Tunniford became a good soldier. Gone was his inner contempt for his superiors; no longer did he smirk to himself at the practice of saluting and the rituals that went with military life. Had he lived, there could probably have been two, or even three, stripes for him, in due course – maybe even a commission. But he did not live, so all speculations about stripes and commissions were fruitless.

On this day, the day that it all came to an end for him, Private Tunniford had waited in the trench with the rest, as seven-thirty approached, enthusiasm giving way to apprehension. In the back of his mind lurked fear, but he put that spectre behind him. On this day, the day when the war would surely begin to end, there was no room in his heart for fear. Some people would not live to see the sun set, of course, but he would not be among them. Neither, he hoped, would too many of his comrades. Some yards down the trench, a private in 3 Platoon leant against the back wall and vomited. Private Tunniford looked at Private Hope, and they shared a rueful smile at the other man's fear. Now, as bravado overcame apprehension, Private Tunniford winked at Private Hope – two comrades about to share the same dangers and, he was sure, the same victory.

After the mines had exploded, and the barrage had stopped, as the officers' whistles were sounding along the front line, Private Tunniford climbed the trench ladder, just behind Private Travis. It was just like it had been in the training exercises – once out of the trench, follow the white tape, through the prepared gaps in the British wire. Once through, they were to spread out in line abreast, rifles at high port, and walk steadily towards the blasted remnants of the enemy front line. It was as easy as that. As he began walking, Private Tunniford saw a line of men, stretching out either side of him, to each horizon. After the unbelievable noise of the barrage, the comparative quiet was almost startling. He could hear his own footfall on the dry earth, a bird singing somewhere, men's voices, and the sound of his own breathing.

"Next stop Berlin," someone yelled.

"Shut up and keep moving," bellowed someone else, probably Lance Corporal Clay

As ordered, he made his way across no man's land at a walking pace. For perhaps half a minute, he began to think that the day would actually turn out exactly as the planners had said it would. Looking at the endless line of soldiers to the right and left of him – and this was just the first wave – he couldn't see how an enemy, even one as efficient and well trained as the German army, could withstand an assault of this magnitude. He told himself to look round him at all times, to impress upon his memory all the sights of the attack, so that afterwards he could make rough drawings of what he had seen, to be reproduced, at a later date, as paintings for sale. This was obviously the pivotal day of the whole war, the day that things began to end, the day, although he didn't know it, that would occupy page after page in the history books. As such, he wanted to have paintings ready to sell. For him, as a war artist, this day was a marvellous opportunity; his best chance of leaving his mark upon posterity. In his pack, which he carried on his back, as well as the large pair of wire cutters he had been ordered to take with him, were several sheets of cartridge paper, a box of pencils and crayons, and a few sticks of charcoal. He had come prepared.

When the German machine guns opened up, he was, for a few moments, sure that his senses were deceiving him. This was not supposed to happen. He had been dwelling on how to reproduce, in a few bold strokes of the brush, the few wisps of cotton wool clouds, that hung against the pure blue of the summer sky. For a second or two, he had even forgotten that he was in a battle. It was a beautiful blue sky. *Cerulean*, he thought, *that's what they call that sort of sky blue*. It was an interesting sounding word, 'cerulean'. As far as he could remember, he had never used it before. He muttered it out loud – "Cerulean" – just to get a taste of it, and, as some words do when you're under great stress or pressure, it stuck in his mind, and it echoed round in his brain as he walked forward. 'Cerulean, cerulean.' Then, to his left, he saw several men fall, one after the other, and instinctively he threw himself flat on the ground, pressing his face into the dirt, trying to make himself as small a target as possible. He succeeded in this, because he remained untouched, except for one bullet that struck his pack, which, apart from giving him a scare, did him no harm at all.

"Come on lads, keep going," shouted one of the sergeants

Private Tunniford did not want to keep moving. He was not a physical coward, not by any means, but he just did not want to stand up and walk into that tempest of machine gun fire. For the time being, he was safe where he was, lying down. But he was a soldier, for the duration only, perhaps, but a soldier, first and last. He did what thousands of men did that day, and he drew upon a reserve of courage, deep inside himself, that he did not even know he possessed. He stood and began to walk, in the soldier's crouch, towards the German lines. For him, as for so many, the enemy barbed wire was the place to get to first. For some reason, it gave the illusion of offering a measure of shelter from the bullets. He began to walk faster and then broke into a trot – as fast as he could go, carrying his pack. The man immediately to his left fell, with a sharp cry, onto the ground, and Private Tunniford, in some corner of his artist's mind, noticed the cloud of dry earth that erupted as the body landed. At one point he stumbled but managed to keep himself from falling, and by good luck more than anything else, he reached the edge of the German wire, where he again flung himself down. For a few moments, as he caught his breath, he wondered what he should do next.

The German wire was an impenetrable belt of hundreds of strands, dozens of yards across. Some of it had rusted, for it had been there for months, or even years, while other strands still bore the shine of new steel. Old or new though, it was an effective barrier to an assault. As Private Tunniford looked at it, one thought struck him after a few seconds – this was not supposed to be there. The whole point of that week-long barrage, they had all been told, was to destroy the German wire, so the attacking troops could walk over it, to the enemy trenches. Obviously, though, the barrage had failed. Perhaps the wire had been disturbed by the barrage, true, but it was still here, as impassable as ever.

As he looked back the way he had come, he saw no man's land littered with bodies in khaki. Who was dead and who was wounded, he could not tell. Here and there, men scuttled towards the German lines, but the enemy artillery had started up now, and more fell, even as he watched. Well, he thought, he had the wire cutters with him, so it was his job to start cutting the wire, to make a way through for any men who managed to get as far as him.

It was very awkward, lying on his front, clutching his rifle, his pack on his back, trying to make himself as flat as he could, to avoid the maelstrom of German bullets that flew above him. As far as he could tell, no one was aiming at him specifically, but of course, that made no difference. The dozens of machine guns spraying no man's land were as indiscriminate as a scythes when the corn is harvested. He didn't want to draw attention to himself and would have been quite willing, left to his own devices, to lie flat, face pressed into the earth, for the rest of the day, the week, or until the whole deadly business was over. But he hadn't been left to his own devices – he was a soldier, part of an attack, and he had his duty to do. The enemy wire had not been cut by the barrage; he had with him a pair of wire cutters. It was obvious to him what he had to do.

These wire cutters, a big, two-handed affair, were strapped to the outside of his pack. To get at them, he had to unbuckle his pack and shrug it off, then reach over it and unstring them. He expected a bullet at any moment, but he managed it, and as he held the tool, one handle in each hand, he contemplated the impenetrable belt of barbed wire in front of him, many yards across. It didn't seem possible that he could cut his way through that, one strand at a time, but that was something he preferred not to think about.

"Just get on with it," he muttered out loud to himself, and he put the jaws of the cutters round one strand of wire pushing the handles together. The blades sliced, almost effortlessly, through the wire, whose severed ends leaped apart with an audible twang, scattering tiny flakes of rust in their wake.

And the next one, he thought, as he cut another strand. Now he had something to do, something to concentrate on, he was not as frightened as he had been. All round him, men were running, falling, taking cover, screaming, dying, but he felt completely on his own. All he was thinking of, was the next strand of barbed wire.

Soon some of the men saw what he was doing and, some running, some crawling, some scuttling over in a crouch, they converged on him. Here was someone who was going to cut a way through the wire for them. Soon, a knot of soldiers surrounded Private Tunniford. They had been warned against bunching up, but now, all that was forgotten, and he was too intent on what he was doing to pay too much attention to the crowd of khaki that was surrounding him. He had cut maybe a dozen strands of wire, which left only a few hundred to go. He crawled forward another foot and cursed, as he impaled his elbow on a rusty barb, that was lying half buried in the dirt.

He may not have noticed the crowd of soldiers round him, taking cover as best they could, most lying as flat as possible, but the German defenders did. Some of them, exposing themselves above the parapets of their own trenches, began shooting their rifles at the crowd of British soldiers, caught in a bottleneck on the other side of the barbed wire, who made such an irresistible target.

One of the British soldiers there was an officer, Captain Case, the battalion adjutant. He crawled up to where Private Tunniford was doggedly cutting, strand by strand, through the wire.

"Good man," he said.

Private Tunniford glanced back at him. "Sir," he replied. There wasn't much more he could say, and he certainly didn't feel this was the right time to make conversation.

Captain Case looked back at the other men surrounding them. "Does anyone else have a pair of wire cutters?"

No reply.

"Anyone? No? Very well then, when this man has cut a way through the enemy wire, follow in single file. Remember the drill. Consolidate the enemy trench one bay at a time."

Useful instructions, maybe, and fully representative of how they had all been drilled when the attack had been rehearsed, but they turned out to be thoroughly redundant. As it happened, no one was going anywhere. For all his good intentions, Private Tunniford had no hope of cutting all the way through the belt of German barbed wire like that. It would have taken hours. Furthermore, the German rifle fire, at the clump of men, was not without success. Several of them lay dead or wounded. A couple of Germans began to throw grenades. One landed just next to Captain Case and Private Tunniford, killing them both. In the twinkle of an eye, death swept Colin Tunniford away. No more painting, no more career as a war artist. Just another dead soldier.

While Colin Tunniford, after climbing out of the trench, had been thinking about the blue of the sky and listening to his own footfall, Private Winslow had been conscious, above all, of one thing – overpowering and all-consuming fear. The same Johnny Winslow who had been the unofficial leader of his little troupe of chums, who had enjoyed the advantage of owning a motor car, even a second hand one, and who had done punishment drill for cheeking the sergeant instructor at Étaples, the Johnny Winslow who had been everyone's cheerful friend, a bit more worldly wise than most of the others; this same man had discovered that, since they had first visited the front line, he was probably the closest thing to a coward in all of A-Company. It was beyond his understanding how so many of his comrades, who had had far more trouble with army drill and manoeuvres than him, could stay so calm, or at least appear to, under fire. When they had been in the front line previously, he had never put his head above the parapet, even for a fraction of a second, unless he had to. When he was on sentry duty, he had performed it at a permanent cringe. He wanted to run and hide in a dugout every time a shell flew overhead, and while his fellow platoon members soon learned to tell one kind of shell from another by their sounds, not even bothering to duck when they heard one flying overhead, which they knew would land many miles behind them, he ducked at every single one. It was an effort to stop himself crying out in fear, and he did not always succeed. How many of his friends had noticed his fear, he did not know. Certainly, no one had said anything to him about it, possibly because he was still so very popular.

When the bombardment had started the previous week, and it had become clear that the long heralded big push, as everyone was calling it, was soon to take place, Private Winslow had seriously considered taking himself out of the fighting by shooting himself, even bayoneting himself, if necessary, in the foot, or the left arm. But, of course, he was not the only soldier in the army to have had that idea, and such acts were considered cowardice in the face of the enemy. After church parade, two weeks previously, the adjutant had read out, to the entire battalion, the news that a corporal in a territorial regiment, stationed nearby, had been court martialled and sentenced to death by firing squad for cowardice, after having deliberately shot himself in the leg. When the men had discussed it afterwards, the general feeling was that the death sentence would probably be commuted, as most of them were, but there had been little sympathy for the corporal in question.

"That's the coward's way out," remarked Private Giddington.

"I can't understand what would drive someone to that extreme," commented Lance Corporal Marvell.

I can, Private Winslow wanted to shout. *I know exactly what he was feeling. I know the terror he must have experienced, that he would risk permanent mutilation, just to get away from here. What is wrong with all of you, that you aren't all trying to get out of here?* But, of course, he said nothing and just nodded in vague agreement with his friends.

Now, the big push was here. After that long, unceasing barrage, and the huge mine explosions, it did not seem possible that there could be any Germans left alive in the enemy trenches – their own officers had reassured them as much – but Private Winslow was not going to take that on trust. Threading his way through the prepared gap in the British wire, then walking in line abreast with his fellows, gripping his rifle so tightly that his hands hurt, he felt fear envelop him like a familiar shroud. With each step, he was softly whimpering to himself.

When the German machine guns and artillery opened up, he screamed, but the sound of his fear was lost in the noise of shells and bullets. He began to run, though he didn't really know what he was running to. In the German trenches, death was surely waiting for him, but it was also out here in the open too, ready to pluck him away at any second. If he ran back the way he had come, the military police would have him, and he would be up before a court martial and then a firing squad. So he ran onwards, weeping in terror. He saw men falling dead and wounded at either side of him, including, many yards away, Private Wilfred Leuchars. *Oh no,* he thought, *not Wilf.* Not his childhood friend, his best pal in the world! Not Wilf; it couldn't be. He and Wilf were supposed to survive this war. This was not supposed to have happened.

A shell exploded near to him – not close enough to do more than knock him off his feet and shower him with earth, even though it killed two other men near him. Private Winslow lay on his front, whimpering, his eyes squeezed tightly shut. This was not fair. He shouldn't have been there; he should have been back at the bank in Rochester, with Wilf and Eddie. Except that Wilf was dead. This was all a mistake. He didn't want to be a soldier after all. He had changed his mind.

He did not remember getting to his feet, but he found himself running again, crouched over, towards the German lines. He was overcome with fear now. What he had to do was get away from this killing ground and, in his terror, he reasoned that there was more safety in a trench, than out in the open. If running back to his own trench would get him arrested and shot, then he had best get to the enemy trenches, preferably after his comrades had taken and secured it. So, he would get to the German wire, take shelter in a convenient shell hole, or similar, give the rest of the battalion time to capture its objectives, and then make his way to the safety of the newly captured trench.

As a plan for his survival, it was not a bad one, and it might even have worked, but as he ran to the enemy lines a bullet struck him in the hip, and he fell to the ground, screaming in pain and frustration. A few yards ahead of him, no more than that, was a slight rise in the ground, only a couple of feet, but enough to afford him shelter. He was wounded now and, by virtue of his wound, he was exempt from taking any further part in the battle. All he had to do was stay alive till the stretcher-bearers came to get him. He unbuckled and shed his pack, the prerogative of the wounded man, before trying to drag himself to the lee of the ridge of earth, but fate was not about to let him escape that easily. A second bullet hit him in the stomach and he collapsed where he was.

The pain was bad, but not as bad as he would have imagined it would be. Shock or something, probably, he reasoned. There was still a good chance, he supposed, that he would be found and taken to a casualty clearing station, before he died. All he had to do was lie still, one hand clamped to his stomach, in an effort to staunch the bleeding. He was aware of bullets flying, shells exploding, and men running past him. Most paid him no attention – they had seen enough dead and wounded bodies in the last few minutes, for the sight to no longer be remarkable. A few glanced at him but kept on going, as per orders not to stop for the wounded. His tunic was soaked with blood now, and his vision was blurring. How long would the stretcher-bearers take to find him? There were so many men running to the enemy lines, those that weren't shot down, and not one of them was carrying a stretcher. None of them seemed to pay any attention to him. Then, suddenly, as a spasm of pain racked him, and white lights danced round the edge of his vision, he saw his friend, Wilfred Leuchars, coming towards him. Wilf – he hadn't been killed after all.

"Wilf," he called. "I'm hit, Wilf!"

But Wilf took no notice; he just kept on running, straight past Private Winslow. Perhaps he hadn't seen him.

"Wilf," he croaked again, and he reached out and grabbed Wilf by the ankle. Taken completely by surprise, Wilf stumbled and almost fell over.

"Let go," he snapped.

"I'm hit, Wilf. I think it's pretty bad. Do you know where the stretcher-bearers are?"

"Let go, will you?" He tried to free his ankle, but the grip of the dying man was surprisingly strong.

"Go and find the stretcher-bearers, Wilf. I can't last much longer out here."

"I'm not Wilf, you silly sod. Let go of my ankle." He was almost tempted to jab Private Winslow's hand with the tip of his bayonet.

"Help me, Wilf!"

"I'm not fucking Wilf. Let me go!" This was ridiculous. Here he was, trying to get across no man's land, and some wounded bloke had stopped him, dead in the middle of things.

"Not Wilf?"

"No, I'm not. Sorry. Let go of me."

Private Winslow squinted up at him. No, it wasn't his friend Wilf. It was someone from B-Company; he couldn't remember his name. He didn't even look like Wilf.

"You're not Wilf." It came out as a wail.

"No. So let go of my ankle." He softened a bit. "Look mate, stretcher-bearers'll be along soon enough. Just lie still till they get here."

Private Winslow stared up at this man, who wasn't his friend Wilf after all.

"Sorry," he mumbled. He was about to let go of the man's ankle but, just then, a well aimed bullet from the enemy lines, fired by a German who found a British soldier standing upright, in the middle of no man's land, too good a target to ignore, hit this man full in the chest, ploughed its way through his heart, before coming out of his back and spinning off into the distance. The man fell dead next to Private Winslow, who still held on to his ankle.

Johnny Winslow released his grip. His stomach wasn't quite so painful now, and his vision was fading. In fact, he felt rather relaxed. He looked at the blurred form of the corpse next to him and, as the life gurgled out of him, he couldn't avoid the nagging feeling that maybe this had, somehow, been partly his fault.

Chapter XXXV

Private Snibley and Private Leuchars

Hundreds upon hundreds of trench ladders had been made for this attack. Rough hewn, unseasoned, two-inch by four-inch beams, cut and fashioned into ladders high enough to allow men to climb out of a six foot trench. Hundreds there might have been, but they were still not enough. In many places in the British front line, pegs had been driven into the trench wall for men to climb, but in the sector occupied by 2 Platoon, there were thankfully ladders enough, each one designated for two men.

Private Hubert Snibley and Private Wilfred Leuchars stood either side of the ladder they were to climb. Everything had been decided – Private Snibley up first, Private Leuchars up behind him. Because their packs were so heavy, and climbing a ladder with one was not as easy as it would normally be, they had arranged that, if necessary, Wilfred would give Hubert a boost by pushing him up. After Hubert had gone, Wilfred would just have to do the best he could.

When the barrage stopped at 7:25am, and a sudden quiet fell over the trenches, each man was left, for a few moments, with his own thoughts. Some remembered home, others made muttered conversation. Some made last minute adjustments to the webbing of their packs, or checked, for the dozenth time and quite unnecessarily, that their bayonets were firmly fixed. Many just stood in silence, like Privates Snibley and Leuchars, waiting for the signal to go over the top.

There was a lump of mud on one of the rungs of the ladder, the fourth rung up from the bottom, Private Snibley noted. It had probably been scraped off the sole of the boot, by someone who had used the ladder before. But when? Maybe it had been in an exercise, or one of the many manoeuvres that had been staged in recent weeks. Or perhaps it had been during the night. The ladders had been fixed in place during the last few days, and last night the working parties had gone out, to cut and mark paths through the British wire. That bit of mud had probably come off one of their boots. That must be it, Private Snibley nodded to himself in satisfaction. There was always an answer to every problem, if you just concentrated and thought it through. There was a blade of grass sticking out of the lump of mud, a flash of green against the grey-brown. If no one trod on it, he thought, that could probably continue growing, and as he pondered that for a few moments, the thought came to him unbidden – by the time it got dark, maybe that blade of grass would still be alive, but how many of his chums would be dead? This was not going to be a difficult attack, they had all been assured of that, what with all the Germans being obliterated by the barrage, but it still would be dangerous. He tried to push his fears out of his mind. Mustn't show you're scared – that would be letting your mates down.

However, there were times when he got so nervous at the thought of being in combat, that he could taste it, sour and malevolent, at the back of his throat. Not now, though – he would not permit himself to be scared, and he definitely shouldn't have been thinking like that. He had confided to Myrtle, when he stayed with her during his embarkation leave, that when he thought about it, really thought about it, he realised how nervous he was about combat. The whole business of joining up had been a lark, an escape from a series of hand to mouth jobs and his unhappy, squalid little home. He enjoyed the comradeship of his new mates and had even enjoyed most of the training. He was good at it, and he had no doubts as to the justice of Britain's cause, but he was frightened of what might happen to him in an actual battle. He did not want to die and he certainly did not want to be mutilated.

Myrtle had patted his hand and told him she quite understood, going on to say that the army had a job to do in defeating the Germans, who were a menace to the peace of Europe. Such sentiments, though, had not stopped her holding a meeting of some anti-war group or other at her flat – half a dozen earnest young people, who preached to each other about the evil of this war – including three young men, in apparently good health, of military age. Hubert, in his uniform, as per orders, had sat at the back of the room, nursing a beer.

"What about Belgium?" he'd asked, after listening to their chatter for about half an hour.

"What?" Half a dozen heads had turned to look at the soldier in the corner, surprised he had spoken. He was Myrtle's latest pet, but he wasn't expected to have any opinions.

"What about Belgium? The Germans are occupying almost all of it and some of France too. How do we get them out if we don't fight?"

"That's typical of the military mind," muttered one of the women.

"What we have to do, my friend," said the young man who appeared to be leading the group, "is make the Germans understand that their position is simply morally unacceptable."

"How?"

"Intelligent discussion, old chap. Civilised fellows sitting down and talking it through."

"Fine, yes, but what do we do if, after all these discussions, the Germans still say they'd prefer to keep Belgium for themselves?"

A barrage of tutting erupted from the women, amidst indulgent smiles from the men.

"You don't understand. If the moral case is stated to them clearly enough, the Germans can't possibly fail to see that we are right. It simply isn't possible."

"Not possible," someone echoed.

"You do realise, don't you, that we are talking about the nation that brought forth Beethoven, and Schiller, and Goethe? They're not a crowd of Hottentots."

Hubert had never heard of those three German gentlemen, so their invocation had failed to impress him.

"They can behave like Hottentots. We've all heard the stories."

"Propaganda, my dear fellow. Fiction, fiction, all the way; invented to sell newspapers of the most vulgar kind."

"And," chimed in a tall woman, with bad acne, "to increase the profits of the munitions manufacturers." The congregation all nodded.

"Look," Hubert persisted. "All I know is that we promised we would help Belgium, gave our word as a country, so that's what we've got to do."

"That's very touching, but of course, I'm not surprised you feel that way. You're a soldier, after all," said the man. "And it's only natural that your outlook has been blinkered by your military training. No need for you to blame yourself."

"I don't."

"Quite. But, what I mean is that, we in our group here, have been studying this war in depth. Looking at it from all angles, so to speak, so it's only natural that we should understand it better than people like you."

"People like me?"

"Yes. Soldiers, sailors, victims of the whole rotten system."

A couple of the women assumed expressions of sympathy, while the other men nodded.

"What's it like at the front?" one asked.

"I haven't been to the front yet. Haven't left England. We're off to France in a couple of days."

"So you haven't been blooded yet?"

"No." Hubert hadn't heard that hunting metaphor before, but it was easy enough to tell what it meant.

"Can you really bring yourself to kill your fellow man?" asked the woman with acne, clasping her hands together.

"If my fellow man's trying to kill me, of course I can!"

"Very sad," said the man, who had then turned his attention away from Hubert and back to the group, beginning a discussion about how to organise a mass letter writing campaign to the Kaiser, to persuade him to cease hostilities and pull back to the August 1914 borders immediately. Hubert was of the opinion that writing letters to the Kaiser, in wartime was probably not possible, but he kept his own council. He had noticed that Myrtle had said not a word during this exchange and he was tempted to leave, but he had nowhere else to go except back to the barracks.

After the group meeting had ended and all the members had left, without so much as even acknowledging Hubert's presence again, Myrtle had taken him to a basement in Camden Town, where they sat through an alleged poetry reading from a tall, fey American called Butch, and Hubert had met several more of Myrtle's friends. They'd seemed pleased to meet him, and no one had talked about the war, as they'd tried to involve him in their artistic circle, but to Hubert, they seemed as though they came from another world. Back at the flat, he and Myrtle had made love and slept in each other's arms. The next day, there had been that incident, when Alec Millcross and Colin Tunniford had turned up and were obviously taken aback, and less than happy, to find him there, which left a bit of a bad taste. He hadn't discussed his feelings about the war with Myrtle again and, the following day, the battalion had left for France.

Now, there he stood, transfixed by a blade of grass, as his platoon commander's watch ticked towards 7:30am. When the mines had gone off, he was shaken from his thoughts and, with everyone else, he watched the columns of earth and debris – and what that debris consisted of, didn't bear thinking about too closely – rise thousands of feet into the sky. After that, the barrage ended, and he had a few moments to let his mind wander again, before Arnold Snow blew his whistle. Without a second thought, he was up the ladder and making his way towards the path through the British wire. He saw Private Leuchars coming behind him.

"So far, so good," he heard Private Leuchars mutter.

"Yes, so far," he replied.

They moved through the wire, then they spread out. A line of khaki, stretching, if they but knew it, for a dozen miles. The edge of the blade that would cut through the German lines. Maybe it would all go to plan after all. He had never read any poetry, that he could remember, and he had never paid more than scant attention when he had heard people quoting it, but from somewhere, some unused and forgotten corner of his mind, the phrase, ''Twas a famous victory', bubbled to the surface.

Yes, that seemed fitting, he thought. Maybe all his pre-battle nerves had been groundless. It was usually the case that nothing was as bad as you thought it would be. Now, he could feel optimism suffusing him. He was positively cheerful.

"Next stop, Berlin," he shouted, to encourage his mates. Was that Lance Corporal Clay who shouted at him to shut up? What an old misery he could be. Never mind. Orders were to walk, but Private Snibley was tempted to break into a run. No point in giving the Hun a chance to catch his breath; if there were any Huns left alive, of course, and that didn't seem very likely. He looked round him; there was Wilf Leuchars to one side of him. All his mates, in fact.

When the German machine guns began to fire, the first indication Private Snibley saw that anything was amiss, was when he saw a line of bullets stitch across the ground, a few yards in front of him. He knew at once what it was, and he realised, in that exact moment, that the plan had gone awry. Next, he saw soldiers falling dead and wounded, and his first thought was to run for cover. There was a shell hole just ahead, and he began to make towards it. Out of the corner of his eye, he saw Private Leuchars fall; the first of his mates, as far as he knew, to be hit. Then he was in the shell hole. It wasn't very deep, and it obviously wasn't new, because grass had taken root on the inside surface. Not that that mattered, because it was enough to shelter him from enemy fire.

However, just sheltering from the enemy fire, regardless of how unexpected it might be, was not what he was here for, and he risked a peek over the lip of the hole, to see what was happening. Dead men, wounded men, men running, men bent over, taking cover. No more long line of infantrymen, no more steady walking. Now, they were advancing in quick, crouching runs, from one point to another. As he looked, Snibley saw two men, running side by side, throw their arms in the air and fall flat. From somewhere within himself, he summoned the courage to climb out of the shell hole and make his way to a group of men, running towards the enemy wire. The Germans had begun shelling now and everywhere in no man's land was dangerous – all shelter was illusory. They had to get to the enemy trench. Above the noise, he heard someone shouting orders, and he looked round to see who it was. It was hard to tell for sure, but it looked like Lance Corporal Clay. He waved back to show that he had heard. No one seemed in charge of this little group – all men from other platoons – but they were all scuttling towards the enemy trench, soon to be there. The shelling was getting worse. He looked round for Lance Corporal Clay, but he was nowhere to be seen.

"Come on, lads," said one of the men, who a moment later fell dead with a bullet in his brain. Before he, or anyone else, could react, Snibley heard a burst of machine gun fire, above all the noises, and he knew, for certain, that it was aimed at him and his new comrades. Two of them were hit, and Snibley threw himself flat; but not flat enough, as a bullet struck him in the lower leg. It was a clean in-and-out shot, through his left calf, that missed the bone completely. In fact, it was one of the luckiest moments in Hubert Snibley's life, though, at that moment, he would have been hard put to appreciate it. Still, thanks to this wound he was almost out of the war.

The trickiest part was the next twenty-four hours, but, on a day when luck was in very short supply, he had the good fortune not to be hit again, as he lay there, numbed by shock. Shells fell all around, but none was close enough to do him any further damage. He had long lost track of the men who had been with him when he was hit, though he was dimly aware of the second wave, those who had not been hit themselves, passing him as he lay there. His leg didn't hurt too much, but he was conscious of a terrible thirst and, presently, he drank the entire contents of his water bottle, lukewarm and tasting of chlorine, hoping that, somehow, help would come before his thirst returned.

It did. In the middle of the afternoon, when there was a lull in the fighting, for some reason, the stretcher-bearers came for him, and he was taken, slowly and uncomfortably, to the regimental aid post, then to the casualty clearing station. Triage was in his favour – he was one of the casualties expected to recover, given suitable treatment. He had received what all soldiers wanted: a Blighty one – a wound not bad enough to disable or disfigure permanently, but serious enough to get one sent back to England to recover. The doctor told him that his wound would heal well enough that he would not to have to use a stick, but that walking any great distance, or standing for long periods, would be uncomfortable. No more soldiering for him. They marked the card above his bed with a large capital B, for Blighty, and told him he was lucky – his war would soon be over. In a day or two, he would be on his way to a hospital in England. Hubert Snibley smiled and wondered if Myrtle would come to visit him.

Private Wilfred Leuchars had, indeed, been the first man in 2 Platoon to fall, as several of his comrades had noticed, but he had not been shot. He had caught the toe of his boot on the exposed root of a tree, that the shelling had long since obliterated, and had fallen flat on his face. His pack, all sixty pounds of it, had made him much heavier than normal, and so the fall had knocked the breath out of him. He lay there, cursing to himself, before getting up. His ankle hurt, but it was not bad enough to prevent his moving forward.

The men with him when he started out had all advanced some distance ahead – those who had not been killed or wounded – and he hobbled after them as best he could. Ahead and to his left, he saw a line of men from 3 Platoon fall, one after the other, as a traversing machine gun cut them down. The enemy trench seemed as far away as ever, even as he scuttled towards it. He realised that he had no idea how his comrades had fared in taking it. In falling flat, and lying there for a minute, he had lost his place in the first wave, and now he did not know how many of them, if any, had taken their objectives. How would it be, he wondered, if he reached the German trench, to find he was the only one to get there?

He needed to take stock, see how it looked, and then decide what to do. There, a few yards in front of the enemy trench, was a shell hole, one of the many tens of thousands created during the barrage. This one looked a bit different – the rim was a little higher than one might expect. Maybe it was deeper. He had to step over some barbed wire to get to it, and then he ran full tilt to it, jumping over the edge and into the crater. To his surprise, he landed on another figure in khaki.

This was obviously an enemy listening post, or maybe a sniper's nest; a shell hole, that had been dug down and ringed with barbed wire. He had expected to find it empty, but instead he found two German soldiers and three British ones – a couple of men from 3 Platoon and his own platoon commander, Second Lieutenant Arnold Snow. The two Germans were dead.

"Bloody hell," exclaimed the man whom Private Leuchars had actually landed on.

"Sorry," he muttered.

"Who is that?" asked Arnold Snow.

"Me, sir, Private Leuchars."

"Someone from my own platoon. Jolly good. We seem to be all jumbled up now."

"Yes, sir."

"Right, listen carefully, you three. This is what we're going to have to do. When I give the word, all three of you will throw your Mills bombs into the trench. Two each, one after the other. As soon as they've gone off, we rush in, shoot whoever is left, and hold that section of trench until we're relieved. Got that?"

"Yes sir," replied all three men.

"Very good. Two bombs each, and save the rest for clearing any dugouts we find."

"Sir."

"Right, bombs ready? Good luck everyone. On my signal. Now!"

The Mills bomb was a hand-thrown grenade, fused to explode two or three seconds after it was thrown. Six of them landed in a stretch of German trench, about a couple of dozen yards long, the explosions seeming to merge into one long blast. Before the debris from the explosions had fallen back to earth, Second Lieutenant Snow, Private Leuchars, and the other two men, were in the trench.

The first Germans they encountered were dead ones, half a dozen or so, who had been killed by the Mills bombs. The next ones they saw, were two who appeared from round the bay to their left, charging with bayonets fixed towards them. Arnold Snow shot them both with his revolver before they could get close enough to do any harm – one dead, one wounded badly enough to die a minute or two later.

For a few seconds, they all stared at the two Germans, one of whom was lying motionless, the other clutching his belly and whimpering –

the first ones they had actually seen die that day. Then Arnold remembered what had to be done and ordered the men to throw grenades into the one dugout entrance that they could see. That done, they were taking stock of the situation, when at the other end of their section of trench, more Germans appeared and fired at the four men, who returned fire at once. In the close confines of a trench, it was remarkable that anyone survived, but in fact, of the British, only Private Leuchars was hit, with a wound to his left shoulder. Two of the Germans were killed, however, and the rest retreated round the bay.

"They'll throw grenades over at us in a moment," said Arnold Snow. "I want everyone up the far end as quickly as possible. After they've thrown their bombs, they'll be rushing round to finish us off. Get ready to shoot into them when they do."

Quickly, the four men moved as far up the trench as they could, but before they could position themselves, they heard voices and saw something white, tied to the end of a bayonet, being waved round the corner of the bay.

"*Kamerad!*"

"Come out slowly," called Arnold Snow, adding, "If they try anything, shoot them all," to his men.

Three frightened, unkempt Germans shuffled into their section of trench, hands up, muttering, "*Kamerad, Kamerad.*"

Two rifles and a revolver were pointing at them. Private Leuchars, wounded, leant against the trench wall.

"*Setzen Sie da,*" shouted Arnold Snow, pointing at the fire-step. The three Germans sat. "*Hände hoch,*" he shouted, and they raised their hands even higher.

"Keep watching them. Make sure they don't move," he said to one of the 3 Platoon men.

"There's an easy way to make sure of that, sir," replied the man.

"Not while I'm in command, there isn't. Is that understood?"

"Sir."

"Right, Private Leuchars, how badly are you hit?"

"My shoulder, sir."

"Let me see."

Private Leuchars let his platoon commander look at his wound.

"Not too much blood. Bullet hasn't come out. We'll plug the hole with a field dressing and get you back to the aid post, as soon as its practicable, but I can't say when that is likely to be."

"Yes, sir."

"Meanwhile, you can watch the prisoners."

So, Private Leuchars sat on the fire-step opposite the three demoralised Germans, pointing Arnold's revolver at them, while Arnold, holding Wilfred's rifle, and the other two men, mounted the parados to be ready for a counter attack, if one came. In fact, none did, and when the soldiers from the second wave of the attack arrived in their bit of trench – six men, who had survived the guns and artillery of the enemy – Arnold took command of them all.

"Leuchars, can you walk?"

Wilfred stood up. It felt a bit odd, and his shoulder was hurting badly now, but his legs were fine.

"Yes, sir, I think so."

"Good. I want you to try to make your way back to our lines, and I want you to take these three characters with you."

"The prisoners, sir?"

"Yes. You can hang on to my revolver. If they try anything, shoot first, and ask questions afterwards. Can you manage that?"

"Yes, sir."

With a mixture of schoolboy German, gestures, and shouted English, Arnold Snow made it clear to the prisoners that they were to go with Wilfred across no man's land.

"*Sie gehen mit dieser Soldat!* He has a gun. You, *Hände hoch*. If you run, he shoot you. Shoot. *Mit Pistole.*"

The three prisoners nodded eagerly, to show they understood.

"Actually, sir, I don't think I'll have much trouble with them," said Private Leuchars.

"I daresay you're right. They seem keen to be out of it all."

They were. They gave Private Leuchars no trouble at all as they crossed no man's land, during a relative lull in the firing. They held their hands up as high as they could, and, as they approached the

British trench, Wilfred shouted: “Prisoners and escort coming in,” before someone shot at them. In the trench, he turned the Germans over to a sergeant of the military police, to whom he also handed Arnold Snow’s revolver, and made his way, with several other walking wounded, to the regimental aid post. Later that day, in a hospital behind the front, they removed the bullet from his shoulder and cleaned his wound the best they could. He would need more treatment, and they needed the bed, so they wrote a big B on his card too.

Chapter XXXVI

Second Lieutenant Charles Snow & Corporal O'Malley

Nobody ever knew – nobody possibly could have known – that Second Lieutenant Charles Snow and Corporal Seamus O'Malley died at precisely the same moment. They were nowhere near each other, and the manner of their deaths differed markedly, but the fact remains that they died simultaneously

Charles Snow was doing what every good subaltern did that day – he was leading his men from the front. His platoon all saw him, all took heart from the fact that Mr. Charlie was with them. He had not hesitated for even a fraction of a second and, when the whistles had blown, he had been first up the trench ladder.

"Good luck everyone," he had called, as he climbed. "See you all at the objective."

One or two of his men had cheered, most were too nervous. So, truth be told, was Charles. Elation, fear, and pride had all stirred within him, as the minutes to H-Hour ticked away, and the distillation of all three made itself felt in him as nervousness. He wanted to pace up and down, bite his nails, smoke, tell someone how he felt. But he didn't. This, he told himself, was why he had joined. This was why he and his brother had cajoled their step-father into easing their way into commissions with Kitchener's Army. This was his duty. Firm resolve overcame nerves.

Calm, he said to himself. *Be calm. This is the big battle, the one that will bring about a successful conclusion to this war. By the end of today, we'll be through the enemy lines, mopping up resistance, and chasing Jerry all the way to Berlin.* Charles had always been proud to be a soldier in the British Army, but never more so than today. He knew, however, that it was an inescapable fact of war that some men would die. There was no getting away from it. Very possibly, some of them would be men in his own platoon, but the dead would be a minority. Most people would survive intact. The seven-day barrage would have left very few Germans alive, and their barbed wire was obviously blown to fragments. In all probability, there would be very little for them to do, other than go forward, do a bit of mopping up, and occupy their objectives. Be calm.

So it was an emboldened, determined Charles Snow who climbed that ladder. He hoped his brother would come through it too. "This way," he called to his men, following the white tape that led to the prepared gaps in the British wire, and as ordered, Charles and his platoon, along with so many thousands of others, walked across no man's land.

They were about a quarter of the way across, if that, when they heard the first shots from the other side. This was not what they had been told to expect, but they were soldiers, and they took it all in their stride. The shots became more frequent, and they heard machine guns open up.

Someone to Charles's left screamed and fell. A few men faltered. "Keep going," he shouted, as more men fell. The man next to him toppled sideways, clutching his leg. Blood welled from between his fingers. Two other men immediately moved to help their comrade. "Leave him," Charles yelled. Orders were very definite – no stopping to help the wounded; the advance had to continue at all costs, the momentum must not be lost.

By now, only a matter of minutes since the first wave had left their trenches, the enemy fire was so thick, that it seemed as though there was no shelter from it. Then the German artillery started too.

"I thought the Germans was all supposed to be dead, sir," one of his platoon yelled.

"Keep going," Charles shouted again, and those two words turned out to be the last he ever uttered. A few seconds later, a shell fired from a German field gun, a little over a mile away – quite low calibre but deadly enough to anyone who got in its way – landed one yard in front of him, and Second Lieutenant Charles Snow was blown to atoms.

A couple of hundred yards to the left, as Charles Snow was stopping his men from helping their comrade, men from 2 and 3 platoons had run into this unexpected German resistance. Corporal O'Malley was taking shelter in a shell hole.

O'Malley was a good enough soldier to have been able to reach the rank of corporal. He could do drill and get his men, one way or another, to perform well, but he never took risks if he could help it. He did everything he was ordered to do, but he never did more. That was not so surprising. Countless thousands of soldiers, in every army that there ever was, had adopted the same approach. So, O'Malley was quite happy to stay in the shell hole until there was a lull in the enemy fire, if indeed there ever would be a lull. He wasn't a coward – it was just that he wasn't foolhardy.

He was not, however, the only one to spot this inviting shell hole, and in a matter of moments, O'Malley was joined by three of his comrades.

"What's going on, Corp? They said there wouldn't be any Germans left to shoot at us."

"Well, obviously they were wrong."

"What we going to do?"

"I don't know."

"If we don't stay in here we'll be killed. Do you think we should stay here till we get new orders? I think we should stay here. Someone's bound to come by with new orders, don't you think, Corp? So we should stay here and wait, shouldn't we?"

"Look, shut up will you?"

"Yes, Corp. It's just that they told us there wouldn't be any Germans left to shoot at us."

In spite of his overpowering wish for self-preservation, O'Malley knew that the four of them could not huddle in this hole in the earth while the battle went on all round them. There would be no orders, and he knew that, because the top brass had got it wrong, again, it didn't mean that the original orders were cancelled.

"You're right," he said. "They did. But there are, and so it's up to the likes of you and me, to make the best of a bad job. Come on lads, let's go."

"But, Corp—"

"Did yez join the fockin' army to pick daisies?" In times of stress. O'Malley's accent thickened. "Or to lie about while yer mates do all the work?"

"No, Corp, but—"

"But nothin', ye lazy bastard! Now, out of this shell hole, all three of yez, or so help me, you'll get my bayonet up yer jacksie. I'm not bloody jokin'! Out!"

The three men climbed out of the shellhole, O'Malley behind them, holding his rifle with the bayonet pointing at them.

"Come on, lads. A steady pace and we'll be in the German trenches in no time."

Orders called for a walking pace but, in the light of the new circumstances, O'Malley thought that a trot would be suitable.

The German machine guns were not firing directly into the oncoming wave of soldiers, they were firing diagonally, with the effect that their attackers tended to run into the line of fire. A bullet hit O'Malley in his right side, just below the ribcage, passing though him and out of his left side. He fell with a moan and lay still.

"Corp, are you hit?" asked one of the other men he was herding across the battlefield.

"He's had it," said another, who did not want to stop moving. He wanted to get across this hell as quickly as he could – just as he and his comrades had all been ordered, in fact. "Leave him."

They trotted on, and one of the three actually did make it to the German trench. The other two both met the same fate as O'Malley.

O'Malley, in fact, was not dead when the other men left him, but he knew that he had been gut-shot, and it was only a matter of time. The time in question was in fact less than a minute, and at the precise moment that a 77mm shell obliterated all trace of Charles Snow, the life of Seamus O'Malley flickered out.

Chapter XXXVII

Private Travis

Harry Travis lay on his back in a shell hole, which he was sharing with Vic Rangle's dead body. There was another body there as well but he couldn't tell whose it was because it had no face. How long he had been there, he wasn't sure. To his left was his pack, though he could not remember having taken it off or whether someone else had done that for him. He didn't know where his rifle and helmet were either. The shell hole was deep enough to shelter him from bullets and shell fragments, and unless he received a direct hit from the German artillery, or an enemy soldier jumped into the hole with him, he reckoned he was safe enough. The earth was dry and grey, crumbling in trickles with every vibration from the shells which exploded all round. At the bottom, was a patch of damp mud. The sky, Harry noticed, was bright blue; the sort of blue he remembered so well, from working on the roads in northern Oxfordshire, in the summer weather. A friendly blue, scattered with patches of white, scarcely more than wisps, that could be blown away by the merest of breezes. It was a beautiful summer's day. What a contrast the sky made with the unprecedented bloodletting that was taking place beneath it.

Both of Harry's feet had been blown off. Try as he might, he could not remember actually being wounded. He could recall climbing out of the trench, following Bert Giddington up the ladder. He could remember walking, not running, as per orders, towards the enemy line, with Bert to one side of him, and Hubert Snibley to the other. As the artillery barrage lifted, Harry had heard the sound of their footsteps on the dusty earth as they approached the enemy lines, where they fully expected to find nothing but devastation and bodies. Someone had even started singing, he seemed to remember, only to be told to shut up by an NCO. Harry was as surprised as anyone when the machine guns started up. This was not how they had been told it would be. All of a sudden, no man's land seemed wider than it had ever been. To think that they used to remark to each other how close the enemy was. Next thing, Harry was on his back, stunned rather than hurt. He had tried to stand up, to resume walking, but he couldn't make his legs work properly. It was probably the shock, but when he raised his head and saw that his feet were missing, he wasn't scared, so much as surprised. He wondered why he hadn't bled very much from his stumps, but they looked as though they had been burned by the explosion. Perhaps that had something to do with it. Maybe the burning had sort of sealed the stumps; he wasn't sure. It didn't really hurt. That was probably the shock too. He was conscious and lucid enough to realise that he needed to get under some sort of cover, any cover, before he was wounded again, and he saw a shell hole a few feet from where he lay. With a great deal of effort, he managed to roll to the edge of the shell hole and over the side, coming to rest on his back a few feet from the bottom. There he lay, passing out and waking, several times.

A young medical orderly corporal, with a Red Cross armband, had jumped into the shell hole. He carried a small green canvas pack, containing what was, in effect, little more than a glorified first aid kit. He could staunch wounds, apply rudimentary bandages, give the odd painkiller or two, but he could do little for those with serious wounds. He just had to do his best to keep them alive until the stretcher-bearers arrived – if they arrived. He had joined Harry at the bottom of the hole, had applied tourniquets to the shattered ends of his legs, had injected him with morphine, and marked an M in indelible pencil on his forehead.

"You'll be right as rain, mate," he had said, as Harry stared blankly up at him, grateful for the lie. "The stretcher-bearers will be along in a tick to take you back to the field hospital."

The morphia took over from the body's own natural anaesthetic, shock, and Harry felt no pain. He just hoped that the stretcher-bearers would come before the drug wore off.

The corporal had lifted his head and bellowed, "Stretcher-bearers," at the top of his voice, as so many had done already that day, but Harry wondered if anyone more than a few feet away would be able to hear him, above the infernal noise of the battle. Perhaps the corporal had read Harry's thoughts, for he smiled down at him.

"Not to worry. They'll be here to fetch you before you know it. The Germans are keeping them busy today, but they're still managing."

Harry muttered something that was intended as a thank you, but came out more as a groan.

"Don't tire yourself, mate. Just wait here. You'll be in some cushy hospital in England in a couple of days, just you wait and see. You're out of this war. Some blokes get all the luck," and he smiled again in encouragement. "They can do wonderful things with artificial legs these days. You'll be walking again soon, no doubt about it."

Harry tried to speak again, but the effort was too great, so he just smiled back at this helpful young man.

"Oh well," said the corporal. "Plenty more customers for me, I'm sure. See you back in England after the war, mate."

He patted Harry on the shoulder, closed his medical pack, crawled to the lip of the shell hole and, when he judged the moment was right, he leapt over the edge. As he did, a bullet took him in the temple, and his body fell backwards into the hole, where he lay, a few feet from Harry. With all that had happened so far that day, this was just one more death among thousands, and Harry could do little more than stare at the dead medic for a few moments, then turn his gaze back to the blue sky above him. He knew that he should feel some sort of regret, or sadness, but it just wasn't in him. Instead, he lay there, continuing to hope the stretcher-bearers would find him soon.

He didn't know whether to be surprised, relieved, or both when they actually did. With so many thousands of wounded men on the field of battle, it was a wonder they found him. Mainly, in fact, because Harry was one of the lucky ones, if one can call anyone in his position lucky. He had been hit not far from his own lines, and he was accessible to the stretcher-bearers, unlike so many thousands of wounded, who lay untended and out of reach in no man's land. The two stretcher-bearers were already exhausted, even this early in the battle, and they did not waste time in chatting to Harry, but simply made a visual assessment of his wounds, lifted him onto their stretcher and, somehow, with much stumbling and cursing, were able to carry him, unscathed, back through the British wire, down into the trench, and to the regimental aid post in the support trench. Harry felt weaker and weaker by the minute, but he did allow himself, at last, to believe that perhaps the orderly's prediction, about him reaching a cushy hospital in England, might actually come true.

Chapter XXXVIII

Lance Corporal Marvell

Since qualifying as a doctor, Quentin Draycott had never actually practiced as a GP, even though that had been his whole reason for following his father into the profession. If truth were known, he had never particularly liked his father. Papa had been loving and caring, in his own way, but his own way was such that he seemed, on the face of it, the face his children saw, cold and remote. Quentin and his three younger brothers were afraid of their father, wary of him, obedient, but they never warmed to him. They did, however, admire him. Even to their young eyes, he was an excellent doctor, with a widespread practice of patients who looked up to him, depended on him, and revered him. From the day he started at prep school, Quentin knew what he wanted to be when he grew up – a doctor, to heal the sick. No other profession had ever occurred to him. After leaving St. Paul's, he went to medical school, qualifying just as war was declared, and like so many others, he volunteered for military service, where, not surprisingly, the army put him in the Royal Army Medical Corps. So it was that on the first day of July 1916, he found himself in a casualty clearing station, a couple of miles behind the lines.

If you had asked him for his definition of hell, he would have perhaps described the traditional hellfire of eternal burning, but what he saw on this day, would have qualified just as well. They had been warned to expect casualties, possibly heavy casualties. In spite of the optimistic talk, and the official view, that the men were going to stroll through the shattered German lines and mop up a few isolated pockets of feeble resistance, more realistic counsels had warned that the fighting was going to be heavy and bloody, and the RAMC was going to be kept very busy.

That was an understatement. Quentin had lost count of how many men had been brought to him that day, and it was scarcely noon. He knew that outside the tent, lay a line of men on stretchers, some on the bare earth, waiting their turns. Another line of men lay unattended – they had died, either before or after treatment, and they now awaited the burial party. Behind the tent was a growing pile of amputated limbs. Quentin had never in his life felt the emotion of despair before, but it was his constant companion on this day. Never before had he felt so utterly useless. He was doing his best, but it just didn't seem to be enough, and he was enveloped in this despair when the unconscious and roughly patched body of a man, from whose chest he had removed a shell fragment, was lifted from the table, and replaced with the shattered form of Lance Corporal Edwin Marvell.

Marvell had just reached the German lines when he had been hit. He had led several men across no man's land, line abreast and at a walking pace, until the German machine guns had opened up, causing those who weren't shot, to run as fast as they could go. It seemed to Marvell that whole swathes of British soldiers were being cut down by the enemy fire, and he wondered if anyone would reach the German trenches. This was not what they had been told would happen. Marvell, however, even though he was not a regular soldier, had all the attitudes of someone who had been in the army all his life. Maybe it was all the years he had spent working his way up from the bottom in his civilian job that did it. At any rate, he did not even begin to question the wisdom of his superiors; if they had got it wrong, it was just one of those things, and you couldn't expect your officers to be perfect.

When he got to the German wire, he found that the barrage had not destroyed it. The continuous shelling had bounced it about, but it was still there, as tangled and obstructive as it had always been. All along the miles of the attacking front, British soldiers were running one way or another along the enemy wire, trying to find a way through, while German rifles and machine guns cut them down. Crouched over, to make himself a smaller target, Marvell found a place where the wire had been partly flattened by the artillery barrage.

"This way," he shouted. "You men, to me!" Several unwounded soldiers ran towards him; some were from his platoon, others were from different platoons, and Marvell guessed that the designated order of advance had gone by the board, once the unexpected enemy fire had started.

"Come on!" he shouted, and they ran through the gap, such as it was. It was wide enough for men to run in single file, although several were picked off. As they got close to the enemy trench, they actually saw, for the first time, German soldiers. One of them, gawping up at the approaching British with horror, looked hardly old enough to shave. He raised his rifle with shaking hands, but the soldiers who had followed Edwin Marvell through that particular gap in the wire, were just a few paces away and panic disturbed his aim. As the British soldiers were jumping into his trench, he fired at Marvell, but the bullet went wide and almost missed. Instead of homing on Marvell's heart, it passed through his left upper arm. Marvell swore, something his comrades had hardly ever heard him do, and fell to one side. The young German never got a chance to fire again, because Private Giddington, with movements that could have come straight out of the army drill manual, thrust his bayonet into the boy's throat, twisted it, and then, placing his boot on his victim's chest, pulled it out again. He was ready to thrust a second time, but it was not necessary – the German was dead.

By now, about a dozen solders had entered this little section of German trench and had accounted for five of the enemy.

"You two," Marvell shouted to two soldiers from another platoon, who had somehow ended up here. He pointed to a dugout entrance to his left. "Take care of that dugout! Duchess, you do that one," he ordered Private Selway, meaning the one on his right.

Nobody wanted to walk down the stairs of an enemy dugout. You never knew who would be waiting to shoot you. So when Marvell gave orders to 'take care' of a dugout, what happened was that the men he had designated simply threw a couple of Mills bombs into each one and stood aside. No one could survive an explosion in such a confined space.

Now, in this little section of German trench, the only German soldiers present were dead ones. Marvell detailed the men to be ready to repulse any counter attack, while they waited for the second attacking wave.

"Shouldn't you get that seen to, Edwin?" asked Private Selway. Marvell's shot arm was bleeding heavily.

"Later. I want to make sure we're all set here, to wait for the next wave."

While Marvell and his men had secured their little section of enemy trench, they had no idea at all what was happening elsewhere. For all they knew, they were the only British soldiers who had succeeded in actually getting this far. This was, in fact, not the case, but round the traverse to Marvell's left, in the next bay, were two very frightened Germans. They could hear the British voices in the bay next to them, and they knew they had to do something about it, so they each threw a couple of potato-masher style grenades over the traverse. One of them went too far and landed over the parapet, doing little more than making a noise and showering several men with earth. The second landed between Edwin Marvell and one of the stragglers from 4 platoon. It landed on the ground with a soft thud, and as both men looked down to see what it was, it exploded. The straggler was killed outright. Edwin Marvell's right hand side was shredded, but he did not die straight away. As he fell to the ground, Privates Giddington, Selway, and Hope threw Mills bombs over the traverse and, as they had been trained to do, rushed round into the next bay, just after the resultant explosions, to finish off whoever was there. They did not have to bother; both Germans were dead.

Meantime, someone had been shouting for stretcher-bearers. There was nothing else anyone could do for Edwin Marvell right then, and Roland Selway organised the posting of sentries at the parapet, as they awaited the next wave.

The second wave had taken almost as many casualties as the first, but some of them did arrive, three of them being walking wounded, so they were sent back, carrying Edwin Marvell with them

Eventually he was carried to the regimental aid post, a dugout in a British reserve trench, where he was injected with morphine and had a large M inscribed on his forehead, in indelible pencil, to indicate that this had been done. From there, he was taken to the rear, to the casualty clearing station, where he found himself lifted onto the examination table. Dr. Draycott didn't need to examine him closely to know that his man would not survive. In fact, he had no idea why he hadn't already died. He looked at the orderly and shook his head. Just then, Edwin somehow lifted his head and his left arm, grabbing hold of the stethoscope that was hanging round the doctor's neck. He saw the name *Redfield & Hawkins, Ltd.* stamped into the metal bell of the instrument, and he smiled.

"One of ours," he whispered, then he lay back and died.

"What do you suppose he meant by that?" asked Dr. Draycott.

"Dunno, sir. Maybe he meant he was hit by one of our own shells."

"Well, he wouldn't be the first, poor sod. Right, take him away"

And that was the end of Edwin Marvell.

Chapter XXXIX

Private Giddington and Private Marren

After the wounded Lance Corporal Edwin Marvell had been borne away, Privates Giddington and Hope picked up the body of the dead man from 3 Platoon and threw it over the parapet of the trench. There was little else they could do with it, and no one wanted a body lying on the trench floor to trip them up, especially in the event of a German counter attack, when there could be a lot of frantic hand to hand fighting. So the corpse was thrown into no man's land, to join thousands of his dead comrades, while the group from 2 and 3 Platoons waited for the third wave, or for the Germans to attempt to retake the trench.

They were all privates. There were no NCOs among them, now that Edwin Marvell had been wounded, but they all looked to Rollo Selway for leadership. It was he who deployed the lookouts. The Germans had the measure of the trench, and were sweeping the area with machine gun fire, and one of them was wounded before he could reach his assigned spot, and crawled, bleeding from his leg, back to the trench.

"What's going to happen now, Duchess?" asked Bert Giddington. He didn't really expect his fellow private to have an answer; he just wanted to make some sort of conversation to relieve the tension.

"I wish I knew, Bert," said Rollo. "I know what's supposed to happen, but who knows if it actually will? The attack doesn't seem to have gone at all to plan in our sector."

"Do you suppose it's just in our sector then? Not the whole front line?"

"Heaven knows. Maybe nobody knows. It wouldn't surprise me."

"I wonder where Mr. Snow is. And Harry and Joe."

"I think I saw Harry get it, I'm afraid. A shell burst, about halfway across no man's land. Looked like it got him, and Vic as well."

"Oh, that's bad." Bert was silent for a few moments. "Poor old Harry."

Before Rollo Selway could reply, there was the sound of grenades exploding in the next bay; first one, then two others in quick succession.

"Cover that traverse," Rollo shouted, and they all aimed their rifles at the traverse between them and the stretch of trench to their right. At the first sight of a German uniform, they would all fire. In fact, what they saw was a man in khaki, under the unmistakable shape of a British steel helmet

"Strewth," muttered Bert Giddington.

"'Allo mates. How long you been here?" It was someone from 1 Platoon.

"A little while. Anyone with you?"

Before the man could answer, three other Tommies came round the corner, led by Arnold Snow.

"Selway, Giddington, Hope – good," he said. "Is there an NCO with you?"

"No, sir," replied Rollo Selway. "Just us and some men from 3 Platoon."

"I see. As far as I know, I'm the only officer from A-Company to reach this far, unless you've seen any others."

"No, sir. None."

"Very well, we'll see if anyone else joins us, then press on to the Jerry second line."

"Sir."

All three of the old comrades could see that their platoon commander was not the same man he had been earlier that morning. It didn't seem possible, but his face had aged; there were lines there now, wrinkles that drew in his mouth and hooded his eyes. It was probably only dust, or earth, Bert Giddington told himself, but it was as though there was grey in his hair now.

A sound from one of the bays, which they were somehow able to hear above the noise of machine guns and artillery, made them all turn round, rifles at the ready, but luckily, before anyone pulled a trigger, they saw it was a British officer and a number of soldiers, among whom were Privates Joseph Marren and Alec Millcross. The officer was the second-lieutenant in command of 4 Platoon, who had previously distinguished himself by falling from his horse at battalion sports day. Like Arnold, he appeared to have aged. No longer a fresh-faced young man just out of school, he seemed bowed under the weight of what he had undergone that morning.

"Oh, Arnold, you here?" he said.

"Yes, Gilbert. Are there many of you?"

"Just us. I have some of your platoon here. Everyone's jumbled up."

"Anyone from B-Company?"

"Haven't seen anyone. They ought to be here by now."

"Meantime, we should be ready for the Hun to hit back," said Arnold, "Are we the only officers?"

"Far as I know."

"I wonder if Major Henderson is nearby."

"Dead."

"Dead?"

"Yes, he got caught on the wire. I saw it. The Huns kept shooting at him long after he was dead. They had him jerking about like a marionette."

Arnold was disgusted. "The bastards."

"Quite. Anyway, the Company Commander's dead. The CSM too."

"Bull got it?"

"Yes, he was one of the first. Shot down, just after clearing our own wire, as soon as the Jerry machine guns started up."

"So we have no idea how many of us made it this far?" Arnold wanted to know.

"No."

"There's only me and these men here. I just sent one of my chaps back with some prisoners."

"As I see it, we must assume we are all who are left of the first wave in this sector, so we should make our dispositions accordingly."

While the two subalterns were talking, Bert Giddington went to greet his old pal, Joseph Marren.

"Still in one piece, Joe?"

"Just about, though how I came across no man's land without being hit is a mystery to me."

"Duchess says he thinks Harry's dead," said Bert.

"Yes, he is. I saw it. He got blown up."

"So it's true. Poor old Harry."

The other officer, Second Lieutenant Hooper, began to call to them all.

"Now listen, everyone," he shouted, but before he could say more, a shell burst nearby, showering everyone with earth. "Listen," he said again. "As near as Mr. Snow and I can tell, we are the only ones from A-Company to make it across to the Jerry front line. So we have to reverse and hold this stretch of trench. We can expect two things to happen. One, is that the next two waves will arrive and, with luck, more of them will make it over here than we did. The other, is that Jerry will counter-attack, so we have to be ready to hold him off."

As though to confirm what he said, two more shells landed close by.

"I see you've posted lookouts already," he said to Arnold.

"I didn't. They were already in position when I arrived here." He called over to the men. "Who positioned the lookouts?"

"I did, sir," answered Rollo Selway.

"Good man," Arnold said. "I think that you had better consider yourself acting lance corporal for the time being."

"Yes, sir."

"Sir," shouted Private Hope, pointing upwards. They all looked up to see a British aeroplane flying very low, above the German trenches.

"That's bloody dangerous," Private Hope remarked, and he was right. Flying in a straight line, at about two hundred feet over a battle zone, with artillery fire going in both directions, was not a healthy pursuit. Nevertheless, the plane kept a steady course, and as it flew past their section of trench, the men could quite clearly see the pilot wave at them.

"At least someone will know we're here," said Arnold to Second Lieutenant Hooper.

Several more shells landed close by.

"Looks like Jerry knows we're here too."

Somehow the remnants of C-Company, the third attacking wave, had made it across no man's land, and eight or nine of them jumped into the trench.

"Well done!" Arnold took stock of his little band. The new arrivals all seemed to be in one piece, except for one man, who had been wounded in the left arm.

"This is as far as we've got, so you're with us now. I expect D-Company will be along presently. Meantime, prepare for a Hun counter attack. When D-Company arrives, we'll have a go at their support trench."

The men nodded acknowledgement. As though to remind them that the Germans knew they were there, machine gun fire swept the parapet, kicking up dirt.

"Won't be long before they start shelling, I reckon," muttered Alec Millcross.

Arnold Snow risked a look over the parados, towards the German support trench, then called to one of his men.

"Giddington, over here."

Bert joined him.

"Sir?"

"See that big shell crater over there?" Arnold pointed to one, larger than the others that surrounded it, about fifty yards away.

"Yes, sir."

"It's a tall order, but I want you to make your way over to it, and make sure you force the Jerries in their support trench to keep their heads down. If we can keep them off balance, we'll be better able to make a run at them when the fourth wave gets here, and you'll be our first defence if they have a go at attacking us."

"Yes, sir."

"Good man. Take those three with you," said Arnold, indicating Joe Marren and two of the men from 3 Platoon. "And when we advance to their support trench, you come with us."

"Sir."

"Good luck to you."

"Thank you, sir."

So Bert Giddington, Joe Marren, and their two comrades got out of the trench, and amidst the bullets and shells that were flying in both directions across the battle area, they all four succeeded in reaching the shell hole in question.

Since Bert had been the one to receive the orders from Arnold Snow, he considered himself to be in charge of this little venture

"Right, the officer wants us to make the Jerries keep their heads down. That's easy enough. And if we do it right, we'll make things that much easier for the next stage of the attack."

"So how do we do that, then?" asked Joe.

"We'll just point our rifles at the Jerry trench and shoot at anything that moves."

The four of them lay at the lip of the shell crater, ready to shoot any German who showed himself in front of them. It was generally hard to tell how successful they were, though Joe Marren definitely got one, but as long as they were making difficulties for Fritz, that was good enough for them.

The Germans were not about to allow that sort of thing to happen unanswered, and after about ten minutes, they were successful in inflicting the first casualty on the group in the shell hole. It was either a very lucky shot or a brilliant bit of shooting; one of the men from 3 Platoon was struck above the bridge of his nose, just below the rim of his steel helmet. He knew nothing about it – one moment alive, the next just a body and a heap of rags.

"Get him out of the way," hissed Bert Giddington, and the other two pushed the body to the back of the shell crater.

"There," shouted the remaining 3 Platoon man, pointing to a spot in front of the German lines. An enemy soldier, either foolhardy, brave, or both, had risen from a shell hole, or a sap, and was fully exposed as he threw a stick grenade towards the three men. The grenade had just left his hand, when Joe Marren and Bert Giddington both shot him dead. The man's throw was not quite far enough, and his grenade fell short of its target. The dead man's heroic last act had no effect at all.

Back in the trench, the two second lieutenants were still in command of the small band of men from the St. Marylebones.

"They ought to know we're here," remarked Second Lieutenant Hooper to Arnold Snow, not for the first time.

"Yes, though I don't really see what they can do about it. It looks as though the fourth wave has had it."

Bullets had been flying above the trench, all the time the men had been occupying it, from the German support trenches, wiping out the successive attacking waves that were still trying to advance. Arnold was right. The fourth wave, D-Company, had come up against concentrated machine gun fire, leaving the field of battle littered with yet more dead and wounded. No one knew what was happening along the rest of the twelve miles of front, where the attack was taking place, but in this sector, scarcely a single man was able to cross no man's land unscathed.

"They've got to be coming," said one of the men from 1 Platoon. Like so many of his comrades, he could not believe that the day was going so badly, completely contrary to what they had been told to expect. He jumped up to the fire-step, to see if anyone was in fact coming to their aid.

"Get down, you bloody fool," yelled Alec Millcross, but the words were scarcely out of his mouth, than the man had been hit, and he fell back dead into the trench.

The same thing, almost, happened at about the same moment in the shell crater. The second 3 Platoon man showed himself, for a moment or two longer than was prudent, and was shot through the neck. He fell back, looking wide eyed at the other two men; his mouth opened and closed soundlessly a couple of times, and then he was dead. Bert Giddington pushed the body to the back of the shell crater, to join the other corpse.

"Just you and me now, Joe," he said.

"We'll be alright if we're careful, Bert."

"Yes, I expect you're right. We'll just keep popping Jerries."

As he was saying that, a shell landed just in front of the German trench and, when the dust had settled, the two men saw a figure in field grey scuttling back to the safety of his own lines. They both fired, and one or other of them hit him. He fell and lay motionless.

"One less to worry about," said Bert.

More shells fell – British or German, they had no way of knowing – and they crouched as low as they could in the crater, as earth pattered down on them. A direct hit onto the shell hole would kill them both. They tried not to think about that.

Someone in the German trench threw a grenade at them; he was too far away for it to come anything like close enough to them, to do any damage – probably thrown as a gesture, or by a man in a panic. The two men saw it quite clearly, the grenade like a small tin can on a stick, looking like a potato masher, tumbling end over end and falling to earth, a couple of dozen yards away, the sharp bang of its detonation almost lost in the noise of the shells and gunfire, that continued unceasing. By accident or design, a rifle bullet struck the ground just in front of them, kicking up a spray of earth into their faces. Both men muttered curses and wiped the dirt from their eyes.

Bert Giddington thought he saw a German about fifty yards away. He couldn't be sure, but he loosed off a shot anyway. Then, he and Joe Marren quite clearly saw a group of three Germans, running from one shell hole to another, probably trying to get within grenade throwing range of the trench that Arnold Snow and his little band now occupied.

"Oh no you don't," muttered Joe Marren, and he and Bert Giddington fired several shots in their direction. It wasn't possible to be certain, of course, but they were pretty sure they had hit some of them.

For a few minutes, they saw nothing to shoot at. The enemy was keeping his head down. Shells exploded, bullets flew, but as far as Bert Giddington and Joe Marren could see, there wasn't another human being in sight.

"Can't see a bloody Hun anywhere," muttered Joe.

A shell exploded to the left of them, throwing them against the opposite wall of the crater and again showering them with earth. Joe Marren swore, wiping his face. Then he heard his friend gasp: "Oh, Joe, I'm hit."

He turned to see Bert slumped against the side of the crater. Something, a shell splinter or a bit of rock, had hit him in the chest. The front of his tunic was soaked with blood.

"Feels pretty bad, Joe," he said.

Joe reached inside his own tunic, to the pocket where his field dressing was nestling.

"We'll just get a dressing on that, Bert, and you'll be fine until the stretcher-bearers pick you up. Just you see."

"I don't think so, Joe," said Bert, "I think I've had it."

"Don't say that, Bert. The doc'll patch you up. You'll be going home."

"Don't think home is where I'm going, Joe." Bert coughed blood. "Say hello to my Alice when you see her. Tell her I love her."

"You can tell her yourself when you get to Blighty. Just hang on, Bert."

But in spite of his friend's entreaties, Bert just shook his head and let a half smile briefly touch his lips.

"Don't think so, Joe. I reckon it's—" He was gone.

Joe looked at his old friend for a moment, not wanting to admit that he had lost him, and then, most uncharacteristically, he swore long and loud, and most foully.

In the trench, of course, they couldn't hear Joe Marren shouting. The battle noise was far too loud to be overcome by one man's grief and anger. In fact, Arnold Snow had little time to think about the four men he had ordered into the shell crater – he had no idea, for example, that three of them were already dead. He had been joined by three more men from 6 Platoon, but one of them was badly injured and had bled to death, a minute or two after tumbling into the trench. While Joe Marren was calling down a thousand curses on the heads of the Germans, and on the war in general, Arnold Snow was conferring with his fellow subaltern.

"I don't think we can stay here indefinitely," he said."We need to press on, have a go at their second line."

"There's hardly enough of us," replied Second Lieutenant Hooper. "If we try anything right now, we're likely to be wiped out."

"That means the offensive has stalled, then."

"It seems very probable."

"So everything we have been training for has come to nothing?"

"Maybe we can wait for the fourth wave to get here. They can't be long in coming now. We can attack at company strength when they get here."

"Company strength? Gilbert, look out at no man's land. Most of the first three waves are out there, dead. We're the lucky ones. Pray God the fourth wave doesn't end up like the first three, but we have to be prepared for that. Our job must be to hold this little bit of trench against whatever the Hun throws at us, then when we can, we follow our orders and try to take a bit of their second line."

When the fourth wave, the four platoons of D-Company, had earlier attempted to cross no man's land, most had become casualties. Eventually, to Arnold Snow's few dozen yards of trench, came six men unwounded, three who were lightly wounded, and one man seriously wounded, whom his mates, contrary to orders, had carried with them. He lasted just long enough to lie on the floor of the trench, emit a death rattle loud enough for those around him to hear, and then they had to throw out his corpse.

A traversing machine gun kicked up earth along the lip of the trench, and everyone instinctively ducked, even those who were safely below parapet level. Alec Millcross cried out, swore, and clapped his hand to the side of his head. As blood seeped between his fingers, he leant against the trench wall.

"Alec!" Rollo Selway ran to his friend.

"Fuck, that hurts, Rollo."

"Let's see how bad it is." Arnold Snow was at his side.

Alec Millcross lifted his hand.

"Lots of blood but not much damage, Private. You ear lobe has been shot off. You'll live to fight another day."

"Sir."

"Stick a field dressing on him, Selway. There's little else we can do just at the moment."

"Yes, sir."

"And when he's done that, Millcross, I need you on the fire-step. We can't spare you because you're wounded."

Two shells landed almost simultaneously, either side of the trench. The concussion knocked two men off the fire-step, stunned but unhurt. Then, Arnold noticed that Second Lieutenant Hooper was lying in the entrance to a dugout.

"Gilbert, are you hit?" He approached is fellow subaltern, but when he got to the dugout and looked in, he saw that Hooper was beyond help. A fragment, from one or other of the two shells, had taken the top of his head off. From the bridge of his nose upwards, there was nothing. Now, there was no one to share command with. Arnold was in charge of these few dozen yards of trench, to be held against the might of the Imperial German Army.

Over the course of several hours, their position was shelled repeatedly, and it was only by great good fortune that the German gunners were not more accurate than they were. Two of Arnold's ad-hoc crew were killed, both from 4 Platoon, and Private Jimmy Hope was knocked over, dazed, but otherwise unhurt, when a shell fragment ricocheted off his steel helmet.

Arnold still planned to advance, when he could, to the next German line of defence. Those were his orders. For all he knew, his was the only sector of the front where the attack had not been pressed successfully to all its objectives. Maybe the Germans in front of him were in a defensive enclave, surrounded on all sides by the British. If so, he had no intention of being the officer in command of the day's only failure.

"Lance Corporal Selway," he called, observing Rollo's unofficial, and probably very temporary, promotion.

"Sir?"

"We'll be going over the top shortly. We can't crouch in here all day."

"Sir."

"I want you to make sure every man has ammunition and bombs. Take what you can find from the dead men and redistribute it."

"Very good, sir."

"What about Millcross? Is he up to it?"

Rollo looked at Alec. The field dressing over his right ear was red with blood.

"That's just a flea bite, sir. I'm sure he'll be fine."

"Jolly good. Go make sure the men are ready, and then I'll give the signal for the off."

"Yes, sir."

No one can say what would have happened to Arnold Snow, Rollo Selway, Alec Millcross, Jimmy Hope, and the band of men from other platoons, had they climbed out of that trench and rushed the defenders of the German support line. As it turned out, they never made the attempt. A few minutes after Arnold Snow had given Rollo Selway those instructions, an exhausted, muddy figure jumped into their trench. It was a battalion runner, with a message, which he passed to Arnold, as the officer in charge. Arnold was taken aback.

"Retire?"

"Yes, sir. Orders is to retire to our front line. They'll be starting a barrage to give you cover."

"When?"

"At six-twenty, sir."

"Any moment now, then," said Arnold, looking at his watch.

"Yes, sir."

"I see." Arnold raised his voice. "Listen, everyone. We're ordered to retire. They're going to put down a barrage to cover us in a few minutes. I want everyone to be ready to go the moment it starts."

No one said anything in reply for a moment, and after that moment, any reply would have been a waste of breath, because the barrage began. It was a beautiful bit of accurate shooting, with shells exploding in a line, no more than thirty yards beyond their position, throwing up enough earth to obscure them from the Germans' view. In an objective moment, Arnold was able to admire the accuracy of the shellfire – explosions planted behind them like a row of trees.

"Right, out of the trench! Quick as you can," he yelled above the noise of the shellfire, and he and his companions climbed out of the trench and ran back to the British front line. The barrage effectively masked them, and they were able to make their way unscathed, though, unnoticed by Arnold Snow, a bullet passed through his sleeve. No man's land was littered with bodies. Even as they ran, they were aghast at the rows of corpses, lying where the machine guns had scythed them down.

Just as they reached the British wire, they came across a man lying wounded, calling for help. Almost without breaking pace, Arnold Snow and Rollo Selway grabbed him by the arms and dragged him back with them. A few moments later, they were back in the British trench – exactly where they had started, over eleven hours before. Arnold looked about him. He saw Alec Millcross, whey faced and bandaged, and Jimmy Hope and Roland Selway who, like him, were both unhurt. He couldn't see anyone else from 2 Platoon. He wondered where they all were. He also wondered how his brother was.

Joseph Marren, meanwhile, was still in his shell crater with his three dead comrades. The British barrage, designed to give cover to the men retiring from the German lines, had effectively cut him off from joining the retreat. He could have tried running through the barrage, but the chances of coming out unscathed the other side, were as close to zero as made no difference.

A certain fatalism settled upon Private Joseph Marren. He had been ordered to slow up the Germans, so that was what he would do. He collected the three rifles that had belonged to the dead men, from whom he had also taken all their spare ammunition, and he lay at the lip of the crater, shooting at anything in the German lines that moved. He knew for sure that he had hit three men, maybe more. As the light began to fail, and he realised how very thirsty he was, he sensed, rather than saw, that the Germans were creeping out of their trench and would probably surround him.

He shot at Germans when he could see them, and he shot at shadows. The barrel of his rifle became too hot to hold, so he cast it aside, picking up one of the other three to continue shooting, all the while sensing that the enemy would soon have him. So be it, he thought. He had no intention of going down without a fight. It was with some surprise, that he suddenly felt something pressed into the small of his back.

"Very good, Tommy," said an unmistakably German voice. "But now you stop. Now you are a prisoner."

Joseph turned his head to see a German officer, pistol in hand, a half smile on his lips. He may not have been the cleverest solider in the British army, but Private Marren was able to appreciate how extremely lucky he was that the German had not simply shot him. He put his rifle aside and stood up.

"Yes, sir. Thank you very much, sir," he said, saluting.

The officer acknowledged the salute with a nod and gestured with his pistol to a couple of German soldiers, who appeared to have been lightly wounded.

"You go with them now. No more fighting for you."

Joseph Marren nodded. "Yes, sir," he said again, and he went with the two Germans to their support trench, and into captivity.

Chapter XL

At The Going Down of the Sun

At the going down of the sun, at the end of that dreadful day, Arnold Snow and the men who had followed him back from the only section of German trench that the 35th Middlesex had captured and briefly held, made their way to the rear, along the communications trenches. Their progress was slow. The trenches were clogged with walking wounded, the more severely hurt, who were waiting their turns for the stretcher-bearers, and the abandoned dead. Priority, at all times, was for the living.

It was some hours, therefore, before they reached the area where the forty men of the minimum reserve were waiting. They greeted each other with subdued and stilted conversation. Those who had been spared taking part in the day's battle, even against their will, felt an unwarranted guilt, while those who had survived against the odds tried not to resent those who had waited in relative safety behind the lines.

That morning, twenty-five officers and eight hundred and seventy-five men of the 35th Middlesex, had gone into battle. Now in this field, muted and collectively stunned, stood two officers and one hundred and seventeen men. The pale, bleaching moonlight of midsummer that illuminated a silent Arnold Snow and a second-lieutenant from C-Company, watching as one of the surviving sergeants called the roll, also shone down on no man's land, where the majority of the battalion now lay, some wounded, most dead. Defying the order that battalion commanders should remain in the British trenches, Lieutenant-Colonel Wintergrass had gone over the top with the third wave. Now, he lay dead before the German wire. The headless body of his second-in-command, Major Fullerton, lay some yards distant.

The roll was taken and the sergeant reported to Arnold Snow, who nodded and thanked him, unwilling to believe that the day had ended thus, but forced by the facts to do so.

"Stand the men easy, Sergeant," he said, and the sergeant gave the order. While Arnold and the other officer conferred, the men made soft conversation.

"Anyone seen Ted?"

"Not since we went over the top."

"I saw Corporal Hakesley get it."

"It was pure bloody murder."

"Where's the C.O.?"

"You were well out of it, Eddie."

"D'you know what happened to Johnny and Wilf?"

"I left my pack out there, in a shell hole. That's two-hundred fags gone."

"I can't believe we're all that's left."

"Some more will probably come in."

"That's the end of this battalion."

"Shut up. Don't talk like that."

"Poor old Dusty. Got caught on the wire."

"I never fired my rifle once. Not once, all bloody day."

"I don't see O'Malley anywhere."

"Was it like this along the whole front?"

"Dunno. Don't suppose anyone'll tell us anyway."

"Bloody Hun threw a grenade right at me, but it didn't go off. I shot him in the belly."

"I'm so fuckin' thirsty."

"I'm dyin' for a fag."

"Does anyone know what happened to Billy?"

After the roll call, with its long lists of men marked dead, wounded, or missing – and missing so very often meant dead, they all knew – Arnold Snow and the other subaltern marched the men back to the field outside Lesmurs. The tents were still up, and the men rested, while the officers awaited further orders.

The Battle of the Somme itself lasted until November of that year, when it was called off after enormous losses on both sides, but no day was as costly to the British army as that first day. One hundred thousand men had attacked on a twelve-mile front; over half of them had become casualties, with twenty-thousand of them killed. After five months, the British had achieved some of their objectives, but others remained as unattainable as they had been that first July morning.

The days of the 35th Middlesex were numbered. Fresh drafts of officers and men were sent from England, but the battalion never again reached full strength. The survivors of the Somme found themselves in a regiment of strangers. Arnold Snow was promoted to captain and was put in command of D-Company. Several other survivors became NCOs. Twice more the 35th Middlesex was thrown into battle, and twice more did it acquit itself with honour.

The army was changing, though, and the hard lessons learned at the Somme, and at Passchendaele the following year, enabled it to become the machine that eventually won the war, after the French collapsed, and before the Americans arrived in strength. Many of the New Army battalions that had been raised in 1914 and 1915, when the volunteers had flocked to the colours, had been all but obliterated in their very first battle. There was very little point in maintaining them.

That was why, in the spring of 1917, the 35th (Service) Battalion, the Middlesex Regiment, known informally as the St. Marylebone Rifles, paraded for the very last time, received the thanks of the brigade commander, and was disbanded, its officers and men being transferred to other regiments.

Strangely, it was as though the war had tried its best to eliminate the men we have followed, in this tale, on the opening day of the battle of the Somme, and afterwards, as though it had shot its bolt, it turned its attention away from those who remained alive when the sun went down. Most of them lived to see victory in 1918.

One of them was discharged from the army after his leg wound had healed as much as it would, leaving him with a permanent limp, and he found well paid employment in a munitions plant in London. After the war, Hubert was given a job in a car factory, rising eventually to a senior position. In 1919, he married someone he had met at the home of one of the strange, artistic crowd he had once mixed with.

One of them fell in battle in September of 1916, on the very first day that he had been in combat. His last thought, as he approached the enemy positions with his mates, was that he was glad that this time he could do his part, not wait safely in the minimum reserve. Yes, it was frightening, but it was, after all, what Eddie had joined up to do. One bullet ensured that he had no opportunity to think anything more.

One of them, minus an ear lobe, was later given a commission in another battalion and was wounded in 1917. He was sent to a hospital for officers outside London, where he met his future wife, one of the nurses who had looked after him. It was while he was recovering from his wounds, that he wrote most of the poems that comprised the slim volume which was published, not at his own expense, in late 1918, called *Verses by an Officer at the Front.* It sold moderately well, but it was just one of many such volumes that appeared towards the end of the war and afterwards. Poetry, especially mediocre poetry, seldom pays enough to support a man, let alone a man with a wife and a baby on the way, so after the war, which he survived without further injury, he opted for a cheerless job in the civil service, and after plugging away at it for a few years, Alec and his young family emigrated to New Zealand.

One of them did manage to obtain a transfer to the Royal Flying Corps. He was able to put all those hours flying before the war, to very good use. In April of 1918, he was lightly injured in a bad landing, and while recovering, he received orders to proceed to an airfield in central England as an instructor. While he was there, helping to train pilots for the war that gave them a life expectancy of five weeks, hostilities ended. Experience such as his was too useful to waste, and after he was demobilised, he managed to make contact with his former employer who, like him, had come through the war in one piece. Lord Beckanhill was about to invest part of his considerable fortune in a business venture whose time, he was sure, had come – a cargo airline – and he could think of no one better than his former chauffeur, a very experienced pilot, to be his number two. The business flourished, and within a few years they were flying freight and mail to several destinations, both at home and on the continent. Jimmy lived long enough and successfully enough to be able to experience transatlantic flight in a first-class seat on a jet airliner.

One of them was discharged from the army with a disability pension, two artificial legs, and a pair of crutches. He recuperated as best as could be expected in his home in Oxfordshire, but he had always been used to working outdoors, to fresh air, to mobility. Such a change demoralises some people more than others. Harry took it badly. He ate little, lost interest in what was happening around him, and eventually fell easy prey to the influenza pandemic that swept the world in 1918 and 1919.

One of them recovered from his shoulder wound and, after recuperation leave, was sent back to France as part of a draft that joined another battalion. He missed his old friends but soon made new ones. During the German offensive of March, 1918, he single-handedly rescued a wounded comrade from no man's land, an act for which he was awarded the Distinguished Conduct Medal. After the war, Wilfred returned to the bank where he had been employed before joining up, and he spent the remainder of his working life there, retiring as area manager, a contented husband and father.

One of them came back from a German prisoner-of-war camp, malnourished and grey, but able to appreciate his good fortune in having survived the war, still remaining the essentially optimistic person he had always been. He returned to the little cottage in the Oxfordshire village where he had been born and raised, and he promised not to roam again. As a prisoner, he had been put to work in a German bicycle factory, and Joe resolved never to work indoors again. His resumed his former employment as a farm labourer, eventually marrying and raising his own family.

One of them ended the war as a company sergeant major, a rank whose duties he discharged with fairness and efficiency. He had constantly resisted all attempts to get him to accept a commission. When he was demobilised, he joined his wife, Erika, and the two of them moved into a pleasant rented flat in Bayswater and, in time, they started a family. There was still a rift, of sorts, between him and his own father, and that needed attention. Rollo had no doubt that, in time, all the old wounds would be healed. The fact was, he had survived the war unscathed, when so many hundreds of thousands of parents were mourning the loss of one or more sons. That alone would make his father glad to see him. From that reunion, would spring the reconciliation he wanted, that Erika, now pregnant, wanted, and that he was certain that his parents wanted.

Arnold Snow let himself into the house in Berkeley Square one afternoon, in February of 1919. He had not told his mother or his step-father exactly when he would be returning, and there was no one to meet him, except for a rather startled butler. That suited Arnold. He went to his room and took off his uniform for the last time. He had ended the war a major, second in command of a New Army battalion that had seen action several times. He had been offered the opportunity of staying in the army after the war, but had decided it was not for him. He was demobilised and returned home. In his civilian clothes, he sat in the drawing room, sipping a dry sherry and waiting for his mother to come home. A very long time ago, it seemed, his mother had proposed a toast to the safe return of both her sons. Fate had granted her half her wish. Arnold knew that any joy at his return would be tempered by her unending grief at the loss of his brother. It was his duty now to live his life well, and successfully, out of respect for his mother, and as a memorial to Charles. He would do his best.

Victory in 1918 did not usher in an age of tranquillity and comfort, but as far as they could, after their own fashions, at their own stations in life. and with varying degrees of success, these men who remained lived reasonably contented lives.

They all did their best.

The End

Author's Note

The Middlesex Regiment had a long and very distinguished record of service with the British army, from its formation in 1881 until its amalgamation with two other regiments in 1966. Several service battalions were formed in the First World War, but there never was a 35th battalion. That means, of course, that the St. Marylebone Rifles never existed, and neither did the officers and men who served in its ranks. They, and those they were related to, married to, worked with, and stole from, are all products of my imagination. Equally imaginary is the village of Lesmurs and that means, sadly, that there never was a Pompette's.

The training camp at Étaples was real, however, and the conditions there were as I have described. The camp was an unpleasant staging post for men on their way to the front, and their treatment by dugout officers and 'canaries' was a source of resentment that eventually boiled over into mutiny in September 1917.

A single platoon of a British Army battalion at full strength was about forty. While this story follows only nineteen men from 2 Platoon, we may assume that the remaining twenty-one men were present before and during the battle, but their words and deeds have gone unrecorded.

The Metropolitan Music Hall in the Edgware Road was real, and Sir Harry Lauder may, on occasion, have performed there. He actually wrote the song *Keep Right On To The End Of The Road* in 1917, but I have taken the liberty of bringing its composition forward by three years.

Something else that was all too real, was the statistic quoted in the final chapter. On the first day of the Battle of the Somme, the British army did indeed sustain over fifty thousand casualties, with almost twenty thousand of them killed, most of them during the first two hours. On no other occasion, before or since, has such a disaster been visited upon the British armed forces, not even later in the First World War.

The general conduct of the opening of the battle was as I have set it out: the barrage, the deep German dugouts, the mines, the order to walk across no man's land, the extra heavy packs, the uncut barbed wire, the devastation wrought by the enemy machine guns and artillery. The deeds of Arnold Snow, Edwin Marvell, Harry Travis, Rollo Selway, and their comrades may have been fiction, but they were mirrored many thousands of times over in fact.

There are many accounts of the battle and the campaign on the Western Front, both by participants and by historians. For readers who are interested in knowing more, in detail, about July 1, 1916, and the battle that started that day, I especially recommend *The First Day on the Somme* by Martin Middlebrook (London, 1971), *The Somme* by Martin Gilbert (London, 2006) and *Somme* by Lyn Macdonald (London, 1971), all of which are outstanding examples of the historian's craft.

N.T-S.

Printed in Great Britain
by Amazon